SMOKE

There were nine people aboard the little rescue ~~~ ~ ~~
the airliner had finally sunk into the Indian Ocean.

Among those huddled together in unwanted intimacy and
fearful danger are an African M.P. from Salisbury, a Trans-
vaal farmer, an embittered Englishman from Kenya, a con-
fidence-man hell-bent on personal advantage, a London
clerk and a rich industrialist now far from the security and
splendour of his City boardroom.

There are women in the dinghy, too. A plain, man-hungry
university lecturer; the only surviving member of the air-
crew, a young air hostess; and a Mauritian woman of great
beauty.

These people have ultimately to work out their destiny on
a coral island from which the bare requirements for survival
can only be wrung with ingenuity, persistence and mutual
co-operation; and to seek means of returning to the world,
and to their relations and friends. The tantalising smoke
spirals that are sometimes sighted seem to promise a chance
of rescue; yet they are almost as distant and elusive as the
world of civilisation, which has lost these people and dropped them into a manner of life that is exotic and romantic but
that holds no charm for them.

Smoke Island

ANTONY TREW

COLLINS
8 Grafton Street, London W1

William Collins Sons and Co Ltd
London · Glasgow · Sydney · Auckland
Toronto · Johannesburg

ISBN 0 00 221774 0

First published 1964
This reprint 1986

Made and Printed in Great Britain by
William Collins Sons and Co Ltd Glasgow

To Nora

"The Chagos Archipelago, a dependency of Mauritius, consisting of numerous islands and coral reefs, lies between the parallels of 4° 44′S and 7° 41′S and the meridians of 70° 47′E and 72° 47′E.

The most remarkable feature in the Archipelago is the general atoll character of the islands, reefs, and banks."

The South Indian Ocean Pilot
Seventh Edition, 1958
*Published by the Hydrographic
Department of the Admiralty*

One

THE AIRCRAFT'S fin stood high in the water, towering, a silvered obelisk splashed with black letters staring in the moonlight. The apex moved slowly, teetering forward and then down with a shuddering plunge until where it had been there was a hissing plume, a swirl and eddy, soon swept away by the wind and sea until there was nothing but the rolling valleys. In the troughs they were a dull oily black but on the moonlit crests a fiery silver, spluttering and hissing as they raced towards the dinghy, thrusting it crazily upwards as they passed, surging on into primordial darkness.

She heard the whistle again; a thin urgent blast, nearer now.

"Swimming towards us," said the black man. "I saw the light."

"More likely we're drifting down on him. No room for the poor sod here, we're packed already." The voice was nasal, high pitched.

One of the Australians, thought the girl.

There was a groan from a wet heap on the other side, and the voice of an older man, authoritative, urgent, English.

"Of course! He can't come in here. He'll upset the dinghy. Keep him away."

The girl was shocked. "Rubbish!" she said firmly, the foreign accent rolling the R. "This dinghy can hold twenty. Of course we must pick him up."

The whistle sounded again, almost alongside.

"There he is," said the black man. He shouted: "Hey! You!" He was looking down on the struggling figure with its small white light blinking feebly in the water; as the dinghy lifted high on the next crest he could see in the moonlight the face, white with staring eyes. Below the black moustache a gash of mouth opened and gasped. "Help me, man! For God's sake help me!" and the arms lifted out towards the dinghy. It came off the crest, took the angle of the slope and bumped into the shape in the water.

The African hung over the side, reaching down. "Hey! Grab!" he called.

From the water the arms jerked upwards and the hands of the two men locked, the black hands pulling and straining on the white hands until the white arms were in over the side of the dinghy. It sagged towards the new weight.

"Look out!" said the querulous voice under the canopy, "you'll sink us."

"That's right." It was the nasal shrill again. "Leave the bastard alone! Why should we drown for 'im?"

"Nobody'll drown," said the girl quickly. "I'll help you." She wriggled over in the darkness, slushing through the water on the sagging floor of the dinghy until she was next to the black man. The dinghy on that side dipped as she leant out and put an arm round the neck of the dark bundle.

"Now!" she said urgently. *"Together*—heave!"

As they pulled, the man in the water lurched upward until his arms and shoulders were on the buoyancy chamber. He lay there gasping. The dinghy climbed up the black slope and as they jerked over onto the crest she called "Now!" and with a final clawing heave they had the legs into the dinghy.

The girl with the foreign accent addressed the darkness. "See, it makes no difference. There's plenty of room."

The new arrival stirred. *"Ek dank my God!* Thank God!" The speech was laboured and guttural. One of the Afrikaans passengers, she thought and looked down; but it was too dark to see the face. Just a pale blob in a shapeless bundle, with the survivor's lamp glowing like an eye in the centre. She disconnected it.

The groaning started again.

"Who's that?" asked the girl.

"One next to me," said the Australian. He prodded in the darkness. "What's the trouble? What you bellyaching for?"

The prods brought more groans.

"Leave him," said the girl. "He's hurt." She remembered helping him out of the water. The young Italian from Milan.

A new voice came out of the surrounding blackness, soft and warm. "Shall we die?" It was the woman with the French accent. She put the question directly, without emotion.

"Of course not," said the girl. "These inflatable dinghies stand much worse weather than this. They'll be searching for us at daybreak." She was trying to identify the French voice. Must be the dark woman who joined in Mauritius—the good-looking one: Creole perhaps.

Somebody was vomiting, and for a moment the acrid sour smell assailed them. God, thought the girl, what's going to happen to us? She was on the edge of collapse, almost in tears, but she couldn't allow that. There was no one else to take charge. There'd be no hope if she gave in. If only some of the crew were here. Iles or Steve or Bud or even Karin.

What had happened to them? She looked out of the canopy. The moon had gone behind the clouds again and it was dark; beyond that there was nothing but the rain and the wind and the climbs up the long slopes of the seas, the jolting at the top and the jerk over to the new angle and the sickening slide down the other side. Nothing but violent motion and the black splash and slop of water. The tears came again and she fought them back.

Distress signals! The two-star-reds! Of course. She began to remember the drill. *The dinghies must keep together. Vitally important. Particularly at night. Chances of rescue greatly enhanced. Lines for securing dinghies to each other will be found in them.*

The two-star-reds! Why had she forgotten them? How stupid!

"We'll send up a two-star-red," she said in a business-like voice. "That'll let the others know we're here."

"How'll that help?" It was the African.

She turned towards him in the darkness. "The dinghies must keep together. Then we can help each other. Much better for rescue."

With the survivor's light from her life-jacket she searched through the emergency pack, found the waterproof torch and the box of flares. They fired two at five minute intervals. But none was fired in reply. There was only the shriek of the wind and sea, the slosh and gurgle of water, the muttering and groaning, and increasingly the sound of vomiting and its foul acrid smell.

*   *

It must have been the beginning of daylight because the blackness was no longer opaque. She could make out some detail now, like the shapes in the dinghy and where the groaning was coming from.

At first she refused to admit it because it seemed too good to be true, then she was pretty sure she was right so she said: "Wind's dropping. Sea's not so big now."

"There's too much water in here," said the anxious voice. "Must be a leak."

"No," said the girl. "It's slopped in. Let's bail."

She found the bailers, gave him one and got to work with the other. He was right. There was a lot of water. Everything was wet; even in the half darkness you could see that because every bit of the dinghy that wasn't in shadow and every bundle in it reflected a grey oily glisten, so that instead of blackness everywhere there was now a wet greyness.

"It's not getting less." The nagging voice was querulous.

He's frightened, she thought. So am I. Why does he talk about it and make it worse?

"It's getting less," she said and looked at him. Now she could just make out the round flabby face and the well-fed jowls, grey like everything else in the dinghy. The top of the bald head was grey too, and tenuous locks of hair hung down from the pate, the ends below the level of the eyebrows. The too-close, too-beady eyes were bright with fear and the mouth hung open, the lower lip flabby and sensuous. She remembered him now and the fuss just before Mauritius because the soda wasn't cold enough, all in that special loud voice which advertised that the owner was used to getting his own way.

She tried to associate him with the passenger list and then it came back to her . . . Canning! Herbert William Canning. They'd checked on him after the row about the soda. He'd joined the aircraft at Jan Smuts, in transit from London. God, she thought, why did he have to be here? Why not one of the young men?

Daylight was coming more quickly now and some of the grey shapes began to stir. The African threw off his sick drowsiness and edged round to an opening in the canopy so that he looked out over the sea. It was better, that, than inwards where there was nothing but the wet blackness changing to wet greyness.

One of the prone shapes in the bottom of the dinghy began to move and scrabble in the water. First the legs flexed, then the toes crimped and after that the arms moved and the fingers worked. Then there was a wriggle of the shoulders under the life-jacket and the man wearing it thought, Nothing wrong there! But his neck was stiff; something had hit him as they struck the water, just before the bright flash of the explosion.

Then he'd had this dream that he was running away from Esau to hide. He had to run fast because he was only seven and Esau was nine at least, though he didn't know his age because farm natives never did. He had to find a place quickly because Esau would uncover his eyes too soon. Esau always did. As he came round the wall of the kraal he heard Esau shout, "*Ek kom, Basie!*" —"I'm coming, little master."

Ahead was the stone surround and inside the narrow earth-rim round the hole. He clambered over the wall and crouched against the inside, bent, huddled, trying to make himself small, gasping for breath. But he looked at the stone wall, not the other side because there he'd see the dark hole and that would frighten him.

"There's a big black mamba in that hole," warned his mother, "bigger than the one that killed Oom Klasie. You must never go there, child."

He began thinking about the big mamba and these thoughts were so vivid that he forgot the game until he heard the scream next to his ear. As he fell he knew it was Esau screaming with excitement because he'd found him, but it was too late and the struggle was on.

It was black and terrifying down there. The water burnt and tore at his lungs, and jagged lights of red and white stabbed in his head as he twisted and clawed. While he was in the water this struggle was timeless, but when he was nearly dead black hands reached down and grasped his. He knew they were black because they locked onto his white hands and there was a light, the moon or something, and he could see the difference. But after that the dream ended: there at that point was the end of all recollection, beyond it there was nothing but the sound of his mother's voice.

Huddled in the dinghy, wet and bruised, he realised with a shock that it wasn't his mother's voice, but this woman next to him who was scraping at the water and throwing it away.

With an effort he sat up and the movement racked his body. There was a hot burning in his neck and chest and his mouth was dry and swollen. He looked at the woman's gaunt face, saw the high cheekbones, the arched eyebrows and hollow brown eyes. Somewhere, someplace, a long time ago, he'd seen her . . .? Then he knew. She was one of the hostesses. But she didn't look young and attractive any more. Her face was pallid and there was a long scratch over the cheek, from the corner of the eye down to below the chin. It was red and angry and along it there were blotches of congealed blood. The brown hair was hanging in rats' tails over her face, and under the orange life-jacket the dirty sodden blouse was torn where a sleeve had broken away and left a bare shoulder.

He looked at her. "How did I get here?"

She stopped bailing and with the back of her wrist tried to push the hair out of her eyes. "We pulled you out of the water—last night."

He looked at her blankly. "Out of the water? Was I there?"

"Don't you remember?"

He shook his head. "Only that we hit the water and the explosion. Then I had a dream."

He felt his neck with his hand. "It hit my neck."

"What did?"

"Something hard. Hell of a crack. It's stiff now."

While he was talking a black hand stretched forward and took the bailer from the girl. "Let me do it," said a man's voice.

The sight of that black hand—so close, so unexpected—was a profound shock. Like a slap in the face. Before he looked round he knew who it was. There was more light now and when he turned their eyes met and there was a frigid moment of recognition.

They'd put them together; the black in the window seat. You paid nearly five hundred and fifty pounds of your own money—not the taxpayers' like his—and they expected you to sit all the way from Johannesburg to Melbourne with one of them next to you! And when he had complained, they'd said he could exchange places with the young Italian, but they couldn't ask the black man to move because he was an M.P. from Salisbury and he'd booked the window seat. They tried to be tactful and explained that Australian Government policy was involved, so that he'd had to move. But all the time he was collecting his things the black man sat there with an insolent smile as if it was all a joke.

Now here in this dinghy that could sink at any moment, with terrible pains all over him and little chance of rescue, he must share his last hours with the native and that coloured woman. He was glad that the people from the valley didn't know.

Anyway he'd stand no cheek from the fellow and now the thing was to use all the strength and skill and cunning God had given him to survive, and from what he could see and feel that wasn't going to be easy.

He looked at the girl again and pointed to his orange life-jacket. "Can I take this off?"

"Not now. Later, perhaps."

On top of all that bailing, the effort to answer was the last straw. The water in the dinghy was foul with vomit and urine and God knows what else and she couldn't stand the stench. Seasickness, shock, the nervous strain and lack of sleep had brought her to the threshold of collapse.

She looked round with misty swimming eyes and the dinghy and the horizon began to circle, slowly at first, then faster until she toppled over.

       *   *

It was daylight and the first thing one noticed was the sea. It was still quite rough but calmer than during the night. The wind was not blowing so hard and between high banks of white cloud there was blue sky and from it the sun touched the dinghy with warm fingers.

Her mouth was terribly dry and she thought of water but then dismissed it. It was light under the canopy. She started to count . . . nine of them . . . ten with herself . . . ten sodden, huddled shapes. Five were still asleep. The university woman who'd been so sick . . . the Afrikaner, the last one they'd pulled out of the water . . . the young Italian . . . the gaunt man with the domed head . . .and the thin man with mournful hooded eyes. It was he and the Italian who'd been groaning during the night. Now he was lying back limply. His mouth hung open and he breathed unevenly. The hair had receded from the forehead, and a jagged cut ran back into the scalp, red and blood-wet.

The young Italian was lying in the middle of the dinghy, knees drawn up, face towards her. He'd not said a word during the night, just moaned quietly at times. Now that the dinghy had been bailed out the water wasn't slopping about him as before. She felt terribly sorry for him; he was young and he'd been keenly interested in the flight; quiet and polite and helpful. Now the face under the dark crew-cut was like chalk and the eyes . . .! Wide open . . . staring at her . . . funny that he doesn't blink, she thought, and then she realised that he was dead.

Canning and the Australian were muttering to each other at the far end of the dinghy. She interrupted them.

"Look!" she pointed. "He's dead."

They started and she could see the horror in Canning's eyes. "Dead!" he said it dumbly. "My God!"

"Let's ditch 'im," said the Australian.

She looked at him hard and realised he was a ferret. Thick black hair, tousled now and quite unlike the well-creamed affair it had been in the aircraft, dark elongated eyes set close together in a narrow head, and below them a long nose with dilated nostrils, a small flat mouth, a narrow receding chin.

In daylight she was able to identify him . . . Arthur Basset, another transit passenger from London to Sydney. She and Karin had soon found that he was a bottom pincher, just as that flabby old man Canning was a breast peeper. When you bent down to hand him something, his eyes darted to the open neck of your blouse. Later in the journey before Perth, they would both have been asking for telephone numbers.

"Got to get 'im out," said Basset. "Can't have a corpse lying 'ere. It's going to be hot."

The girl shook her head. "Not just yet. Wait until everybody's awake." She was playing for time. They'd have to get rid of the body, but she couldn't bear to see the ferret do it.

"Look! . . . This isn't the aircraft, you know . . ." Canning grumbled, "better listen to *us* now . . ." Above heavy bags the eyes were a watery bloodshot grey, the thin windswept hair round the bald pate a washed-out brown, but over the face and neck the bristles were white.

Her silence encouraged him. "No point in keeping it." He looked down at the young Italian fearfully. "Not healthy."

The gaunt man nodded deferentially. "Quite right, sir."

She said: "I'll wake the others." She started with the big Afrikaner because he was nearest, and when she'd done that she nodded at the African. He understood and tapped the shoulder of the man with the scalp wound. It took time to waken the university woman, and when they'd succeeded she leant over the side of the dinghy and was sick. She fell back into a coma again.

The girl spoke to the Afrikaner and the African because she felt that they were the most reliable; but it was evident that the Afrikaner was still weak, slumped against the side, his neck awkwardly bent.

"There are things we must discuss," she explained. "That's why we woke you." From sheer force of habit she said: "I am Nada Katic, your air hostess, and I'm the only member of the crew in this dinghy." She stopped for a moment, not knowing how to go on. Then she gathered her thoughts. "First we'll have to . . . bury this young man."

She looked hopefully towards the Afrikaner. But Basset had edged forward. " 'Ere you," he pointed with his chin at the African. "Lend a hand."

They started to work the body up and over the side but it stuck, the head and shoulders still in the dinghy and the rump and one leg outboard, the cold white face pressed against the floor.

The Afrikaner raised his hand. "*Wag!* Stop! Not like that. No man must go to his God like that."

He crawled over to them, hanging onto the steadying line. "There must be prayers."

"Indeed there must be," said the bald man.

"Come on," Basset interrupted. "Over with 'im."

The Afrikaner reached out and pushed the Australian away.

"Keep yer paws off me, digger!" shrilled Basset, but the big man ignored him.

"I will say the prayers—not in English. I know them better in Afrikaans. God will understand."

Canning looked like protesting but thought better of it.

The Afrikaner bent his head and prayed in a slow deep voice:

> *"Bly by my, Heer, terwyl die skadu's daal,*
> *Laat tans u lig my donker pad bestraal!*
> *Daar is geen ander hulp of troos vir my . . .*
> *Hulp van die hulplose, staan my by!"*

Then he beckoned with his eye to Basset and Canning, and put his hand on the dead Italian's shoulder.

> *"Die waters rol om my, ombruis my al geheel*
> *Omsingel my in hoëvloed en reik tot aan my keel."*

"Come on," he said.

With the help of the bald man, whose lips had been moving in prayer, they man-handled the body over the side and it settled on the sea, face downwards, the rump floating clear of the water, a pocket of air trapped in the seat of the trousers. And so for a long time the mortal remains of Pietro Brucci of Milan kept station on the dinghy, five feet distant, rising and falling to the warm undulations of the Indian Ocean.

*   *

Nada Katic thought that she knew most of the names but some she'd forgotten like the Creole woman and the man with the scalp wound, so after the burial she organised a roll-call. It was part of the drill, although she hadn't got the passenger list to tick them off against . . . that had gone during the struggle in the water.

After Canning and Basset had given their names, she looked at the Afrikaner. "And you . . .?"

"Lombaard of Soetwaters. Jos Lombaard."

Like MacDonald of the Isles, she thought. "And you . . .?"

The African's shoulders went back a little. "Ezekiel Wanalu, M.P. from Salisbury."

Despite the precarious circumstances, the carefully articulated statement, the heavily emphasized "M.P.", betrayed the owner's pride in his name and achievement.

Then it was the dark-skinned woman.

"Angelique Lee of Mauritius."

Hair awry, face dirty and shorn of make-up, sodden clothes steaming in the morning sun, she was still calm and handsome.

The red-eyed university woman with the taut, pallid face said: "Sarah Tripp," in a prim, slightly self-conscious voice and then, "From Johannesburg." She pulled a pair of spectacles from where she had tucked them inside her brassière and tried to clean them with the edge of her petticoat.

The bald man with the kind face said: "Sebastian Goldsworthy, London." He gave Canning an apologetic smile.

Nada thought, what a strange man. It is almost as if he were not here. He's so quiet and inconspicuous. But he's afraid of Canning.

Last to introduce himself was the thin man with the scalp wound. "Christopher Robin Mecky," he announced in a high voice. "From Nairobi . . .," he glared at Ezekiel Wanalu and added, "Kenya." He pronounced it "Keen-yah."

"Thank you," the girl looked round.

Now what, she thought? Better not tell them about the emergency radio. She passed her hand across her eyes. If only Iles or Steve or Bud had made it. She felt pitifully inadequate. Anyway, thank God they'd got the emergency pack and they still had the Sarah Beacon and the radar reflector aerial. It could have been worse.

The emergency pack had been a near shave!

Iles had thrown it out, but with the explosion the ditching procedures had ended suddenly. After that she was in the water swimming towards the lights on the dinghy, fighting for her life in the darkness. Then she bumped into something and instinctively clung to it. In the glow of her survivor's lamp she saw that it was the emergency pack.

The dinghy was only five feet away, but the struggle to reach it with the pack was ghastly and endless. Fortunately she'd not been badly hurt and in her terror she'd found new resources of strength so that at last she reached the dinghy in spite of the waves. She saw a light in the canopy entrance and shouted from the water, "Take this! . . . Make it fast!"

With one hand she held onto the life-line round the dinghy and with the other she held up the securing line on the emergency pack. For a dreadful moment she thought she'd made a mistake because there was no longer a light at the canopy entrance. Then she screamed: "Quick, quick! Help me!"

After that the light re-appeared and an arm came down and took the line.

A man's voice said, "O.K.!" but she couldn't see who it was.

"Tie it very tight . . . there . . ." she pointed.

Then she felt with her feet for the cord ladder, found it and struggled into the dinghy with the man helping her.

She knelt in the water in the bottom of the dinghy and gasped for breath and when she looked up she saw in the light of his survivor's lamp that it was the African. He said: "You all right?"

She nodded. "We must get the emergency pack on board. Right now!" she said emphatically.

Together they knelt at the opening, the lights on their life-jackets reflecting back from the gleaming wet side of the dinghy. They pulled on the securing line first and then clawed at the pack, waiting for the next wave to pass. When they reached the bottom of the trough she shouted, "Heave!"

After it was safely on board she leant on it in the darkness, hugging the dripping pack as if it were a child.

She was almost in tears.

"Wonderful . . . Oh, wonderful!"

The drill came back to her. "*Stream the drogue . . . close the curtains if shipping water.*" They could stream the drogue but they couldn't close both curtains—there were still others to come. She crawled across the soggy yielding floor, clinging to the steadying line until in the darkness she found the drogue. All this she did in slow time because of the violent motion and the wet, clinging darkness.

When she'd streamed the drogue and closed the curtain of the up-wind opening she felt round in the cold sloshing water for the paddle bag, the Sarah Beacon, the safety knife and the radar reflector. They were all there. Thank God!

She struggled over to the down-wind opening and looked out into the darkness, shuddering at the scream of the wind and the hiss and roar of the water.

The African was near her. She couldn't see him but she could hear him moving, the water splashing and slopping as he wriggled alongside.

She said: "We must look out for the others."

Two

"WE'LL OPEN the emergency pack and muster the equipment." She said it firmly, anxious to avoid argument. Mecky complained about the pain in his head and asked to be excused. He huddled up against the side of the dinghy with closed eyes. The bedraggled shapes gathered about the emergency pack like vultures round a kill, each head framed in an orange life-jacket, each face drawn and dirty.

The pack was opened and morale rose as its contents were examined and Nada explained their purpose. There were desalting units for converting sea water to fresh; six ten-ounce tins of fresh water; two dozen tins of glucose sweets; a tube of anti-mosquito cream; sea-marker dyes; a steel signalling mirror; a sponge; compass; waterproof matchbox; first-aid kit; the box of twenty two-star-red distress signals which she'd already opened; a bottle of salt tablets; two bottles of chlorine tablets; and two fishing lines with six hooks. Thoughtfully and providentially a little booklet entitled "Sea Survival" was included.

When they'd repacked everything they talked about rationing food and water, and she explained that strict discipline was essential to survival.

"Water's the vital thing," she said. "Mustn't be used on the first day. After that we'll use rain-water whenever possible . . . then desalted water. The tins of fresh water mustn't be opened except as a last resort."

She showed them the depression on the canopy top and the small catchment pockets on its sides for collecting rainwater, and the inlet pipes for tapping it.

The Sea Survival booklet reminded her of many things. One of these was the allocation of duties and she began on that. This led to some argument, but eventually it was agreed that Sarah Tripp and Angelique would be responsible for the inside of the dinghy; the six men would take turns as lookouts, fishermen and signallers. Nada was to be solely responsible for issuing rations, and in general charge as the only crew member on board.

When she'd shown the two women how to sponge the floor dry, and inflate the double bottom of the dinghy and top up the buoyancy chambers with the bellows, she left them to it. Next she dealt with the lookouts.

"We must always have two on duty—night and day—doing a stretch of one hour. It's terribly important to keep a good lookout of the sea and sky."

She was thinking of the emergency radio pack, an orange cube bobbing about in the sea somewhere near them. It shouldn't be too far away: it was subject to the same wind and sea as the dinghy. But she didn't want to tell them yet.

"Especially look out for other dinghies . . ."

"If there are any," interrupted Canning gloomily.

She frowned at him. ". . . and for orange things like the babies' survival cots . . . and other things."

"What other things?" It was Canning again.

"They may have put extra water and blankets . . . and anything useful, like that . . . in the survival cots that weren't needed for babies . . . that's part of the drill. We only had one baby aboard. The crew may have put things in the other cots."

Angelique was sitting with her hands folded on her lap, her chin resting on the collar of the orange life-jacket.

"The baby," she whispered, her eyes misty with compassion. "What do you think?"

"We put it in a survival cot. Told the mother what to do." Nada shrugged her shoulders. "But she was hysterical." She looked away, and tried to shake off the vision of the baby alone in

26

the tiny cot. "I don't know. But we must keep a good lookout in case. Look for ships and aircraft. We'll probably hear aircraft before we see them, so always listen. You two . . .," she looked at Jos Lombaard and Ezekiel Wanalu, . . . "please be the first lookouts. One at either end."

Ezekiel and Jos went to the canopy openings and began to scan the distant circle of water and the vast clouded sky. Lombaard still held his head awkwardly on one side, twisting his shoulders when he wanted to move his head.

Canning sat with his back against the side, jowls puffed out by the life-jacket, the eyes still bloodshot and watery, but the colour was returning to his cheeks.

"What are our chances of rescue?" he asked.

That's what I'd like to know, thought Nada desperately. She looked at her watch. "It's nine a.m. Mauritius time—we're about three hours overdue at Cocos now. The search will have started."

Canning's eyes were frightened.

"D'you think that distress signal got through?"

In her mind she was pretty certain it hadn't. Iles knew what he was talking about. She looked at Canning.

"I hope it has. But it doesn't really matter. We have to report to Mauritius or Cocos every half-hour. When a report's five minutes overdue they start the first phase of the alert. They keep trying to contact the aircraft and . . . well," she shrugged her shoulders again, . . . "by the time the fuel-burn-up time's expired, they're all set to start things moving."

Everybody in the dinghy was listening now, even Mecky who'd given up pretending to be asleep, and Sarah Tripp whose bouts of nausea were getting fewer.

"What things?" Canning's eyes narrowed. He polished his glasses with a grubby handkerchief.

The bald man thought, The Chief's got a good brain. He misses nothing.

27

"Well . . . it's terrific," she said, and then for a moment she thought she would burst into tears because the exaggeration was so ridiculous. How could it be terrific? That huge endless stretch of water reaching out for thousands of miles in every direction, and this little dinghy bobbing up and down, a tiny speck of flotsam somewhere in the Indian Ocean between Mauritius and Cocos . . . a speck in an unknown position, proceeding in an unknown direction to an unknown fate.

She was sure the distress signal hadn't got through. They were without the emergency radio which was the mainstay of survival, and though Operations might guess the dinghy's position within, perhaps, three hundred miles had they been on course . . . well, they hadn't been and she knew it.

There was that big storm right ahead, and Hughie had tried to avoid it by going north for nearly half an hour. God knows how far off course they were when they ditched.

They watched her closely.

"You were saying?" . . . it was Canning's bland voice.

She gulped. "I was wondering where to start. We were four hours out when we ditched. That'd put us about 1,400 miles from Mauritius and . . .," she made a rapid mental calculation, ". . . about 1,500 miles from Cocos. Just about halfway so the search'll come from both sides.

"The Australian and South African Shackletons'll be out and the R.A.F. Shackletons from Gan—Oh!—and the special transport aircraft from T.O.A.L., South African Airways and Qantas. All ships will be alerted and . . ."

Canning's business brain was at work.

"Where do the Shackletons start from?"

She wasn't quite sure about that, so she chanced her arm: "Durban and Perth usually, and the R.A.F. from Gan in the Maldive Islands."

For a moment he had a vivid picture of the flying schedule. He'd pored over it in London once it was clear that his directors expected him to fly, and at night he'd lain awake thinking of those vast, chilling over-the-ocean hops: South African coast . . . Mauritius, 2,100 miles; Mauritius . . . Cocos 2,850 miles; Cocos . . . Perth, 1,900 miles. And the Maldives were somewhere up near India.

Terror seized him. Physical courage was not Mr. Canning's strong suit.

     *   *

Appalled at the prospect of the journey he huddled up against Winifred in the wide expanse of the Canning double-bed.

Tittery, gigglish, coy, wee-girlie Winifred, 53 last summer, so often subject to headaches when Canning reached out for her in the night.

"Not tonight, Bert! . . . Oh! *Please* not tonight!"

"It's not that," he said irritably. "It's the journey. That long flight over the sea. You know I'm not easily frightened, but frankly . . .," he sighed. "Well . . . it's just that I don't like it."

"Of course I know you're never frightened, darling," she lied. Then she turned her back on him, gently, sighed happily, and thought of her grandchildren and tomorrow's Yoga class.

They were finished with *Yama* and *Niyama*, and Urdan was taking them on to *Asama* . . . Winifred wasn't quite sure what it was because she could never concentrate when he was talking . . . there were so many other things to think about. But it was something to do with bodily posture and breathing. It sounded terribly exciting!

Dear Urdan! He had already complimented her on her suppleness. "Your body," he whispered daringly, the dark eyes consuming her, the laughing teeth ivory white, "Eet ees jost like a yong vooman!"

She hugged herself and giggled ever so quietly in the darkness, but Canning heard her.

"What's so funny?"

"You, darling. The idea of you being frightened."

       *   *

There was a tremor in Canning's voice.

"So that if you take the fuel-burn-up time as six o'clock this morning, a Shackleton can't be here before four or five this afternoon."

"That's about right," Nada said, "But to be on the safe side we'll start the Sarah Beacon at about two o'clock."

"What does it do?" It was Sarah Tripp.

Nada noticed the sibilance for the first time and wondered about the teeth, but they were all there and they were real; no self-respecting dental mechanic could have produced anything quite so protruding and uneven.

"Once it's plugged in, it sends out the international distress signal automatically. Ships and aircraft pick up the signals and home on us. The radar reflector aerial bounces back their radar signals," she added confidently.

Canning frowned, rubbing his hands together slowly and sniffing as he always did before asking an important question.

"What's its range?"

Nada thought, You wretch! Why can't you leave it alone?

"Up to about 80 miles . . . I mean aircraft flying high pick up the signals at that distance."

"And a ship?" He watched her fearfully, knowing that the life of Herbert William Canning hung upon a thread, stretched out precariously to meet another such thread.

"About five miles," she said quietly, and he winced as if he'd been hit between the eyes.

       *   *

When the compass was produced Art Basset broke the surprising news that he'd been in the Royal Australian Navy during the war; a petty officer, he explained modestly, and though it was seventeen years ago the sea was the sea, and a man didn't forget those sort of things.

"Perhaps . . . then . . . you can tell us where we are?" Mecky cleared his throat and the hooded, pale eyes watched Basset coldly.

"Got no instruments. But I c'n read the compass and set a course . . . and I know the weather and all that." He cocked a knowing eye over the sea, taking in the vast expanse of sky and water in a comprehending glance.

"Thing is . . . about lookouts." Basset blinked and looked down at the circle of feet opposite him.

"What about them?"

"Well, if I'm navigator, I got to keep fresh. Like sleep at nights. See what I mean, digger?"

Mecky's nose twitched. "So that's what you're after, is it?"

"Whadya mean?" Basset snarled, shaking his finger, with exaggerated fierceness. "Not trying to get out of anything."

Canning tried to pacify them. "I think we must all do our stint, old man. Fair shares you know."

"That's right, sir," the bald man nodded.

"Of course," said Nada. "Besides it won't be easy to sleep at nights with this motion. I mean you won't want to," she added hurriedly. "Doing a spell of lookout helps to keep one occupied . . . makes the time pass."

*   *

After that Art Basset withdrew into himself and sulked. Lousy lot, he thought, looking round furtively at his tattered companions, their unshaven unwashed faces grotesquely framed in the orange life-jackets.

Across the centre of the dinghy a few sodden garments were strung out on the steadying lines to dry, and they swung about jerkily as the dinghy swung and bobbed and slid and climbed. The sun was well up in the tropical sky and the humid steamy air under the canopy was stirred now and then by an occasional gust of fresh air as the dinghy yawed under the impact of the seas.

and the canopy entrance caught the sharp breeze which had taken over from the gale of the night before.

A lousy lot, he repeated to himself, and hunched up against the side of the dinghy, knees drawn up, the compass in his lap. The markings seemed familiar enough, but he couldn't make out how to set it to get the direction in which they were drifting. Perhaps he'd overplayed his hand in saying he'd been a petty officer? Of course he hadn't said what branch, but he'd meant to convey that it was the seamen's. Once accepted as navigator, life would be easier in the dinghy and an obvious duty to dodge was lookout.

Fancy having to do hour on and hour off right through the bloody night and day? Like doing time! It was that thin bugger Mecky who'd bitched his plans . . . but now this compass? How the devil did the blasted thing work?

He thought back to the time when he was a steward in the armed merchant cruiser *Bulolo*. They'd often done boat drill and he tried to remember the little compass in boat no. 4 on the starboard side. It was in fact the only compass he'd ever seen, because his duties never took him near the bridge. But it was no use; he couldn't remember what it had looked like or how it had worked.

He sighed nostalgically for those six months in *Bulolo*. They'd seen the beginning and end of a naval career which had started and finished solely on account of the law. Started because he had to get away from Sydney in a hurry before a certain matter caught up with him, and finished six months later when it did . . . and he was returned to Sydney under armed escort to stand his trial for forgery. The law, of course, won and confirmed his view that those particular dice were heavily loaded against him. After that he'd done five dreary years in Long Bay gaol.

Much water had flowed under the bridge since then and it was a strange chain of circumstances which had put him down here in this inflatable dinghy somewhere in the middle of the Indian

Ocean. But he couldn't think of all that now. He had to get the hang of this goddam compass!

*   *

The lookouts changed at eleven o'clock, Canning and Basset relieving Wanalu and Lombaard. Mecky was excused duty because of his scalp wound.

Lombaard sat in the dinghy feeling the bristles on his cheeks and neck with the back of his hand.

"It's all right there." He nodded towards where he'd been sitting at the canopy entrance. "Nice and fresh . . . you can see things . . . albatross and flying fish."

Long sentence for him, thought Nada, he must be thawing.

"How's the neck?" she asked.

"No good, lady. Still stiff." His dark eyes screwed up, emphasizing the crow's-feet at the corners.

"Shall I massage it?"

"No," he said. "It'll be okay. I'm going to try for fish." He looked over to where Ezekiel Wanalu sat against the side of the dinghy, trouser-legs rolled up to the knees, rubbing his calves. "You too, hey?" It was more a command than a question.

The African didn't look up, but his voice was calm. "When I'm ready."

Lombaard gave him a long look and crawled over to the emergency pack and searched for the fishing line and hooks.

The girl looked at his broad back. He didn't like the African, she could see that. The trouble in the aircraft about the seats, she supposed.

He found a line and hook and held them up, looking at her. "Bait?"

She shook her head. "The survival booklet tells you what to do."

For some reason he smiled. A slow quizzical smile, the strong white teeth shining under the dark moustache.

"I don't need the book, lady . . . I know."

33

It was said quietly and modestly, but beyond contradiction.

He scrabbled in his trouser pocket for something and she saw the red tie. She remembered it—a little too red, a little too flashy, crushed and sodden now, but the same dazzling number that'd hit her in the eye when he boarded at Jan Smuts.

With a pocket knife he cut off a small strip a few inches long, and started to work it round the hook. He looked up and saw she was watching.

"Good bait, lady," he said seriously. "If they're here."

"What sort?"

He shrugged his shoulders. "Could be marlin, or tunny, or barracuda or bonito. I don't know." He worked away at the lure.

Nada wondered about him. He was big, muscular, strong, and the hair on the square head set on broad shoulders was dark, almost black, and cut short.

The face was strong too. Ugly in a nice way, she decided. Bushy eyebrows, dark eyes. The nose a little too full, perhaps, but the mouth was good and firm and the chin determined. He often frowned, his forehead wrinkling. He was burnt a dark brown and the stubble gave his face a shadowed tinge.

"D'you think they'll bite?" She hoped her voice didn't betray how vital the answer was to their survival.

He looked up.

"If God wants them to, lady."

She hoped fervently that God would, and then her thoughts were interrupted by a shout from Basset.

"I can see something."

Hopes in the dinghy soared. Sarah Tripp was nearest to Basset and in a moment she was leaning far out through the canopy opening.

"What? Where?" she shrilled.

Basset pointed over to port and there, not a hundred feet away, drifting parallel to them, was an orange-coloured object not much bigger than the overnight bags the airline had given them at the start of the journey.

Nada laughed happily. "It's a survival cot . . . how marvellous!" She felt slightly hysterical.

The paddles were quickly produced and by common consent handed to Wanalu and Lombaard. The drogue was pulled in, and they climbed astride the buoyancy chambers at each end and paddled hard in the direction of the floating cot. But progress was slow and though the lateral distance was closing the dinghy was drawing slowly ahead, travelling faster downwind than the cot.

Wanalu stopped and handed his paddle to Basset.

"Here, take this."

He crawled back under the canopy and pulled off his clothes until he was naked but for his underpants.

The others were leaning out of the canopy openings watching the survival cot and the African passed unnoticed until he said: "I'm going to swim it."

They looked round and Nada said: "Don't . . . the dinghy drifts much faster than you can swim. You'll never get back . . . there are sharks!"

The African grinned. "They don't go for brown skins, miss."

"That's not dinkum." Basset blinked. "I seen a black boy taken."

Wanalu tied the dinghy life-line round his waist, climbed onto the buoyancy chamber and went in neat and clean like an otter.

Surfacing, he flung his head clear of the water, turned and grinned at them, and was off at a fast crawl.

Basset was paying out the life-line.

"That coon c'n swim," his voice was full of admiration.

"Not too bad," Lombaard said grudgingly. He had a vivid picture of swimming with Esau in the cold clear waters of the dam at Soetwaters, around them the green hills dotted with sheep and far down in the kloof the sound of orioles calling.

Angelique's hands were clasped together in a gesture of supplication, her dark eyes tragic. "The baby . . . oh, I hope for the baby," she whispered.

Sarah Tripp shuddered. "What on earth will we do with a baby?"

"He's *terrific!* . . . He's nearly there!" Nada was kneeling on the buoyancy chamber, almost on the outside of the dinghy, clinging to the canopy opening.

They could see the African at times when he rose on a passing wave and then, just as Basset said: "Bloody rope's not gonna be long enough," Wanalu reached the cot. He held on to it and turned on the next wave, raising his arm in a signal.

Lombaard crawled across to Basset.

"Here," he said and took the line and started to pull on it slowly.

At the other end the African held the cot in front of him and kicked as he was pulled back to the dinghy. When he got alongside they lifted the cot inboard, and then helped him out of the water.

Under the canopy Nada knelt by the cot and unclipped its cover. The survival light was still burning; she pulled the cover back and looked in, eager, fearful, ready to lift out the small bundle. Let it be a warm bundle, she prayed. Then she laughed brokenly. "It isn't the baby. It's . . . it's other things."

They took them out . . . a fire-axe from the aircraft cabin and a whisky bottle. She pulled the cork and sniffed.

"It's water!" she said excitedly. "That's Iles. Just what he'd think of."

As she thought of him she felt an ache of misery and came near to tears. It wasn't that she was in love with Iles . . . she was supposed to be in love with Dieter . . . but Iles was a wonderful, wonderful man.

*   *

Ezekiel Wanalu M.P. sat on the side of the dinghy drying

himself in the downwind opening; he had no desire to dress
again because the wind and the hot sun and the occasional
flutter of spray from a passing sea were balm to his body, cramped
by the hours of sitting in the dinghy. Slowly he massaged his
muscular thighs and arms.

*   *

It had been hot on that other day, too, when the launch had
gone onto the sandbank. It was three o'clock . . . and there they
were hard and fast in midstream with the Zambezi, vast and
brown, flowing endlessly past them. There were plenty of flies
and mosquitoes and you had to keep slapping at them with your
hand if you were black, or with an important-looking horse-
hair switch if you were white like the Governor and his aides.

Ezekiel was wearing the khaki shorts and white singlet that
the rest of the crew wore, because theirs was not a swagger boat
in the Zambezi hierarchy and they did not have uniforms like
some of the big company boats downstream. The launch belonged
to bwana Flynn who had the trading-store at Gensa and he was
not a very rich bwana, but the Governor had to be content with
the boat because it was the best on that part of the river, with
quite a reliable engine. In fact, after that boat there was really
nothing much else at Gensa other than Father O'Harrigan's boat
which leaked badly and had an erratic two-stroke engine. Next
on the list was Chief Imasiku's dug-out, twelve paddles, big and
fast, but not suitable for important white men . . . especially after
a big lunch.

They shouldn't have gone on the sandbank, of course, but
bwana Flynn wished to impress the Governor, so he'd taken the
tiller himself instead of leaving it to Titus Musialela who knew
the Zambezi thereabouts like the back of his hand. It was because
of this good impression which had to be created that they'd all
been issued with white singlets . . . "You can pay for them later,"
explained bwana Flynn.

And so there they were hard and fast on the sandbank with all the bwanas talking at once, the Governor amused at first and then . . . when full astern and pushing and pulling made no difference . . . slightly annoyed, and finally . . . when the District Commissioner explained that they might be there some time . . . furious and very rude to poor bwana Flynn who had exhausted himself telling Titus Musialela—in the Barotse language—what a bloody fool he was not to have warned him about the sandbank. Titus had apologised profusely, admitted he was a bloody fool, and returned to his thoughts of Namangolwa, his newest acquisition, ripe and lush at seventeen, bought for the unusually high lobola of twelve cows, but on her showing so far worth every one of them. What was more, she got on well with his other three wives. Indeed, it was Namangolwa who was directly responsible for their predicament because had he not been so engrossed with thoughts about her he would assuredly have reminded bwana Flynn about the sandbank.

The Governor glared.

"Are you seriously suggesting we may have to spend the night here, my dear chap?"

The District Commissioner looked uncomfortable. "Just possible, sir. If a native boat doesn't come along before sunset."

"Good God!" The Governor was appalled. "These confounded mosquitoes will eat us alive."

But bwana Flynn was not the man to accept defeat lightly. He looked across to the nearest shore, just over one hundred yards away.

Yes! Why not? If he kept the Governor out all night he'd never get those concessions.

He was prepared to go up to a fiver . . . that was more than three months' pay for one of these chaps. Once one of them had got to the bank he could leg it back to the store and get Imasiku to send down the dug-out to take off the Governor and his party. Then they could take their time about getting the launch clear, using some of Imasiku's boys.

Flynn spoke to Titus Musialela. "Tell the boys I'll give a pound to the one who swims ashore with a message for Imasiku."

The four young Africans tittered quietly but respectfully, hands in front of their mouths, and only stopped when Titus told them to mind their manners. After a short conversation with them during which he raised his voice and became extremely insulting, he turned to bwana Flynn and said: "These sons of snakes say there are crocodiles."

"Of course there are!" snorted Flynn. "What do they think the bloody pound's for?"

The bargaining and haranguing went on until Ezekiel Wanalu . . . who was fourteen and had never seen five pounds together in his whole life . . . could resist the temptation no longer, and so with quick powerful strokes he swam to the shore, his mind shut to the terror of the crocodiles by the vision of those five crisp notes.

But the spirits of his ancestors, resting in the bodies of his father's cattle, had been with him throughout that swim as they had been ever since and Ezekiel reached the shore unmolested, delivered the message and the Governor and his party were rescued.

In itself the event was unimportant but the consequences for Ezekiel were epochal because the Governor was not only impressed and grateful but influential, and Ezekiel found that he had, so to speak, swum his way out of the mission school down to the secondary school at Livingstone and then on to Oxford . . . and finally, with a tremendous breasting of adverse and improbable tides and currents, that swim had taken him into Parliament and made him what he was . . . Ezekiel Wanalu, M.P., an aspirant cabinet minister in the next Government—and Ezekiel knew that it was not quite as far away as Whitehall hoped it was.

*   *

Shortly before noon Nada suggested setting up the radar reflector aerial. This was not easy because there was a good deal of motion in the dinghy, and the long pole with the bird-cage aerial on top had to be stepped into sockets on the buoyancy chamber outside the canopy. Normally, the drill was to lean out of the canopy opening and slip the pole into the sockets, but in that sea it proved impossible. However, Basset was small and agile and they accepted his offer to go outside and stand on the buoyancy chamber above the sockets. Once there they could pass him the aerial.

When Basset had crawled out, Lombaard knelt in the opening holding on with one hand, leaning out in the Australian's direction. Nada passed up the aerial and Lombaard took it. When the dinghy was on an even keel he called: "Here! . . . Grab!" holding it out to Basset who leant towards him.

"O.K.," shouted the Australian. "Let go!"

Lombaard released his grip and Basset swayed back, the aerial in one hand, the other clutching fiercely at the rim of the canopy's rainwater bowl. A sea loomed up, the dinghy took on a dizzy down-slope tilt, and Basset swung round, his back arched against the canopy, one foot on the buoyancy chamber, the other out over the water.

Lombaard shouted, "Look out man!"

There was an agonised "Jesus!" from Basset as he dropped the aerial and swung back to the canopy to hold on with both hands. They heard the aerial plop into the water as it sank into the Indian Ocean.

There was a stunned silence, broken by Canning. "Criminal stupidity!"

The voice was a mixture of fear and recrimination. The remark was addressed to Nada.

"Why did you suggest it in this weather? You're supposed to be in charge . . . you pretend to know everything . . . now you've ruined our chances of rescue."

Nada was pale and trembling. No one knew better than she what the loss of the aerial meant.

40

The search aircraft could cover huge areas of water with speed and exactitude using radar, but without the reflector aerial in the dinghy there would be no proper "blip" and if the searchers had to rely on their eyes the chances of finding the dinghy were remote—even in a flat calm, and it certainly wasn't that. She shook her head hopelessly.

Canning went on. "You've had too much say, that's the trouble." He was determined to press home his advantage. He was tired of taking orders from this girl with the foreign accent who pretended she was an Australian. "From now on . . ."

Jos Lombaard's deep voice broke in, curt and peremptory. "Leave her alone!"

The Afrikaner was crouching on the floor of the dinghy, his back to Canning.

Canning's eyes bulged with indignation. What right had this ignorant fellow to talk to him like that?

"You mind your own business!" he said sharply.

Lombaard turned round slowly, still crouching, his eyes screwed up, dark uncommunicative slits.

"Shut up!" It was a slow guttural threat. "Or I'll kick your arse!"

"Please! Please!" It was Sarah Tripp, tight-lipped, cold and prim, her long neck pushed up high above the life-jacket to register disapproval.

*   *

At noon Nada opened a tin of glucose. She gave them each a lozenge and explained how it should be held in the cheek and not crunched.

When he saw the tin Lombaard said: "Can I have that lid, lady?"

"What for?"

"They *might* take this," he held up the hook with the red lure, "but with that," he pointed at the lid, "it's *nearly* certain."

"What about God's will?" she asked and then was sorry because it sounded like blasphemy, and she could see he was not pleased.

"I said *nearly*." His voice was gruff.

After he'd unwound the lid from the opener he straightened it out and cut off thin strips with the surgical scissors from the first-aid outfit. He worked a strip through the hook until the lure was a two-tailed red and silver. He threw the lure into the water and slowly paid out the line until it streamed far up-wind and sea from the dinghy. Then with the warm sun on his face and the glucose lozenge sticky and sweet in his mouth, he settled down to wait, his thoughts going back to the last time he'd fished that ocean—far to the westward.

*   *

Less than an hour after they'd shoved off from the beach at Santa Carolina, they rounded Ponta da Carlos and began to feel the wind and sea. There was a light chop on the big indigo swells and they were coming in with the tops ruffled by the south-easter, not much but enough to make them look like old lace.

Andy told José to ease her down and then when they'd turned and were running to the south off Bazaruto they started a slow troll, the rods in the holders and the lines running up through the outriggers.

At eleven o'clock José turned the ski-boat and after about twenty minutes they took the sea temperature and it was dead right at 80°. The water was getting bluer too, just about the colour of Reckitts' which was a pretty good sign . . . but the outriggers went on springing and swishing and nothing came.

Soon after that there were a couple of alarms and the garfish baits were chopped by barracuda, so they put another garfish on one and a dorab on the other . . . just for the hell of it.

Then they sat there waiting, thinking plenty and watching the bait skittering in the water and the outriggers flexing and whipping, and sometimes by way of a change just looking at José's friendly black face. You can't move about much on a ski, you've just got to sit and wait and hope.

Round about the time they were chatting about one thing and another . . . Ferreira's marlin two days back . . . the honeymoon girl from Jo'burg who'd got drunk the night before and run down to the beach naked . . . just about then they heard the reel scream and he shouted: "Yours, man!" and he thought, So it's that dorab they've taken.

The line was singing as it raced off the reel and he was watching Andy and saying to himself, take it easy man! . . . count twenty slowly . . . take out a cigarette and light it . . . put it in your mouth and *then* strike!

When he reckoned sufficient time had passed to do all that and enough of the four hundred yards of line was off for the metal of the reel to show through, he thought, God! He *must* strike now! . . . and then he saw Andy tighten the drag.

Andy's shoulders went forward and he struck; once—twice—thrice, powerful blows, and the hook was in.

There was a moment of pause, of agonising shock deep under the water, and then the line started to sing again as it spun off the reel.

He shouted: "Follow him!"

José brought the ski-boat round and Andy recovered some of the lost line as he scrambled into the fighting-chair, where they strapped him in good and tight. Then the fish began to sound and Andy shouted, "Hell! Wonder if it's a bloody shark!"

He knew better than Andy that it didn't pay to guess . . . better to wait and see.

You can't afford to give him more line now, he thought, and then he saw Andy holding on tight, the line vibrating and singing. Just when he was wondering how long that could go on, the strain eased and José shouted as a black shape rocketed from the water more than two hundred yards from the ski. You'd have had to've been blind to have missed the long beak.

Quite unnecessarily he yelled, "Marlin!" and then he sat down to watch the fight, the sun blistering down from right overhead and Bazaruto away to starboard a smudge of land now, with the Mozambique coast out of sight below the horizon.

For two hours he watched the marlin fight off death with all its wild strength and anguish . . . surfacing, greyhounding, tail-walking and sounding, and all the time José was working the ski round so that a long bight of line was laid out through the water to add to the death load. Twice he got up and doused Andy with a bucket of sea-water, because he could see how the fight and the heat were getting him.

After a long time it became easier for Andy to recover the line; the marlin's runs were getting shorter until he was lying down deep in the water below them . . . a dark quivering shadow . . . and after a bit the marlin had to give again and finally—with broken heart and spirit—he'd come up spent to the surrender. He lay there wallowing, eleven feet and four hundred pounds of stream-lined, dying majesty. That was José's chance and he plunged the gaff into the shoulder. They slipped the chain round the tail and hauled the big fish up over the stern.

Watching the glory and light of the marlin fading as it died, he felt sad for the great fish, and wondered once again if it was right to kill for pleasure.

It seemed to Jos that he was still pondering that problem, the dying marlin lying at the stern with its long beak through the gap between the outboards, while José's serious face searched the sea as he steered, when he felt the tug . . .!

Then he was pulling in the line slowly, hand over hand, and Nada and Goldsworthy and Angelique were laughing and cheering and Basset was handing him the axe he'd shouted for when he felt the tug.

Three

AT TWO O'CLOCK in the afternoon they put out sea-marker dyes and began using the Sarah Beacon, but Nada had grave doubts. The neon-tester did not glow and although she said it must be faulty she had an agonising suspicion that the trouble was the beacon. But she was careful not to let the others know this and the drill for using the beacon was faithfully observed while the survivors huddled in the dinghy waiting hopefully for the distant note of aircraft engines which never came.

The widening spread of yellow water left by the dye markers streamed out behind the dinghy as it ran before the south-east trades.

*   *

Nada continued to be the centre of authority but the attack by Canning had not been without effect and there were signs that an English-speaking group—suspicious of all foreigners and therefore of Nada, Jos, Ezekiel and Angelique—was emerging in the persons of Canning, Goldsworthy, Basset, Mecky and Sarah Tripp, with Canning preparing himself for the role of leader now that the first catharsis of fear had cleared his mind.

After all, he reasoned, who is there here with anything like my background of experience and authority? If one is used to directing the affairs of a great organisation, to giving orders and making decisions which affect the lives of thousands of workers . . . well . . . one is naturally fitted to take charge in an emergency.

His head went up a little at the thought, and his eyes took on the glint he affected when dealing with subordinates . . . but then he sighed, for it was so different here in the dinghy where he was ill-equipped to deal with the realities of this frightening situation. Nostalgically he remembered the walnut-panelled office in the city: the mahogany desk; the fine chairs; the discreet walnut bookcase-cum-cocktail cabinet-cum-safe, made to his own design; to the left the table with the tape recorder and the telephones. He had only to depress any one of those twenty keys to summon some deferential aide; attentive, willing, eager to please and slightly apprehensive.

A downward flick of the first key on the right would bring in Goldsworthy; the third key from the left, Miss Williams. Neat, trim, a trifle grey now after fifteen years of Mr. Canning . . . but quick, efficient, patient and understanding.

*　　　　*

Nada shook her head.

"I don't know. I was in the after-cabin when it happened. I felt the engines being throttled back and then Iles came and told me there was a fire in the port outer engine. He said the extinguishers couldn't cope and we were going down because it might spread to a fuel tank or the spars. We were only at five thousand feet because they'd been losing height to get round the edge of that bank of cloud where the storm was. Iles said they were trying to send an SOS, but there was bad interference and they hadn't got a reply. Then he told me we were going to ditch and to stand by for the Captain's announcement."

She looked round at them.

"Well, you know what happened. He told you what he was going to do, while Iles and the radio operator and I got the dinghy and everything ready."

Sarah Tripp shuddered. It had been too ghastly. The Captain's announcement . . . those dreadful preparations . . . "We who are about to die salute you."

The eerie brightness of the flares over the water, the darkness in the cabin when the lights were switched off, the sinister hiss of air coming in through the ventilating ports, the crying of that baby as they strapped it into the survival cot . . . drowned suddenly by the hysteria of its mother. The acrid smell of smoke picked up in the ventilating system and drifting down through the cabin, the horror and unbelief in the eyes of the people near her, and then the straightening out as the pilot levelled off and held the aircraft just above the waves.

The paralysing terror of waiting to hit the water while one sat in that ridiculous position, head down on one's arms, arms resting on the tiny cushion on one's knees. Then the unbelievable violence of the impact as if one's body were being torn apart.

She couldn't remember much more. They hit the water and there was an explosion and she was struggling in the sea, trying to remember what the air hostess had told them to do.

Miraculously, in the wet blackness she found herself near two bobbing lights and they turned out to be the dinghy, and the air hostess and the African had clawed her into it. She'd crawled as far back as she could under the canopy to lie there half-dead, while the dinghy battled with those dreadful seas. Then mercifully she'd passed out.

*   *

When Mecky complained about the pain again she looked at the wound and saw it was inflamed. She poured water from the whisky bottle into a drinking-box from one of the purifiers and dissolved a chlorine tablet in it.

With cotton-wool she cleaned the wound with this solution, afterwards painting it with mercurochrome while Mecky complained.

Then he pleaded for water and she gave him an inch of it, in the bottom of the drinking-box after she'd rinsed it out in sea water. Still complaining he huddled up against the side of the dinghy and slept.

Later, Angelique insisted on examining Nada's cut cheek. Despite the air hostess's assurance that it was not worrying her, Angelique cleaned the cut and painted it with mercurochrome.

Ezekiel was at the canopy opening working on the barracuda with a pocket knife, the fish on the dinghy's buoyancy chamber, its blood running down the rubberised side into the sea. Nada watched him and wondered if many members of parliament could gut a fish so expertly.

"How shall we eat it?" she said.

"Dried," said Ezekiel. "In the sun." He pointed to the top of the canopy.

"Will it stay there?"

Lombaard hadn't said anything yet. It was his fish and here was this native cleaning it and deciding just what was to be done with it. It was about time somebody else had a say.

He looked at Nada, pointing at Ezekiel with his thumb. "When he's cleaned it, we'll cut it into strips and salt it first."

Ezekiel looked up. "Why salt it?"

"Keeps the flies away."

The black man stopped cleaning the fish. "There are no flies."

"There's no salt either," said Nada. "Only the tablets for us."

Lombaard glowered at them both, shrugging his shoulders. "*Ag*, man! Do what you like with the *verdomde* thing . . . I don't care."

When the African had cleaned the fish he dissected it neatly along the spine, making two halves. He threaded the end of the dinghy's life-line through the gills, stretching it over the canopy with the fish outside and the ends of the line drawn taut and made fast inside.

"In a few days it'll be good to eat."

Sarah Tripp shuddered. "God! What a thought!"

*　　　　*

The African was singing quietly to himself, an endless repetitive theme. He'd just come off lookout and he sat with his back to the dinghy's side, rubbing his calves.

"Can't we take these off now?" He looked at Nada and pointed to the life-jacket.

48

She spoke to the others. "What d'you think?"

Angelique began untying the tapes.

"Please," she sighed, "it is terrible . . . so hot, so awful the smell."

Nada watched Lombaard. He'd said nothing, but he too was untying the tapes. Quite soon everyone had shed their life-jackets, except Canning.

"I'm not parting with mine. Not while there're still these waves."

"We can use them as pillows," suggested Nada. "Right next to us if we want them in the night."

"Don't say I didn't warn you," said Canning prophetically.

Ezekiel started his quiet song again and Jos Lombaard coiled up the fishing line, slowly and deliberately as if he wanted this particular task to last a long time.

*　　　　*

It was while he was singing that Nada noticed Ezekiel had a special sort of face. In the aircraft he'd been a voice and a body and for the rest just another black face, but in the fourteen hours in the dinghy she'd been aware of a personality emerging. Now she saw that it had a distinctive face with its own set of features, that somehow fitted the personality.

Below the crinkly hair a broad forehead led to well-defined eyebrows which almost met on the bridge of the nose and then rose steeply, only to straighten out and fall again, giving the face a permanent expression of interrogation. The eyes were almond shaped and regarded one steadily without blinking, but they were truly African because what should have been the whites were yellow. They were challenging eyes and what Lombaard would have called cheeky. There was nothing humble or deferential about them, but they had not always been so. The humility had only lessened at Oxford, and the steady uninhibited look had come with the owner's successes, the results of many skirmishes on and off the political platform, some not without violence. The nose was broad and retroussé with elongated nostrils. The mouth was full and the lips ample and fleshy above a determined chin.

The face was more brown than black, and the skin shone as if it had a fine film of oil.

The general impression, decided Nada, interested in the discovery, was of a strong personality and, like Lombaard's, the face of a good man.

* *

The dinghy was designed to take twenty people so with its nine occupants it was not crowded, but since it was circular with a diameter of only ten feet, they were very close to each other and there was no privacy. Nature, however, took no account of these circumstances and as the day progressed from morning to afternoon some at least of the bladders and bowels had to be emptied. This could only be done if their owners sat at a canopy opening facing inboard, holding on with one hand at least, and extending the rump as far as possible outboard.

Their circumstances were so precarious, and the need to survive so paramount, that they attended to these requirements with considerably less embarrassment than they could have imagined in prospect. None the less, on the first occasion that Nada was compelled to squat in a canopy opening a situation developed.

Lombaard, who always turned away from the engaged side on these occasions, found that Ezekiel hadn't done so. Worse still he appeared to be watching the white girl and this filled the South African with such rage and disgust that he shouted: "Hey, you! Look this way, my boy!"

Ezekiel at once took exception to being called "boy".

"I'm not your *boy*," he said truculently. "Keep that for your kitchen."

If they'd been standing up Lombaard would have struck him, but hunched on the heaving floor of the dinghy it was not possible.

The Afrikaner was dark with rage. "If I see you looking at a white woman again at such a time . . ." he breathed heavily, "I'll smash you." And if there were any certainties in the dinghy it was that he would do just that and they all knew it . . . even Sarah Tripp who thought, You lout! Why bring colour into this?

After that there was a tense ten seconds while Ezekiel Wanalu's eyes burned as he looked at the white man. He turned away. "I wasn't looking. I was thinking." His voice was surly.

*   *

Nada sat at the up-wind opening, her arms on the side of the dinghy, chin resting on them, while she breathed in the fresh salty air and looked out at the wastes of blue water, over the endless rows of charging white horses. The air was hot and damp under the canopy, foetid with the odours of rubberised canvas and human bodies. The pungent mixture of fresh and stale sweat, an acrid sour synthesis, predominated.

Basset was on lookout next to her but they had nothing to say to each other, so she sat there in silence watching the seas coming up to the dinghy, lifting it so that at the top of each wave a ridge formed on the floor with the two halves sagging a little on either side. Every now and then the crests would throw off spray and the cold tingle of it splashing into her face was refreshing.

She looked at the time. It was nearly four o'clock in the afternoon. Only fifteen hours since they'd ditched and it seemed like a lifetime. The problem of survival was so urgent, so much one continuing crisis, that she'd had no time for thought. It seemed to her now in these few minutes, sitting there doing nothing for the first time since she'd climbed into the dinghy, that there really was no other life than this. Life had started with the dinghy. When she'd struggled in the water and seen the canopy lights winking in the darkness, she'd known that once in the dinghy life would start again.

Only *now* was important, not the future. Two days before she'd thought that death might not be a bad thing. That was when she'd read Dieter's letter with its endless excuses. Why didn't he just write: "I've had all I want of you, Nada, and I'm now busy with another girl."

But now Dieter didn't seem at all important, nor was it important who crawled onto the studio couch with him in the little flat in Hillbrow, so carefully furnished for seduction. What did it matter? Life was the only thing that mattered. The assurance that one would go on waking up each morning to see the brightness of the day, to enjoy the simple wonderful things that one had always taken for granted, because one was so busy making life complicated that there was no time to notice them.

How wonderful if now, at this very moment, an aircraft were to come over and circle before diving low to dip its wings in greeting and then climb again to circle, while it directed other aircraft and ships to the scene so that quite soon there would be a ship alongside, then a lifeboat with clean freshly shaven sailors manning it. Strong arms would lift her out of the dinghy and into the boat and soon she would be on board the steamer, drinking and eating, soaping herself in a steaming hot bath, dressing, performing the rites of initiation for return to that wonderful prophylactic world where everything was done for you and where you were always safe.

She looked round to where the others were sitting or lying under the canopy . . . at the dirty unkempt faces, the ragged disaster-stained garments, creased and torn, the jumble of life-jackets and shoes which they dared not part with, the pieces of dried fish—brought in after the Afrikaner had caught his second barracuda and they'd decided against putting it all on the canopy in case the albatrosses took it.

The only person who looked anything like normal was the Mauritian woman. She'd taken off her coat, shoes and stockings and wore only a dark Terylene blouse with short sleeves and a dark Terylene skirt. The long hair was pulled back and tied behind her neck with a piece of tape which she'd taken from the survival cot. Somehow she'd contrived to wash her face with sea water, and there was a healthy glow in her cheeks above the soft open lips which looked permanently red and moist in spite of all their owner had endured.

For the first time Nada noticed the jewellery. A ray of sunshine came into the dinghy as it rode the crest of a wave, and Nada saw the flashes of light. They came from Angelique's fingers: a large solitaire diamond in one ring and a set of three lime-coloured diamonds in another; an eternity ring studded with tiny diamonds between two lines of sapphires, and a simple gold wedding ring. Pinned across her blouse, just above the neck-line, there was a lover's knot in diamonds. Fabulous, thought Nada, but how useless here!

She saw that Angelique was sucking something and wondered what it was, until she remembered she'd told them to suck buttons to assuage their thirst until the first issue of water the next morning.

Beyond the half-caste, Sarah Tripp was asleep, sprawled sideways, her head resting on a life-jacket, the mouse-coloured hair a tangle of knots over a dirt-smudged face. She slept with her mouth open, breathing deeply. The summer frock was dirty and crumpled, and next to her lay a bundled up green cardigan she'd taken off because of the heat. She was still wearing stockings and they were torn and laddered, hanging in wrinkles.

Other than the lookouts, Basset and Canning, the men were asleep. Jos and Ezekiel had taken off their coats and shirts and hung them across the steadying lines, and they wore nothing but singlets and trousers.

Basset, Canning and Goldsworthy had kept on their clothes and Canning was still wearing his life-jacket and shoes and socks. These at least Basset had removed, but he had refused to take off his coat . . . not even to let it dry early in the forenoon when they had all been drying clothes. Nothing would part him from it and Nada wondered if he were wearing a dicky or some other strange garment he preferred not to disclose? Or was he ashamed in some strange way of that skinny figure?

*   *

Canning was still smarting from the clash with Lombaard for he knew he'd met his match in the Afrikaner. Lombaard was a powerful brute, and he'd obviously stop at nothing. Besides he was a foreigner and you could never predict what they'd do. Evidently he had no respect for age or position, or he would never have dared to speak to Herbert William Canning like that. He'd have to be watched very carefully. Fortunately Lombaard and the African didn't like each other. Just as well, because the African was another man who'd have to be watched. He was young and well-built and pretty quick on the uptake. You could never tell what these black fellows were thinking.

Canning knew that the girl didn't like him and she clearly didn't appreciate his importance and the influence he could wield with her Company. After all, Trans Ocean Air Lines was a newcomer looking for support, particularly in the freight field. She was anti-British, no doubt, like all the other foreigners, although she claimed to be an Australian. Must have been one of that immigrant bunch they'd swept out of the gutters of Europe after the war.

By and large he realised he'd have to use all his wits and cunning to survive, particularly as he was by far the oldest person in the dinghy. A wave of self-pity swept him and his eyes misted up so that he had to clear them by rubbing a finger over the lids.

The thing to do about the Afrikaner and the African was to divide and rule. Good old British policy! Somehow keep them at loggerheads so that they didn't gang up and take advantage of him. Or of the others. Make no mistake! Whatever he did would be in the interests of all.

*   *

An hour after sunset, when it was quite dark, there was a sudden storm of wind and rain. The wind came first in tearing gusts which threatened to whip up a big sea and then, just as they were filled with despair at the prospect of another night of storm, the wind dropped and the rain came, a heavy downpour—and they began to behave like wild animals.

Nada screamed at them not to take the water but they ignored her, and there they were shouting and pushing each other and drinking, three at a time, from the catchment inlets. She begged them not to drink too much or too quickly, but they took no notice until Sarah Tripp began vomiting . . . then they calmed down.

But the rain was kind and they were able to fill two life-jackets and these were put under Nada's care.

Frightened by the lack of discipline during the rainstorm, she asked Lombaard and Wanalu to accept responsibility for the water supplies and their rationing, and she emphasised the gravity of the situation. Shamefaced at their own lack of control, they undertook to do this and to change their lookout shifts so that they wouldn't be on duty at the same time. Nada agreed to do Jos's next lookout stint to make the change possible. She saw that Lombaard was not happy about sharing this duty with Wanalu, but evidently he realised that none of the other men could exercise the necessary physical control.

Mecky entered a squeaky protest against these arrangements, and he was supported by Basset and Canning. But the latter was in no mood yet for a test of strength with the Afrikaner, so the matter was not pressed.

Nada breathed a sigh of relief. Now they would get some discipline in the dinghy.

*

As the day wore on the south-east trades and the upward thrust of the south equatorial current continued to drive the dinghy away from the ditching position, and although its inmates were unaware of this they were moving steadily in a north-westerly direction. To them it seemed that they were wallowing aimlessly and uncomfortably in the same place, while the endless seas capped with foaming ridges sped by, tipping the dinghy derisively in their flight.

In the late afternoon, lookouts were doubled and all conversation ceased so that they might not fail to pick up the distant note of engines. The Sarah Beacon was held aloft at regular intervals, and in their minds they saw its pulsations winging outwards through the atmosphere until they struck the complicated electronic devices of the searching aircraft. Then the nose of the aircraft would turn quickly so that the distant bearing of the dinghy would become the course to steer to find it.

But nothing came, and in the west the sun lost itself behind a high bank of cumulus, edging it with salmon and painting the western sky a fiery bronze where distant wisps of cloud drifted like golden feathers. Soon the sun dropped below the cumulus and sank in a final blaze until all daylight was gone, and the swift night of the tropics had taken over.

Soon after dark they fired two more distress signals at five-minute intervals. After each they waited with muted hope for some answering signal, but none came.

Instead there was the insistent sigh of the wind, the endless hiss and slap of the seas as they passed, and beyond that nothing but the heavy breathing in the dinghy.

Lookouts were posted and under the canopy they settled down in a mood of deep depression to face the long night, to be harrowed by false alarms, imagined sightings, and restless dreams.

Four

EXHAUSTED though she was she knew she couldn't afford to sleep. The search aircraft were out, shipping had been alerted, this was the night . . . the first after ditching. Whatever had happened the dinghy could not be too far from a broadly defined area of probability. If the point of ditching had been estimated by Operations within three hundred miles, then the square of search had sides of six hundred miles. Aided by the dinghy's radar reflector aerial, emergency radio and the Sarah Beacon . . . or any one of them . . . two aircraft doing a squared search should find it within six hours . . . and from almost every point of view night was better for that than day.

But they had no emergency radio . . . they had no radar reflector aerial and the Sarah Beacon . . . well, was it working?

What then?

A good lookout! That was the essential for survival. Nada knew she must listen, not sleep. Perhaps she would hear the aircraft before the others. Then they could fire the two-star-reds. One every twenty seconds while you heard the aircraft. It might not see the first or the second or the third, but it would definitely see the fourth or the fifth or the sixth . . . and then they would be found and this ugly, frightening dream would be over.

And so listen! . . . Don't relax! . . . Listen!

She would not sleep.

Rest?

Yes, perhaps!

Except for a brief period of unconsciousness after she'd fainted, she hadn't slept for nineteen hours. In that time she'd drunk four ounces of water and eaten two glucose lozenges. Her body and mind had been subjected to shocks and strains far beyond their normal thresholds . . . but sleep was not to be contemplated. It was nine o'clock, Mecky and Canning were on watch. Leave it to them?

Impossible!

The life-jacket was not a bad pillow. Unpleasant odour . . . hot damp rubber, faint suggestion of vomit and urine, but soft under the head. And the movement of the dinghy? Not too bad really, now that one was used to it. A rocking, cradling motion and . . .

And her father saying: "A good day in the school. The children were excellent. We had the chief inspector from Belgrade . . . Ivo Milic . . . the same as last year. Very anxious to please his new masters. Toeing the party line, of course. But in the privacy of my study . . ." he shook his shoulders, ". . . apologetic, my dear. Even a little ashamed, I daresay."

Then her mother said, "Run along, Nada. This is not for you. Your father and I wish to talk."

She ran out onto the terraced vineyard in front of the house and climbed the white stone wall to gaze out to the islands before Peljesac . . . out over the Adriatic to Korcula, Lastovo and Mljet.

Farther down the terrace the moon shone on the white of other walls, and the spring air was heavy with the scent of vines and figs and blown almond blossom and underlying these the musky smell of wine in the cellar.

Far below a dark thing no bigger than her hand entered the path of the moon splashed across the sea in iridescent silver, and she heard the creak of oars.

A shadow spilt over her foot and she pulled it back into the moonlight. The shadow came from the olive tree and though *pretty well everything* could be explained one could never be quite free of fear. Not if one had been in Peljesac when *they* came. Not if one had experienced *those things*. They were not talked about now but they were always with you, even if you were three when they came and seven when they left. You remembered the hushed voices, the drawn curtains, the stealth by night, the knock on the door in the darkness of early morning, the sound of shots, the noise of guns, and the flames and crackle of burning houses. And of course the bombs. The noise of bombs which made one's parents laugh though they were frightened. Made them laugh for reasons one could not comprehend.

That was before she had gone to school in Dubrovnik—that moonlight night—sitting on the wall, the creature of adolescent dreams and fears, wondering what her parents were saying.

Then she heard the whistle . . . low, discreet, repeated three times, at each the note rising higher, to make something stir within her, exciting, unknown, forbidden, the blood racing to her head, her stomach churning.

It was Dimitri Pavic. He had seen her in the moonlight from the terrace above her family's house.

There it was again, much nearer. He must have come down with incredible speed because he was next to her now, saying: "Did you hear it? Did you hear it?"

*   *

"Did you hear it?" Canning's voice was urgent. "We must do something at once!"

She scrambled up. "What is it?"

They were all awake now.

"An aircraft—I heard the engines."

Mecky's voice broke in. "I didn't. Not a thing."

She realised that Mecky and Canning were still the lookouts. I couldn't have slept for long, she thought, but then she looked at the luminous dial of her watch, and saw that it was two o'clock in the morning . . . she'd slept for five hours!

Canning was insistent. "I heard it, I tell you!"

"Funny, I didn't."

"No good arguing," it was Jos's guttural voice. "Let's do something."

"Of course." Nada was wide awake now. She felt in the emergency pack and brought out the tin of two-star-reds.

"Here!" she said frantically. "Fire them at twenty second intervals!"

After each was fired there was an agonising wait while they searched the clouded sky and the unseen horizon for some answering sign, but none came. When they'd fired four they stopped. The stock of flares was dwindling and Mecky was so sure that Canning had imagined the noise that no one really believed it had been an aircraft. But hope died hard and they listened breathlessly, every nerve strained for the distant thrum of engines above the noise of the wind and sea. But there was nothing.

For a long time afterwards they sat huddled in the dark, unable to see each other, discussing the chances of rescue, going over and over the same ground. Canning bitter and apprehensive, Goldsworthy trying to placate him, Mecky cheerless and dispirited, Basset whining and threatening—Jos and Ezekiel silent and non-committal, each wary of what the other might say. Of the women only Sarah Tripp gave way to despair, abusive of everyone . . . the airline, the crew, the emergency equipment, the rescue set-up and of course Nada.

"You *would* be asleep. You're one of the crew . . . you should have acted the moment the noise was heard."

Angelique's gentle voice broke in. "She is tired. *Sacré Dieu*, she cannot be always without sleep. But for her we would be already drowned."

*   *

Daylight came suddenly and brought with it knowledge of another set-back: during the night the drogue had been lost. Jos had been on lookout and he'd noticed just before dawn that the dinghy was swinging slowly one way and then the other, sometimes completing a full circle, at others rotating only halfway round and then swinging back, the pace of rotation varying as much as the direction.

He'd watched this for some time, puzzled. Then he'd leant over and seen that the drogue line was slack. When he pulled it in the end was frayed where it had parted.

They considered using the paddles as a drogue but eventually decided against it because of the danger of losing them, although Mecky pointed out that there was unlikely to be any use for paddles in the middle of the Indian Ocean. But they remembered they'd been some help when the survival cot was sighted, and they felt they might be of importance again.

Now as they drove before the south-east trades the motion was more uncomfortable, and the lookouts found themselves constantly in difficulties because the dinghy would turn suddenly and present an entirely new sector of the horizon, only to snatch it away a few moments later in favour of another.

*   *

Somebody mentioned the compass—forgotten since it had been handed to Art Basset the day before, to become for him a symbol of the mysterious and unfathomable.

"What we should know is the direction in which we're travelling." Canning's jowls overflowed the life-jacket, the white stubble of another day's growth emphasized by the redness of his complexion.

Signs of privation were beginning to show. The cheeks were thinner, the mouth not quite so full, the sensuous lower lip dry and cracking.

Mecky was fingering his wound. "What's the use? Haven't a clue where we are."

"At least we would know something."

"Something that can't help us . . . that we can't do anything about."

Jos looked at Basset. "Where's the compass?"

"Over there," Basset yawned, pointing with his thumb. "N.B.G. anyway. Don't wonna work."

Jos crawled over the heaving floor and fetched the compass.

"Looks all right to me."

He fiddled with it, moving it this way and that, then cupping it in his lap, waiting for the revolving card to settle. But the turning and twisting of the dinghy was too much and when he'd managed to get the rough direction of the wind he gave up.

"Wind's from the south-east," he said.

"Of course," said Ezekiel.

"Of course what?"

"From the south-east. The sun and stars tell that."

Jos gave a surly grunt.

Nada remembered, then, the ocean chart she'd looked at in the cockpit. "It's the south-east trades."

Jos nodded. "*Ja*. We're drifting north-west."

Canning's eyes flickered. "Where does that bring us? I mean—what's ahead?"

Jos was trying to remember the spread of the atlas, the big green one in his workroom at Soetwaters. Africa was on the left if you were looking north. Then Madagascar immediately to the right of the east coast, and after that a great sweep of ocean right across the page—way over to the east where the edge of Australia showed around Perth.

The dinghy was somewhere in the middle of that great sweep. To the south he remembered there was nothing . . . you went clear away down to Antarctica . . . and to the north was India. But they'd ditched about half-way between Mauritius and Cocos, and they were drifting north and west . . . so where could that land them? That was the part he couldn't remember.

Up there?

What was up there?

Sarah Tripp had been doing the same mental exercise but with a better picture of the spread of the atlas, and she brought to the problem a university mind and a photographic memory.

"I imagine," she said dryly, "that *if we survive* we'll hit either the north-eastern tip of Africa somewhere near Cape

Guardafui or we'll drift to Saudi Arabia, provided of course the wind keeps like this and there are no currents against us, and we all stay merry and bright."

Canning's knowledge of geography was perfunctory, but what Sarah had said sounded reasonable. He clutched at the straw. "That would be how far?"

She did some mental arithmetic, thinking in terms of latitude ... ten degrees to six hundred miles ... it was a simple little sum, but the answer frightened her.

"About two to three thousand miles," she said in a strangled voice. "Anything from one to two months at say three miles an hour ... and I suppose we're doing much less."

The implications of this were too much for Canning. He crouched back, his breath coming in short gasps ... then he began to whimper.

Jos looked at him with contempt. "That won't help you."

Canning's brain took over quickly. Emotion and survival didn't go together. Sorry as he was for himself he mustn't let self-pity take charge and put him at a disadvantage with these others.

"I wasn't thinking of myself," he said brokenly—and Winifred Canning would have been astonished at what came next—"But my wife is a—a—helpless soul ... and ... I had a sudden picture of the poor woman ... trying ... trying to manage on her own." He sniffed and dabbed at his eyes with a grubby handkerchief.

Goldsworthy looked at him and thought, Dear me—who'd have thought the Chief could be so fond of someone. They'd never believe it in Fenchurch Street.

"Expect you're well heeled, ain't you, Chief?" Basset broke in irreverently. "I mean, she'll collect some mazuma?"

Canning ignored him, and Basset once again resolved that he'd take over the waterproof gold watch with the heavy strap if anything should happen to the old bastard.

"As an ex-naval *petty* officer," Sarah Tripp was heavily sarcastic,

"you haven't contributed much to this navigational problem."
She fixed him with the chilling look she reserved for inattentive
undergraduates.

"Whatsa good?" Basset whined. "Miles and miles of sweet
fanny, and we gotta go where the wind blows us."

"Personally, I doubt if you *ever were* in the Navy."

Basset's eyes narrowed as he rolled up the sleeve of his coat
and turned his forearm round so that she could see the foul anchor
with *H.M.S. BULOLO* tattooed below it. He bared his teeth in
an exaggerated snarl. "See, Miss smarty pants?"

She turned away in disgust and began to clean the thick lensed
glasses on her petticoat.

But all the same Art Basset never again laid claim to any special
nautical knowledge. The golden rule was never to work a racket
unless you got away with it, and he hadn't with this one.

*　　　　　*

Soon after dawn Jos and Ezekiel issued the first ration of water.
Four ounces each, with the promise of more at noon and in the
evening.

Later, Nada read aloud to them from the Sea Survival booklet
about food and water rationing and the need for rest—to conserve
body moisture by reducing perspiration to the minimum. She
gave them each a glucose tablet.

Angelique and Sarah cleaned and dried the dinghy as best they
could, bailing out the water which had splashed in during the
night and sponging the floor dry.

They topped up the buoyancy chambers and double bottom with
the bellows and made some attempt to square off the inside by
pushing the life-jackets and odd shoes into separate heaps and
hanging the discarded clothing over the steadying lines.

Nada again washed and painted Mecky's scalp wound. The
inflammation was subsiding, although he complained that the
pain was as bad as ever and that he'd not had a wink of sleep.

Of the other casualties, Lombaard reported some improvement

in the stiff neck—he was now able to turn his head slightly either way without pain—and Angelique again doctored the cut on Nada's cheek which was healing.

Most of them were suffering from dried and cracked lips and these were rubbed lightly with burn cream from the first-aid outfit. In spite of the canopy there was some sunburn but nothing serious.

They'd discovered that it was advisable to accept a little water in the dinghy from the crests of the seas, rather than fasten the curtains over the openings. With both entrances open a refreshing breeze swept through blowing away the stale air under the canopy and lowering the temperature.

By eight o'clock in the morning, their various tasks completed, all but the lookouts settled down to rest. It had been agreed that fishing should be left to the comparative cool of evening as they'd not yet touched the fish caught the day before.

Little of consequence happened during the rest of that forenoon while the dinghy ran on before the wind and sea, twisting and turning now added to the motions of dipping and climbing. The worst pangs of seasickness were over, although they'd left in their wake an exhausted Canning and a somewhat emaciated Sarah Tripp. But even she was showing more signs of life and now joined in much of the conversation; if only to lash Basset with her tongue, for she seemed to loathe him.

*   *

Mecky watched the circle of water with a dull eye. He seemed to have been doing lookout duty for weeks, for months, for years . . . instead of only for a day. Hour on, hour off throughout the day and night . . . what a ghastly existence. He wondered how long they'd go on like this, drifting aimlessly under a tropical sun with little food and water and no hope unless you were the most congenital optimist.

He thought back over the sequence of events which had brought him to this point.

"It's due to Africanisation, Mecky," the general manager looked out of the windows of the large cool office in Delamere Avenue.

"You know it's the company's policy to have a trained cadre of Africans in certain key points before independence."

The eyes came back from the window and lighted on Mecky with cold disapproval. "You're a bachelor—high up on the list of those suitable for early transfer."

While he talked he shuffled the papers on the desk.

"That's why Head Office has arranged for the transfer to Melbourne. In the circumstances," he gave Mecky another cold appraising glance, "I think you'd be well advised to accept the arrangements."

Of course he'd accepted them! He hadn't any option. They both knew that "the circumstances" were not Africanisation. They were Paul.

Pale, artistic, gentle Paul . . . Paul, with twice the G.M.'s brains and a sensitivity that the whisky-swilling "types" in the club could never comprehend because to them he was queer; an intellectual. Just as well they didn't know what he and Paul thought of them.

How he longed to be back in the flat up on the Hill. It was on a corner on the top floor and from it one looked out over a vast panorama from the Ngong Hills in the south-west to the dark hump of Ol Donyo Sabak in the north-east. In the centre, across the city, lay the thorn-scrub and rolling grasslands of the game plains and the thin line of the Athi River. Below the flat there was a broad sweep of lawn with indigenous trees in which bougain-villaeas climbed and twisted to festoon the crowns with splashes of Gauguinesque colour. Beyond the lawn, in the middle distance, the suburbs led up to the business centre where towers of concrete were bathed in equatorial sunlight.

Mecky's mind quickened at the thought of the flat. It was exquisite, but of course Paul had been the main source of inspiration. He had a genius for colour and texture. Who but he could

have thought of the bedroom. It was eccentric in shape, narrow
at the back but widening towards the large contemporary window
which looked out over Nairobi. The symphony of indigo and
ivory and gold was breathtaking. The walls were papered in a
rough ivory silk, the indigo curtains were corduroy with golden
cords. This theme was caught up in the bedspreads of heavy
satin in purest gold. A final touch of genius was the snow white
carpet.

The living-room was austerely simple. Wine-coloured wall-to-
wall carpeting, a contemporary settee and chairs finished in dove-
grey suède, an ivory white coffee table, the walls papered in
Japanese grass, a heavenly setting for the abstracts Paul had
collected in Paris.

Mecky could never think of them without a wave of indignation
because of the night "the types" had invaded the flat, arriving
disgustingly drunk and behaving as if they were in a bear garden.
He winced at the recollection of their boorish insensitivity. How
he loathed them . . . "the types" who had been responsible for
his transfer. It was they who had pinned that senseless jingle on
the club notice-board:

> "*Mecky has a little flat,*
> *It's really awfully queer,*
> *But not as queer,*
> *My dear, I swear,*
> *As who he lives with there.*"

Of course it had been the most dreadful shock to both of them,
but what was so criminal was that the whole thing had been taken
up at Head Office level. Then had come the news of the transfer
to Melbourne and after that the parting from Paul.

*   *

If only she could remember some of the detail on the ocean
chart. She'd looked at it often in the cockpit, but somehow one
always looked for the places one knew. There's Mauritius and

that little atoll over there's Cocos—Keeling. There, if you follow the course line eastwards, is the Australian coast with Perth and Fremantle on top of each other . . . and there's . . .?

But if you come off that course line what do you find to the north, especially to the north-west if the trade-winds are blowing you in that direction?

It was no use . . . she just couldn't remember.

She had a vague recollection of the Seychelles to the north of Madagascar, and of the Maldives south of India. But was there anything else? Or must they drift for months as Sarah Tripp had suggested before hitting the north-east tip of Africa or, beyond that, the coast of Arabia?

Terror struck her and she sensed that Sarah was right . . . *there was nothing else*.

So . . .?

Shipping lanes, of course!

With the hazy picture of the ocean chart still in her mind she tried to remember the shipping lanes.

The dinghy was too far north for the South African-Australian run. The Aden-India-Fremantle run? No! That was at least a thousand miles west of where they'd ditched.

So what?

The answer which one had to face was that there weren't any other shipping lanes that one could think of.

So it was the air-search then . . .? Well, this was only the morning of the third day. Operations wouldn't give up easily—or would they?

Even if they didn't hear one peep from one emergency radio in one dinghy. Even if there were no transmissions from Sarah Beacons. Not even one blip on one radar screen?

But there weren't any other dinghies after that explosion. They'd got away with it because they were in the tail unit that had stayed floating for nearly five minutes. There'd been no other lights on the water . . . no answering two-star-reds.

She gave it up.

It was easier to look out over the endless circle of water. It was nearly ten o'clock in the morning, the chores were all done, and now there was nothing for it but to sit and wait . . . and listen. The lookouts might miss something, so go to one of the entrances and back them up. Search with smarting eyes carried in a sore head on a smelly, itching body . . . and stare and stare at the horizon as if concentration must bring something . . . the top of a funnel or a mast . . . or just the sound of aircraft.

Suck away at the button, lick with a dry tongue over the cracked lips, listen to the belly-rumbles as the stomach gases effervesce, feel the skin as it dries and wrinkles, urinate the dark foetid liquid and suffer its burning protest at the wanton act of dehydration.

Scratch at the embryo eruptions where the salt water sores are forming, pick with a dirty nailed finger to ease the itch of mucus filled nostrils, scratch the cracked and drying scalp below the dank knotted hair.

But above all keep your pecker up! Remember, you're the only crew member on board!

"The chances of survival for all will depend to a great extent upon the resourcefulness of members of the crew and the example they set."

Lecture number three, and you turn to Iles who is sitting next to you and say: "Are you resourceful, Iles?" and he winks and says: "Try me, baby!"

If one could muster the energy to interest oneself there was really plenty to see.

The flying fish! They started so suddenly, so full of energy, emerging explosively as if they'd been catapulted out of the water; then whirring like locusts until, with a brief glide, they bump-splashed into a swell and found themselves once again in the sea.

And the porpoises which brought everyone to the canopy openings, and somehow made one feel less lonely. Twice she'd seen the fins of sharks, enigmatic and menacing, as if they were watching the dinghy, and she'd shuddered. But she loved the albatrosses. There was a solemn majesty about them; that effortless glide and . . . her thoughts trailed off. She was too tired to think.

The sky was filled with high banks of cumulus with here and there patches of blue, and dark shadows scurried across the water so that sometimes the dinghy was in shadow and at others in sunlight.

* *

She sat with her hands on her lap, back against the buoyancy chambers, feet drawn up, eyes half closed. Her face was serene, but she was afraid.

They should have arrived in Sydney the morning before and Kwan would have been there to meet her. By now the news that the aircraft was down in the sea would have been flashed all over the world, and Kwan would know and be desperate. He would reveal nothing of those feelings and people at the airport would say: "That Chinaman never moved a muscle when he heard the news . . . funny devils!"

That absurd myth of Chinese inscrutability and lack of emotion. If only they knew Kwan as she did: the deep emotions, the rapid changes of mood and expression so evident once you knew him; above all his devotion to her.

This was something she could never feel for him . . . the difference in age was too great. He was nearly sixty. Gratitude and respect, yes, but not love. He was a Cantonese; Kwan Lee to the Chinese on the island, but Douglas Lee to the Europeans with whom he did business.

They knew him as a wealthy merchant but they scarcely knew her at all for there was an unofficial colour bar in Mauritius and Europeans and Chinese rarely met socially.

Angelique was not Chinese and Kwan had done an unusual thing in marrying her. In the early days of his merchant successes he saw her once when she was fifteen and vowed she would be the mother of his children. Despite the protestations of family and friends . . . and leading members of the Chinese community . . . he swept her out of the indifferent house of her foster parents and installed her in his fine house in the better part of Port Louis' Chinese quarter.

She had only the vaguest notions of her origin, but resented any suggestion that she was a Creole. Her mother who had died at her birth was French, and had worked in a shop owned by a Chinese family. These were the people who had adopted her. Her Chinese "aunt" often spoke of this mother but never a word about the father. Every inquiry Angelique might make evoked a tight-lipped shake of the head, and she'd long since given up asking.

So all that she really knew was that she was half French. But as a small girl she had for her own peace of mind invented a father. She was dark, so she'd decided he must be Greek. Ever since she'd carried in her mind a rather hazy picture of a dashing cavalier with black moustachios and a dazzling smile. The picture had been there so long that Angelique was sometimes not sure whether he was fiction or fact.

Once installed as Kwan's wife, she'd devoted her considerable talents to justifying his choice and in this she succeeded well for she was a capable woman.

Capable of everything, except having babies. That she apparently could not do and though it was a great sorrow to her, Kwan did not seem to mind.

Perhaps it was because he found Angelique all satisfying. She was handsome, intelligent, quiet and calm. She spoke Chinese and English in addition to the peculiar French of the Island and she ran his house superbly.

Paradoxically, it was because she meant so much to him that she was in the dinghy. He had gone to Australia on a business visit which had had to be extended. After four weeks he could stand it no longer and he cabled her to join him in Sydney for the remainder of the visit. From Australia he planned to take her on to Hong Kong, and then back to Mauritius by way of India.

With customary serenity Angelique had read the cable, packed her luggage and boarded the aircraft . . . all within forty-eight hours . . . and now here she was floating around on the Indian Ocean in a dinghy, with Kwan near breaking point somewhere in Sydney.

*   *

Sebastian Goldsworthy did not know whether he was dreaming or thinking. It was a recurring jumble of old recollections, always new in their terror; the screech of rubber tyres locked against bitumen; a little body flying into the air, turning slowly at the top of the parabola, legs and arms spread-eagled, then falling back heavily on the road, the toy bucket clattering to rest beyond the inert bundle.

There were screams and shouts and people running and she was in front of them, horror in her eyes. Now she was speaking to him from a great distance, her voice urgent, supplicant, strangely blurred. "I need you, Sebastian, I *need* you."

But he couldn't speak, it wasn't that sort of telephone, so he waited in muted terror, his heart breaking, for what he knew must come.

Twice more she called his name, then there was a despairing sob and the line went dead. He was left with nothing but the echo of her sobbing.

Somewhere a door opened and a slight pallid young woman came in, notebook and pencil in hand. "I've done my best, Sebastian. He can't give you a time now, but he'll see you as soon as possible."

Then he was standing at the door waiting, the familiar knot of anxiety in his belly, his chin thrust up and away from the collar in an attempt at reassurance, but all he could say was: "The line went dead . . . the line went dead."

Goldsworthy kept muttering the words in his sleep, and Mecky who was lying next to him shook him once more.

"Shut up," he hissed. "For God's sake shut up, man."

*   *

"Hey, watch it! You're peeing all over me, you silly bastard!" Basset's whine ended on a high note.

"Sorry," said Ezekiel. "When I started I was doing it down wind, but we've swung round again."

Sarah Tripp shuddered.

"Must you use that foul word?"

The Australian's lips curled. "Listen, smarty pants! Don't try your airs and graces with me. Won't pay, you know. Dinky-di it won't."

She recoiled, turning her head away.

"You've got a foul mouth, Basset. Better watch it!" Jos's voice was threatening.

Basset scowled, his narrow eyes a mixture of fear and dislike.

"What I could do with," said Jos, changing the subject, "would be a nice piece of fresh mutton with plenty of potatoes and some pumpkin and mealie samp."

"The last thing I want is food," Mecky made a disapproving noise in his throat and glared at Jos. Instinctively he disliked this heavy taciturn man.

"That's because you've not had much to drink," explained Nada. "The less you drink the less you want to eat."

Jos Lombaard stretched his arms and yawned. He'd taken off his singlet and was wearing nothing but trousers. Squatting on the floor of the dinghy, his face covered in dark stubble, he looked to Nada like a good-natured bear. As if he could read her thoughts he began to scratch, plucking ponderously at his hairy chest.

"I could still eat," his forehead puckered. "If I had the chance."

"Don't want no tucker . . . give me a fag." Basset blinked round the dinghy. "Just one bloomin' fag. Not askin' much, is it?"

Canning was looking anxious.

"How long will our water and provisions last?"

Nada sighed. He was at it again.

"Before we collected the rain-water we had enough in the emergency pack, and with the purifiers, for twenty people for three days."

Canning squeaked with alarm.

"Three days!"

"Yes, but for twenty people. There are only nine of us and we've still got the rain water. If the water discipline's strict . . .," she frowned ". . . and *it must be*, we've enough for weeks. And it's bound to rain again."

"And the glucose sweets. We're using eighteen a day, aren't we? How many have we got?"

Nada thought for a moment.

"Twenty-four tins with twenty sweets in each . . . how many's that?"

Canning put the tips of his fingers together.

"Enough for twenty-five days." He looked happier.

"There'll be plenty of fish," said Jos.

Mecky sneered. "Want to know what the survival booklet says about that?" He waved the book at them.

"I'll read it." He read in a high strained voice:

"*The flesh of fish is valuable food, but remember that it can be included in your diet only when you have sufficient water for its digestion, roughly two parts of water for one of fish.*"

"Two ounces of water for every ounce of fish," Sarah Tripp's mouth curled. "We won't be eating much fish."

Angelique unclasped her hands and looked at the others. "It is now time for the south-east trade winds, you know. It will rain very much. This it does every day in Mauritius."

Sarah Tripp shrugged her shoulders. "Unfortunately, this is not Mauritius."

"We are not so far. The same winds and moistures. There will be much rain. You shall see. Especially in the time of the evening. Am I not right, Miss Katic?" she smiled, a warm encouraging smile.

"Yes, of course. We're always dodging storms on this run at this time of the year."

A cold fear took hold of Canning. "This . . . this isn't the season of cyclones, is it?"

Nada and Angelique looked away.

"My God!" he breathed heavily. "My God!"

Five

HE SAT at the opening fishing in the late evening, his muscular back, hirsute and streaked with long white scars, towards the others. On the fourth day he'd found that two life-jackets filled with sea-water made a fair drogue when towed on fifty feet of life-line. Although the dinghy still yawed widely the rotating had stopped and the motion was more comfortable.

As he watched the fishing line he sang in a deep voice:

> *"Want Hy het gespreek en 'n stormwind laat*
> *opsteek wat die golwe daarvan opgesweep het.*
> *Hulle het opgerys na die hemel, neergedaal*
> *na die dieptes—hulle siel het vergaan van wee."*

Angelique touched Nada's arm. "What is this song? It is sad?"

"I don't know. Sounds religious."

Ezekiel clasped his hands round his knees. "It is. It's Psalm one hundred and seven."

Bowing his head, he started to sing with Jos, softly, but in English and in a higher key so that while the words were different there was harmony:

> *"He maketh the storm a calm, so that the waves*
> *thereof are still.*
> *Then they are glad because they be quiet; so*
> *He bringeth them unto their desired haven."*

When he heard the singing Jos stopped, and Ezekiel stopped too so that there was a sudden silence.

76

The Afrikaner turned round slowly, his dark eyes friendly. He could not believe it for this was the first time anyone else in the dinghy had shown interest in anything religious. Well, not quite the first time because Angelique prayed sometimes in French; but she was bound to be a Roman Catholic and since the Pope and the devil walked hand-in-hand, he had never spoken to her about religion.

He smiled. "Who sang with me just now?"

Nada pointed to Ezekiel. "He did."

Puzzled, frowning, Lombaard looked at the African.

"*You* . . . you know the Psalms?"

"Of course!"

"How d'you mean *of course*?"

"I went to a mission school."

Lombaard sighed. Mission schools . . . mission schools and education and cheeky natives were synonymous, and now you had these people becoming politicians, putting "M.P." after their names and travelling first class in European aircraft. It showed a man what Africa was coming to.

"So you're a Christian?" he said doubtfully.

"Not really. I suppose I was *once*. When I grew up and learnt to think for myself I decided I wasn't."

Lombaard shrugged his shoulders and turned away. "So you're a heathen?"

"Call it what you like. At Jesus they called me an existentialist."

Lombaard looked back quickly. "Listen man!" he said severely. "So long as I'm around you don't blaspheme, understand?"

Ezekiel smiled. "It wasn't blasphemy. It was the name of my college at Oxford."

Lombaard looked at him warily for a few moments, then he turned back to his fishing. So this native had been to Oxford, that was why he was so cocky. That was what the English didn't understand: that you can't send these people to a European university without making trouble. He brooded about the English.

Only a cynical, thoroughly hypocritical people like them could commit such blasphemy. Fancy calling a university college "Jesus!"

And how had Wanalu known what Psalm it was unless he understood Afrikaans?

*　　　　*

Sarah Tripp was whimpering in her sleep and twice Ezekiel heard her say "Lennie." Once it had been "Lennie, you devil!" and the next time "Lennie, oh, Lennie!" It could not be a nice dream, he thought, because she was twitching and sometimes grating her teeth.

The others appeared to be asleep. Canning snoring as usual, and Art Basset talking horses . . . which was funny because he'd not yet spoken about them while he was awake.

Angelique and Nada were lying close together which was a habit they'd developed in the last few days and it seemed to him that the Mauritian, who couldn't be much more than thirty, was more or less mothering the girl. That was funny, too, because if there was anyone in the dinghy who knew what she was about it was Nada. She was tough and sensible and she didn't lose her head or complain or despair like the others . . . well, most of the others. The Afrikaner hadn't shown any signs of despair either, but then he didn't show much of anything. You couldn't make out what was going on inside there. You knew what was ticking inside Canning and Basset, and even to some extent in Mecky and Goldsworthy, but not in Lombaard.

All you knew about him was that he thought he was so goddam superior because he had a white skin, and you had a brown one.

*　　　　*

It was between two and three in the morning of the ninth day. But it seemed more like nine years than nine days.

Ezekiel wondered about the outside world. The search would have long since ended. The relatives, the friends, the interested

78

ones, would begin now to accept the position . . . that there were no survivors . . . that there was no hope . . . that the various legal processes must be started in due course.

In Canberra, the meeting of the Commonwealth Parliamentary Association would be over and the delegates would be doing a conducted tour of Australia. No doubt all the appropriate things had been said at the meeting about the tragic disaster that had befallen the promising young politician from Africa.

*   *

From far out on the starboard side the line of phosphorus raced towards the dinghy, brightest where it cleaved the water in its forward rush, fading behind until its wake was swallowed by the darkness. On it came, ruled through the seas by a giant straight edge, and when it reached the dinghy it went deep . . . deep down and under and Ezekiel heard the whistle of the porpoise.

Two nights ago he'd seen a bigger, slower light-track coming for the dinghy and as it passed under he'd looked down on the phosphorescent outline of a whale. Then it spouted ahead of the dinghy, a brilliant jet of water sparkling with luminous sapphires and emeralds, before it sounded and was gone.

Ezekiel looked over to the opening where Basset was on lookout. "See that porpoise?" he called softly.

"Beaut, wasn't it?"

"I like to see them . . . makes me feel we're not so alone."

"Know what I was thinking?"

"Cigarettes?"

"No . . . mutton and veg. A bonzer helping. Ice-cream after. *Had* this dried fish. Makes a guy feel crook."

"It's keeping us alive."

"I'm not so sure. Look at the sores we got. What's gonna happen when they get worse?"

"That's not the fish. It's because we're so often wet. They're salt water sores."

79

"What's gonna happen to us anyway?"

Ezekiel thought of his forefathers and the herd of sleek cattle beyond Gensa. They would be grazing there in the morning as they were every day, tails flicking at the flies, the cattle egrets—white and vigilant—pecking the ticks from the shining coats; the coats of the oxen in which reposed the spirits of his ancestors. Lombaard depended on God, but Ezekiel believed that these spirits were more to be depended upon than any god. They had a more personal and direct interest in his well-being than could any universal deity.

That was why it had rained almost every day so that they'd had plenty of water and built up a reserve of five full life-jackets of it. That was why they always caught fish and had ample supplies, dried and waiting to be eaten.

"I think," said the African slowly, "that we're going to be all right."

"You're crazy, Zeke! It's on account you're black you got this sorta fatalistic gimmick."

"I'm brown, not black."

"It's all the same, Zeke, You're not white, see?"

Ezekiel looked again at the sea, black under the night sky, the wave crests gleaming; the dark slopes sometimes splashed with phosphorescent patches where flying fish broke surface.

*   *

Sarah Tripp was whimpering in her sleep because Lennie was threatening to beat the daylights out of her if she didn't shut up; filling the tooth mug with that cheap brandy and sitting there drooped over the table. In his mouth a cigarette with an ash he'd let grow until it sagged and fell onto his lap or the cheap little carpet. In front of him there was a white saucer full of cigarette ends and the room smelt of them and of brandy.

He drank again from the plastic mug, "Shut up!" he said heavily. "For Christ's sake shut up!"

She was crying bitterly; noisy, face-contorting sobs.

"Aw, shut up!" he said again. "You're just a bloody whore, like the rest of them."

As he leant forward and stretched for the brandy bottle she threw up her arms. Then she woke up, terrified.

She realised that she was in the dinghy and that she'd been dreaming. She could hear Wanalu and Basset talking in low voices.

She shuddered.

God, what alternatives!

To be asleep with nightmares of that dreadful little room with Lennie, or awake in this dinghy where they were slowly dying.

Yes . . .! Slowly dying! Whatever that girl or Jos or Ezekiel might say. Canning and Mecky and Basset at least admitted it, and even if they did give way to despair at times at least they didn't try to bluff themselves.

Everyone was weaker and more sore-ridden and thinner, and the routine was slacker so that the dinghy was never properly dried out nowadays because they hadn't the energy. Their stomachs were distended and full of disgusting gases and their eyes were red, and the men bearded and gaunt. She and Nada were like scarecrows—only Angelique seemed in some miraculous way not to be much affected.

She still had that dull stomach-ache which constipation always gave her. In moments of terror she wondered how long she could go on before something dreadful happened inside? She'd discussed it with Mecky because he was badly constipated too . . . it was about the only thing they had in common.

It was after Nada had given them laxatives from the first-aid outfit . . . for the second time . . . that she broached the subject.

"We seem much worse than the others," she smiled wanly.

"I've always had trouble." Mecky was gloomy. "Never really been able to get on without laxatives. But you needn't worry. I've often talked to my doctor about it. You can go for two or three weeks without doing it, especially if you're eating and drinking practically nothing."

When she found she couldn't sleep she huddled up against the buoyancy chambers and looked out of the canopy at the night sky. There were few clouds, but so many glittering stars that the sky seemed to vibrate with distant light.

She wondered if the same night sky could be seen in Johannesburg? The latitude there was about 26° south. Mauritius, she remembered, was on the 20° parallel of South latitude; so of course Johannesburg would see the same sky, but later because the dinghy was far to the eastward. She estimated the difference in longitude at about forty-five degrees, say three hours of time.

She crawled over to where Goldsworthy was on watch and looked again at the sky and wished she knew more of the stars. She knew some of them, of course. Like the Southern Cross with its pointers Alpha and Beta Centauri. Starting there, Canopus and Sirius were easy to find. From them she went on to Orion's Belt where she identified Betelgeuse, Rigel and Bellatrix, and they led her to Aldebaran and the Pleiades. But then there was a whole vault of sky where she knew nothing until she came to Formalhaut.

She thought, I should have gone more often to the planetarium. I should have gone out more. I shouldn't have read so much and spent so much time brooding.

Her life was an awful mess, that was why she'd accepted the offer of a lectureship in philosophy at Melbourne and had decided to leave South Africa for good. It was a difficult decision because she was a moral coward . . . she knew that . . . and she feared change. But lately things had contrived to make it easier. There had been the Separate Universities Act. She would have been lecturing in a university no longer open to all, and what she had found particularly stimulating there had been the smattering of non-white students. For her they breathed new life into the place and sharpened the wits of all, white and coloured alike.

But now to the paraphernalia of apartheid which she found so dreary and depressing, had been added this new legislation which meant that the university could no longer enrol non-white students; they had to go to their own ethnic universities. She felt she just couldn't stomach that one. She disliked everything about apartheid, but nothing quite as much as that. It was an unforgiveable assault upon her social conscience. Then, just about the time she learned about the lectureship in Melbourne, staying with her parents on the farm near Graaff Reinett, she overheard a conversation which decided her.

It was a hot night and she couldn't sleep, so she went onto the stoep in her pyjamas. She'd not been there long when she heard the low voices of her parents through the open French windows of their bedroom.

She hadn't realised at first that she was the subject of their conversation; until she heard her father say: "But she's thirty-four. She hasn't a hope of finding a man. Besides let's face it—even if she is our daughter—she's damned plain."

"Oh, not really, Jack. She's got a sweet smile. Anyway, men don't just want a pretty face. It's the girl herself that matters."

"Quite. That's the trouble. I mean . . . be honest, old girl . . . it's no disgrace! She's a bluestocking. She's too damned brainy! Men don't like that! And she's such a sourpuss. I mean she won't laugh. She's not even interested in men. It's a damned shame, but there you are. No good worrying."

Choking with humiliation, Sarah fled back to her room and cried herself through to daylight.

The dreadful thing was that she knew her father was right. She was plain; her teeth were bad; she hadn't a single decent feature; and, as if that were not enough, she had to wear thick lenses to correct her short sight.

But how could her father be so insensitive as to think she was not interested in men? Did he think that because she was plain her body was somehow different? Did he think that the urge in her to reproduce was less strong than in other women? Could he imagine what it was like to long for a man and never have one?

If only he knew what a mess all this had made of her life. The dreadful frustrations; the sort of men she'd had to settle for when she became too desperate? Men like Lennie who came to her not because they were attracted but because they could make use of her.

These then were the things that had decided her to accept the Melbourne offer; these were the things that had landed her in this dreadful little dinghy where anyone but a complete moron could see they were dying slowly.

*   *

They were getting to know each other better and first names were now used by some, although there were exceptions. Canning, for example, who had made an early bid for popularity by inviting them to call him "Bert", was still "Mr. Canning" to the women, and "Canning" to the men. Not to all of them, for to Goldsworthy he was "Sir".

Nada and Angelique were called by those names but no one seemed to have got round to calling Sarah Tripp "Sarah". She was rarely addressed, because somehow they seemed to miss her out. This was, perhaps, due to her sharp tongue. A defence mechanism compensating for inadmissible feelings of inferiority.

Goldsworthy, silent, self-effacing, almost a cipher, always kind and ready to help in a fumbling ineffective way, continued to be "Mr. Goldsworthy" except to Canning who called him "Sebastian" or "Goldsworthy" depending upon his mood.

Basset was "Art" to most of them, and Lombaard and Ezekiel were "Jos" and "Zeke" . . . but not to each other because this business of names had flared up into a row a few nights back. For a moment it had looked like being a very ugly row.

There had been some argument about lookout duties for the night and Lombaard had said: "I tell you, man, Wanalu goes on at ten."

Mecky disagreed and appealed to Ezekiel: "What d'you say?"

"You're right! Lombaard goes on at ten."

Jos interrupted angrily: "Listen, Wanalu! When you use my name say 'mister' first! Understand?"

It was dark under the canopy and they couldn't see the faces of the two men, but after a short pause they heard Ezekiel say: "Certainly, Lombaard. When you use 'mister' before mine."

Lombaard moved towards the African in the darkness and they could hear his heavy breathing . . . but he must have thought better of it, because nothing happened. They were getting weaker, it was necessary to conserve strength, and it was blowing fairly sharply that night and there was a lot of movement in the dinghy so that it was no place for a fight.

But after that neither of them used the other's name and when they spoke to each other—which was seldom—they had to get along as best they could. It soon became understood that when Jos said "him" in a rather contemptuous way he meant Wanalu— and when Ezekiel said "him" in the same sort of tone he was known to mean Jos.

*   *

When daylight came on the tenth day it was raining and over-cast, but towards noon it started to clear. It had been getting hotter, and this confirmed their belief that they were drifting to the north-west. The south-east trades had blown almost without pause and though their force had varied it had been remarkably consistent on the whole. There had been rain on most days. Heavy showers about an hour after sunset were an almost daily occurrence. Some of the survivors stripped down in the darkness and went outside the canopy to be drenched by these showers, but as time went on only those who were strong did so. For the last two nights only Lombaard and Wanalu. Basset, still wearing his coat despite the heat, refused to have anything to do with these ablutions, even when Jos told him he stank like a polecat.

In the early afternoon Lombaard was on lookout at the upwind canopy opening, talking to Nada.

They had been making an estimate of their reserves of fresh water and dried fish . . .

"So we've no water problem in sight yet, Jos?"

He nodded. "But we must not think we'll always get this rain, hey?"

"No, of course not. Let's . . ."

But he wasn't listening to her any more, instead he was leaning out, pointing up-wind.

"First time I've seen those."

"What d'you mean?"

"Those birds."

She looked where he was pointing and saw a flight of sea-birds circling high above the water in confused formations from which an endless succession of attackers plummeted down in long stoops, white plumes of spray marking the strikes long before the faint "plops" reached the dinghy.

"What are they, Jos?"

"Gannets, I think. That's a shoal of fish they're after. They'll be small fish. Under them there'll be big fish: bonito, barracuda, tunny, marlin, perhaps. Forcing them up."

"Could we get some of the small ones if they come this way?"

"Maybe. But we've plenty."

"I know. I just wondered."

*   *

Reluctantly his eyes went back to her. She was dozing in the heat of early afternoon, like all of them except Ezekiel and Mecky who were the lookouts. There was nobody watching, so his eyes went first to the curves of her breasts and then to her thighs where the skirt had slipped up and he could see above her knees. She was sitting sideways and where the dark Terylene blouse was torn at the shoulder he could see the round of her breast almost down to the nipple. They are fine breasts and strong thighs, he thought, and their brownness adds something. Is it because they're forbidden to me? Then he felt ashamed that he should be thinking such things at such a time.

Forcing his eyes from her, he thought of Maria and the children at Soetwaters. Undoubtedly they must believe he was dead, and she and Dirkie and Marietjie would be grief stricken, with the relations coming in from far and wide to comfort them.

His old father would be there, gaunt and straight for all his years, enjoining them to find comfort in God since it was His will.

Jos thought of the green valley with the river winding through it, the mealies standing high now on the lands and the sheep grazing on the koppies. Down in Heuningneskloof the bees would be taking honey from the mimosa blossom and the otters would be fishing under the overhang. It would be hot there now. Not this humid tropical heat but the dry heat of strong sunlight in high country.

The valley was Lombaard country. Uncles and brothers and cousins farmed seven big farms there and in the surrounding hills. It had been Lombaard country ever since Hendrik Lombaard rode in at the head of his wagons in 1835, his rifle in one saddle holster and Bible in the other.

He had stopped his horse at the top of the valley and looked down over two hundred square miles of fertile country untouched by man but for an occasional wandering tribe, and he had said: "This is our country! Here we stay! God in His wisdom has sent us to bring His light where there was darkness!"

The wagons had gone down into the valley and outspanned for the night and that was how the Lombaards had come to Soetwaters, to tame the wild valley and to multiply. It was the will of God.

*   *

It was five o'clock that afternoon when the colour of the sea changed, and there was more green than blue in it. The number of sea-birds had multiplied steadily, their shrill cries a welcome new sound to those in the dinghy for whom, for so long, the only outside noises had been those of the wind and sea.

Jos's eyes took on a new brightness and he constantly examined the sea and the distant horizon. At last he said what had been on his mind ever since he'd seen the gannets in the morning.

"The water's not so deep, and there are plenty of sea-birds. This means . . .," he looked round at them with narrowed eyes, ". . . we could be getting close to land."

"To what land?" Canning was lying in the dinghy, his white-bearded face resting on his arms, his eyes hollow and listless.

"I don't know. I don't know if we'll see it even. But it can't be too far."

Mecky's voice was irritable, slightly hysterical. "You say that! Why do you? You're mad! You know we've worked it out dozens of times. The nearest land's more than a thousand miles away. Much more! Why d'you say that?"

Lombaard shook his head. "I told you already I don't know, man. But the water's getting shallower and these sea-birds don't go too far from land."

Basset blinked at him. "How do you know?"

The Afrikaner shrugged his shoulders. "I've done plenty of fishing from boats . . . on the Mozambique coast."

"I'm sure he's right." Nada was excited. "I'm *sure* he is. We've only had our memory to tell us where land is. Perhaps there are some little islands or something we don't know about?"

Sarah Tripp groaned. "Perhaps there're not. You're just imagining things."

"Well, no one's imagined land yet," said Ezekiel and he crawled up onto the buoyancy chamber and knelt there, holding onto the rim of the canopy. "Let's keep a good lookout. We certainly haven't seen these birds before. Just albatrosses so far!"

Angelique crossed herself. "I think Jos is right. The land cannot be far."

Lombaard gave her a quick look. It was the first time she'd called him Jos.

After that the dinghy's occupants bubbled with suppressed excitement and even pessimists like Canning, Mecky and Sarah were inwardly affected and began to accept that their fortunes might change.

For a long time Jos concentrated on a point to the eastward where a cloud bank seemed anchored to the horizon, stationary while the further clouds were moving. There was a thin dark line at the base of the cloud and he watched it until his eyes burned with the concentration. An hour later, he could contain himself no longer. He meant to say it quietly, impressively, but the occasion was too much and he ended by shouting:

"I can see palm trees, man! Palm trees! *Kyk julle mense!*" he broke into Afrikaans. *"Ons is gered! Ons is gered! . . .* We are saved!"

Everybody came to the canopy openings, all talking at once, laughing, shouting and crying. Ezekiel was the first to confirm Lombaard's report.

"There!" he pointed excitedly. "There . . . I can see them too! He's right! He's right!"

It was a thin row of palms, a darkly etched line against the clouded horizon, and it was just visible when the dinghy rose on the crest of a sea, disappearing as it slid into the trough.

For the next few minutes excitement ran high. They slapped each other on the back, laughed hysterically, joked like children, clapped their hands and gesticulated at the distant palms, the tears running down their cheeks. But not for long. Their hopes were shattered by Art Basset's whine.

"Jesus! We're drifting away! Look! The palms finish on the left there! That's the end of them! We're drifting away."

Lombaard saw that Basset was right. The palms were about

four or five miles away to the east and the stiff breeze was carrying the dinghy to the north-west. There was no hope of stopping the drift with the two small paddles.

Canning's despairing moan was followed by Nada's cry: "The two-star-reds! The two-star-reds!" She scrambled across to the emergency pack, grabbed them and shouted to Lombaard: "Here! Quick! Fire them!"

During the next hour they fired six flares and in that time the distant line of palms vanished from sight and the light-coloured water was left behind. As daylight went their wild hopes quickly receded and most of them gave way to black despair.

Canning and Mecky were all recrimination, as if some special responsibility attached to Lombaard because he'd first sighted the palm trees. Sarah Tripp slumped into the bottom of the dinghy and wept quietly, while Art Basset whined and swore. Goldsworthy sat quietly by himself, looking unutterably sad.

Lombaard and Ezekiel redoubled their efforts at lookout but the light was fading and they could not see the horizon.

On Jos's suggestion they fired two more flares once it was dark. One at half past eight and the other at half past nine. But in spite of their passionate and insistent belief that there would be some response there was none. The stock of flares was down to four.

Later that night the wind fell away and the dinghy lay becalmed under a louring sky. They found sleep impossible; it was intensely hot and their minds were in a turmoil. Land had loomed up from nowhere and they had been confronted with the thrilling prospect of rescue. Then, just as suddenly, the land and all that it promised had gone and they were back in the limbo of the last ten days . . . but to all their other misfortunes was now added bitter disappointment.

*   *

In the early hours of next morning Basset and Ezekiel were on watch when daylight came, faint and grey, and with it the wind from the south-east. But it was blowing harder than usual and before long the ground swell which had come up in the night became a confused sea with short steep waves. The motion became so uncomfortable that soon everyone was awake and querulous.

Suddenly they were electrified by Jos's shout: "Listen! I hear breakers!"

They listened and he was right. From the west there came the unmistakable sound of seas breaking and as the light got stronger they saw a distant line of surf breaking on a hidden reef.

Soon afterwards Basset shrieked: "Land . . . O! Listen you lucky bastards. Land . . . O!"

There, a mile away to the north-west, they saw the island. It was small, edged with a white strip of beach above which tall palms rose like masts from the green undergrowth, their fronds dancing in the wind. The sea-birds swooped and screamed about the dinghy now with new vigour and purpose, as if they were welcoming friends instead of strangers of the ocean wastes.

Six

Soon after sighting the island they saw more land ahead; right on their course this time, which was fortunate because the wind was taking them well clear of the first island. The sea was again a lighter colour and it was evident that the water was shallowing.

Jos was not going to make a second mistake, so he commanded the others to silence while he offered a brief prayer of thanks to the Almighty. Though he prayed in Afrikaans he heard several others join in the "Amen", apart from Goldsworthy who always did so, being himself a devout man. They're improving, Jos thought. He looked at the tense, strained faces:

"We must make ready for landing . . . pack up the emergency kit . . . get ashore with everything we need."

Although they were weak, from somewhere they found new energy to re-stow the kit. They put some of the reserve stocks of dried fish into the empty glucose tins and packed them in. Then they secured the watertight cover.

Ezekiel picked up the fire-axe.

"This is something we can need badly."

Nada pushed the survival cot across to him. "Put it in this." She gave him the whisky bottle filled with water, and the rest of the dried fish. "These, too."

Canning frowned. "Why not leave everything in the dinghy?"

"That's dinkum," said Basset. "Why're we getting all steamed up?"

Jos pointed ahead. "That's a weather shore we've got to land on. You see those breakers on the reef? We'll find plenty like that."

Canning's face sagged.

"We'll be all right in the dinghy, won't we?"

"Maybe. Perhaps not."

"Why? What can happen?" His voice trembled.

Time was short and Jos was getting irritable.

"*Ag*, man! Trust in God for a change!"

When all was ready for the landing, they considered the problem of getting the stocks of rainwater ashore. Five life-jackets were being used as water containers, and these would now have to be worn for the dangerous journey through the surf.

Eventually it was agreed to haul in the two which were serving as drogues. These were Lombaard's and Wanalu's, but they were strong swimmers and felt they'd manage better without them. Thus, with the life-jacket which had belonged to the young Italian, three were available for rainwater and these were tied by their tapes to the steadying lines in the dinghy. It was decided to leave the emergency pack and the survival cot loose in the dinghy, ready to float off independently if necessary.

Their absorption in these tasks was interrupted by a shout from Basset who was on lookout.

"We're getting close to the point! There's bloody big seas breaking!"

They saw that the end of the island was less than a quarter of a mile away. Big seas were racing in on it and breaking well short of the beach. The dinghy was being blown along almost parallel with the eastern side of the island, but the distance from the line of surf was closing and they could already see the beach ahead where they would land; a white strip of sand fringed with green scrub and coconut palms.

"There's a reef along here," said Jos. "That's what the seas are breaking on. Must be high water now. At low water we'd see it."

Ezekiel picked up a paddle. He was frowning with concentration.

93

"Let's see if we can help her over the reef."

Jos picked up the other one, looking at Nada.

"We'll try, but the seas are big."

They sat astride the buoyancy chambers at either end and began paddling but they made no impression. Without the life-jacket drogues the dinghy was rotating slowly as the seas carried it to the beach.

There was no time to look for signs of life on the island. They were too busy bracing themselves for the coming struggle, and the frantic joy of sighting land and the prospect of early rescue had given way to fear. The thunder of the surf was obscene, menacing, the seas racing past the dinghy huge and pitiless, their crests foaming and frothing, the air misty with blown spume.

Beyond the hidden reef where the seas were breaking there was a stretch of calm water and across this the remnants of each spent sea swirled on towards the beach.

"Won't be long now," Jos shouted.

The fourth sea after that lifted the dinghy high in the air and tumbled it forward in a flurry of spray and water. It took on a crazy down-slope angle, and the sea broke over it foaming in through the canopy openings. Then they hit something hard and unyielding.

Jos shouted: "Get out! Jump!" but before they could move, another sea raced up and capsized the dinghy.

Nada felt the heavy pressure of water and a roaring in her ears, and then she was somehow clear and struggling in the sea. She saw others near her. Jos was holding onto the emergency pack. She remembered thinking about the fresh water and the fire-axe. The sea drained away and her feet touched bottom . . . she felt herself being dragged back over the coral and she fought wildly against the backwash.

Somewhere near her there was a despairing shout and a third sea swept by and threw her forward; it broke with a monstrous

94

roar and she was over the reef and in the deep water nearer the beach. She saw Mecky just ahead, a look of such abject disgust on his face in its ridiculous life-jacket frame, that she almost laughed. There was blood on her forearms, but she felt no pain and when she used them everything seemed to work.

She looked round for the others and saw someone beyond Mecky swimming for the beach. Behind her Ezekiel was helping Angelique who looked dazed. Over on the right she saw Jos pushing the emergency kit through the water, kicking hard as he headed for the beach. She counted seven of them. Where was the eighth? Then she saw someone lying on the beach just clear of the water.

So they've all got ashore, she thought. Thank God for that! But the dinghy was nowhere to be seen and she was puzzled. Such a big conspicuous thing could hardly have vanished into thin air? She swam towards the beach again, slowly because the life-jacket hampered her.

Before long her feet touched bottom and she staggered out onto the firm white sand. She threw herself down and wept with relief; then she lay there exhausted, shivering occasionally in spite of the morning sun, breathing in the musty, spicy smell of the island.

*　　　　*

By eight o'clock most of them were sufficiently recovered from their ordeal to take stock of the position.

Although they had got the emergency kit ashore, various things including the fire-axe, the bellows, the paddles, the safety knife, life-lines and the Sarah Beacon had been lost with the dinghy. Jos thought he could trace them. "That second sea after we hit broke up the dinghy. The coral ripped out the bottom and the buoyancy chambers went. What's left must be in the water on this side of the reef."

"Look at your foot," Angelique pointed to a bloody gash on his left heel.

95

Lombaard nodded. "My shoe came off . . . the reef got me."

Most of them had been injured by the coral. Angelique had a cut on her thigh; Canning's back was lacerated . . . fortunately he couldn't see it or he'd have made much more fuss. Sarah Tripp's shoulder was cut and bruised; Mecky's head wound had re-opened; Goldsworthy's legs were cut, and Nada's fore-arms were badly scratched. Using the first-aid outfit Nada and Angelique attended to these injuries, but none of them was serious.

Now that they were safely and so unexpectedly ashore they were overcome by a curious lethargy, due largely to their poor physical condition and the rigours of the last ten days, and also to reaction to the escape from disaster.

For the rest of the morning they lay on the beach resting and sleeping, about them their soiled and stained clothing laid in the sun to dry; and the life-jackets, shoes, and emergency pack.

*   *

In the early afternoon Jos was wakened by the heat of the sun. He stood up, yawned and scratched himself slowly like a waking animal. He looked at the others sprawled about in various attitudes of sleep. The men's beards were showing some growth. Mecky's mouse-coloured and tenuous; Canning's revealingly white against the weak brown hair which had paled steadily as the dye faded.

Though most of them had stripped to bare essentials once they'd got to the beach, Basset still wore his double-breasted jacket. Fifty feet from them Ezekiel lay on his back, sleeping soundly in spite of the fierce sun.

Jos saw that Angelique's eyes were open. She half-smiled and he looked away quickly, afraid she might read his thoughts: that she was a handsome woman and that somehow she had kept herself cleaner and neater than the others. Beyond her, Nada was lying on her stomach one arm flung out across the sand, the other pillowing her head. She was burnt a dark brown, the skin peeling from her face and limbs, her hair tangled and the scar down the right cheek still livid.

Jos felt a glow of affection for this girl who'd done so well in the dinghy. They owed a lot to her . . . he particularly, because she'd rescued him from the water. Sometime he'd thank her for that. The struggle to survive had been too urgent to worry about such things. She was like the women in the valley. They were bigger than she was and stouter but they, too, were strong and resourceful with plenty of courage. That was how women should be. Not painted up, smoking and drinking, monkeying about with fine clothes . . . chasing men and wasting their husbands' money on hairdressers and beauty parlours, like those thin English women in Johannesburg with high voices and teeth stuck out in front whom he'd seen sitting on the stoep of that club the McMurrays had taken him to during the last Rand Show.

He looked across the lagoon . . . the tide had gone out, and the coral reef stood clear of the water where it ran parallel with the beach. There were two breaks in it where the sea came boiling through.

The dinghy must be lying on the bottom somewhere inside the reef. There were things there that they must have. The life-jackets filled with water and the fire-axe. Somehow the survival cot must have got stuck inside when the dinghy collapsed. He might even find the shoe he'd lost. One shoe was no good.

Now he noticed things they'd missed in the urgency of getting ashore: the remains of an old boat jetty made from lumps of coral; a rusty pipe leading down into the water from the undergrowth which lined the beach. He followed it up through the bushes and found the dilapidated remains of a small settlement. Rusted sheets of corrugated iron and old timbers lay about in careless confusion, concrete foundations, pieces of rusty steel cable and odd scraps of tin.

An air of bleak desolation, of long desertion, hung over the place. Jos felt an unreasoning resentment that the settlement should have been deserted; it was as if its former inhabitants had committed an act of calculated treachery against the survivors.

He went back to the beach and northwards to where the palms swung to the right along a point of land which ended abruptly in the sea.

Was this an island?

What was beyond that point?

Perhaps there were people on the the other side; the side away from the south-east trades?

With a sense of urgency he realised that, weak as they were, there was much to be done before night fell. First he would offer a prayer of thanksgiving to the Almighty. After that he would waken the others.

He knelt and prayed.

*   *

Jos told them about the ruins, and they went to inspect them. When they returned it was agreed, after some argument, to split into two parties: one to salvage the equipment from the dinghy, the other to carry out a quick reconnaissance to see whether they were on an island and if there were any inhabitants.

Jos looked at the clouds gathering on the horizon. "Look out for water and a good place to make a camp for the night. Looks like rain."

Canning frowned. "We're not children, you know. We're quite capable of thinking of these things ourselves." He motioned to Goldsworthy and Mecky. "Leave it to us."

Ezekiel pointed to the palm trees. "Coconuts are good food. And we can make cups from the husks."

Canning nodded. "Leave it to us. You get on with the salvage."

Ezekiel's white teeth flashed in a smile. "Know how to open them, Canning?"

"I've no doubt we'll manage." He turned to his party. "Now I suggest we divide into two groups. One to go up the beach, the other inland."

"Wait a mo!" Basset held up his hand. "This is a democratic outfit. I don't take orders from nobody. We gotta agree it all first."

"Let's fix a time to meet," Ezekiel interrupted. "It's dark at seven. What d'you say? Half past five? Six? We've still got to find a place for tonight."

Jos frowned but he said nothing. This native had too much to say.

Canning looked at his watch. "It's three now. That gives us plenty of time." He spoke to Basset and Mecky. "That meet with your approval, gentlemen?"

Mecky was picking at his scalp wound, gazing aimlessly out to sea. He shrugged his shoulders. "I don't care what we do, long as it's not too much. My head's hell!"

Basset slapped his legs where the midges were biting him. "So's my arse, but we gotta live, bluey. Can't lie down and die."

Sarah Tripp had a stained, man-sized handkerchief stretched over her head and tied under her chin; below the handkerchief her hair was knotted and dirty, and skin was peeling off the end of her nose. She peered shortsightedly through her spectacles. "For heaven's sake let's do something instead of standing here nattering."

After further argument the two groups parted. The strong swimmers, Jos, Ezekiel and Nada, were in the salvage party, and the others went off to reconnoitre. Of these Canning, Goldsworthy, Sarah and Angelique went along the beach to the north, while Basset and Mecky struck inland. It had been arranged that they would all meet at six that evening on what they now called "Rescue Beach".

When Jos last saw the beach party it was nearing the point, Sarah Tripp plodding ahead in the lead, Angelique following, and Canning dragging far behind with Goldsworthy.

*　　　　*

When the others had gone, the salvage party prepared for its

99

task. The men took off everything except their underpants; Nada wore an improvised bikini of brassière and panties.

Jos was not happy about this. Her body turned out to be a lot more attractive than he'd expected, which was undesirable with a black man in the party.

He knew their survival depended on the success of the salvage operations and that he must accept the situation, just as he'd accepted so much in the last ten days which was foreign to his principles and upbringing.

Ezekiel waded in ahead of them and Jos observed the lithe body of the African with critical, measuring eyes, watching the back and thigh muscles ripple as he walked. He's strong, thought Jos guardedly, but I'm heavier and stronger. I could fix him! I can lift a two hundred bag of mealies onto my shoulders and walk with it. I bet he can't do that.

As Nada went into the water behind Lombaard she thought, This man has a back like a gorilla and he still looks strong after all we've endured. It was strange that these two men feared and disliked each other. They were the best in the dinghy and without them she knew they wouldn't have survived.

* *

The water was cool and refreshing after the heat of the beach, and they swam slowly conserving their strength. Once on the reef they walked gingerly along the coral peering down into the clear water of the lagoon where brilliantly-coloured fish darted between the staghorns and porites of the coral colonies.

Jos knew pretty well where the dinghy had broken up, and before long they found the tangle of rubberised canvas lying in water about eight feet deep. After more than an hour of diving they got it up onto the reef. The coral had damaged it beyond repair, but they were able to salvage the survival cot, the life-lines, the safety knife, the bellows, the spent Sarah Beacon, the fire-axe and the whisky bottle of rain water. One of the water-containing life-jackets was torn, but the others were intact.

The salvage work finished, they swam between the reef and the beach getting the equipment ashore. Throughout these operations Nada saw that Jos felt he was the leader, but it was equally clear that Ezekiel did things at his own pace and in his own way, often ignoring the Afrikaner's instructions. Then Lombaard would have to do the job himself . . . with an ill grace because the black man was showing a will of his own. But Jos was not ready yet to make an issue of it and he wasn't happy about his throbbing heel.

*   *

The beach party walked on firm white sand until they reached the point where a flat table of coral barred their way. It had to be negotiated carefully, and Sarah Tripp put on the shoes she'd been carrying.

They named it "Coral Point", and found that once round it the beach turned westward before swinging in a semi-circle to the north-east to form a bay rather larger than the one into which the dinghy had drifted. The northern point of this bay was about a mile away. Beyond it they could see only water. With the sea on their right they continued along the narrow beach, the screen of undergrowth and palms blanking off the view to the left. Occasionally the undergrowth gave way to sandy glades reaching into the palms, then the view would be lost again in the shadows where the palms thickened. To seaward the reef ran parallel to the beach and the roar of the breaking surf never ceased.

They were well along this sandy stretch which they had named "Second Beach", when they first saw things moving in the soft sand up near the line of undergrowth.

As she got nearer Sarah Tripp realised with a shock that they were huge crabs.

She ran back to the others. "Ugh! . . . they're crabs."

"Maybe good to eat," said Angelique serenely.

The men joined them and while they stood talking, Canning lowered himself onto the sand.

"You're going much too fast," he grumbled. "I'm still very weak."

"I am sorry," Angelique was contrite. "I did not know."

"You're soft," Sarah Tripp was disapproving. "You'd better start back now. We'll go on."

"He's not himself, you know," Goldsworthy pleaded.

"Well, now," Canning's eyes avoided hers. "I wouldn't normally hear of such a thing, but I've had a bad time these last ten days—a bad time indeed. But Goldsworthy will go on with you."

Sarah peered anxiously at the crabs, and her voice was distant. "So have *we* had a bad time. Anyway . . . see you later."

Goldsworthy and the two women went on, leaving Canning on the sand examining his feet.

On reaching the point they found that the beach swept round it to the west and south-west so that they were soon walking back in the reverse direction but on the other side of the island. They named this northerly extremity "Casuarina Point" because of the grove of casuarina trees which reached almost to the water there; here, too, they found colonies of terns, gannets and frigate-birds. Angelique was again severely practical. "More food, that is good."

"What, sea-birds?"

"No, the eggs."

Sarah Tripp sighed. "I'm tired."

"I, too. We are still weak, Sarah."

Now the beach widened and to their left a sandy glade shone white in the afternoon sunlight. This was the lee side of the island, well sheltered from the south-east wind. The tide was low and across the lagoon the reef showed grey and glistening. There was little surf on this side. It would be wonderful for bathing, they agreed, and in a moment of unusual levity Sarah Tripp named it "Bikini Beach". Angelique was puzzled.

"Why this name?"

"What else'll we bathe in?"

"What matter? There is nothing wrong with our bodies."

Sarah flushed. "Not with yours."

"But you have a good figure." Angelique regarded her seriously.

Sarah Tripp shook her head and looked away.

*　　　　　*

After they had gone into the palm plantation, and walked in a northerly direction for about twenty minutes, Mecky and Basset found themselves in a clearing at the end of which, to their left, they could see the sea.

Mecky pointed. "This is either a peninsula or an island."

"Forget the geography! I want people. Let's go and have a dekko."

Mecky looked at Basset coldly and thought, What an indescribable little bounder you are! God help Australia if there are many like you! But he said: "All right. Let's go."

On their way they came upon the forlorn and decaying remains of old cottages.

They reached the western beach and walked north up it for about half a mile. For the third time Basset complained of the heat.

"Why don't you take off your coat?" Mecky snapped. "Apart from anything else it smells."

Basset's eyes narrowed. "When I want it off, it comes off . . . see, cobber! Till then it stays flippin' on. Get me?"

"I couldn't care less. *You* complained about the heat."

"Well. Any reason why I shouldn't?"

"Oh, for God's sake dry up."

Before Basset could reply Mecky shouted, "Look! Look at those huts! They aren't very old." He pointed to a large clearing on their right where three huts stood in the shade of the palms.

Basset blinked. "Maybe there's people there."

They found that the huts were long neglected, though of more recent construction than anything else they'd seen. The wooden frames were tied together with coconut fibre, and coarsely woven palm leaf matting was stretched over them. The roofs, roughly thatched with palm leaves, were in poor shape. Inside there was nothing but fallen palm thatch, spiders' webs and a few large spiders.

Basset cleared his throat and spat in the sand. "There's been people 'ere. We may find they shifted round to another spot. We gonna get rescued soon, digger, mark my words."

Mecky shook his head. "I doubt it," he said gloomily.

Near the huts they found some rusted tins, pieces of desiccated khaki cloth and rotting paper caught up in the undergrowth.

"Musta bin some poor bastards like us," said Basset. "Castaways, I reckon."

But the discovery was exciting. Human beings had been there, perhaps a year or so ago, and somehow it made them feel less alone.

They went back to the beach and suddenly Basset yelled, "Look! There's some people over there!" He pointed and Mecky saw them.

"Into the edge of the palms, digger! See who they are before we show ourselves."

They slipped quickly in and watched the figures coming down the beach. When they were about a hundred yards away Basset laughed.

"It's old Goldyguts and our own bits of skirt. Angelique and smarty pants."

*　　　　　*

When they met again at Rescue Beach that evening notes were compared, and it was agreed that though they had not yet explored the southernmost end, first sighted in the morning, they were on an island about two to three miles long which varied in width from five hundred to fifteen hundred yards.

Canning rubbed his hands together slowly.

"Other things we know . . . one—people used to live here, and may still do on the southern end, though that's unlikely because they'd've seen us drifting in this morning and been here by now. Agreed?" He looked round confidently.

"Two," he slapped at the cloud of midges round his head. "We know that food supplies are reasonably ample if a little—er —monotonous. Much less so than over the last ten days, though . . . agreed?"

Mecky picked lugubriously at his head. "And water?"

Canning frowned. "Not so good I admit, but we've the purifying apparatus, the tins of reserve fresh water, the whisky bottle and three life-jackets of fresh water . . ."

"One and a half," Jos folded his arms across his chest.

"What d'you mean?"

"We only salvaged two, and we've drunk half one already."

"Plenty of rain about, bluey," Basset pointed to the gathering clouds. "Needn't worry on that account. There wouldn't be all this green," his arm went round in a wide sweep, "if it didn't pee like a sonofabitch every time the bell strikes."

Sarah Tripp stiffened. "I wish you'd clean out your mouth or shut up."

Basset made a nose at her. "Go an' Lady Chatterley yourself, smarty pants! No one else will."

Sarah's eyes blazed. "How dare you!"

Mecky swept imaginary cobwebs from his forehead. "Is there any point in this wrangling? I mean, it doesn't help."

Jos got up from his squatting position. "*Ag!* It'll be dark soon and we've made no camp. You talk too much. You're like a lot of *kaffers*!"

Ezekiel switched over from right to left; tense, ready to move quickly. "Like a lot of whites, I'd say!"

Jos felt a strong desire to give this native the kick in the pants he so richly deserved, but no one else in the party had taken exception to his remark. Jos had complained about their behaviour, so he could hardly make an issue of it. But he'd remember it for the future.

He looked at the sky. "It's too late to make a proper camp. We'd better go into the plantation. Get out of the wind. We can make a fire."

"Why?" said Nada. "It's warm and we've nothing to cook."

Jos brushed away the midges and sand-flies buzzing round them. "It'll help keep these away. Other people may see it."

A fire was made from the dry wood and coconut husks lying about, and lit with a match-stick from the watertight tube in the emergency kit.

They were too exhausted to set about collecting coconuts. Squatting disconsolately round the fire they ate the dried fish from the dinghy. Nada gave them each a glucose sweet to round off the meal.

Before they went to sleep that night, Ezekiel scooped a heap of glowing embers into a hole he'd scratched near the fire; he covered them with green leaves, then sand, leaving a small breathing hole.

Nada looked at him. "What are you doing?"

"We won't always have matches. This way we'll have embers tomorrow. Start another fire with them."

"Oh, how clever! Were you a Boy Scout?"

Ezekiel knew Jos was watching him. "No. I was a *kaffer* in a kraal. Couldn't afford matches." Smiling he flashed his teeth, pleased with the sally.

Jos stretched his arms and yawned loudly. The remark angered him. He, too, had kept embers glowing like that when he was hunting in the bushveld . . . that was how the Voortrekkers had kept their fires alive during the Trek when there were no matches. Pride wouldn't allow him to claim that achievement for his people now, and this *verdomde* native knew it.

*   *

In the lee of a thick tangle of undergrowth, the palm fronds above them swishing and rustling in the south-easter, the roar of the surf in their ears, the survivors settled down in the sandy grass for the night. But it was not to be a peaceful one because storms of wind and rain were to come before midnight, and again in the early morning, to leave them drenched and miserable.

Jos was far from pleased to see Ezekiel lie down among them as he had done in the dinghy. Then, there was no option. Here, he should have known better.

"Tomorrow," Jos told them firmly, "we build shelters."

Seven

THEY WERE up at dawn, glad to have finished with the discomfort of the night, determined to lose no time building the shelters. The clearing with its three neglected huts on the lee side of the island was, they agreed, the best place.

After a meal of dried fish and water they started gathering the equipment. There was some argument about who would carry what, and this was further complicated by Ezekiel's insistence that the southern end of the island should be explored without delay.

Jos looked at Canning; he always avoided speaking directly to the African. "No point in that. When we drifted in yesterday we saw nothing there."

Ezekiel shook his head. He, too, spoke to Canning. "There's thick trees and bush there. We've only seen this side. What's on the other? Maybe people. It's out of the wind."

Canning looked at the Afrikaner and then at the African. These two must be encouraged to disagree. He said: "I think Ezekiel has something. Why build shelters if there's a settlement of some sort down on that side?"

Jos's shoulders shrugged irritably. "There's nothing there. It's a waste of time. Let's get on with making a camp."

He picked up the fire-axe, the two life-jackets of water and the survival cot and began arranging the load.

Ezekiel got up off his haunches. "I'm going to have a look at the southern end, anyway."

Jos swung round. "Look! There's heavy work to be done! You'd better come along with the rest of us." There was no mistaking his tone. It was an order.

But it was wasted on Ezekiel. He shook his head and his eyes were sullen. "I'm going down there first. I'll be back to do my share of work before long." He started off towards Rescue Beach.

"Hey, you!" shouted Jos angrily. "Come here!"

Ezekiel ignored the shout and quickened his pace.

Jos looked at the others in disgust. "Cheeky swine," he said bitterly. "That's what you get from these blacks nowadays."

To his surprise Angelique walked off in the direction taken by Ezekiel. Jos started after her. "Where are you going?" It was friendly but puzzled.

She made no answer so he quickened his stride until he was alongside her. He put his hand on her arm. "What's the trouble?"

She brushed the hand away and walked faster. "Leave me alone! I'm going to help Ezekiel."

"Why? Come with us. He doesn't need help."

For a moment she looked at him, her dark eyes flashing. "That's my business. I'm going with him."

Jos realised it was hopeless. He shook his head and rejoined the others. "You never know what goes on in a woman's mind."

Sarah snorted. "You've got to be pretty dim not to see what's going on in hers."

Jos could deduce nothing from this. "Come on," he said, "let's go."

Soon his mood changed to anger. Angelique had not only sided against him in his clash with Ezekiel, but she had gone off with the African indicating that she preferred his company to theirs. He could not begin to understand her.

*   *

On the way to the camp site they struck through the centre of the island, past the ruins of the old settlement. Soon they came upon a sandy path and followed it until, in a slight depression, they found a cairn built of coral. There was no indication of its purpose so after a brief examination they continued along the path which inclined now to the north-east.

Some time later Basset, who was leading, saw the sun shining in a clearing ahead and in a few minutes they'd reached the deserted huts.

When they'd examined them Canning clasped his hands together and ran his tongue round his lips. "Don't look very wholesome. But we can use the frames. That'll save a lot of work."

"No," said Jos firmly, "We can't."

"Why not?"

"You mustn't re-build deserted huts."

"Why not?"

Jos wondered if he should tell them the real reason: that it was something you never did; that it brought misfortune. Some people in the valley believed that deserted dwellings were haunted by the people who'd lived in them. He didn't believe that— it was an old wives' tale—but he did believe it was unlucky. This Englishman would never understand that.

There was, however, something which he'd understand, so Jos said: "It's a question of health. The people who lived here may've had T.B. or leprosy or something. You never know."

Canning gave the dilapidated huts the sort of look usually reserved for bad smells. "T.B.! Leprosy! I never thought of that."

Jos pointed to the other side of the clearing. "We should make the new camp there. Away from these."

Basset was sitting on the sandy grass with his back against a coconut palm, sucking at a pebble. "One of these is good enough for me." He looked at the old huts. "I'll fix up the roof an' walls and it'll be bonzer."

Unexpectedly, Mecky agreed. "I think he's right. Why go to the sweat of putting up a new framework when we've got these. With all the wind that blows over this benighted spot there shouldn't be any germs."

Canning puffed out his cheeks. "I must say I agree with Lombaard. One can't be too careful."

Nada kicked her foot in the sand. "How long will it take to build a new hut?" She pushed back the hair from her eyes and looked at Jos quizzically.

He thought for a moment. "One hut'll take about five or six days. We'll have to cut the poles for the frames and you women'll have to make the matting from palm leaves . . . like this." He pointed at a piece of matting which had fallen from the wall of a nearby hut. "Then we'll have to put it on. We can use the fibre from these huts for tying. We can unravel some of the lines from the dinghy if we need more."

"Only five or six days?"

"That's for one. We'll need three."

"*Three*, why?"

"One for you women, and two for the men."

Nada looked at him in surprise. "You'll only need one for the men. Art and Mecky are going to fix an old one."

"What about Wanalu?" said Jos. "He's got to have somewhere to sleep."

"But he'll be in the men's hut."

Jos wondered if he'd heard her correctly. "You mean him . . . a black man . . . sleep with us?" His tone was incredulous.

"But of course. He's been sleeping with us all the time."

"That was in the dinghy. We had no option. Now we have."

Sarah Tripp peered at him suspiciously. "Are you trying to be funny?"

Jos's sincere brown eyes met hers unwaveringly. "Of course not. He must have his own hut. He doesn't want to mix with us any more than we do with him."

Sarah Tripp clapped her hand to her forehead. "My God!" she said, "I can't believe it!"

Nada touched Jos's arm. "You know he saved your life. D'you think it's right to do this to him now?"

Jos wheeled round on her. "How did he save my life?"

"In the dinghy. He pulled you out of the water."

"I thought that was you."

"I couldn't have done it, Jos. I was too weak."

He looked at the others. "And these? They were there?"

Nada remembered Canning and Basset's insistence that no more survivors should be allowed into the dinghy. She shook her head.

*　　　*

It was decided to build two new huts, one for the women and one for the men including Ezekiel, Jos having given way under pressure from Nada. Basset and Mecky stuck to their intention to repair one of the old huts. The deciding factor for them was the much smaller amount of work involved.

While Jos cut timber for the poles, Canning and Goldsworthy carried them to the camp site and the women collected palm leaves. The work went slowly, for they were all weak.

In the middle of the forenoon Ezekiel and Angelique came back with a report that there were no people on the southern end of the island, although there was a sheltered beach on the south-western end with a crude jetty made from coral. There was natural bush on one side and mango groves on the other and many trees with colonies of sea-birds. They had found eggs and chicks in the nests.

As there was only one axe it was agreed that Jos would go over to Second Beach to catch fish in the lagoon and collect eggs from the sea-birds' nests at Casuarina Point, while Ezekiel cut timber.

Angelique joined the women and showed them how to make matting from palm leaves. If necessary, she said, she could make rope from the fibre of the husk, but for that she would need much help.

Nada noticed that Angelique and Jos now ignored each other. Mecky and Basset worked at an old hut, patching and mending but they could do nothing about the roof until the new coconut matting was ready.

*   *

The meal that evening was the best since the aircraft had crashed: fresh fish cooked in young palm leaves with coconut flesh, and coconut milk to wash it down. The only people who didn't really enjoy it were Sarah and Mecky who were still suffering from acute constipation. Jos cheered them by promising rather mysteriously that as soon as he could find certain ingredients he'd give them something which really would work.

They begged him not to delay.

*   *

There was a moon and some of them went to Bikini Beach to swim because it was oppressively hot in the camp, and there seemed no point in settling down so early to another night in the open.

Ezekiel and Nada were the last to come out of the water. As they walked along the beach to join the others they discussed the day's doings.

"D'you agree that we shouldn't have tried to fix the old huts, Ezekiel?"

"Of course. Can't use them again."

"Why?"

"It'd be unlucky. It's just something you can't do."

"But why? Isn't what you say superstition?"

In the moonlight his face was serious. "It's more than that. It'd be desecration. The spirits of those who lived there would worry you."

"D'you seriously believe that?"

"Let us say, I believe it *will* be so, Nada. Just as devout Christians believe that Christ *will* come a second time. My people have seen the misfortune which befalls those who disregard these customs."

"But that's mysticism . . . if you attribute misfortune to that."

113

"Call it what you like. There are possibly other explanations. There's a great deal that's not understood. Why not this, too?"

"Mecky and Basset don't agree with you."

"That's their business. I'm sorry for them."

*   *

Six days later the first of the new huts was finished and the women moved in. During this time Mecky and Basset made good progress repairing the old hut.

A number of problems were settled in those first days including the vexed one of collecting and storing fresh water. For a catchment they had scooped out a hollow depression in the sand on the beach opposite the camp and about a hundred yards from it. The place was well clear of the palms and got a free fall of rain. They lined the depression with the largest pieces of unbroken dinghy material held in place by lumps of coral. The catchment area was about six by eight feet, and some eighteen inches at its deepest point. The first night after it was built there was no rain, but on the evening of the second day a heavy downpour came and repeated itself during the night so that there was ample water in the catchment next morning.

It was Jos who thought of the catchment and supervised its construction, but it was Canning's idea to use life-jackets for storing water supplies. These were marked with the survivors' names and hung from a crude gallows they erected near the huts. Every morning each life-jacket received the same amount of fresh water from the catchment. It was scooped out with drinking boxes from the purifier outfits, the rationing being controlled by Jos and Ezekiel.

Another early problem dealt with was that of lookouts. This was after Angelique had suggested that the island might be visited seasonally by coconut harvesters. This happened, she said, with certain islands in the Seychelles group. The many coconuts lying on the ground suggested that it was some time since the island had been visited, and she believed the next visit might be near.

"Where would the harvesters come from?" Canning watched her intently.

"I do not know. Perhaps from the island we first saw."

Canning turned to Jos. "How far's that?"

The big man shrugged his shoulders. "Thirty or forty miles."

They decided not to post regular lookouts, but to try to keep the sea under observation during the greater part of the day as they went about their work. If anything showed up they would fire the last of the flares or start a smoke fire. Jos was not very optimistic about the chances of attracting attention from the sea.

"From what's been said," he avoided Angelique's eyes, "anybody seeing smoke here will think we're picking coconuts. They won't know we're in distress unless they see the flares; and there's not much chance of that against the background of this island?"

*　　　　*

Work on the second hut went quicker because of the experience gained with the first. To avoid friction Jos and Ezekiel didn't work together. If one was building, the other would fish or collect eggs or coconuts.

This system was good, since none of the others approached Jos or Ezekiel as fishermen. But it did mean that the only other men on the huts were Canning and Goldsworthy. Mecky and Basset refused to have anything to do with the new huts on the grounds that they'd received no assistance in repairing their old hut. It was pointed out that they'd used coconut matting made by the women, but they were obdurate.

On this morning, Jos, Canning and Goldsworthy were working on the hut, while the women under Angelique's direction made matting from the long sword-like palm leaves.

Jos was on the roof and had to move gingerly because of his

weight. From time to time he asked Canning to pass up material.

For the third time that morning the plump man had disappeared and Jos's temper was fraying.

"Canning!" he shouted, "Where the hell are you?"

From his left he heard Canning's, "Keep your hair on!"

He looked across and saw him sitting against a palm, holding a coconut from which he was drinking the milk.

Jos prickled with irritation. "Hey, Canning! Leave that bloody stuff and come here and help."

Canning put down the coconut and shuffled back to the hut. Although he'd shed much weight in the last two weeks, he was still rotund. His face and balding head, burnt red, were benevolent above the white beard. He wore his shirt outside trousers which he'd cut off above the knees because of the heat. The sweat poured off him and as he walked he wiped his face with the tail of his shirt.

Jos scowled at him. "Why d'you keep on buggering off when you're needed?"

Canning glared. "Look here, Lombaard, if you want co-operation you must learn to make yourself agreeable. I'm not accustomed to being talked to like that."

"If you did a fair day's work and stuck to the job, you wouldn't be."

"Are you suggesting I don't pull my weight?"

"Of course you don't, Canning, and everybody knows it. You're bloody lazy. And you're greedy too. You've been at that coconut milk twice in the last hour."

"Can't I quench my thirst?"

"There's plenty of water. You don't have to go off and sit down in the middle of the job."

Canning ignored the remark. "Anyway, what d'you want?"

"Pass up some of the matting."

Canning gathered up the matting. Standing on his toes he passed it up to the Afrikaner. He thought, Just you wait, my friend. I'm not putting up with this much longer. I'm sick and tired of being humiliated.

* *

It was late evening and she sat on the beach near Casuarina Point watching the sun set. Angelique and Sarah Tripp were bathing but she'd not felt like it, so she sat there, her mind in Sydney with her father and mother. The time would be different there but she was too tired to work it out. Maybe it was early morning and they'd be getting up, Mother fixing the tea and Dad reading the newspaper, looking desperately for news about survivors but knowing at the bottom of his heart that it was too late. That if there'd been any, why they'd for sure have heard about it by now.

Poor old Dad!

He'd been a school-master in Yugoslavia . . . a school principal at a small school. Teaching was his life and without it he was not a complete person.

On reaching Australia he'd found that his poor, almost non-existent English was a fatal bar to school-mastering, so he'd had to settle for what he could get which was clerk in a warehouse down near the harbour.

Her mother worked in a small grocers' shop and what with that and the help Nada gave they were not too badly off; and though they had moments of desperate longing for Peljesac and the bright beauty of the Dalmatian coast, they knew they were fortunate to have started life afresh in a young and prosperous country.

Nada was their pride and joy and that she, a new Australian, had been made an air hostess . . . and lately, what was more, on overseas flights . . . confirmed their belief that she was a quite exceptional girl. It was their constant prayer that she would marry an "old" Australian and give them grandchildren.

Looking out across the sea from Casuarina Point, she wondered when, if ever, she'd see them again.

She thought about her last Sunday at home. Iles had arrived in his funny old car and announced that he was taking them off to Hawkesbury for the day. Her mother who adored Iles had said: "No, it is very sad, we cannot go. We are expecting visitors, but you two run along. For you it will be so lovely."

Nada glared at her and snapped, "You know I can't go, Mother. I've got too many things to do."

Her mother shook her head, shrugged her shoulders and left the room. Poor old Iles had given her that sad friendly smile and said: "Well, better luck for me next time, Nada."

He drove off in the jalopy, waving madly as if this were the good-bye of all good-byes, though he knew perfectly well that they would be flying off to Perth together in the same aircraft in three days' time.

When he'd gone her mother said: "Shame, Nada, he likes you so much."

Nada glared again. "You seem to forget about Dieter."

Her mother shook her head vigorously. "I wish you'd forget that German."

*   *

The clouds came clear of the moon and the beach shone white, the shadows of the takamaka trees reaching down to where the silvery water lapped the sand.

Jos knelt in the undergrowth, rigid, scarcely breathing, his eyes scanning the beach. To his left was the coral jetty, in the lee of Danger Point where it curved briefly to the west.

He had named this long white beach "The Strand", because it reminded him of its namesake in False Bay, across the water from Simonstown.

It was here that he had first seen the spoors a few days earlier. For two hours he'd been waiting but nothing had come. But most of the time the moon had been obscured by clouds so he could not be sure. Now that the moonlight had broken through again he concentrated afresh, nerves strained, his right hand gripping the heavy stick.

A hundred feet from him he saw in the water, for the first time, the flat rocks.

Were they rocks?

As he posed this question, two of them moved up the beach towards him. Trembling with excitement, tensed for the hunt, he leant forward.

So you've come at last, he thought, just like your spoors told me you would. I mustn't move. Not until you're *much* closer.

For a minute or so he knelt there, immobile, a part of the surroundings. In that time five more shapes moved up the beach from the water. Jos looked at the sky and saw there was not much time.

A bank of dark cloud shut out the moon, and he rushed the nearest two. With a quick movement like a rugby player collecting the ball on the run, he turned the turtles onto their backs, and was shocked momentarily by their weight. In vain he searched in the darkness for the others, before he went back to his captives. They were bigger than he'd expected and he knew they'd be heavy to lift. But he wouldn't try that yet. Not with the jaws and claws still in action.

Stick in hand, he waited patiently. Sooner or later they'll put out their heads, he thought. Then I'll fix them. He thought of Mecky and Sarah Tripp. He'd make them a *muti*, rich with turtle fat and their bowels would work, though it was not for that he'd caught the turtles. Soon there would be rich steaks. Their first meat for nearly three weeks.

*   *

Twelve days after they'd landed the huts were finished and life on the island was acquiring a pattern. The men fished, collected sea-food and sea-birds' eggs and coconuts. From the survival booklet they identified a vegetable food: purslane, a soft-stemmed weed which tasted like watercress when fresh and like sour spinach when cooked.

The women did the cooking, or rather Angelique did with their assistance. She was resourceful and within the limitations of the island—and the absence of any cooking vessels, empty glucose tins and purifier boxes being all she had—she did wonders over an open fire.

Jos and Ezekiel were the fishermen and they maintained a steady supply from the deep pools inside the reef off Second Beach. Among other sea-food they found mussels and clams and from these Angelique made soups.

The day on the island was divided into three parts: the mornings which started early and were devoted to collecting food, to filling the water containers, and to preparing and cooking the meals— the object being to get as much done as possible before eleven o'clock when the sun was getting high and the heat and humidity began to make themselves felt. They had two meals each day . . . one at about half past eleven in the morning and the other in the evening. During the middle of the day they would rest. In the afternoon, after the worst of the heat, there would be more fishing and foraging for food, followed by preparation of the evening meal. Sometimes, before the sun set, there would be a move to Bikini Beach to round off the day with a swim. Twice they had bathed by moonlight.

When it was dark they sat round the fire in front of the huts and talked. This was the time when they fell prey to nostalgic thoughts of the outside world, and inevitably they would discuss the chances of rescue. How it might come, and when, and from where . . .? Always they would end up with the conundrum . . .?

Where were they?

At about nine or ten, they would leave the fire and wander off to their huts to sleep on the beds of palm-leaves which grew more comfortable as the days passed.

The weather, too, had a fairly set pattern, the wind blowing night and day with remarkable consistency; mostly from the sector between east and south, and generally directly from the south-east. On most days there was a good deal of cloud, and rain fell almost every other day, most often about an hour after sunset and an hour before dawn.

The men lived more or less in their cut-down trousers, often without a shirt or singlet until the evening. The women usually wore a skirt of sorts and a blouse, or just a brassière. In the last few days, the huts finished, there was more time for leisure and the men began to cut their hair, and trim their beards with the scissors from the first-aid outfit. But not Basset, who seemed to revel in scruffiness.

Even in the dinghy Angelique had kept herself reasonably neat and clean, but now both Nada and Sarah Tripp followed her example and were often to be seen using the signalling mirror.

But life on the island was far from idyllic. They were worried by midges and sand-flies, and all but Ezekiel suffered from prickly heat and athlete's foot. He attributed his immunity to the colour of his skin. "It doesn't worry brown skins. Like sharks!" He laughed.

*   *

Nada realised that on the island the authority she'd exercised in the dinghy had gone. The leadership position was now confused and a decision was rarely made without argument which left a trail of disagreement. In so far as there was a leader it was Jos, because the more practical ideas came from him and he was the hardest worker.

Ezekiel was good-natured and intelligent and once on a job worked at it, but he seemed to lack Jos's urge to get things done. He'd been inclined sometimes—when he remembered his M.P.— to pompousness but had dropped it when he found that badges of former office were of no account among the survivors. Nada felt that he would readily have accepted their lot rather than exert himself to alter it. Either that or the tension between him and

Jos, which often resulted in the African expressing a contrary or negative view, gave that impression.

Canning was resentful of Jos's authority while Basset and Mecky had already made clear their dislike of the Afrikaner, and their aversion for work of any sort. To a constant background of grumble and complaint they did the unavoidable minimum.

To Nada it seemed that Sebastian Goldsworthy had an almost saintlike quality. He was diffident and withdrawn but kind to everyone and always helpful however ineffectually because this lanky bald man with the domed head was not practical. He seemed afraid of Canning, whom he served with dog-like devotion. Canning for his part treated him very much like a dog, though sometimes with less consideration.

*   *

In the afternoon Jos left the camp and walked through the palms to Second Beach. There he turned south, his eyes searching the horizon. It was high tide and big seas were breaking over the reef. Occasionally a thin mist of spray, cool and refreshing, blew against his face. At Coral Point he went back into the palms to avoid the sharp edges of the polyps, but once round the point he made for the white sands of Rescue Beach. It seemed to him a long time since the orange dinghy had hurtled shorewards there and crashed on the reef. The wounds from that encounter had mostly mended now, but for his heel. The scar was red and angry and sometimes in the night it throbbed.

He would have spoken to Angelique about it but she was not friendly nowadays and he could not bring himself to ask for help. He had no idea what the trouble was. Since that second morning on the island when she and Ezekiel had gone off to explore she'd been cool and distant.

When he had walked for the best part of twenty-five minutes he was near the southern end of the island and the palms gave way to trees and scrub.

The beach petered out and mangroves grew down to the water;

beyond them the undergrowth and trees began. Sparse trees with a curious gauntness from their lifelong struggle with the wind which made them lean to the north-west as if they were reaching for something. From Angelique he had learnt their names. The casuarinas she called "filaos" and others were "bois blanc" and "takamakas".

In the glades of sand beneath the trees there were patches of coarse grass and on one of these, under a large takamaka tree, he sat down. He had found this place some days before. From it he could watch the seas racing in to the reef and at the same time command a wide arc of the horizon. But it was the sea-birds which really drew him there.

The gannets and frigate-birds roosted and nested in the trees to the south of him; there were terns, too, which laid their single egg on a fallen palm leaf or patch of grass.

Jos never tired of watching the abundance of bird life which, once he was in position, paid him little attention. There was a gay liveliness about this colony with its quarrelling and chattering in the trees where many of the rough nests had chicks. The gannets were prominent in this noise making, their quacks and grunts alternating with shrill whistles of surprise. Nothing entranced Jos more than their flight across the water, hugging the surface in single line ahead. When fish were sighted the line would climb to fifty or sixty feet, then they would come plummeting down, wings folded, until they disappeared into the water with a splash. A moment later they would reappear, their beaks shining with the silver of fish.

A black shape would then detach itself from the cloud of frigate-birds hovering overhead and hurtle down. A short swift chase would follow and the scurrying gannet would disgorge the fish; immediately the frigate-bird would snap it up, often seizing the fish in mid-air while it was still falling.

Of the sea-birds, Jos thought the terns the most beautiful. With their delicate hovering flight, their white wings translucent against the sun, they were fairylike creatures. If the black frigate-bird was the villain of the piece, then the white tern was the hero. He arrived at this conclusion quite independently, not knowing that Charles Darwin had said ". . . so light a body must be tenanted by some wandering spirit." And when the terns set about their neat thoughtful hunt, Jos was with them, as if it were his. The careful search of the sea, bill down at right angles to the body; the hover over the target and at the critical moment of the kill the quick closing of the wings and the neat drop into the water. Then the tern would reappear after the briefest of immersions with a fish in its beak.

While he sat watching, his thoughts went back to Soetwaters. He wondered what was happening there and whether they had finally accepted that he was dead. It was ridiculous and frustrating to be alive and well, and yet to know that one's family was enduring all the shock and misery of mourning one's death.

Sooner or later they would be rescued, his faith permitted no other conclusion, but in the meantime it seemed that a lot of people would suffer.

He wished he'd never made those inquiries which had led to the decision to study pasture grasses at the experimental station at Cunnamulla. It was that which had landed him on this island.

*   *

"*Lwami lwa wiki mando yamana*", the African was chanting a canoe paddling song he'd learnt on the Zambezi as a boy. His arms were high above his head, his hands clasping the green husk of a coconut. But for cut-down trousers he wore nothing, and his head, neck and bare chest, so brown that they were almost black, glistened with sweat.

"*No ku mana linyotwa ni ndala*," he chanted, his eyes on the point of the husking stick. He shifted key to a deep "*Ah Shoo-o*!" and his arms came down in a strike, the husk splitting in two. He wrenched it from the kernel and threw it onto the nearby heap.

He picked up another husk as Sarah Tripp appeared.

"Guess what?" Her eyes shone with excitement.

Ezekiel shook his head. With his hand he wiped the sweat from his forehead.

"We've seen smoke . . . a steamer!" She beckoned eagerly. "Come and look! Come on!" She ran along the sandy path through the plantation.

At the beach he saw the others at Casuarina Point and broke into a run, overtaking Sarah Tripp. Before he reached them he could hear their excited cries. To the east he saw a thin whirl of smoke on the horizon, streaming off to the north-west in the fresh breeze.

"Basset spotted it first," said Canning. "*Very* good effort."

Ezekiel looked round. They were all there except Lombaard. "How long ago?"

Basset blinked. "'Bout ten minutes, I s'pose."

"Which way's it going?"

"Can't say yet. Doesn't seem to be moving."

"Too far away," explained Canning. "We'll soon know."

Ezekiel frowned. "Where's Lombaard?"

"Messing about with the fish-trap."

Nada said: "I'm going to get the two-star-reds. We'll have to use them to attract attention if it comes this way." She disappeared.

Ezekiel looked at the smoke again, then at the others.

"We must make a big fire. Let's get plenty of wood."

He went over to the casuarina trees with Goldsworthy and the other men who, for once, showed some enthusiasm for work.

During the next half-hour a large bonfire was laid. They were about to light it when Ezekiel, looking out towards the distant smoke, stopped them.

"Know what?" he said, "it's not moving. Look! It's in exactly the same position."

With troubled eyes they saw that he was right. It had not moved. They watched it for fully an hour but it did not move. After long discussion they decided it was a ship at anchor, possibly a trawler. They watched until sunset and next morning they found that the smoke had gone. They were filled with despair. It re-appeared in the afternoon and once more they were elated. When this happened again on the next two days, the smoke appearing at various times but always in the same place, they realised that it must come from another island.

With this new discovery their excitement increased.

"You know what," said Jos, "Must be a group of islands here. There was that first island we sighted the day before we landed . . . and there's that small island about two miles south of Danger Point. Now there's the smoke over there. Land there, too. Another island. Must be people there."

Canning's eyes glistened. "How far would you say it is?"

Jos looked at the smoke. "Can't say. Could be quite a way off. We can see five or six miles from here, but the land's not in sight."

"Can't someone climb a palm tree?" Sebastian Goldsworthy said thoughtfully. "Maybe we could see the land then."

Ezekiel volunteered for the job on the grounds that he'd done it before.

"In Dar es Salaam," he grinned, "when I was undergoing political instruction."

Jos watched him mistrustfully. Political instruction my foot— I expect you're a Communist, he thought, a *verdomde Kommunis*.

With the aid of a short length of dinghy life-line round the trunk of the palm and his body, Ezekiel struggled up the tree, taking frequent rests, until he reached the top. After waiting and watching the smoke he shouted: "It's no use. I can't see any land."

"Must be more than twelve or fifteen miles away," said Jos lugubriously.

"D'you think they'd see a two-star-red if we fired one?" Nada held up a flare.

Jos shook his head. "Not by day. Perhaps we could try a couple tonight. But I think it's too far."

"How many have we left?" asked Angelique.

"Four."

Sarah Tripp gave a despairing shrug. "It seems hopeless. Shouldn't we keep them in case something comes really close?"

Jos nodded. "I think so."

*   *

Round the fire that night they discussed the day's events, and before they slept the unseen land had been named "Smoke Island." The smoke had been reassuring and the knowledge that there were other human beings in these waters, not far away, was immensely comforting. They no longer felt alone.

Eight

THE SMOKE was there next morning.

When they'd watched it for about ten minutes, speculating endlessly about its origin, Canning voiced their thoughts. "Well —*there* it is and *here* we are. How do we get there?"

Mecky was thoughtful. "The 64,000 dollar question, isn't it?" Instinctively he watched Jos.

Ezekiel looked across to the horizon. "We could build a raft. When the weather's right we might get there."

Jos turned to Canning, shaking his head. "The weather won't be right. We're in the south-east trades. The smoke's over there in the east and the wind blows to the north and west. We'd never make it."

Ezekiel knew that Lombaard was right. "It was just an idea." His voice was sullen.

Basset chimed in. "There's people where that smoke is. *People* . . . about ten miles away! If we keep a bonzer fire burning with plenty of green leaves on, they'll see our smoke just like we see theirs. They'll be here soon enough."

"That," said Mecky, "is the first sensible suggestion I've heard for a long time."

They lit the bonfire built the day before and when it was well ablaze they fed it with green leaves. At sunset they let it die down.

Next day the smoke from the island had gone. Notwithstanding, they stoked up the fire and piled on the green leaves until thick billows of white smoke climbed into the sky.

But nothing came and on the third day when the distant

smoke had still not appeared they abandoned the bonfire and once
more their hopes faded.

*   *

Ezekiel squatted on his haunches beyond the people round the
fire. He did not wish to talk and he had withdrawn himself so
that his thoughts would be undisturbed. At first they were of
Lombaard because it had happened again, and it worried him.
The Afrikaner had been sitting opposite him and Ezekiel had
suddenly become aware of the dark eyes staring. Not so much at
him as at his hands held out towards the fire.

There had been a wild look in Lombaard's eyes as he got up
and walked off into the darkness. For some time the African
contemplated the mystery of the white man's behaviour. Then
his mind emptied.

Squatting like this, his bare feet flat on the ground and his
knees reaching up towards his chin, clasped hands on the ground
in front of him, he could rest almost as well as if he were lying
down. The intermittent crackle of the fire, the smell of wood
smoke, the murmur of voices, the noise of leaves rustling in the
wind, and the clouds scurrying across the moon reminded him of
the kraal at Gensa.

He felt lonely because for three weeks he'd seen nothing but
white people.

Angelique? Was she white? He wasn't sure.

It was not the sort of question you asked in Africa. It *could*
be a deadly insult. But she was not from Africa and sometime,
maybe, he would ask her. She was a friendly creature, a fine
looking woman and a wonderful cook, but she was not easy to
know. You threw her the ball but she didn't throw it back, and
you never really knew what she was thinking except that it was
unlikely to be unkind because she always had that warm gentle
smile.

Munalula came into his thoughts. He pictured her going down
to the river, tall, upright, the earthenware jar balanced on her

head, brass anklets jangling. She had borne him four children over the last seven years, two girls and two boys. One had died.

They were fine children and the future for them was good; much better than it had been for him when he was a child.

Munalula was a good woman: his only wife so far, though he could well have afforded more. But his political career had been too strenuous for much home life and he'd seldom been at Gensa in recent years.

The time would come when he would have to make the decision: to leave Munalula and the children there or bring them down to Salisbury to be with him.

*   *

"I thought you were going to rinse out that shirt for me this afternoon, Sebastian?" Canning's voice was querulous.

"I was helping Lombaard with the fish-trap, sir."

Canning held up a peremptory hand. "I've told you before that I prefer you not to help him."

"It's difficult to refuse when one's asked to help in the common good, sir."

"Poppycock, Sebastian. We don't need a fish-trap. They're catching enough fish with the handlines. It's most unsatisfactory. After all I've done for you." He shook his head. "Am I to conclude that you regard Lombaard's wishes as more important than mine?"

"No sir, it was just that . . . "

Canning's podgy hand went up. "In that case, Sebastian," his voice hardened. "Take the shirt now and rinse it . . . and Sebastian . . ."

"Sir?"

"Don't let this sort of thing happen again, will you?"

"No, Mr. Canning, sir, I can assure you I'm very sorry."

*   *

Sebastian was troubled as he knelt down to wash the shirt in the lagoon. Using small handfuls of sand as an abrasive he tried to remove the dirt where it was worst. At least the rinsing got rid of the sweat and when the shirt dried in the sun the salt water acted as a bleaching agent.

Not, he reflected, that any shirt . . . even one of this quality . . . could last very long under these conditions.

But he was deeply troubled and although it was eleven years ago, Canning's voice still rang with cold pomposity:

"*I have no pity for you, Sebastian. You have only yourself to blame . . . that is not a justification, it is an explanation. It in no way detracts from what you have done. What right have you to act as judge in your own cause? Circumstances alone cannot authorise us to decide these matters for ourselves. I am well aware of the illness, but I fail to see that it makes the slightest difference. If, of course, you would prefer the matter to be decided elsewhere, I have no doubt that can be arranged . . . but would it be advisable, Sebastian? You are, you say, twenty-eight; I would have thought that by now you would have saved something. It is, of course, easy to be improvident and I have little doubt that you have taken the line of least resistance and lived beyond your means. I would certainly not have reached the position I have, had I pursued such a course. To retain at all times a proper regard for one's responsibilities is, I admit, not easy and requires character, Sebastian, but it brings its own rewards. In the circumstances, then, you are fortunate that I have decided on this course of action . . . will you sign here . . .*"

*　　　　*

It was Sunday and nothing but the essential work of collecting and preparing food was undertaken. It hadn't rained for two days so that there was not even the task of transferring water from the catchment to the life-jackets.

They might, by now, have lost count of the days had it not been for Mecky's calendar; ever since the third day in the dinghy he had kept it religiously, on the inside back pages of the survival booklet.

He checked the entries. They'd come down in the sea at one hour after midnight on Monday the 17th September, and they'd landed on the island on Friday the 28th September. This was Sunday the 14th October. As he wrote it into the booklet he sighed. It was now twenty-seven days since they had crashed. How much longer would this God-forsaken existence continue? Living in these obscene rags, wearing this ludicrous sweat-soaked beard, tormented by midges and sand-flies and prickly heat, and waking each morning to the knowledge that another deadly day lay ahead? What was this absurd struggle for survival about anyway? The dreary existence of a minor executive in an oil company in Australia, slaving away in an office abounding with "the types"? But they'd be Australian "types" just as bad, no doubt, as the loutish extroverts in Nairobi. There'd be nobody like Paul in Australia. He'd have to eke out an existence more or less by himself, relying upon his own resources. He thought gratefully of the large packing-case which should by now have reached Melbourne. At least he'd have his books and music . . . but what was life without someone to confide in, to share one's thoughts, one's revolts, one's satisfactions and one's desires?

How much longer could he stand these others?

Canning, Lombaard, Wanalu, Goldsworthy, Basset . . . God! What a bunch to be imprisoned with.

Basset? What a companion! Not a thought that wasn't a profanity. And yet somehow he was less offensive than the others, this pert incorrigible sparrow. Perhaps there was a certain kinship; the mutuality of misfits? The women he dismissed with scarcely a thought: he wasn't interested in women.

Lombaard? What was Lombaard? A huge ape with exaggerated survival values. How he loathed the man.

And Wanalu? A jumped-up African, riding the wave of African nationalism, dragged from the obscurity of the kraal, endured at Oxford, a humble offering on the altar of the British social conscience, determined now to atone for its past sins, even if others must do the penance.

*   *

In the late evening Nada saw Ezekiel fishing on the reef off Rescue Beach. The wind had fallen and there was a haze over the sea. She waved and he beckoned her across. It was low water and she waded out to the reef, the water below her knees. When she reached the reef she climbed onto it and walked over to him.

Ezekiel was fishing in a deep pool; at his side were four or five mullet and as many "stripeys".

"Clever boy!"

"Poor fishes. They fall so easily."

"Fall?"

"For the bait."

"They must be hungry."

"They are greedy, Nada."

Through their gills he threaded a spiky leaf from a palm frond. "What have you been doing?"

"Helping Sarah mend her skirt."

"She's a funny woman."

"Very unhappy, Zeke."

"She's frightened. Thirty-five and she hasn't found a man yet. Time's getting short."

"It's a nuisance this man—woman thing, isn't it? Life would be much more simple without it."

"Then we wouldn't exist."

Slowly he coiled the line, anchoring the hook in it when he'd finished. "Let's go."

He picked up the fish and they waded across to the beach. They went into the palms and along the path past the coral cairn to the other side of the island. The sun was setting and the distant cloud banks were splashed with bronze and carmine. The patches of sky between them were cerulean blue, pale lemon, and deepest salmon, and their reflection laid a glittering path across the water to the beach. Here in the lee of the island, the water lapped the sand gently, tiny wavelets turning in with a mild splash.

"Beautiful, isn't it, Zeke?"

"Yes. Let's sit and watch it."

After a pause she said: "Still optimistic about rescue?"

"Of course. And you?"

"I suppose so really. But for different reasons."

"How do you mean?"

She looked at him sideways and smiled shyly. "Not because of the spirits of my ancestors."

"You think that's funny?"

"So primitive, Zeke."

"What about Goldsworthy and Jos? They're good Christians. They think we'll be rescued because they believe in God."

"Yes. But that's different. That's faith! Christianity."

Ezekiel frowned. "It's not different, you know. I admire Christianity. It's a flame that's endured. But it's rooted in mysticism, too."

She shook her head emphatically. "I don't know much about these things and I'm not much of a Christian, but you can't call Christianity mysticism."

There was a ghost of a smile on Ezekiel's face. "I think we mustn't question these things. They're too alike."

* *

Jos was in a thoroughly bad mood that night. He'd seen Nada and the African sitting on the beach together at sunset and it had upset him.

It was unfortunate, therefore, that when they were sitting round the fire eating their fish Mecky should have said, "God, how *sick* I am of this eternal fish," and that Basset had added, "Human otters that's what we are! Fish, fish, glorious fish, what a lousy bloomin' dish!"

From the darkness Angelique said: "I am sorry. It is all you have given me to cook. You men must catch more turtles."

134

That was too much for Jos.

"*Men*," he snorted, "They're not men. They're pansies!"

"Mind what you're saying, digger," snarled Basset.

Mecky looked across to where Jos was sitting and then said to Basset in a stage whisper: "What's our muscle-bound friend getting so worked up about?" It was evident that he intended the remark to be overheard.

It took a few minutes to sink in but when it did, Jos lumbered to his feet and moved round the fire until he stood next to them. With the red firelight flickering on his rugged bearded face, his hairy chest showing in the large V of the unbuttoned shirt, his massive shoulders inclined forward, and his hands hanging at his side, he was a fearsome figure.

"You said something?" the inquiry was slow, ominous. Mecky and Basset looked into the fire and kept quiet; anything they could say now would be dangerous.

"Because if you did," said Jos thickly, "I just want you to know you're a couple of rats. If you don't like that you know what you can do!"

There was an agonised silence, a moment of awful suspense, broken at last by Sarah Tripp's high voice:

"Personally, I thought the fish very good tonight, Angelique."

＊ ＊

That night Jos dreamt that the Lord came to him; a bearded figure clothed in dazzling white with a lantern held on high, the light so bright that he had to look away. Then he heard a voice speaking from afar: "With thine hands shalt thou fashion a boat and go out upon the waters."

Jos knew that it was he the Lord had commanded, and he trembled in his sleep.

＊ ＊

It was a hot day and the wind had dropped; overhead the louring sky was thick with grey cloud. Ezekiel was splitting wood with the axe. His body glistened with beads of perspiration and below his eyes there were pools of moisture. Near him Sarah Tripp was sitting in the shade of a palm mending her blouse.

Ezekiel interrupted his work for a moment to clear his nose, closing one nostril with his thumb in the manner of Africa, and blowing freely through the other. When he first did this in the dinghy there'd been hard looks, but in the absence of handkerchiefs it had since become the habit of them all. They had learnt from him, too, how to clean their teeth with a moist forefinger dipped in wood charcoal . . . another African custom which they'd originally thought odd. Some of them now squatted on their haunches, but none with his ease and grace.

Near them Jos was making cups from coconut shells. In the glowing embers of a wood fire he had heated a length of wire from the Sarah Beacon. Then he seized the ends, using two sets of flat pumice stones as pliers, and wound the wire round the coconut about a third down from the top. It burned deeply into the shell and the acrid smoke penetrated Jos's half-closed eyes and tears ran down his cheeks. When the wire had burned through the shell he smoothed the edge of the cup with a pocket knife. At his side there was a row of finished cups.

Nada and Angelique were collecting purslane along The Strand; Basset was picking up coconuts; and Canning and Goldsworthy had gone to Second Beach to gather mussels. In fact Canning was sitting with his back to a palm watching Sebastian work.

On reaching the beach he had opened with his usual gambit. "My back's worrying me today, Sebastian. Mind if I don't join you?" It was in no sense a question.

"Of course not, sir. You take a good rest." Sebastian's voice was solicitous. The Chief had suffered a lot from his back since they'd reached the island, but it had been agreed between them, early on, that Sebastian would not mention this to the others.

They'd been gathering sea-birds' eggs on that occasion and Canning had said with simple dignity: "I prefer to suffer in

silence, Sebastian, rather than have those women fussing over me.
My only regret," he had added, settling himself more comfortably
in the shade of a tree, "is that I can't help you as much I'd like to."

Because he'd waited on Canning hand and foot for eleven
years, Sebastian accepted the position without question. It did
not occur to him that the sore back might be a subterfuge and,
even if it had, it wouldn't have made any difference. After all,
the head of a great organisation like the Company couldn't be
expected to do menial work. Sebastian had noticed that if the
other survivors were present the Chief helped with the work;
too proud, presumably, to let them know about his back.

*   *

It had rained shortly after sunset and drops of moisture still
fell from the palm tops, their "tick-tick" breaking the silence
of the night.

The evening meal was finished. Around the fire the ground was
moist and steaming. A long silence was broken by Angelique.

"It's days since we saw the smoke on that island."

"Five," said Sarah Tripp.

"You know," said Jos, "I've been thinking. The other day
somebody suggested a raft. But that's no good. It couldn't make
it against the wind."

Somebody, thought Ezekiel indignantly. He knows damn' well
I did.

"What I think," went on Jos, "is . . . why shouldn't we build
a catamaran? Fit it with a sail and when the wind's more southerly
than south-easterly we could reach the island."

Basset felt that as an ex-sailor something was expected from
him. "You mean tack up there, Jos?"

Canning's eyes brightened. "What's a catamaran?"

"Sort of canoe, made from the hollowed-out trunk of a tree.
Got outriggers so that it can't capsize."

Nada was enthusiastic. "Jos, that sounds terribly exciting.
What a *marvellous* idea!"

Ezekiel frowned. Why hadn't he thought of this? He'd grown up with dug-out canoes: helped to make them, paddled them. But for the outriggers and masts and sails, they were the same as catamarans.

"We can make sails from palm leaves." Angelique's voice was gentle, but she wouldn't look at Jos. "The pirogues do this."

Sarah Tripp peered at her. "What's a pirogue?"

"A small fishing-boat. We have them in Mauritius."

Jos and Zeke avoided addressing each other directly and this inhibited the conversation because certain pauses and evasions were necessary.

"On the Mozambique coast," said Jos at last, speaking to Nada, "I've seen catamarans. Only trouble is—we've no tools." There was a long pause while he brooded over this.

Ezekiel saw his chance. "We've got the axe. That's all we need. We can build one."

The others looked at him.

Jos was silent; annoyed that the African had cottoned onto the idea and was now enjoying the limelight.

"How can we build it, Zeke?" Nada's eyes were bright.

"Put a dried palm trunk on trestles. Work the top flat with adzes." He paused and looked at the faces round the fire. "We can use the fire-axe. When the top's flat you make a fire along it . . . away from the sides. It burns down into the log. After that it's easy to cut out the charred wood. You go on with these fires, and you go on cutting out the burnt wood until the log's hollow. Then you shape the ends."

Jos decided it was time he spoke. "We'll have to fit outriggers, and put in a mast to take the sail."

Canning's eyes sparkled. "How many people could it hold, Jos?"

"Depends on the size of the trunk. Three or four perhaps . . . with trees the size we've got here."

"Only three or four? But then . . ."

"That's fine," Mecky interrupted. "Even if it only took one we'd be rescued if he reached Smoke Island."

"*If*," echoed Sarah Tripp gloomily.

"Of course," Nada nodded emphatically. "I think it's a fabulous idea!"

Art Basset came in again. "How long to build it, Jos?"

"Don't know. A month, perhaps."

"Chr . . . I mean cripes! A month! We'll be rescued anyways before that."

"I doubt it. It'll be a lot of work, but I think we should build the catamaran." It was not often that Ezekiel agreed so readily with Jos's suggestions.

The Afrikaner looked at him . . . not at his face so much as at the black hands which the African was holding to the fire. Then he got up slowly, and without a word disappeared into the darkness.

Angelique had seen the strange light in the big man's eyes, and it frightened her. This had happened before and it was beyond her understanding.

Work on the catamaran began the next day.

*   *

In the pool she saw herself: the firmly drawn eyebrows; the well-shaped, slightly tilted nose; the moist red mouth; the brown eyes; and the long tresses of blue-black hair pulled down over her shoulders.

She tired of her reflection and looked round to make sure no one was in sight. Slipping off her brassière and skirt, she sat there for a few minutes. Then, naked, she let herself down into the shaded part of the pool and enjoyed the cool intimacy of the water. She looked down on her breasts and sighed. She was beautiful: a woman knew these things. But why couldn't she have babies? What was the use of those breasts if no small mouth ever tugged at them?

The house in Port Louis would be transformed with a child;

it would become a home not just a house. Life would take on a new and wonderful dimension if she had a child. It seemed so pointless at times, this life without children. One day Kwan had found her on the bed weeping and after much persuasion she'd told him she was sad because she had no children.

Kwan's kind face had puckered. "Why not adopt a baby, Angelique?"

"No! I should be terrified! What if it turned out to be . . . strange? Perhaps a criminal, even?" Her hands went out in a gesture of hopelessness. "How can one know?"

"Many people have found happiness in such a way."

"I could not, Kwan."

That was the first time they'd discussed her secret sorrow so openly, but not the last for afterwards, at long intervals, they'd gone back to it and Kwan had made other suggestions.

*　　　　*

The light from the campfire flickered and made strange patterns on their faces.

"What I miss most is a fag." Art Basset's eyes were on the diamond brooch on Angelique's blouse. "And me gin. Life's really not worth living if you can't 'ave 'em. I mean . . . what is there?" That brooch, he thought, must be worth every penny of three thousand pounds, maybe more.

Nada smiled. "Oh, many things, millions more important. Like music and clean white sheets and nice soap and perfumes and proper lights."

Angelique looked at Ezekiel. "What do you miss, Zeke?"

"Newspapers, radio. News. We don't know what's happening. Time has stopped here."

"That's because you're a politician." Angelique teased. "You're out of the picture."

He laughed. "I know."

"What I miss most," said Canning. "Is the office . . . and my good little woman . . . all the comfort of our lovely home. This place . . . ," he looked round disapprovingly, "is so crude. There's no . . . atmosphere, you know. No character . . ."

"People make atmosphere," said Sarah Tripp, an uncompromising light in her eyes.

"Yes, I know . . . ." Canning saw the pit he'd dug for himself. In that moment, looking at her in the half-light, he thought, She's really not bad looking; quite a decent figure. "You're right, Sarah." He added gaily, "*And* I miss my Scotch and soda and my cigars."

Mecky was dreamy. "I miss the roar of traffic . . . the lights . . . the smell of the city. I can't stand . . ." he looked round into the darkness behind him, ". . . the deadly monotony of this place . . . the noise of these seas breaking. The wind . . . the rain. Much more of it and . . . and . . . ," his voice rose, "I'll go mad. I *swear* I will."

"I would like," said Jos in his deep guttural, "to have my Bible. This is something a man should always have with him. To remind him of God." He looked at Angelique, his dark eyes enigmatic.

"Oh, I *do* agree," said Sebastian.

There was an embarrassed silence.

"But I also miss a nice brandy," Jos regarded them gravely. "After a day's work a man needs a few spots, you understand?"

"It's difficult to know what one misses most." Sarah Tripp gazed thoughtfully into the fire. "Books and intelligent discussion . . ." She gulped at her own tactlessness. "Salt and sugar are rather important too. The sameness of life here is deadly. One day's so like another . . . nothing to look forward to, really."

"What about you, Angelique, you never say what you're thinking?" Canning's eyes travelled over her well-developed figure.

Angelique smiled. "I don't think much about anything. I am content with the day as it is. I do not ask for more. If you wish for things you have not, then you are unhappy. It is better like this."

Nada looked across the fire. "You, Sebastian?"

He smiled nervously. "You know, I . . . er . . . must be honest. I don't think I miss anything. I mean life here's so . . . so adventurous. Such fun. Like . . . well . . . Robinson Crusoe really. Not like the office . . ." The words froze in his mouth and he gasped. "I'm truly sorry, Mr. Canning, sir. No reflection on the Company, I assure you. What I meant . . ."

"Oh, forget it, Sebastian," Canning said irritably, his thoughts elsewhere. "We couldn't really care what you think." He leant closer to Sarah Tripp. "Could we?"

"I wish," she said icily, moving away from him, "that you'd stop nudging me."

Canning looked explosive. "I *beg* your pardon."

"Smarty pants fancies herself," chuckled Basset. "Didn't know you was one of them, Canning . . . blimey! Glad I'm not *your* room-mate."

*　　　　*

That morning Ezekiel had again been involved in a humiliating row with Jos. They had almost come to blows. That was why he was thinking about Jos: about the white man in Africa; about white men anywhere. How little they knew of the black man; to them a black skin meant ignorance and savagery. Its wearer was anonymous; disembodied; just *another* black face.

They thought of the black man only as *for* or *against* the white man. They couldn't concede the African ethos; that such a thing as the African personality existed. It puzzled Ezekiel that the white man could not understand that the African was neither pro-West nor pro-Communist, but simply pro-African. Another thing which worried him was the white man's assumption that because the black man was pro-African, he must be anti-white.

Ezekiel put a thumb to his nose and blew it.

They had no conception of the ambivalence of the black man's feeling for the white man; the bewildering complexity of the love-

142

hatred relationship which made so much anti-white emotion chicken-hearted.

Ezekiel wondered whether the white man would ever understand the black man's yearning for dignity, for freedom from humiliation, for recognition, and for acceptance as a full member of society.

He switched at the flies with a twig of green leaves and thought more about negritude. How did it fit into the pattern of Western civilisation? And what really *was* Western civilisation?

In moments of cynicism he thought of it as an affair of pep-pills and tranquillisers—of ulcers and coronaries—of status symbols and race persecution—of hydrogen bombs and aids to longevity—of stupendous crop surpluses and grotesque famines—of artificial insemination and gas ovens—of super highways and super hospitals for their users. But in rational moments he recognised it for something more than that. In any case, whichever way one looked at it, it was the direction in which Africa was headed.

His thoughts went back to Jos.

Jos and his people believed with messianic fervour in the basic incompatibility of black and white: were moving towards partition of the land because they were convinced that in the context of Africa multi-racialism was not politically viable, founded as it was on what they regarded as a complex myth: that people were colour blind; that the abstractions of moral philosophy were more powerful than the realities of race; that the black man could be moulded into a compliant neo-white man who would seek no more in his own land than to share power.

In Southern Africa the majority on both sides of the colour line rejected this myth; yet to admit as much was to give affront to the Western world to whom *separation . . . partition . . . apart-heid* were dirty words. Strange, thought Ezekiel, that the West engineered partition in Palestine, condones it in India, yet condemns it in South Africa. Fortunate, though, for the political axe we have to grind, he concluded with becoming honesty.

But the Afrikaner had no illusions about these things. He had had power, lost it and regained it. Power was not something one shared except with one's own people. It was not a divisible commodity. It belonged to those who held it: as long as they could hold it. The African was not looking for power sharing arrangements: he was looking for power.

At least, reflected Ezekiel, Jos's people acknowledge our right to free and unfettered sway in our own lands. But if they are sincere, if separation is really meant to work, then the sharing of the land will have to take account of the realities however unpalatable they may be. Justice will have to be done. What is more, it will have to be seen to be done.

He switched again at the flies. It was hot and he was sleepy. He could not worry too much about these things. There was always tomorrow.

Nine

It was not only Jos who knew about Ezekiel's and Angelique's disappearances; others, too, had seen them leave the camp separately on these occasions, usually in the early afternoon. And though they never returned together, the coincidence of their absences was remarkable. This irritated Jos. In fact, though he would never have admitted it, he was jealous.

One afternoon when Angelique left the camp in the direction of Second Beach, and Ezekiel not long afterwards disappeared towards Needle Point . . . that is to say in quite the opposite direction . . . Jos took to the palms, keeping the African under close observation. Jos had grown up in the veld and could stalk a kudu or lion to within thirty yards, so that for him this shadowing was not difficult. Silent, unseen, the big man slipped from tree to tree, always about a hundred yards from his quarry.

At Needle Point, Ezekiel turned south and walked along the beach stopping now and then to examine the pools left by the tide. Beyond the curved sand spit which they called Hook Point he hesitated and after a long and elaborately casual look round went back into the palms to cross the island in a south-easterly direction. This sudden alteration of course reduced the distance between them to about fifty yards, and Jos had to slip behind a large palm to avoid detection.

He heard a low whistle away to the left and this was answered at once by Ezekiel. Jos felt the blood rushing to his head. His suspicions of a clandestine meeting were well founded. Tense, smouldering with jealousy, he stood waiting, his eyes searching the side from which the whistle had come.

Then he saw her, not thirty yards away, and she was waving to Ezekiel who called out, "Hallo there!"

She answered, "Well met, Zeke!"

Jos remained as motionless as the palm behind which he hid; he would see this thing out to the bitter end before he betrayed his presence—*if* he did.

But the expected embrace did not materialise and to his surprise they turned south, Angelique following the African along the sandy path through the palms. Jos moved forward, a silent shadow, turning with them as they veered back towards The Strand. Soon they reached the beach and walked down it. Ten minutes later they went into the dense undergrowth fringing the beach.

Slowly, with infinite patience, Jos had followed them, keeping always to the shadows. Now he knew from their voices that they'd stopped and as he got closer he went down on his knees, then onto his stomach, inching himself forward under a thick overhang of scrub, to lie there motionless. Their voices were close now.

"Up you go," laughed Angelique. "It is a good cause."

Ezekiel said: " A little tighter," and Jos heard Angelique ask, "Too tight?"

The African answered: "No. That's okay."

Noises of chafing and heavy breathing followed and Jos realised that Ezekiel was climbing a palm. After a while he heard Ezekiel's shout, "Know what? The tin's full."

Angelique called back, "Good! Be careful! Lower it to me with the line."

At that moment the worst of all things happened. Jos felt a dry tickle in his throat and realised with anguish that he was going to cough and that nothing could stop him. It came. An explosive cough—like a gunshot.

Then Angelique was bending down peering at him through the undergrowth, looking as if she'd seen a ghost.

"*Mon dieu!* What are you doing, Jos?"

Enormously embarrassed he crawled out.

"I went for a walk. Then I was sleepy. I lay·down here. Then you came along." He looked away from her.

"But you were in the camp when we left? You have not had time for this."

Jos realised that his story didn't hold water so he swung to the attack—glaring. "What are you doing here—with *him*?"

There was a strange look on her face. "What do you mean?"

"I saw you leave the camp separately. Then you met in the plantation . . . and came here. What's the idea?"

Angelique's eyes were cold. "So you have been following us?"

"Yes."

"You . . . you disgust me! You are a *peeg*!" The way she said it hurt Jos terribly, and what made it worse she looked as though she was going to cry.

She turned on him again and he did not know whether she was angry or amused now because there was a funny look on her face. "We are making calao."

"Calao? What's that?"

"Coconut *toddy*, the English call it. Alcohol. It is for you men who talk of nothing but the drink you cannot get."

"You mean," he said dubiously, looking up to Ezekiel working sixty feet above them, "that he's making a drink?"

"Pouf!" she said, pouting her moist red lips at him, "I do not wish to talk to you." She turned away.

*　　　　*

A friendship of sorts was developing between Jos and Goldsworthy, although their characters were so different.

But they were both God-fearing men, and evidence of this had not been lost upon them. Goldsworthy had noticed how Jos would often sing a psalm, particularly if he thought he were alone. Jos, in turn had observed Sebastian's humility, and with what reverence he spoke of the Almighty.

Both disliked blasphemy, Sebastian wincing when he heard it, and Jos usually admonishing the blasphemer.

They had not discussed these matters but each noted the other's devotions with an increasingly warm and friendly eye.

The nearest they had come to an exchange of confidences was when Sebastian, with a shy gesture, agreed with Jos that to have a bible on the island would have been wonderful. After that he'd said, "You're not C-of-E are you?"

Jos frowned at first and then laughed. Thumping his chest he said: "What me, Joshua Lombaard, Church of England? That'll be the day. No, man," he added seriously, "I'm Nederduits Gereformeerde Kerk. Biggest church in South Africa."

"That's the Dutch Reformed Church, isn't it?"

"That's right. The English call it 'the DRC', but they don't know whether they mean the Hervormde Kerk or the Gereformeerde. The English in South Africa," he frowned, "are not religious people. But for us . . . we Afrikaners . . . the Church is our people . . . we are the Church. It saved us after the Second Freedom War . . . when we had lost everything. It rallied us, gave us back our pride. Gave us hope. Made us a people again, you understand?"

Sebastian frowned. "The Second Freedom War? What was that?"

"The English called it the Boer War."

"Oh, that! It was so long ago. We've forgotten it."

Jos's eyes gleamed, dark and fiery above the sunburnt bearded cheeks. "*We* haven't. You didn't lose twenty thousand women and children in concentration camps."

Sebastian shook his head. "I don't approve of war."

"Nor me," agreed Jos. He looked curiously at the lank, awkward figure, topped by the bald head and sparse face. The pale grey eyes, uncertain above the nondescript beard, proclaimed their owner's meekness.

"What's your church, Sebastian?"

The thin man smiled nervously. "Baptist, Jos. A wonderful church. When I was . . .", he hesitated, "*very* unhappy . . . it saved me."

Jos nodded with deep conviction.

"Without God man hasn't a chance, hey."

*　　　*

A downpour of rain had driven them away from the fire and early to bed; there were no lights in the huts and no real alternatives to sleep.

But Canning could not sleep; he lay there wide awake in the darkness, thinking, listening to Jos and Zeke's heavy breathing. He and Sebastian were on one side of the hut, Jos and Zeke the other. There was, of course, no furniture; nothing, but the palm leaves on the ground to lie on and, in the centre of the hut, supporting the roof ridge, two timber props. From these hung their few pieces of clothing, hooked over the stumps of severed branches.

Outside the rain fell more persistently than usual, and Canning heard the steady splash of water from the roof.

Beyond these sounds was the elegy of the surf and the wind in the palm tops. An occasional stab of lightning pierced the outside darkness, casting dazzling shafts of light into the hut.

For more than an hour he had been trying to sleep but something, the turtle meat probably, had given him indigestion and he was nagged by his thoughts. Mostly they were of Lombaard and Wanalu whom he hated and feared, and to a lesser extent of the others. Goldsworthy, a perpetual source of irritation, yet the only link with the substance of Canning's real life—the Company and Fenchurch Street. A faithful servant, but a confounded bore. Then he thought of Nada and Angelique; both attractive in their own way and . . . well, let's face it . . . becoming more attractive each day. Whether it was the regular hours, the fairly austere diet and the physical work, whatever it was . . . he had not felt so fit for a long time. And this sense of bodily well-being induced unusual ardour. Yes, Nada and Angelique were an attractive pair. He would have to do something about that before long. It was really just a matter of opportunity. Of timing.

His thoughts returned to Jos. In the darkness his anger and resentment grew as he remembered the indignities which the Afrikaner heaped on him. How dare the clumsy oaf behave like that! Ordering him about, treating him like dirt without regard to his age, position and background. Once again Canning resolved that the English-speaking passengers should get together and take over the leadership. It was preposterous to allow this uncouth peasant to take charge. The only person who ever stood up to Lombaard was Wanalu, but he was an African . . . black, unreliable, no background, not to be trusted. And recently Wanalu had shown some disposition to fall in with Lombaard's plans. Like that ridiculous decision to build a catamaran.

Not only ridiculous but dangerous. Canning was sure that if and when the catamaran were finished, Jos and Ezekiel would set off for Smoke Island alone. What would happen to those who remained? The catamaran would probably never make Smoke Island and they would be left to rot on the island, to fend for themselves with the two most resourceful men gone. Sooner or later . . . and preferably sooner . . . the leadership would have to be taken over by the English speakers.

Canning fell asleep.

* *

The steel flashed in the sunlight, wood chips flying into the air as the blade bit into the trunk, the axe-head ringing with each stroke and the muscles in Jos's forearm and biceps flexing as he wielded the axe. It was three days since they had started on the catamaran and the upper side of the palm was nearly flat. The long trunk was supported by trestles tied together with fibre rope which the women had plaited.

Jos's body was moist with sweat as he worked in the sun, his bare feet surrounded by wood shavings. He was the only person at work on the catamaran, but near him Sarah Tripp sat on a stump watching and talking.

She too was bare-footed. A ragged skirt and a brassière were all she wore, besides her floppy hat made from young palm leaves. Through the thick spectacles, worn low on her nose, her eyes looked larger than they were.

Jos worked with his back to her and she watched him, fascinated. He was enormously strong and muscular and the play of his body, the rolling and knotting of the muscles in his shoulders, in his back, in the powerful brown thighs and the strong neck, were to her an aphrodisiac.

It was absurd, she thought, hitting out at the midges buzzing round her neck, that women have to wait for men to make the advances. It was a deadly handicap, with an unimaginative, reserved man like this.

She rearranged herself on the stump, pulling her skirt above her knees, wondering whether he would notice them when he turned.

My legs and thighs are about the only decent things I've got, she thought sadly, looking down at the brassière supporting her too small breasts. She saw the jagged seams of scar tissue which ran down his back and disappeared under the top of his shorts. Once again she wondered how he'd got those scars? They were too long and regular, too parallel, to have been caused by a car accident or anything like that.

The ringing thud of the axe stopped. Jos turned and leaned against the palm trunk, his face streaming with sweat, the raven black beard, roughly trimmed, shining with moisture. He put down the axe and wiped away the sweat.

"Hell! . . . It's hot, hey, Sarah?"

She looked away and nodded, wondering whether he'd noticed her knees. When she turned back she was sure he hadn't; he was gazing out to sea, his thoughts obviously far away.

She sighed. "Tell me, Jos, how did you get those scars?"

His head came round and the dark eyes pierced hers. "These?" He pointed over his shoulder.

"Yes."

"Cat scratched me."

Before she could answer he had turned, picked up the axe and swung it at the trunk with renewed energy.

She looked at her knees and pulled her skirt down. It was no use. He hadn't batted an eyelid.

Her eyes filled with tears.

*   *

Lying in the hut Jos fought with his conscience; a long hard fight, but in the end he knew his conscience hadn't won. For two nights now he'd found himself sitting at the fire near Angelique, struck by her beauty. And it was not only that he was near her: it was the effect she had on him, as if he were hypnotised by her round breasts and strong thighs as she sat there, quiet and withdrawn, the firelight flickering over her face; her eyes, calm and inscrutable, forever searching the fire; her lovely mouth soft and moist; a silent invitation that sent his blood racing. She was all woman, warm, appealing. But there were no gestures of encouragement, no artifices. She was detached, alone, yet tremendously there. Vital. Alluring. The blood swam in his head.

Why should he feel like this? She ignored him, was as near being rude as she could ever be, for rudeness was not a part of her. But he knew, and they all knew, that she was displeased with him, avoided him.

He fought these thoughts with others. The church in the village near Soetwaters; the church where he had been christened, confirmed, married; where Anna had been buried. The church where his father and grandfather—and his mother and grandmother—had been christened and confirmed and married. The church where his great-grandfather and great-grandmother had been buried. Lying in the hut, he saw the dusty brown stone of the church, quarried from the kloof at Soetwaters, the grey slates of the roof and spire, the red dust and cypresses of the churchyard, and beyond them the cemetery where the bones of his forefathers lay. He could see the *dominee* . . . hear him:

> *"Whoso sheddeth man's blood, by man shall his*
> *blood be shed: for in the image of God made*
> *he man."*

Jos closed his eyes to shut out the pain of these thoughts and the pain of other thoughts: of Angelique, of her dark beauty.

Dark beauty: the words drummed in his mind.

She had lived in Mauritius all her life. In the tropics. It was surely no more than the dark tan of the tropical sun?

*   *

Opposite Jos, Canning lay awake in the darkness thinking of the same campfire and the light of the same flames, but they were reflected on Nada's face. In the dinghy he had disliked her intensely: her continual bossiness; her slight regard for him; but here somehow it was different. For one thing she'd taken a back seat since they'd reached the island. She'd become quieter and more thoughtful, obeying orders instead of giving them. She'd become more womanly; much more attractive.

That evening they had been sharing the same log, and after he'd put more wood on the fire, he sat closer so that his shoulder was against hers, his elbow pressing into her side. She had not seemed to mind. And then, when they'd got onto the eternal subject of the things they missed, she said: "And what do you miss most?"

There was a gleam, he fancied, in her eyes; a gleam he returned with interest when he said: "Home comforts, me dear. I'm a married man, you know," and he winked.

She smiled, a provocative smile it seemed, and he felt sure his message had got through. Strangely elated, he squeezed her arm but just then that confounded woman Sarah Tripp had called out: "Nada! Come to the hut! I've got something for you."

Before he could follow up his opening, the two women had disappeared.

Canning turned over and sighed happily. At last there was something positive to look forward to; something which put a new zest into him; something which promised to make even the dreary business of life on the island exciting.

*   *

Next morning Mecky came running into the camp with important news. Collecting eggs at Casuarina Point he had again seen the smoke.

There was once more a sign of life on Smoke Island.

For three days they were in high spirits. The camp was filled with laughter and chatter; the bonfire was lit; lookouts were posted; and work on the catamaran went forward with new vigour.

But nothing came from Smoke Island, and by high noon on the fourth day the smoke had gone.

Ten

ANGELIQUE tasted the calao. It was properly fermented. All of the older brew. Enough to fill the eight coconut shells.

"Tonight we shall show them a surprise. But not too much, Zeke. It is strong. We do not want trouble."

Ezekiel tasted it again, smacking his thick lips. "It's good," he said. "As good as in Dar es Salaam."

After he'd found them collecting the sap in the plantation, Jos had thought of telling the others about it. Later he'd decided not to. It might encourage Angelique to talk of his skulking in the undergrowth, and he wouldn't have liked that. So when the calao was produced that evening it came as a pleasant surprise. Only Sarah Tripp, harrassed by thoughts of Lennie and his drunken orgies, objected.

"It's the *last* thing we want here," she said decidedly.

"So what," Basset whined. "Time this place had a little fun anyways." He held out his cup.

"Another snort, Angie, dear."

She looked at him suspiciously. "How many have you had?"

"Only one. Dinkum."

She poured him some more.

"Thanks, Angie."

Canning rolled the calao round his tongue. "Very good I must say. Clever of you." He looked at Angelique approvingly. "How did you make it?"

"First," she said, "you must collect the sap. Climb the top of many palms." She looked at his large stomach. "Then tie the ends of the flower spikes together and cut them so that the sap drips into the tins." She looked at Ezekiel. "Hard work, is it not?"

He nodded. "Very!"

"It's not at all bad," Mecky drank it bleakly.

Nada said: "Have some, Jos?"

He looked away, glowering. "*Ag!* No thanks. Not for me."

"But you always say how much you miss your brandy."

He got up, stretched his arms and yawned. Then he walked off into the darkness towards Needle Point.

Angelique smiled. He's like a small boy, she thought.

Goldsworthy refused the calao Ezekiel offered him. "I don't approve of strong drink, you know," he said firmly.

"Strong drink?" Basset's eyebrows rose steeply. "It's like mother's milk . . . 'armless."

"Are you sure?"

"'Course. Try some." Basset held out his cup. "Sort of ginger beer."

Goldsworthy looked round the circle of faces in the firelight. He smiled shyly. "Wonder if I should?"

"I wouldn't touch the foul stuff," said Sarah severely. She scratched at her prickly heat.

Goldsworthy hesitated, then tasted the calao. The look of apprehension changed to approval. "Very refreshing. *Very* refreshing." He began to drink again, but Basset snatched the cup away.

"Hey! Don't hog the flippin' lot. You'll get a guts ache."

Sarah put her hands to her ears and her eyes filled with loathing. "Oh, you *foul*-mouthed little rat!"

The Australian took a long draught of calao, wiped his mouth with the back of a hand, watching her with his beady eyes.

"All right, smarty pants! Keep your hair on! We all know what *you* need."

Sarah reached him in a sudden furious spring and slapped his face, her eyes blazing. "You vile little guttersnipe," she shrieked.

Basset jumped up, his face contorted, but as he raised his arm Ezekiel caught it in a firm grip.

"Leave her alone," he said quietly. "She's right. You've got a foul mouth."

Basset swung at him with his free arm, but the African grabbed that as well and had the Australian in a vice-like hold.

Ezekiel smiled. "In my country we say 'Little dogs bark loudest'."

*　　　　*

After ten days of painstaking labour, the top half of the big palm trunk had been worked flat. Jos and Ezekiel had done this, keeping to separate shifts to avoid friction, wielding the small fire-axe with increasing skill, keeping its blade sharp with pumice stones from the beach. With sticks tied together with coconut fibre, Jos made a gauge for measuring the hull form and with this they had achieved the even surface necessary for the next stage.

Canning and Mecky were given the task of skinning the bark from the green casuarinas and takamakas. From these the mast, outrigger poles and paddles would be made. Skinning the bark with pocket knives was a tedious business, and Jos had constantly to harry Canning and Mecky who had no appetite for this work. Once skinned the green poles were laid in the sun to dry, but so far only half had been done.

Basset and Goldsworthy spent their days collecting sea-birds' eggs, shell-fish, coconuts and purslane. Jos and Ezekiel, when they were not working on the catamaran, fished in the lagoon.

Led by Angelique, the women were making coir ropes for the rigging and outriggers. This was a time-consuming task. The husks had to be beaten with wooden clubs to loosen the fibres which were teased into short lengths and loosely intertwined. Then short lengths of fibres, their ends over-lapping, were rolled with the palm of the hand against a trunk until they knit together into long lengths. These were then plaited to make a strong and serviceable coir rope, or they were left single for lighter tasks.

Since meals had still to be cooked and prepared, this work went slowly and they had not yet started on the lateen sail which was to be made from dried palm fronds.

The catamaran was taking shape on a site to the south of the camp, about 150 yards from the huts and half-way between Hook and Needle Points. The trestles holding the trunk were just inside the palms to give some protection from the tropical sun.

The women worked on their tasks nearby, surrounded by heaps of coconut husks and discarded fibres.

On this morning Ezekiel, with Mecky's help, was laying a small fire along the flat top of the palm trunk. This would burn the core which could then be cut out easily. Canning had been skinning the bark from one of the takamakas, but he'd disappeared.

Ezekiel straightened his back and examined the line of tinder. It was ready for lighting. "That's fine," he looked at Mecky. "Get some embers from the camp so that we can light this."

Mecky's eyes were rebellious. "Couldn't get them yourself, I suppose?"

Ezekiel looked surprised. "What's the trouble?"

"Must I always do the fetching and carrying?"

"The axe needs sharpening. I'll fetch the embers if you like, and you can sharpen it."

Mecky shook his head. "I'll go," he said forlornly, and set off for the huts.

Canning came back from the direction of Hook Point. Ezekiel looked at him curiously. "Hallo! Where've you been?"

Canning sat down on the sand next to the casuarina branch and began to strip the bark.

"Minding my own business," he said curtly.

"What was it this time? Drink of water, coconut milk, empty the bowels, sore back or what?"

"Don't be impertinent," said Canning. He pulled a strip of bark down to the end of the trunk, but it caught against the stub of a severed branch. He tugged at it, but it wouldn't budge.

He got to his feet. "Pass over the axe. I'll have to cut this."

Ezekiel gave it to him and Canning attacked the branch with heavy blows, wielding the axe awkwardly. There was a sharp crack and the handle broke. It was the third handle they'd made since they'd landed. To do this with a pocket knife, took time. Ezekiel was annoyed because Canning had broken the handle through sheer clumsiness. The African picked up the axe-head and the remains of the handle, and shook his head.

"You're clumsy, Canning. Shouldn't have let you use it."

"It was worn. Could have broken at any moment."

"That handle's only five days old, man."

There was a pause. The men eyeing each other sullenly. Ezekiel said: "Wait till Jos hears of it."

Canning wiped the sweat from his face with the tail of his shirt. "To hell with Jos!" he said.

* *

In due course Jos did hear of it. "Who broke it?" His eyes smouldered.

"Canning. It was an accident."

"Who said he could use it?"

"I did. He had trouble with a branch."

Jos's thick eyebrows bunched together and he glared at the African. "I said only you and me could use the axe."

Ezekiel saw the rising temper and he decided to be careful. He knew that, provoked enough, his too might rise. A fight was pointless. The thing was to finish the catamaran and get away from the island.

"He had trouble with the branch," he repeated doggedly.

"Why didn't *you* fix it? You know he's no good."

"It was nothing. I thought he'd manage okay."

Jos's eyes bored into his. "You mean," he said, "you were too damned lazy."

Ezekiel burned with inward rage and humiliation; he knew that the accusation was untrue. There were only two men on the island who worked hard—he and Jos—and Jos knew that too. He was trying to provoke him. He fought down his resentment and said: "I'll make a new handle this afternoon."

*   *

The scars on Jos's back were very much on Sarah's mind as she walked through the plantation. She had seen him leave the camp and go towards The Strand. That meant he'd be working on the fish-traps. She allowed a decent interval before taking the path to the coral cairn. There she changed direction so that she'd come out on the beach not far from the traps.

It was only the scars, she assured herself, nothing more. She was going to ask him to be serious and really tell her about them. They made her think of his muscles knotting and rippling as he worked. She'd never known a man who was so strong. It fascinated her. She wondered what his wife was like. He so often spoke of his children, but never directly of her . . . unless she was Maria? He sometimes spoke of Maria and she seemed to be at his farm where the children were. And yet, somehow, he never spoke of her as if she were his wife. Jos was not the sort of man you could question about these things.

At first to Sarah he was the image of all that she disliked: prejudice, intolerance, arrogance. But the more she saw of him the more she realised that he was a good man, tough but sincere, and invaluable to their survival. Without him and Ezekiel, she knew they would never have reached the island. Nor, having got there, could they have survived.

It was a pity, she thought, that there was this dangerous antipathy between him and Ezekiel. It was absurd that the two men who ran things on the island and upon whom all depended, rarely spoke to one another directly. Yet Ezekiel was a pleasant, intelligent, well-educated man once you knew him. No longer the politician he might so easily have been; always ready to co-operate. There was, indeed, every reason except prejudice for these men to be friends. They had this in common, too, that they both disliked Canning, Mecky and Basset, who in turn loathed them.

She came out onto The Strand and stopped. At first she could not see Jos. Later she made out his blurred shape and went over to him. He was working at the thin palisades he'd built with sticks.

He straightened up and smiled.

"Walking, hey?"

"Yes, I've come to see how your traps are getting on." She looked at them. "Nearly finished?"

"Nearly. I don't get much time."

"How do they work?"

He took a deep breath. Now that she'd arrived he wouldn't be able to do much more. Anyway the light was going.

He pointed to the seaward end of the trap. "It's low water now. At high water the whole trap is in the sea. They swim into its mouth," he indicated the two wings of saplings which formed a V with its top facing the sea, "and then along the wings, looking for an opening." He pointed again. "There it is! That's where they come through. Then they're trapped in this square part, and they can't find the opening to go back."

She looked at him with admiration. "You're clever, Jos."

He shook his head.

"Not me. It's from the survival booklet. Don't even know if it'll work."

"Do we really need fish-traps?"

"The hand-lines won't last for ever. They're badly worn already. And we must take one in the catamaran."

He came out of the shallow water and had a last look round, nodding at the setting sun. "There'll be no light soon. Let's go."

She fell in alongside him and they walked up the beach towards Hook Point. When they got there she stopped.

"Just look at that sunset! Isn't it beautiful, Jos?"

He looked at it and scratched his tousled head. "*Ag!* It's okay," he said drily.

"Surely you see its beauty?"

"I'm a farmer. I'm always seeing sunsets. I live in them. Work in them. They're only important to me for what they say. If they say rain is coming on Soetwaters when it's dry, they're beautiful. If it's wet and I can't take my tractors into the lands, and they say more rain is coming, they're ugly."

She sat down on the beach. "Keep me company. I want to see it set."

Jos sighed again and sat down. This woman was like that school mistress in the *dorp* who'd made a set at him after Anna's death.

Sarah peered at him. "Now tell me how you got those scars?" She took off her floppy hat. "I can't stop thinking about them. Wondering what happened."

"I told you. It was a cat."

"Don't be silly, Jos. I'm serious."

"It was a big cat. A leopard."

"Good heavens! How thrilling! Tell me."

He shook his head. "It wasn't thrilling. It gave me a helluva fright."

"And a *helluva* scratch," she imitated him with unexpected frivolity.

His dark eyes were grave. "*Ja!* Helluva scratch, too."

"How did it happen?"

Jos knew he'd have to tell the story. There was no escape now.

"It was on my brother's farm in Bechuanaland. He had about 5,000 morgen 20 miles from Thompson's Drift. There was a good herd there. Afrikanders, you understand. Fine beef producers." His eyes glowed. "Very immune to disease.

"I was 22 then. Before I married. It was far from Soetwaters. About 300 miles. But Danie asked me to come and help drill a new borehole.

"We worked hard. Sunrise to sunset. One Sunday afternoon

I went down to the Limpopo with a sixteen-bore and Danie's pointer to get some guinea fowl for the pot. It was winter and the veld was dry. There was no water in the river except some small pools in the sand." He drew a deep breath. "That was a very dry time.

"On the banks there was thick bush and big trees, *withaak* and *stinkwood*, and *jakkalsbessie* and those big wild figs. There were plenty of guinea fowl. When I'd got four I was ready to go back. The sun was low and it was three miles.

"Just under the bank there was a pool of water and Sarel . . . he was the pointer . . . went down to it. He'd worked hard.

"By the pool there was a thick clump of reeds. After his drink Sarel picked up a scent and went into them. While I was still on the bank, Sarel began making a helluva noise and I heard something moving in the reeds. I thought it was a warthog. Then Sarel began howling the way I knew he was hurt. So I went in after him—to where I could see the reeds trembling—because I knew he was there. He was badly hurt when I got to him and I reckoned a warthog must have ripped him.

" I put the gun down and knelt by him. That was a dumb thing to do. Next I knew there was a noise behind me, and before I could turn something heavy hit me. Like a hard rugby tackle. Then I was fighting for my life and it was this leopard, you understand."

Jos stopped and looked at Sarah in the gathering dusk. His expression was serious. "I was fit then, thank God."

She stared at him through thick glasses. "You're fit now, Jos. You're *terribly* strong."

He patted his stomach. "Too much weight now. About two hundred and thirty pounds. Then I was only one hundred and ninety. I was like a young bull. Well, this leopard had its jaws on my shoulders and it was stretched out along my back. Its head was pressed against mine and its growling sounded like thunder. I could smell its breath. It stank.

"I couldn't get the gun, so I thought of the sheath-knife in my belt. But the leopard was covering it and I knew I hadn't much time. I felt funny, like I was going to pass out.

"I got my right arm round the leopard's head and put a lock on it. With a helluva pull I got my left hip clear . . . only about six inches.

"When I did that he clawed my back with his hind feet. If you've seen a leopard's claws you'll know why my back's that way.

"Well, I worked my left hand down onto the sheath-knife but it seemed to take a helluva time." He looked at her gravely. "You must have a leopard on your back to know what a long time is.

"I got the knife out of the sheath and brought my left arm up. Very slowly—and quietly—until it was at his neck. I put the knife in, hard and strong. Gave it a helluva twist. He started coughing, and jumped clear and out of the reeds. I was feeling pretty bad so I crawled out and Sarel came with me. I saw the leopard again. He was about ten feet away, near the pool, half lying down, the blood pumping out of his neck.

"So there was me and Sarel and the leopard not looking too good and wishing we hadn't ever met each other. I was losing blood fast. Going blind, too.

"I couldn't get up. It seemed pretty hopeless there in the river bed with the dying dog and the leopard. It was getting dark. Same as now. I knew I couldn't last the night on my own. So I prayed, like I always do when things are bad. I mean, then a man prays his best and the Lord knows that he's in a tight spot. It's not like the prayers that a man says just because he knows he must pray each day."

Sarah's eyes widened. "Do you pray each day, Jos?"

"Of course," he said. "I'm a Christian."

"Anyway, the Lord didn't waste much time. About ten minutes later two *umfaans* came along driving a stray cow up the river bed. They walked right into us in the dark and when they heard the leopard coughing they nearly passed out. One of them went for my brother while the other stayed with me, watching me with one eye and the leopard with the other. By the time my brother came the leopard and Sarel were both dead. I was nearly dead.

"They flew me to the hospital in Pretoria, and after a long time and plenty of trouble with the wounds I was all right, so I went back to Soetwaters."

He sighed audibly.

"What a fantastic story, Jos! How marvellous that you killed it. I mean," she said earnestly, "it was *terribly* brave of you."

Jos cleared his throat and spat over his shoulder.

"If you got a leopard on your back you must do something, you understand. But I learnt my lesson. Not to go into reeds like that, and not to put a gun down." His eyes looked past her as if she were not there. "There was a more important lesson."

"What was that?"

"Not to shoot on Sundays. I had desecrated the Sabbath."

The sun was just below the horizon and it was getting dark. Jos got up. "Come on. Let's go."

They walked in silence, Sarah wondering how she could convey to him what was so urgently on her mind. She dropped back and her opportunity came when he turned and said, "Tired?"

She gulped. "D'you sometimes . . . here I mean . . . well, to be honest Jos, do you sometimes feel you need a . . . a woman?" I could scarcely be more direct than that, she thought, appalled at her own audacity.

"What for? We got three anyway. You look after us fine."

"No, Jos. I don't mean in that way. Frankly I'm talking about sex. I mean . . . we're not children . . . we have these needs . . . why can't we be honest about them?" She moved closer to him and her head swam as their arms touched. She looked up but it was too dark to see his expression.

Stopping suddenly, she faced him. "Jos!" she said dramatically, "I . . ."

"Hell!" he interrupted. "Look out, Sarah, there's some of those big land crabs!" He ran forward, his voice urgent. With a shriek, due partly to her fear of land crabs and partly to the humiliating suspicion that he was rejecting her, Sarah tore after him.

They reached the camp and it began to rain.

* *

Some days later Ezekiel was sitting near the palms on the edge of Rescue Beach, enjoying the late afternoon sun. It was Sunday so there was no work on the catamaran, and with the food collecting done in the forenoon, the afternoon was free.

For a time he watched the horizon, then he slept. Now he was awake again, thinking.

Thinking what a strange leveller life on the island was. There was Canning, an important man in the City of London according to Sebastian . . . and he would be the last to exaggerate . . . yet in this environment, without the trappings of office, Canning was nothing.

Take me, thought Ezekiel. Look what the island has done to me. I'm a demagogue. Fiery oratory's my line. Give me a platform, put a few hundred of my people in front of me and I can do things, make headlines. But look at me here. I haven't made a speech since I left Salisbury nearly two months ago, and how could I make a speech? There's no cause here, no grievances . . . nothing. Anyway, these people wouldn't listen to me and there are no newspapers, so what's the point? And if I start on politics one evening after supper they'll think I've gone round the bend, and Sarah Tripp'll get all serious and try to involve me in Hegel and Marx again. I've never understood them anyway. And Lombaard will certainly want to fight. What's the point?

I can't make speeches here so I'm no longer an important person. I'm without my stock in trade. I'm just one of the survivors.

The afternoon was drawing on. He guessed from the sun that

it must be near six. He got up and started through the plantation towards the camp.

He'd not gone far when he heard a jumble of voices ahead. As he approached they sorted themselves out: a man's voice, low and insistent; and the high, angry sound of a woman's. He quickened his pace.

*　　　　*

In the late afternoon Canning had suggested a walk. Nada had not been keen, but as they were alone in the camp it was difficult to refuse.

They set off for Rescue Beach. Canning said he wanted to get pumice stones. Plodding through the sand under the palm trees, they chatted about one thing and another and then, when they'd been walking for about ten minutes, they came to the end of the plantation where thick undergrowth guarded the line of the beach.

Canning pointed to a gap through which the sea showed: indigo blue, laced with white horses blown up by the south-easter.

"Always refreshing on this side, Nada!"

"Lovely!" she said. "I never get tired of it."

Canning looked at her thoughtfully. The wind had blown strands of hair across her face, and above the high cheekbones her slanted brown eyes had little crow's-feet at the corners.

His eyes went down to her breasts cupped tightly in the worn brassière, and below that to the smooth brown stomach. She's a well-built girl, he thought, and felt an overpowering urge to do something about it.

He sat down in the sand and patted the place next to him. "Let's watch the view for a moment. There's no hurry."

She glanced down at the top of his nearly bald head with its few wisps of hair, white now as the beard. He was one of those men who burned badly and the ample stomach and chest were red above the cut-down trousers worn low on the hips.

Nada took a deep breath and sat down.

There was a long pause with nothing but the noise of the surf and the cries of the sea-birds. He looked at her, calculatingly.

"Remember you asked me the other night what I missed most?"

"Yes," she said doubtfully.

"Remember what I said?" It was meant to be a roguish smile. She shook her head.

"Come, come." He put his hand on her arm with an obvious touch of paternalism. Mustn't frighten her at the start, he thought. Go at it gently. She'll be game in the end.

"I said I missed my home comforts." He watched her carefully.

"So?" Nada looked blank. Was this dreadful little man going to make a nuisance of himself?

Canning took the blank look for acquiescence.

"So . . . well . . . what about a little fun?" He darted out an arm and pushed Nada's shoulders down until she was lying in the sand; then with a quick sideways movement he was half on her, his flabby lips on her mouth, his right hand fumbling under her brassière. The movement was so sudden, and he was so heavy, that for a moment she could do nothing, not even cry out because his mouth smothered hers.

Slight though she was she was strong, and a few seconds later she had pushed him off and struggled to her knees. He was kneeling in front of her now in an absurd attitude, his arms round her waist, saying: "Steady, my dear. A little struggle's one thing, but . . ."

"Leave me! Leave me at once!"

"Come, come, Nada." His voice was suave. "You must have had plenty of experience. Why all this fuss?"

She pushed furiously at his arms. "Let me go at once or you'll be damn' sorry!" Her voice had risen.

But Canning's ardour was up and he wasn't at all sure that this was not an act intended to impress him. The kneeling position was uncomfortable, so he got up and stood there breathing heavily. Nada stood, brushing the sand off her skirt, and just as she was congratulating herself on having brought him to his senses, he seized her again, this time in a hug which pinned her arms. He kissed her ravenously.

Her head went back and she shrieked. "Let go, you damned swine!" She struggled to free herself but he held her firmly, so she attacked him with her knees where it would hurt, but he was too strong and then, just as she was about to shriek again, a black hand appeared on Canning's shoulder and spun him away from her. With astonishment she saw that it was Ezekiel, his body taut and his eyes blazing.

"What's going on?" he said roughly, his hand grasping Canning's fleshy arm.

Before she could answer Canning had hit out at the black arm holding him. "Take your filthy hands off me, you damned nigger!" he screeched.

Ezekiel looked at him in mild surprise; then, as the words sank in, he let go and slapped Canning's face.

Above himself with rage and humiliation, Canning repeated his mistake. "You swine of a black bastard!"

Once again, but not so lightly this time, Ezekiel slapped his face.

*   *

It was not only Ezekiel who had heard angry voices. On his way back from Danger Point, Jos had heard them too and he hurried in their direction. He would have gone faster but the sand was thick, he was heavy, and his heel hurt.

As he came round the corner of the undergrowth he took in the scene with an all comprehending eye. There was Nada with drawn and agitated face, one hand supporting a torn brassière. Near her, Canning arguing with Wanalu. It could mean only one thing.

Before he had gone ten feet towards them, he saw the black man slap Canning's face. Mechanically, compulsively, Jos's eyes sought the African's hands. Something in his mind snapped. In five seconds he had closed the distance and the first punch he threw would have ended the fight had not Ezekiel heard the thud of feet in the sand and turned in time to roll the blow from the side of his head.

Eleven

As Jos swung another blow at Ezekiel, Nada rushed in and clung to his arm; but he shook her off and she reeled back.

"Stop! You fool!" she screamed. "He was protecting me."

She might not have spoken for all the attention Jos paid as he got one arm round the African's neck and gathered his strength for the throw.

Caught by surprise, Ezekiel had concentrated on avoiding the blows aimed at him. Now his neck was seized in a bearlike hug and he felt Lombaard bracing for the throw. Ezekiel realised he was in a fight—perhaps for his life.

Nada came in again hammering with her fists on Jos's back. "Stop it! For God's sake stop it! You'll kill him," she shrieked. But Jos didn't feel the punches or hear a word. He'd known this fight must come sooner or later and now that it had started he blacked out to everything but the kill. It was him now, or Ezekiel. Every second of concentrated energy and alertness counted and nothing on earth could stop him until they'd fought it out.

Canning's anger and humiliation at being slapped in the face had changed to astonishment at Lombaard's sudden intervention, and to deep satisfaction at the shape it had taken. Not only would Wanalu receive the punishment he deserved, but Lombaard would suffer. The rift between these two had at last passed breaking point, and to Canning, whose constant desire it was that they should disagree, this unexpected turn of events was bliss. There might be some awkward explaining to do afterwards about Nada but that could wait. In the meantime let these brutes batter each other. With these thoughts uppermost in his mind he slipped quietly from the scene.

Ezekiel relaxed as he was thrown. Striking the sand he rolled away to open the distance, finishing on his knees. Then he sprang up, facing Lombaard, his back to a palm tree, outwardly relaxed but inside tensed, arms motionless at his side, hands flat against the trunk behind him, knees bent. He lifted a foot clear of the ground and pressed it against the trunk.

Lombaard came in crouching, arms out, ready to strike or grapple. Their eyes were riveted on each other, the strain of concentration dominating the hate and fear which was there. They breathed heavily. Not so much from exertion, for the fight had just started, but with the excitement of danger.

Lombaard closed the distance warily, going slowly forward, waiting for the spring.

He cursed himself for his slowness after throwing the African. Should have anticipated that roll, he thought. He'd meant to kick Wanalu into quick submission but the roll, ending with an upward spring, was too fast. He watched Wanalu with narrowed eyes, waiting for the tightening of the muscles that would signal the spring.

The distance was closing. Six feet! . . . five and a half! . . . five! Wanalu's muscles tensed! Lombaard whipped back but the black man didn't move. The distance opened and Ezekiel's muscles relaxed.

Let him come for me, he thought. I'm okay here . . . like this. Catch him moving in. His eyes never left Lombaard's. He saw the distance closing. Stay relaxed, he cautioned himself. Stay relaxed!

Lombaard came in to five feet. Kicking a spurt of sand into Wanalu's face, he jumped left and mule-kicked with his right. Blinded by the sand, Ezekiel snaked sideways as the kick grazed past him and thudded onto the trunk. Lombaard grunted with pain. Ezekiel rocketed off the palm tree head down, seeing his opponent dimly through smarting eyes. Lombaard turned, taking the blow on his thigh and clamping his right arm round the African's neck.

Ezekiel countered by locking his legs round Jos's waist and gouging his eyes. Lombaard's head-lock broke and he fell heavily on the African, trying to pin him. Ezekiel was too agile to be caught like that. He broke away, leapt up, leaving Lombaard on the ground.

They faced each other with deadly concentration. Ezekiel no longer had the palm tree behind him. They crouched, circling and weaving, feinting for openings, gasping for breath, their bodies running with sweat. Their eyes were bloodshot: Ezekiel's from the sand; Jos's from the gouging.

The African was faster than Lombaard though lighter, and he decided to use his speed. He went in swiftly, feinting with his right and landing a heavy left to Lombaard's chin. The white man grunted, shaking his head. Wanalu feinted again, but Jos let loose a hay-making right catching him on the head and sending him reeling.

Lombaard followed up wildly, fists flailing, and Wanalu held on for life. Jos threw him off with his shoulders, then landed heavy lefts and rights. They were killing punches but the African was backing away and that took the sting out of them. All the same he turned sideways and dropped his hands, looking as if he'd had enough. Lombaard went in for the kill then, but as he came Wanalu kicked him in the stomach.

While the Afrikaner was doubled up with pain, Wanalu attacked again. With his shin Lombaard countered another vicious kick.

Then it was close quarters with a gruelling exchange of punches before they broke away. Nada watching, terrified, saw that their faces streamed with blood. Ezekiel had lost a tooth. With a wild cry she made a final effort to separate them, but the African pushed her away and she fell. She stood up and ran off in the direction of the camp.

They were still circling, more warily now. Lombaard dropped his hands and looked to the right, away from Wanalu. The black man's eyes followed. In that split second Lombaard put his head down and charged. Ezekiel weaved, lifting a knee into Lombaard's face. There was a sickening crunch. The Afrikaner groaned.

He sagged onto one knee and the African dived. But it was a trap and as he landed Lombaard threw him again with a shake of those bull-like shoulders. They faced each other then, crouching, arms out, feinting, weaving, trying for an opening.

During the fight they'd moved down from the palms to the beach. As they fought their way nearer to the water the sand hardened, giving a surer foothold.

They'd been fighting for some time. Daylight was going, they were nearing exhaustion, and the pace had slowed down. It wouldn't have lasted so long but they were well matched, despite the difference in weights and Wanalu's comparative youth. Supremely fit, immensely strong, old hands at street fighting, neither had given or expected any quarter. It was a struggle of the utmost ferocity.

But for their will to survive, they might have destroyed each other. As it was, when the light had all but gone and they squared up again after a heavy exchange of blows, the African gasped: "Want to go on?"

They were the first words spoken since the fight had started.

Lombaard, arms extended, crouching, wheezed back: "Had enough, hey?" But the tone belied the threat.

Wanalu nodded. They broke off the fight and staggered away into the darkness. Battered, blood-soaked hulks.

The fight had ended as unexpectedly as it had started.

*   *

It was the talk of the camp for days and somehow the idea got about that they'd fought over Nada. But since neither she nor anyone else concerned were prepared to discuss it, its origins remained obscure and were the subject of much conjecture.

Nada's friendliness with both Jos and Ezekiel, her distant chilly manner towards Canning, added to the mystery.

The fighters were a grim sight with cut and bruised faces, black eyes and swollen lips. The gap left by Ezekiel's missing tooth was painfully evident. Jos limped from the wound on his heel which had re-opened with the kick against the palm tree.

Angelique and Nada did their best to patch the two men with hot water and mercurochrome, but it was clear that only time would heal the damage.

Ezekiel and Jos observed a state of armed neutrality, avoiding each other. They wouldn't have admitted it, but each now had a healthy respect for the other's strength and courage. They knew that they wouldn't easily become involved in another such fight.

Neither had gained a victory nor suffered a defeat. They knew that, too.

*   *

Next day Nada found Jos on the beach, an opportunity she'd eagerly sought. Her eyes were stern and her voice withering. "Now will you please tell me why you attacked Ezekiel in that disgraceful fashion?"

Jos looked away. "When I came round those bushes I could see he'd been getting fresh with you . . . that Canning was telling him off. Then he hit Canning in the face, so I . . ."

"Well, for your information," she interrupted, "it was *Canning* who got fresh, and *Ezekiel* who came to my rescue."

He looked at her incredulously. "Wh-a-a-a-t? You mean Wanalu didn't try anything?"

She stamped her foot furiously. "No, he did not. Except to help me."

"And it was Canning that got fresh?"

Her eyes flashed. "Yes!"

"Why didn't you tell me?"

"Are you mad? I tried to tell you . . . to stop you . . . but you were like a wild beast."

He hung his head. "I don't remember."

"You should be ashamed of yourself. You owe Ezekiel a *terrific* apology. Don't be surprised if he won't accept it."

His dark eyes gleamed, the sockets swollen in the bearded face. "Listen, Nada. I don't apologise to any man. Anyway, he'd no right to strike a white man like that."

"What difference does the colour make?" Her voice was withering. "Canning insulted him."

Jos frowned. "How?"

"When Ezekiel made him let me go, Canning called him a 'filthy nigger'."

Jos was silent. Then he said: "Canning had no right to say that. He was asking for trouble."

"Yes, and in the end it was poor old Zeke who got it." There was a pause. "Thanks to you," she added bitterly.

He said nothing.

"Are you going to apologise *now*?"

Jos shook his head. "No, but I'm going to have a word with *Mister* Canning."

*   *

Canning was supposed to be collecting mussels on Bikini Beach, but when Jos found him he was dozing under a palm tree. Jos nudged him with his foot, not very gently.

"Listen, Canning," his voice was hard, "I've just heard about what really happened yesterday between you and Nada."

Canning pulled himself up until he was sitting bolt upright against the trunk. His eyes were querulous.

"Oh yes. Who from?"

"Nada."

Canning blinked. "Silly girl. Can't imagine what she got excited about. My feelings for her are—er—entirely paternal. She mistook my friendliness for something quite different."

Jos raised a hairy arm. "Listen, Canning, I didn't come to hear your lies. You listen to me. And for a start," he nudged him with his foot, "get up off your fat arse!"

Canning scrambled to his feet.

"You're a pig, Canning. That girl's young enough to be your daughter and you try things like that. And when Wanalu comes along and stops your nonsense you insult him. And when I think it was him getting fresh with Nada and get stuck into him, you just slink off into the bushes." He glared and the fat man trembled.

"Well, what've you got to say for yourself?"

Canning looked away.

With a large forefinger Jos indicated his own battered face and swollen lips. "It's you that's responsible for this," he said grimly, "and for Wanalu's too. What're you going to do about it?"

With a despairing shrug Canning transferred his weight from one foot to the other, but he said nothing.

"Well I'll tell you what. You're going to apologise to Nada and Wanalu—right now—and it's going to be a helluva good apology or I'll skin you alive. Get going!" He moved forward threateningly.

With a last malevolent look at the big man, Canning scuttled across the beach into the palms.

*   *

Knowledge of the mistake which had led to the fight lessened the bitterness between Jos and Ezekiel. Neither would have admitted this but each was aware of it, and Ezekiel's sullen hatred after the fight dissipated with Nada's explanations. And when Canning apologised . . . with ill-grace, and prompted only by fear of what Lombaard might do if he failed . . . Ezekiel knew within himself that he couldn't altogether blame the Afrikaner.

But he couldn't forgive the white man's failure to inquire before starting the fight.

For his part, Jos acknowledged to himself, but to no one else, that he'd wronged Ezekiel and he felt strange but inadmissible pangs of sympathy for the African.

Twelve

SOME DAYS LATER Jos set out for the reef off Second Beach to fish, leaving Ezekiel to work on the catamaran with Goldsworthy.

He didn't feel well. The heel was inflamed and he'd had a restless night full of feverish dreams and hallucinations. The wound had been troubling him. Last night it had been bad, the pain and swelling moving up to the groin.

Because he couldn't sleep he left the camp early. The sun was just rising but the heat was oppressive. His head swam and he walked slowly, the spring gone out of his step, one foot dragging after the other, his mouth dry, tongue swollen.

There was no question of giving in. Fish had to be caught, so he'd have to make the best of it. But his body was not supporting this resolve: his legs weakened and the palms began to revolve slowly. He put down the fishing line, rubbing his eyes and shaking his head to get rid of his blurred vision, but the throbbing in his head and the dazed feeling persisted, so he sat down and rested, back to a tree.

Someone was shaking him and he heard the sound of voices. There were people standing above him. He couldn't make out who they were.

He tried to get up. "Sorry," he mumbled gruffly. "Didn't feel too good. Be okay in a minute."

Nada shook her head. "You're sick, Jos. Sebastian found you here. He fetched us. It's nearly noon."

Jos rubbed his eyes and tried to make out the faces but he couldn't. He must have heard what was said, though, because he mumbled again: "Noon! Hell! Must catch fish." Then he rambled off into delirium.

*   *

It was blood poisoning and it took three days of nursing by Nada and Angelique to control it. They opened the wound on the heel with a pocket knife sterilised in boiling water, and with the aid of hot poultices and chlorine from the first aid kit, they drained the pus and his temperature came down. But nothing that they could have done would have pulled him through, had it not been for his iron determination to get better.

In the first few days he was dimly aware, through a mist of pain and delirium, that Nada and Angelique were nursing him, and he was filled with childlike confidence. He felt warm gratitude, but couldn't express it. It was not his way.

On the fourth day, weak but free of fever, he could think rationally. For the first time then he noticed that Angelique, for so long distant and off-hand, was kind and friendly. He realised the illness was responsible for the change, but he was happy.

Lying in the hut that evening with the rain beating down outside, he thought about this and determined to ask her why she had turned against him after they'd reached the island.

The opportunity came next day when she was examining his heel. "It's getting better. You're lucky, Jos. You might have died. We have so little here."

He touched her arm. "It wasn't luck. It was you and Nada."

She shrugged her shoulders. "We did our best."

There was a moment's silence while Jos gathered his courage. He propped himself up on one elbow and looked at her, frowning. "Tell me, Angelique; why've you been so funny all this time?"

She looked away and her eyes dropped. "Because of what you did."

"What I did?" He gave her a look of blank surprise.

"Never mind, Jos. Forget it."

"But I did nothing. How can I forget it. Tell me," he insisted.

She looked at him thoughtfully. "It was the morning after we landed. When Ezekiel went off to the southern part of the island."

He was beginning to understand. "That's right. It was after *that* you changed. But why?"

"You spoke contemptuously of coloured people. It is awful to show contempt for people because of their colour."

He was dumbfounded. First, that such a harmless remark should so seriously have affected their relationship and, second, that she should be surprised that he regarded non-white people as inferior. Surely she knew they were?

And then suddenly, agonisingly, the truth struck him. *She* was coloured! That was why his harmless remark had upset her!

What could he say? He thought desperately before lowering himself back onto the coconut leaves and closing his eyes.

"I see," he said heavily.

She sighed.

He turned on his side, away from her. "I'm sorry, Angelique, that I said that. I didn't mean to hurt anyone."

"People are people, Jos." Her voice was gentle. "Whatever their colour."

*   *

Jos's illness evoked different emotions in different people and while Angelique and Nada felt sympathy and compassion, others did not.

Canning derived a sort of grim satisfaction from the knowledge that Lombaard might die. This was tempered, however, by a gnawing fear that if anything happened to him they would lose their most resourceful man. They would then have to depend largely on the African, whom Canning feared and disliked.

On reflection, therefore, he hoped that Jos would survive, but he saw in the big man's sickness a heaven-sent opportunity for effecting long-nourished plans. This decision made, he lost no time in confiding in Goldsworthy.

Basset shared Canning's feelings about the illness. He, too, feared and disliked the big man and was sick and tired of being harried by him. If Jos came to a sticky end he would, in Basset's view, be getting his just deserts. It would be good to see the last of him, and with the catamaran coming on well he had little doubt that they could, with the African's help, finish it and get across to Smoke Island.

Mecky, whose dislike for Jos was assuming pathological proportions, frankly hoped that the Afrikaner wouldn't recover.

Goldsworthy, deeply concerned because he admired and respected Jos, continually asked Angelique and Nada about his progress and offered help. But he had to conceal his feelings from Canning, who frowned at any evidence of friendship with the Afrikaner. Nothing, however, could stop Sebastian praying for Jos's recovery, which he did with passionate sincerity.

Ezekiel found his feelings for Jos strangely confused. When he first learnt that the illness arose from damage Jos had sustained in the fight, he felt that justice was being done. But as it became evident that Jos was gravely ill he found, with much surprise, that he was worried and wanted him to recover. For one thing he and Jos had from the start run things in the dinghy and on the island. They were the leaders of this strange community. Although they had disliked and feared each other they were in a sense partners and Ezekiel wondered how things would go without the Afrikaner. He knew that he and Jos were detested by the other men—except Goldsworthy—and he knew instinctively that he could not trust them. As long as he and Jos were there, and working together, even at arm's length, all was well.

Sarah Tripp derived an almost sadistic satisfaction from Jos's illness. She had for some time, and with increasing humiliation, been brooding over the rejection of her advances. Then there had been Jos's savage fight with Ezekiel, apparently about Nada. She supposed Ezekiel had made advances . . . but after all there was nothing peculiar or unnatural about desire. She sighed.

She understood it only too well. But that Jos should have thought Nada worth fighting about made Sarah furiously jealous, and added to her newly acquired dislike of him. She now felt a new warmth and sympathy for Ezekiel and resolved that she would pay more attention to him. With studied indifference she refused to be associated with Jos's nursing and professed little interest in his progress. Indeed, she was nauseated by the fuss Angelique and Nada were making of him.

"Nursing him," she sniffed to Mecky on the third day of the illness. "It's obvious what *they're* after."

Mecky's eyes drooped. "What's that?" he said bleakly.

Sarah snorted. "If you can't see you should have your head read."

*   *

The clouds scurried across the moon and darkness and moonlight followed each other in quick succession, so that at one moment he could see far down Second Beach and the next it was shrouded in darkness.

The wind came in fresh over the sea and the palm fronds leant against it, rustling and sighing to the roar of surf breaking along the reef. Things were moving in the right direction but he felt a vague apprehension nevertheless. Would he get their agreement? The moon came clear of the clouds again and the wet sand at his feet reflected back its brilliance. He looked at his watch. It was just before nine o'clock. Only a few minutes to go.

The time for action was undoubtedly ripe. It was the fourth day of Lombaard's illness and from what Nada and Angelique said he was very bad. At best it would be some time before he recovered.

He wondered if Goldsworthy had managed to tip them off without arousing suspicion? Had they got away from the camp unnoticed? The decision to include Sarah Tripp was right, he was sure. Originally he'd excluded her because of her friendship with Lombaard, but during the last week she'd made it clear

that she disliked the big Afrikaner. Her support could be important and he was pretty sure that she would join the British group.
A few moments later Basset appeared out of the darkness. The
moon came clear of a cloud and they could see each other's faces.

Basset blinked. "What's all the cloak and dagger stuff?"

In short quick sentences Canning unfolded his plan and
explained the importance of the pistol. Basset disagreed about that
at first, but once he'd got over his initial shock and surprise he
quickly saw the advantages of throwing in his lot with Canning.

There was a subdued whistle. Canning answered it and they
saw three figures coming down the beach. As they approached
it was possible to make out the faces of Goldsworthy, Mecky and
Sarah Tripp.

Canning welcomed her effusively, "I'm so glad you've come,
Sarah. Your judgment will be invaluable. Nothing like a trained
mind."

He led them up the beach to the undergrowth. "Let's sit
here. Won't be seen if we keep against this."

When they'd all sat down, Canning cleared his throat.

"Now," he said. He rubbed his hands together and his beard
looked whiter than usual in the moonlight. "I've convened this—
er—little meeting because I felt that we—shall I say—British
types . . . should get together and discuss the way things are
heading."

He looked round at them. "I'm a great believer in democracy.
Good old British system. One man, one vote. Let the majority
decide."

"What's democracy got to do with this?" said Sarah Tripp
grimly.

"You may well ask. Trouble is just that. We haven't *got*
democracy here. That's why I've taken the liberty of calling you
together."

She swiped at some midges. "I haven't the faintest idea what
you're talking about. Why not come to the point?"

"The point, Sarah, is that Lombaard from the start . . . in the dinghy and here . . . has appointed himself leader without ever consulting us. He is rude and insulting and—well—I for one find the situation intolerable." He put his thumb to his nose and blew it. "After all, one has to think of one's self-respect."

"Quite," said Sarah.

"And," went on Canning, "the situation may well become dangerous."

Sebastian regarded them seriously. "The thing is . . . Jos is so—very practical . . ."

Canning glared at him. "Of course Lombaard's practical! But I do suggest our leader should be chosen by popular vote, and that in choosing him regard should be given to one or two rather important points."

"Such as?" It was Mecky.

"For example, I suggest that with a majority of Britishers on the island we might well choose a British leader. Then I would feel that the man chosen should be one who is used to—er—exercising authority and who has—er—established a reputation for himself in the . . ." he paused, "the wider world outside."

"Like yourself?" prompted Mecky.

Canning ignored that. Blandly trading on their fear and dislike of Lombaard and the African, Canning got them to agree that elections for the post of leader should be held as soon as possible.

Basset, taking his cue, proposed that when the elections were held Canning should be the leader; after a short but awkward pause Goldsworthy seconded the proposal and though it was accepted without enthusiasm, there was no opposition. It was clear to them all that there was no one else suitable in the British group.

"But look here," Mecky said. "I agree we'll have the majority vote at the elections and can elect you leader. But how can we enforce our will if Lombaard and Wanalu don't agree?"

Canning eyed him thoughtfully. "You realise, of course, that they hate each other?"

"Of course. But they've always managed to agree on big issues. Here and in the dinghy. Once those two agree there's nothing we can do."

"Not quite *nothing*, Mecky. We've a trump card up our sleeve." Canning sounded unusually confident.

"What's that?"

There was a long pause. "An automatic."

Mecky started. "A what?"

Canning smiled. "Basset's automatic pistol."

There was a stunned silence. Mecky was sceptical. "How did he get an automatic?"

"He's always had it."

"How's it we never saw it?"

Canning smiled again. "*I* saw it. Long ago. In the dinghy. He wore a shoulder-holster under his coat."

"Where's it now?"

Canning winked at Basset. "Shall I tell them, Art?"

"Okay by me."

"It's hidden. *At the moment*, in a place known only to Art and me."

"I see." Mecky sounded dubious.

"And, what's more," went on Canning. "Art's automatic will enforce the rule of law here."

"Isn't this all rather far-fetched?" asked Sarah Tripp. "Why should we use a firearm. It's an extremely dangerous thing to do."

"You're quite right, Sarah. It is. But I doubt very much whether it'll ever be necessary. Once we let Lombaard and Wanalu know we have the pistol that'll be enough. They won't like it, but they'll respect it. They know that the risk of disregarding its existence won't be worth taking."

"What if they steal it?" said Mecky.

"They'd have to find it first." Canning's voice was as suave and convincing as if he were addressing a meeting of shareholders in the City. "But I don't expect trouble. We'll be rescued in due course. Once we have a leader *chosen by popular vote*, Lombaard and Wanalu will have to toe the line. They know they'll have to account to the outside world sooner or later."

The moon went behind the clouds and they could no longer see each other. The wind had freshened, coming in gusts and flurries, bringing with it occasional mists of fine spray, cool and moist in their faces.

Canning got up. "That's about all, then. Tomorrow or the next day we'd better get onto this subject, round the fire in the evening. Perhaps you'll bring it up, Mecky? Just mention the need for a properly chosen leader and we'll chip in and support you."

Mecky thought about this for a moment; then he said: "Lucky Lombaard's ill. I wouldn't be very happy if he were about."

"Quite," said Canning. He helped Sarah from the sand with exaggerated gallantry.

*   *

The next night the elections took place and everything went more or less according to plan. Mecky raised the subject and Basset and Canning came in in support. Notwithstanding doubts . . . well expressed by Ezekiel . . . as to whether it was necessary to have an official leader, and further doubts by Nada about choosing one while Jos was so ill, it was decided to hold the elections.

Canning appointed himself chairman and called for nominations. Goldsworthy proposed Canning; Basset seconded, and Nada then rather hesitantly proposed Jos. There was an awkward pause. Angelique whispered: "I second him."

Canning vacated the chair on the grounds that as one of those nominated it would be improper for him to preside while the voting took place. It was agreed that the African should take his place in the chair. Ezekiel ruled that the matter should be decided on a show of hands and said: "Those in favour of Canning, please signify."

Goldsworthy, Basset and Mecky raised their hands but— unaccountably—Sarah Tripp hesitated. Alarmed at this development, Canning rather shamefacedly raised his hand. At that moment Sarah, who had found the entire proceedings rather nauseous and a childish mockery, heard Jos calling from the hut for Angelique. Whereas before that she had decided to have no part in this nonsense, she now became so enraged with jealousy and mortification that her arm shot up. This act of loyalty, delayed though it was, brought a grateful smile from Canning. She studiously ignored him.

They waited for Angelique to return to the fire. "He wanted some water," she explained. "He has very much fever."

Ezekiel looked grave. "Canning has secured five votes. I will now ask those in favour of Lombaard to signify."

Three hands went up: Ezekiel's, Angelique's and Nada's. Ezekiel thought, Five to three . . . even if Lombaard'd been here and voted for himself it would have made no difference.

"Lombaard has secured three votes," announced Ezekiel. With evident displeasure he added: "I declare Canning to have been elected."

Canning got off the log and looked at the circle of faces around the fire. His voice was bland and unctuous. "You have done me a very great honour. I would like to assure you that I shall do my very best for each and every one of you. It will be my policy to consult you always, and to ensure that all decisions are in future made by popular vote, and in no other way. We shall work on the basis of *one-man-one-vote*: the will of the majority. Nothing could be fairer than that."

Sensing Ezekiel's hostility he looked at him and added, "I take it those are sentiments you'd support?"

The African shrugged his shoulders. "I don't know what this is all about anyway. I can't see that we're going to get off the island any quicker because you've been elected leader. The catamaran's coming on fine now. That seems to me the most important thing. To get it finished. Why worry about a leader?" He got up and began to move off from the fire into the darkness.

"Just a minute!" Canning's voice was peremptory. "It may be," he said, "that some may feel they can disregard the will of the majority. But if there is any trouble, I want you to know that *it will be dealt with sternly*."

Ezekiel smiled. A lazy indolent smile. "Big stuff," he said quietly. "Who'll do the stern dealing?"

Canning's eyes narrowed. "*We* will." He gestured to Mecky and Basset. "*We* have means of enforcing our will. Perhaps you'll demonstrate them, Art?"

"Sure thing, digger." The Australian walked off into the darkness, following the path through the plantation.

Nada, Angelique and Ezekiel were mystified by these proceedings, the more so when Canning said: "We'll have to give him a few minutes. Do anything you like, but please remain within the camp . . . *in your own interests*."

They stood about talking in low voices. Suddenly, unmistakably, above the distant roar of the surf, they heard a gunshot.

Canning smiled. "There will be another one, almost immediately." A second shot rang out. He smiled again, "See what I mean?"

"A gun?" said Ezekiel dully.

"An automatic pistol, to be exact." Canning's eyes held his. "There's no chance of taking it from us. It is always kept hidden . . . *just in case* . . . it's needed. And three of us know where it's kept."

Canning sat down on a log. He chuckled. "Now let's all relax and forget the dramatics. We'll never need the pistol. Just a little joke of mine, really. *Of course* we'll all co-operate. We're bound to be rescued in time and once we're back in circulation we'll all have to account for our behaviour. It wouldn't look too good if one of us had disregarded the wishes of the majority . . . or challenged the authority of the *elected* leader, would it?"

He stopped and looked round at them.

Silently, in ones and twos, they left the fire and went to their huts.

* *

They didn't tell Jos about the elections and Canning's appointment as leader for some days. When they did he looked at them unbelievingly. "*Him* . . . leader? They must be mad."

Nada told him about the voting: five to three. He propped himself on his elbow. "Who voted for him?"

"Basset, Mecky, Sarah Tripp, Goldsworthy and Canning himself."

"And Wanalu?"

"He voted for you."

"For *me*?" He was amazed.

She nodded. "Yes."

"I don't understand." He lay back on the floor of the hut, his eyes clouded.

* *

Deftly Nada plaited the fibre strands into rope, but her thoughts were far away and she was depressed. If there were a God, and she firmly believed there was, why did He let people like Iles and Hughie and Steve and Karin die, while others like Basset, Mecky, Canning and Sarah survived.

Was it all pure chance or was there some obscure grand design which, if only one knew it, explained the prodigal waste of the good and the preservation of the bad? Now that that dreadful man Canning and his cronies were in charge, and Jos was still so weak, anything might happen.

She thanked the Lord for Ezekiel and, to a lesser extent, for Sebastian Goldsworthy. He was kind and good although he was terrified of Canning who seemed to have an extraordinary hold over him. Something which couldn't be explained away by the simple fact that Canning was his boss.

Sarah Tripp was an enigma. She had often made it clear that she disliked Canning and loathed Basset, and yet she'd thrown in her lot with them in the elections. She seemed to have turned against Jos, too, although not long ago she'd made a set at him.

Nada drew a deep breath. There was nobody on the island who really meant anything to her. She liked Ezekiel and Jos in their funny individualistic ways, and she liked Angelique although she was not a person you ever really got to know. Even now, after living together so intimately for nearly two months, she didn't know much about the Mauritian woman or what was going on behind the lovely serene face.

Nada's thoughts drifted away from the island, across the sea to Johannesburg, to the night at the Langham when she was in the lounge having a drink with Dieter before dinner. They'd not seen each other for three weeks and Dieter was at his flattering best, admiring her eyes, her hair, her voice, her figure, everything about her. He did it all so convincingly, so sincerely, that Nada almost believed she must be rather special.

"After dinner," his smile was confident, "we go to the flat. You must hear my new hi-fi, Nada." He made a circle with his thumb and forefinger. "*Fabu*lous!"

His German accent seemed more attractive every time she heard it, and yet why should she of all people find that accent attractive?

He stopped a passing waiter. "Two more." He pointed at the nearly empty glasses and held up two fingers.

"Not another, Dieter. I've had two."

He raised his eyebrows in mock disapproval. "Yes, you are quite an alcoholic already, *liebchen*. But you *must* have another. We are *cele*brating. A most important *occa*sion."

"What, meeting again after three weeks?"

He sighed. "It seems like a *thou*sand years."

Nada looked away. She was disappointed. Somehow she'd thought he was going to propose. They'd seen a lot of each other on and off for a year and as far as she knew there was no other girl. Besides, he'd made it pretty clear in various ways that they were meant for each other; not that he'd ever said anything *definite* about marriage.

Then she heard a familiar voice behind her.

"Hallo there, honey-child!"

It was Iles of course. Large, cheerful, incredibly pleased to see her though they had left the aircraft together at Jan Smuts only that morning.

"Mind if I sit down?" He beamed at Dieter whom he had met before and who roundly disliked him. Without waiting for an answer he sat down and lit a cigarette. "Let's have a drink."

"I have already ordered," said Dieter stiffly.

"Fine. When he comes he can fetch me one, too."

Nada could see that Dieter was far from pleased. It really was too bad the way Iles always assumed that because he was pleased to see you, you must be pleased to see him.

His good-natured eyes were warm with affection. "What you doing tonight, honey-child?"

She frowned: she couldn't very well mention the flat.

"Dieter and I are going to the pictures."

"Mind if I come along?" It never occurred to him that he was butting in. They were strangers in a strange town and it seemed a friendly thing to do.

She looked at Dieter and he gave a faint but unmistakable gesture of disapproval; a raised eyebrow, no more.

"I'm sorry, Iles. Not tonight. Dieter and I have some private things to discuss."

It was crude and brutal, she knew, but you had to be that with Iles. He was like a big kind dog. She was sorry, though, when she saw the hurt look in his eyes, before he laughed and said: "I was only kidding. Got a flash date myself tonight. Be seeing you."

He got up and left and Dieter said: "Thank God! He's such a *bore*."

The recollection of that night worried her. It was one of many times that she'd been less than kind to Iles and it was on her conscience. And to think that she had been rude to him in order to be alone with Dieter. A two-faced scheming womaniser, if ever there was one.

*   *

The smoke was sighted again—early in the forenoon—by Basset and Mecky collecting sea-food near Casuarina Point. They came running back to camp with the news and no time was lost in lighting the bonfire and feeding it with green leaves. It was nearly two weeks since they'd last seen it and excitement ran high.

Cut off for so long from civilisation they found this occasional but tenuous evidence that other people were not far away a heady stimulant which changed normal patterns of behaviour. Work was abandoned and a spirit of festivity took over.

Except for Jos, still convalescing, they were all at Casuarina Point, watching the smoke and discussing it animatedly.

Basset blinked. "Won't be long now, fellows. Third time lucky." He couldn't keep still and kept climbing into the casuarina trees to get a better view, then jumping down onto the sand and running to and from the fire, chattering and pointing. The others were little better.

Two hours later it was agreed to leave Basset and Mecky to feed the fire while the rest went back to their tasks.

Zeke worked on the catamaran with renewed enthusiasm, and the women plaited even more industriously.

The smoke showed intermittently throughout that day and was still there at daybreak on the next. In the early afternoon it disappeared.

Again their hopes sagged and the mood of almost reckless optimism gave way to one of bitter disappointment. Try as they could, they found themselves unable to rationalise the distant smoke. Under what circumstances did it appear at these lengthy intervals, and then never for long?

They began to understand why they could see the distant smoke, yet their bonfire failed to attract attention. It was Ezekiel who first pointed out that the south-east trades blew the smoke from Smoke Island obliquely *towards* them, whereas the same wind blew their smoke directly *away* from the direction of that island.

They were now more than ever convinced that their salvation lay in the catamaran. As it progressed their hopes grew with it . . . all except Canning's, for whom the catamaran was at best a dubious venture. He doubted if it would ever reach Smoke Island, and he doubted even more if those left behind would be able to survive without Lombaard and Wanalu, much as he detested them. The safest thing to do, he felt, would be to abandon the catamaran and wait for the coconut harvesters to visit the island. He couldn't imagine that the rich harvest of nuts would be left there very much longer. But although he was now nominally leader, he knew he could never convince the others that work on the catamaran should stop. Enthusiasm for its completion was running too high.

*　　　　*

Mecky and Basset were talking to Angelique.

"That brooch," said Mecky, "is sheer poetry! Mind if I examine it?"

Angelique wondered if this were flattery or appreciation. Coming from Mecky, she decided it must be appreciation. She unpinned the brooch and passed it to him.

For a minute or so he held it, turning it so that the light from the fire danced and sparkled in the diamonds. He passed it back to her, his face expressionless. "It's incredibly beautiful," he said.

"Must be worth a packet," Basset's eyes never left the brooch as she pinned it back on her blouse. "What say, Chris?"

"I haven't the faintest idea. What's value got to do with beauty?"

"Go and buy one, digger. You'll soon see." He blinked at Angelique. "Where d'you get it, Angie dear?"

"From my husband. On our tenth anniversary."

"Blimey! He must have some lolly."

*   *

Next morning Basset waylaid Angelique down at the water catchment. "Mind if I say something? Friendship's sake."

Her eyes were mildly surprised. "Of course not, Art."

He looked round quickly to make sure they were alone; then he whispered conspiratorially. "Wouldn't wear those jewels if I were you, Angie. Only lead to trouble."

"What, here?"

"Yes. Notice Mecky's interest last night?"

"But he . . . I mean, what can he do here?"

Basset leaned towards her. "He's a funny guy. I share a hut with him. Wouldn't like to tell you some of the things I know. Wouldn't be right. Only worry you. He's not all there you know. Last night, after we left the fire, he talked about the brooch. Said he's set his heart on it."

"But if I don't wear my jewels, Art, where can I keep them? I have nowhere here except the hut, and I cannot leave them there—loose on the ground?"

Once again he looked round to make sure they were alone. "*Bury* them, Angie. In a secret place. Don't even let me know where they are. Then, when the day comes that we have to leave, just dig 'em up again."

"But what can I put them in? I do not wish that they must lie in the sand."

For a few moments he was lost in thought, then he said: "Tell you what, Angie. I'll give you a coconut shell with a small hole in the top. Put them in that. Plug the hole with leaves to keep the sand out. Then bury it."

She looked at him doubtfully. "Do you really think this is necessary?"

"It's up to you, Angie. I've warned you."

She smiled. "Thank you, Art."

"It's nothing. Only I was worried the way Mecky was talking."

There was a silence broken by Basset's snigger. She looked at him, puzzled. "What is it?"

"Just thinking. Say you forgot where you buried 'em?"

For a moment she looked distressed. "Could that happen?"

"Not if you do the job properly. Choose a place near some big object like a palm tree in a special, easily remembered position. Then have a formula."

She frowned. "What is that?"

"Well, like this, see. You could say it's 48NE. That would mean it was four paces north of the tree and from there eight paces east. So before you bury it, choose your tree: step out four paces to the north, then eight paces to the east, then dig the hole. But you must always remember the tree, and the formula. See?"

"That is a good idea. Thank you." Her voice was husky and gentle and her warm breath fanned his face.

Blimey, she's a lovely bit of skirt, he thought. Don't suppose she'd have anything to do with the likes of me.

Thirteen

CANNING'S PERSONALITY which had been sagging badly under the pressures of life on the island, now began to reassert itself. With the semblance of authority restored by his election as leader, he was feeling himself again. With an inward self-congratulatory eye he noted how easily the wielding of authority came to him. He walked with a lighter step, surrounding himself with an aura of confidence and optimism which had been sadly lacking since the night of the disaster. But he was tactful in asserting authority, and went to considerable pains to consult the others and to secure agreement on the smallest matters.

There was, however, little room for change or improvement in a routine which had been dictated by circumstance and established with general consent, though more often than not on Jos's initiative.

If life on the island was little affected by the change in leadership, at least for Canning it meant freedom from discipline and a change in duties, for he lost no time in getting agreement to his proposal that he should exchange chores with Basset. Stripping bark and otherwise assisting directly with the catamaran, he pointed out, was better done by a younger, fitter man. Canning was now back on the comparatively pleasant task of foraging for food—moreover with Sebastian Goldsworthy, who well understood his Chief's back troubles and need for rest.

During the time that Jos was unable to work on the catamaran, it was agreed that Basset should help Ezekiel. This suited the Australian in many ways, but progress was slower.

A week later Jos was fairly well back to normal and he began work again, doing shorter shifts because Nada and Angelique insisted that he must rest his heel. In this way, and with Ezekiel working longer shifts to compensate, work went forward satisfactorily.

*   *

It must have been the calao, Ezekiel decided as he went down to the lagoon at Bikini Beach early in the morning to see if a swim would clear his head. It had been quite a party!

Perhaps, he reflected, the monotonous routine and uncertain future had been more demanding than they'd realised. It was almost two months now since they'd arrived on the island. None of them had ever really thought they would be there for so long. The signs of former habitation; the rich crop of nuts on the ground; the smoke on the horizon; these things had led them to expect early rescue. But it had not come, and but for the distant smoke they had seen nothing but the empty sea.

We had the party, thought Ezekiel, to let off steam; to get rid of all the frustrations and irritations, the tensions and frictions, which grow with each day.

It was unfortunate, though, that in letting off steam he'd insulted Sarah Tripp. He'd never have done that if he'd been stone cold sober. But it was just one of those things. *In vino veritas*, as Brownson never tired of saying at Jesus when he apologised for having called him "my swarthy friend" the night before. Something he did often because he was often *in vino*. Dear old Brownson! How insulting the English could be!

No doubt Sarah was now his enemy for life. Once the calao had started to flow she'd become very serious. Her voice was blurred. "Living on this island with these—morons," she cocked a hostile eye in their direction, "has—been quite an experience, Zeke."

"Sure," he agreed.

She moved closer. "Y'know," she said confidentially, "I like you, Zeke. You've got a mind. You c'n think."

He took a swill of calao. "Sure, sure," he said soothingly.

"Now take Jos f'r instance." She glared at the big man who was laughing loudly at something Angelique had said.

"Take Jos," repeated Ezekiel mechanically.

"He's jussa great big brute."

"No fool you know."

"Jussa big ape," she said dreamily. "And what's more," her voice was serious and confidential again. "Double-dyed racist! Out and out *bigot*! *Herrenvolk* . . . y'know what I mean?"

Ezekiel was bored. The calao made him feel gay. He wanted to sing and dance, not sit and listen to Sarah's maudlin outpourings. He made a move to get up. "Let's go and talk to the others." He pointed to the far side of the fire.

Sarah clutched his arm and pulled him back. He sat down resignedly, but she kept her hand on his arm.

"Lissen," she looked at him owlishly. "Y'know, Zeke . . . I'm different . . . South African without colour prejudice. *You* know that, don't you. Just can't understan' how colour can make any difference . . . c'n you?"

"Yes," said Zeke. "I *can* understand why colour makes a difference. I'm conscious of it myself. Doubt if there's anyone who's not."

"So you meana say you condone Jos's attitude towards colour?"

"I didn't say that. I said I can understand colour prejudice. I feel it myself."

Sarah saw the conversation going away from the direction in which she'd hoped to steer it. She decided to act quickly. Leaning towards him, she wagged an admonitory finger "Naughty boy. You're thinking about politics. But when it comes to personal things, Zeke—like you an' me . . ." she squeezed his arm again. "You *can't* admit to colour prejudice."

Zeke looked at her eyes, magnified by the thick lenses of her glasses, and lost patience. There was only one woman on the island who appealed to him and it wasn't Sarah. He was bored to death. He wanted to escape. To sing . . .! To dance . . .! The calao was at work. Life was gay! Life was good! To hell with being serious! He tried to get up, but she clutched his arm tighter.

"Hey! Let go, Sarah!"

"Zeke . . . you're . . . you're spurning me because of my colour?" The tone was incredulous.

Then he said it: the remark he now so much regretted because although it was true it was unkind and unnecessary. "You're talking a lot of balls, Sarah."

With that he left her. Now, walking down to the beach in the early morning with his head splitting, he knew he'd made a mortal enemy.

       *   *

It was a languorous night and they were swimming in the lagoon; all but Sarah Tripp and Sebastian who were sitting on the beach watching. Jos was floating on his back near Angelique, and the others were farther out in the deep water.

Jos was happy. The breach with Angelique had been healed and their relationship was now friendly. This induced a new peace of mind and did much to compensate for his irritation at Canning's assumption of the leadership.

The water was warm and enervating and Jos felt he could almost go to sleep. Bikini Beach was in the lee of the island and they were sheltered from the wind.

Angelique splashed at him with her feet and he turned over in the water and swam after her. She squealed in mock terror as his strong arms pulled her under.

When she came up she said: "You are a *terreeble* man! Look what you have done to my hair."

He laughed. "You look okay when you're cross."

"*Okay*—what is this?"

"You know—kind of pretty."

"Pouf!" She made a mouth at him in the moonlight. "Only pretty. Am I not beautiful then?"

He looked at her quizzically, his eyes screwed up. "Not bad," he said. She was beautiful, of course, but how could he say that? It was not for men to say such things.

When they got back to the beach he said: "Let's walk down to the fish-traps. The tide's out."

The bathing costume he wore was his one pair of underpants, kept especially for these occasions. Angelique wore a brassière and her only panties. These sodden, scant garments clung to them so that they might as well have been wearing nothing, but they were long accustomed to the limitations of their clothing and wore them only as a gesture to propriety. Tenuous evidence that they were holding on to the shreds of civilised behaviour.

From where she was sitting with Sebastian, Sarah Tripp saw them go. Though Sebastian didn't know it, she'd had eyes for nothing else for the last ten minutes.

"They're in a hurry," she said sardonically. "Can't think why. They've got all night."

Sebastian frowned. "I think you're a little unkind, Sarah."

She snorted. "Rubbish. I know my human nature. What I've learned from life is that things are usually a damned sight worse than one suspects."

"Dear me," sighed Sebastian. "You must have been very unfortunate. I find there is so much unsuspected goodness in people."

"We're probably talking about quite different things," she said curtly. "Anyway, let's go. These midges are giving me hell." She slapped at her legs.

As they walked to the camp, Sebastian resolved that he must try to help Sarah find happiness, for she seemed such a lost and bitter soul. She suffered, he was sure, from a feeling of not belonging, of not being wanted. Sebastian had for so long suffered that, that he understood her unhappiness. His problem had long since been solved: he'd found the Baptist Church; he belonged to it; felt wanted by it; and he was content. Of course he was not as happy as he had been when Mary and Timothy were alive. Life by oneself in a small room in a semi-detached house off the Finchley Road was bound to be lonely. Like the work at Fenchurch Street. He hadn't any friends in the Company. Being the Chief's personal assistant made friendships with the staff almost impossible.

The Chief was not liked—"*You can't be efficient and popular, Sebastian. The two don't go together.*" The Chief didn't approve of Sebastian making close friends on the staff—"*As my P.A., Sebastian, you must keep aloof. To do otherwise can only lead to difficulties and embarrassment.*"

What the Chief said was law for Sebastian, so he kept aloof from the staff and paid the price in loneliness.

But here on the island he was content. There was always companionship: he got on with everybody—even Canning, to whose nagging and rebukes he was so accustomed that they were a normal part of life. He'd never felt fitter in mind and body.

If only he could contrive that Sarah should feel as he did, he knew she would be happy.

*　　　*

There were seven fish in the traps!

This was the first time, although the last stakes had been driven days before. None was large, but there they were plainly visible in the moonlight. Three mullets, two stripeys, a sandjack and a damsel fish. A meal for six people. Jos was delighted.

"Hell, man!" he said. "It works."

Angelique knelt in the shallows. "What shall we do with them, Jos?"

"Leave them for tomorrow. They can't escape."

They started back along the beach towards the camp. They'd not gone far when Jos on a sudden impulse took Angelique's hand in his. He'd not done this before though often tempted to. Her hand was warm and soft in spite of the cooking and plaiting and other chores. The feel of it thrilled Jos so that he felt slightly weak at the knees and his head swam. And the wonder of it was that Angelique's hand rested in his, warm and unprotesting.

Without saying a word he changed direction and led her up through the undergrowth into a sandy glade laced with coarse grass. The wind, gusting and flurrying, brought the musky odour of over-ripe coconuts from the plantation and the acrid smell of guano from the sea-birds' roosts.

The moon was full and they were isolated in a small world of their own. A world of silver-white sand splashed with the dark shadows of undergrowth and palm. Underfoot the sand was warm and yielding. There were no night noises beyond the muffled chorus of surf and wind.

Jos stopped. They faced each other and her head lifted towards his, her eyes questioning, her breath warm and sweet on his face. His arms went round her and their lips met in a long kiss which took them back to the beginning of time.

*

Since their arrival on the island, the monotony of the original diet had been relieved in various ways: they'd found a smaller variety of crab in the lagoons and these Angelique turned into a pleasant dish; they'd discovered that the terns were quite good eating and surprisingly unfishy, and Ezekiel was adept at bringing them down from their roosts with a quick throw of a stick. They'd learned, too, to like the turtle eggs which they often found in the sand, high up on the beach along The Strand. They were seldom without turtle meat, and Jos made a coarse but serviceable soap from turtle fat and charcoal. He'd also made them crude lamps from coconut shells, filled with oil squeezed from the rancid flesh of coconuts, and with wicks of plaited fibre.

Except for heat rash and athlete's foot, their health remained remarkably good. They were leaner, fitter, than before. Made so by the daily round of work and the simple diet. Occasionally they had attacks of diarrhoea accompanied by violent griping pains. A form of enteritis which they'd learnt to associate with eating too much coconut flesh. Sometimes they had feverish chills and ran temperatures, but these bouts never lasted for long.

Sarah Tripp now avoided both Jos and Ezekiel and as her attitude towards Angelique and Nada was cooler, she spent more time with Canning, Mecky and Sebastian. Art Basset she continued to regard with a hostile wary eye, as he did her.

*   *

Canning was sitting in the shade near Coral Point with his back to his favourite palm. But for tattered shorts, and rough sandals of dinghy material, he wore nothing. Out beyond the point he could see Sebastian poking with a stick into pools on the reef, looking for shell-fish and other delicacies for the evening meal.

Hands clasped behind his head, Canning reflected how strange it was that Sebastian . . . so much the clerk from the City of London, timid, subservient, obsequious . . . should have adapted himself so easily to life on the island. Canning could hear his whistle borne down on the wind. Sebastian was forever whistling. The oldest of tunes and always off key, but joyously.

This frank enjoyment of a serious predicament, the aftermath of a disaster which had all but cost them their lives, and *had* cost others theirs, irritated Canning intensely.

Canning was by no means happy. Relieved, of course, that he'd put the leadership on a proper basis and that he no longer suffered the indignities of working with Lombaard and Wanalu and of being ordered around by them. But it was no more than that. Indeed, he was intensely worried at the possibility of being left on this god-forsaken island to fend for himself with the others once the catamaran was built and Jos and Ezekiel had gone. Worried by the gnawing uncertainty of ultimate rescue, and worried by other less important but in a sense equally harrassing thoughts. What was going on in Fenchurch Street? It was dangerous to be away too long. There was always the chilling thought of Porrit, his ambitious and highly capable second in command, who had his eyes firmly on Canning's managerial chair.

No doubt Porrit had done all the right things. Expressed horror at the disaster; sent appropriate messages to Winifred and to Sebastian's aged father; ensured that the salaries continued to be paid to them; and then set about consulting the Company's attorneys as to when death might be presumed. For Porrit, of course, the sooner the better. Canning couldn't for the life of him remember what the legal period was. Three months . . .? He wasn't sure. No point in guessing. They'd been on the island for two months now.

Then there were the important matters of Canning's expense account and income tax. He'd looked forward to a good deal of profitable fiddling in these directions, for this Australian trip had been full of that sort of promise. And what on earth was happening on the share market? Not that it really mattered because no one could deal in his shares. He'd left no power of attorney. He trusted no one.

All his plans had gone awry. He'd no idea what sort of fiddle he could work in respect of several months on a desert island in the middle of the Indian Ocean. He wouldn't even be able to claim for subsistence expenses, let alone travelling or entertainment. Not even medical expenses . . . everything had been free! It was an appalling thought! A disturbing vision presented itself of an income tax assessment larger than any he'd ever experienced.

Of course, if they were rescued, opportunities for the expense account might present themselves in due course. But in the meantime the outlook was decidedly gloomy.

*   *

Out on the reef looking into the strange world below the coral fringe, Mecky found himself listening again to the geologist in the hotel at Nyali Beach. "Darwin first evaluated these things in 1836 when he visited the Cocos Islands. He realised that coral was the end process not the beginning. First came the island, forced up by volcanic action; then the phase of subsidence, the island falling back into and below the sea, and finally the colonisation of the subsiding slopes by countless millions of coral polyps thriving in the sunlit depths. When they died their skeletons were the foundation for future generations of polyps. As they built on the remains of their forebears the reefs began to form, fringing the island with necklaces of coral while it continued to subside until, in the end, there was only the circular atoll with the lagoon in the centre."

This island, thought Mecky, must still be in a sort of half-way stage. There was a reef on one and a half sides of it only, and no sign of the island disappearing.

In some ways he liked this life. It was infinitely preferable to the drudgery of the oil company. But while he liked the uninhibited life of the island he loathed its inhabitants. One needed to choose one's companions for a venture like this. He wouldn't have chosen a single member of this party. With somebody like Paul and one or two others like him, life would have been tolerable.

But these men! God! He thought of Jos, whom he loathed with a blind pathological hatred. What was it about him that was so ominously evocative?

* *

The morning after the moonlight walk back from the fish-traps, Jos woke early and knew there was something wrong. As the picture of the night came back to him, his conscience tightened round his mind like a steel band. He had erred and strayed! He had fallen in the way like a lost sheep! He had all but broken the seventh commandment, for Angelique was a married woman. And it was thanks to her and not to him that he'd not. But he'd sinned grievously for he'd broken the tenth commandment. He'd coveted her.

She was such a kind and beautiful woman. So intelligent and thoughtful! A magnificent cook! So resourceful! He thought of the calao, and the way she could cook a crab and plait fibre rope and make hats and skirts and matting out of coconut leaves.

She was everything a man could look for in a wife. And now he knew she was also a good woman.

"*No, Jos! Not that! We mustn't. I must think of my husband.*" With passionate entreaty he'd tried to persuade her, but she was adamant.

Yes! She was a good woman! Her husband could be proud of her. He found himself wondering what he was like and was conscious of a quick surge of jealousy. The name was Lee—that meant he was English, he supposed. He shook his head. A *rooinek*! That made it worse. His thoughts went back to Angelique and the night before; but his conscience interrupted them. He sighed. He'd have to work harder and take more exercise so that his mind wouldn't dwell on these things. He jumped up, pulled on his shorts and went out of the hut leaving the others asleep.

He'd go for a swim. Then a hard run like in the old days when he was training for the rugby match against Lydenburg. *Wragtig!* Streuth! How he'd trained then! He almost sweated at the recollection.

Near the lagoon he took off his shorts and ran into the water, ending up with a flat dive. He was sorry the sea was so warm. A man needed cold water to get fit! Farther out in deeper water he threw himself about in an orgy of vigour, like a huge porpoise possessed by the devil. Ten minutes later he swam back to the beach. Once there he was tired but he determined to punish his body. He forced himself into a long run. He must have covered a mile before he turned back towards the camp. He felt better now. Cleansed by the exercise.

On his way back he saw Angelique by the water-catchment. She was sitting on the beach, cross-legged, combing her hair.

At first he pretended not to see her, but she was a magnet he couldn't resist. He was glad of the excuse to speak to her, but he knew he was playing with fire. He wondered how she looked after last night. Was she angry with him now she'd had time to think. But obviously she wasn't, because she smiled. "Why all this violent exercises, Jos?"

He blushed through the brown tan. "How d'you mean?"

"I woke early. Then I came here. I saw you swimming and running. It seemed you were in a great competition. Such *strong* things you did." Her eyes opened wide to illustrate her surprise.

"*Ag!* A man must keep fit, you know." He looked away when he said it.

She smiled. The warm knowing smile mothers reserve for boastful small boys.

"Of course," she said simply.

*　　　　*

It was long and hollow, a little irregular in shape, but beginning to look like a dug-out canoe. Except for a portion about six feet from the bow where the mast was to be stepped, the burning and cutting out of the core was finished. Jos and Ezekiel were busy on the mast-step. They'd started working together several days before because the stage had been reached where each needed the skilled help of the other. Ezekiel lit the small fire inside the palm trunk, and the flames ate into the wood under the mast step. Both men watched closely making sure the fire did no more than it should. They raked and tended it with short sticks.

Whether it was the fight, or the knowledge that Canning had used the bad blood between them to take over the leadership, or because they knew they were the key men on the island: whatever it was, these two worked together now without friction. Their manner was still guarded but there was no doubt that it had changed. Dislike and suspicion had given way to mutual respect.

"How d'you come to be called 'Ezekiel'?" Jos didn't look up as he asked the question; his eyes were fixed on the fire where it was eating into the wood.

208

"My mother's idea," said Ezekiel. "She went to a mission school. Read the Bible there and thought a lot of Ezekiel."

"He was the prophet who lived in Babylon, wasn't he?"

"Some say that, but many think that most of his prophecies were made in Jerusalem."

Ezekiel was blowing with puffed cheeks into the small fire, fanning the flames as he fed them with small pieces of dried wood.

"And you," he said. "How did you come by the name ' Joshua'?"

Jos looked at him. Two weeks ago, before the fight, he'd have regarded the question coming from an African as an impertinence, but now he knew it was not. Ezekiel was educated, he had a good brain. Jos knew there was no intention to be cheeky.

"Same as you," he said. "From the Bible. I was called after Joshua."

"He conquered and settled Canaan, didn't he?"

"That's right. He led the Israelites across the Jordan. How do you know these things? In the dinghy you said you were a heathen."

Ezekiel puffed at the embers. "I said I wasn't a Christian."

"But you know the Bible so well?"

"Religious mother—mission school—I was a keen reader—I found the Bible a wonderful book. I still do."

Jos was puzzled but he looked at the African with new respect. "There's a question I've wanted to ask you for a long time, Wanalu."

"What's that?"

"You understand Afrikaans?"

"*Natuurlik, meneer* . . . naturally, sir."

"*Hoe? Waar het jy dit geleer?* . . . How? Where did you learn it?"

"At my first mission school. Before I went to secondary school. A Gereformeerde Kerk mission at Gensa. I worked in the kitchen there, too. I learnt fast."

Jos nodded. "*Nou ja. Ek het al lankal gedag jy kan mos ons taa praat* . . . yes, I've thought for a long time you can speak our language."

That conversation was the turning point in their relationship. Thereafter they spoke often in Afrikaans, and to Jos who had used nothing but English now for two months the relief of conversation in his mother tongue was enormous.

But to Canning, Mecky and Basset this was a new and chilling threat: Lombaard and Wanalu could converse in a language which the others didn't understand. To Canning it was especially ominous that this had been revealed only when the catamaran was so near completion.

Fourteen

SQUATTING on their haunches round the fire—most of them now preferred this to sitting on a log—they ate the grilled fish with their fingers, pinching it out of coconut bowls with three fingers the way Ezekiel had showed them. Between mouthfuls they discussed the things they'd do back in civilisation. Once again Basset found himself confronted with his own nagging problem. It was all right for the others. They had something definite to go to. For most of them it was just a picking up of the threads again. It wasn't like that for him. His talents required special employment and much preliminary work. A careful survey of the field, so to speak, before they could be brought into play.

There was, too, the ticklish question of whether that last English job had caught up with him. That was the curse of this aircrash. He was badly out of touch. Two months late already. Anything might've happened by now. A fine how-do-you-do if the police were waiting for him on the airport at Perth with an extradition order!

The Aussie police knew him as Harry Craggs and in London he'd last operated as Johnnie Brown. If he kept out of Queensland, it could be a long time before they caught up with him. But he didn't like being out of touch with the news. The newspapers were important. They gave timely warnings! . . . *"the police are anxious to communicate with . . ."* They gave gen on potential clients. From others you could learn where old friends and enemies were operating—and plan accordingly.

An idea was taking shape in his mind. Why go back to Australia?

He was not irrevocably committed. Why not go to some quieter place—more of a backwash? Once the survivors reached Australia it would be world news. "*Return of the dead! Amazing story of survivors of air/sea disaster.*" Everybody who'd been on the island would be headline news for days. With a sudden shock he realised what that would mean. It would be fatal! Photos on the front page of every Australian newspaper. Even if he kept his beard—he stroked it reverently—the Queensland police would recognise him. They were trained to see through those sort of disguises. And the reporters would dig out *everything* there was to be dug out. He knew! He'd been fixed by the bastards once before!

Why not go to Kenya? Or Madagascar? Or South Africa? There was racing there. Not on the English scale, but still racing. Ought to be possible to do a little business in Johannesburg, Durban and Cape Town. Wherever there were race-horses there were clients, and there were skads of racehorses in South Africa. Plenty of time to decide. Of course, if a man wanted to disappear altogether a smaller place would be better. Kenya for example.

First you get to Mauritius. Rest there until things have quietened down. Then head for Beira. From there slide quietly up the east coast into Kenya. Unnoticed, unsung! Plenty of time to make onward plans once you'd got there!

*   *

Mecky was arranging small burnt ends of wood which had fallen from the fire. Arranging them in neat orderly rows like soldiers on parade. Like the pens and pencils and paper clips and pins with which he was always fidgeting on his desk in Nairobi. Getting them into neat orderly rows. If they were not set out with iron precision he felt insecure. Must have got it from his mother. She was incredibly neat and tidy. One saw it in her house. Yes . . . one saw the immaculate tidiness in her room and in her garden. The garden was like a municipal park—everything so orderly. Set out in stiff rows with geometric exactitude. He drew his hand across his eyes. His head ached. Come to think of it there was something rather municipal about his mother. The hygiene and cleansing department, perhaps. Hygiene and cleanliness had been her consuming passions, and how he had suffered from them as a small boy! He was forever being scrubbed and changed, or having his face washed with a cold flannel . . . how he'd hated that! . . . or being chided because there was a dirty mark on his blouse.

Yes, *blouse*!

She'd had the most extraordinary ideas about what small boys should wear. Loose blouses with floppy bows, as if one were a toy doll. For him she chose the brightest and most exotic colours, and she kept his hair long and induced it to curl, so that other small boys made his life a misery.

And the crowning indignity. *Christopher Robin*! That horribly pretentious compound. A. A. Milne! Ye Gods!

Christopherrobin!

What a cross that'd been to bear!

He got back to the job of arranging the small burnt ends of wood.

*   *

Goldsworthy was back at the pools, whistling happily, the sun beating down, the south-east trades blustering by laced with spray from the breakers creaming in on the reef beyond him; mighty convolutions of sapphire and green capped with frothing foam, their roar blanketing all sound but the high scream of the sea-birds. There was the smell of sea and coral and weed in the air.

To think, thought Sebastian, that I might be in that dreary office in Fenchurch Street waiting for the Chief's bell to go, or battling on the telephone for his theatre tickets, or arguing with the wine people because they'd invoiced his last order at retail prices!

He looked into a deep pool, waiting for his eyes to become

accustomed to the shadows. A swarm of damsel fish threaded their way through the branches of coral, their scales flashing turquoise in the sunlight. Three translucent fishes, minuscule, with feathery tails and solemn eyes came from the shadows and hovered in the sunlight.

There were brightly coloured flower-like sea anemones, prickly sea-urchins, floating tendrils of fernlike weed and many shells, some of great beauty. Sebastian glowed with happiness. It was a wicked thought, he knew, but he almost hoped they'd not be rescued! He looked inshore over the lagoon to where the Chief was sitting, as if he feared his thoughts might be overheard. But the Chief was dozing under the palms. Sebastian turned back to the pool and got on with his task of collecting clams for the evening meal.

At times he would pick up a delicate salmon-pink fanshell and put it in the pocket of his shorts. He was collecting these for a necklace for Sarah Tripp. It was to be a surprise.

*   *

The hull of the catamaran was finished and they'd fitted the outriggers. Long poles set athwartships, with streamlined floats cut from palm trunks secured to their ends. Jos and Ezekiel went to immense trouble to do this, burning holes through the floats and the ends of the outriggers with white-hot wire from the Sarah Beacon. When the holes were the right size, they hammered in wooden pegs. The outriggers were secured to the hull in the same way.

The mast was now rigged and stepped, held upright by the mast-step and the shrouds and stays of coconut fibre which the women had plaited. The paddles were ready, and a steering oar. In the stern were two thole pins to house it.

The women had almost finished weaving the lateen sail and the gaff for hoisting it lay ready. The gaff would be hoisted with a fibre rope led through a hole in the mast-head.

It would take, perhaps, three more days to complete the finishing touches. Knowledge of this had infected everyone and excitement was running high. Everyone but Canning who still regarded the journey as a dangerous and ill-starred venture. A new factor had, however, reduced the worst of his fears. Jos had decided that the dug-out could take three people, and it had been agreed that these should be Jos, Ezekiel and Goldsworthy. It was Canning who suggested Goldsworthy. He'd done this because he knew that Sebastian got on well with the other two, and they would not wilfully let him come to any harm. If Goldsworthy were in the catamaran, and if it reached Smoke Island, Canning knew that those left behind would not be neglected.

✻   ✻

That night while they ate round the fire, the discussion was entirely of the coming journey. Jos pushed a lump of fish into his mouth and looked at Ezekiel. "We've got to be careful choosing the weather! Must be dead right! I've been testing the currents round Casuarina Point for some time now. When it's blowing hard from the south-east, it sets north-north-west on a rising tide. When the tide's going out the set's to the west, and that's no good for us."

Ezekiel tore with his teeth at the turtle meat he was holding with both hands. Sitting back on his haunches he chewed solidly. "How d'you test the currents?"

Jos wiped his mouth with the back of his hand. "Threw in dried sticks and watched them."

"Is it much?"

"Two or three knots, sometimes." He leant forward and reached for a cup of coconut milk. "Funny thing is . . . when the wind drops the current goes stronger. Got to watch that!"

Basset's face puckered. "What are the best conditions for the journey, Jos?"

"Strong south-easter on a rising tide. Then the current's across but slightly with us. When it sets west it'll take us away from Smoke Island, maybe faster than we can sail. Another thing

215

—we've got to make our long beats *into* wind and short ones *down* wind. We'll never make it otherwise. The more the wind's in the south, the better."

"Sounds very complicated." Canning was gloomy.

"It's okay, man, but we've got to choose the right moment." Jos spat out a fish bone. "If we do that we'll make it okay. We've got to try and keep up to windward so that if we can't make Smoke Island we can get back here."

Canning sighed with relief. "That sounds like good common sense."

Jos gave him the sort of look reserved for bad smells, but said nothing.

"You think there are people there, Jos?" Angelique's eyes were on him.

"Must be," he said emphatically. "Fires don't light themselves. There's either people living there or visiting fairly regularly. That's a dead certainty."

"It's a marvellous thought, isn't it?" Nada's voice was full of suppressed excitement. "Smoke Island . . . people . . . *rescue!* Then back home! I can't believe it!" There were tears in her eyes.

Sarah Tripp snorted. "I refuse to get worked up about something that will probably *never* happen! Not that I don't *want* to get off this benighted island."

There was a long pause, broken by Basset. "When d'we launch the catamaran, Jos?"

"In a day or so, I suppose. What say, Zeke?"

Jos looked at the African and smiled—the smile of a friend.

"I think so, Jos."

"We'll have to reorganise our duties quite a bit while they're away," said Canning. He looked round at the others, apprehensively. "Won't we?"

"We'll manage all right, digger." Basset blinked. "There'll be me and you and Mecky and the three dames."

Jos spoke to Angelique. "Now that the fish-traps are working, you don't have to fish unless you want to. There's plenty of crabs and mussels, and coconuts of course. Maybe I'll get you a turtle the night before we go."

Angelique smiled. "Thank you, Jos. We shall be all right. It is you men in the catamaran who must be careful."

Canning frowned. "What's the date, Mecky?"

"Twenty-third of November."

"Jesus!" said Basset. "How long've we been 'ere?"

"Fifty-six days at midnight," Mecky's voice was sepulchral.

*   *

The firelight flickered, the wind sighed in the palms high above them, and in the distance they heard the roar of the surf. From the tins beyond the fire came pungent reminders of the finished meal. Sickly sweetness of turtle meat. Musky odour of fish. Spicy, rancid smell of coconut.

In the ten days since he and Angelique had first gone down the beach in the moonlight, Jos had taken her for other nocturnal walks to other places. Twice in those ten days he had awoken in the morning stricken by his conscience, and again he had driven himself to early morning swims and vigorous runs. But now as he looked at her in the firelight, his conscience was once more forgotten and her eyes answered the question in his.

Later, when the chores had been done, they left the fire and disappeared in the darkness in the direction of Needle Point. They would examine the fish-traps, they said. After they'd left Art Basset looked across at Nada. She was sitting on a log, gazing into the fire, chin in hand. He saw the fullness of her breasts in the tight shabby brassière and below them her well proportioned suntanned limbs. I wonder, he thought, what she'd say if I suggested it? She's only human like the rest of them, although she made that fuss about Canning. Maybe I will suggest it— sometime. He thought, I haven't got much time.

217

That was the third consecutive day on which it had not rained, and the water level in the catchment was falling fast.

*　　　　　*

Because it was Sunday, there was no work but for unavoidable chores. But there was an urgent problem—water! Another day had gone by without rain and the catchment was nearly empty; and even when that had been shared out there wasn't enough to fill the life-jackets.

Ezekiel scraped up the last of it while his companions stood watching, a motley handful with new fear in their eyes. "We'll have to ration again," he said.

"It'll rain soon, why panic?" Basset's eyes blinked their owner's disapproval.

"It's not panic," said Jos. "It's common sense. If it doesn't rain in two days, we'll have no water unless we ration. Then *you'll* panic."

Canning scratched at his stomach. "As your leader I feel this is a question I must put to you. We're all equally concerned."

The dried skin on the end of her nose added fierceness to Sarah Tripp's glare. "Surely the question decides itself? Why play this tedious committee game?"

Canning held up a peremptory hand. "*Please*, Sarah! Leave it to me, will you?" He turned to the others. "Now—those in favour of water rationing please signify!"

All but Basset and Sarah put up their hands.

Canning counted them. "One—two—three—four—five. I make six. Well! That decides it. Water rationing is introduced as of now." He gestured towards Jos and Zeke. "Water's your responsibility. Kindly suggest a ration."

Jos looked at the sky again before he spoke to Ezekiel. "What d'you think, man?"

Ezekiel shook his head. "Have to work it out. We've still got the six ten-ounce tins of fresh water, and the desalting units from the emergency kit. But we want most of them for the catamaran—

in case." He yawned. The gap left by the missing tooth fascinated Nada.

Jos nodded. "Most of the life-jackets are half full."

"Not mine!" Canning squeaked in alarm as he held up his life-jacket. "Look! It's nearly empty!"

"You got the same amount this morning as the rest."

"Yes, but mine was nearly empty when we started."

"Whose fault was that?"

"How did I know that rationing was coming?" His tone became conciliatory. "Shouldn't we all start with the same amount, Jos? Fair shares in an emergency, you know."

"Balls!" said Jos. "You had the same share as anyone else. But you used more." With Ezekiel he started off towards the camp.

They discussed the matter at length, making various tests. Eventually they agreed on a ration of three cups a day each, apart from the water needed for cooking. The contents of all life-jackets would now become a communal supply. Jos and Ezekiel would draw the rations, and then only first thing in the morning. On this basis they had enough for six days.

Even Canning expressed satisfaction with these arrangements for he would get the same share as the others. There were unlimited supplies of coconut milk on the island but they knew that too much coconut milk was a powerful laxative. Water was essential.

With an eye to possible needs, Jos and Ezekiel dug a well following the instructions in the survival booklet. They chose a place about a hundred yards inland from the beach, and using large scallop shells dug down into the sand. At five feet the water seeped through and soon there were six inches in the bottom of the hole. But it was too brackish to drink so they followed the advice in the booklet and skimmed the fresher water from the top. It was still too salty.

*　　　*

Nada looked at Angelique and wondered again why it was she

looked different; then suddenly she knew—Angelique was not wearing her jewels. Nothing but the simple wedding ring.

"Angelique!" she cried. "Where are your lovely jewels?"

The Mauritian shrugged her shoulders. "I have put them away. One of the stones in the brooch is loose. I think it is better not to wear these things."

"I don't think they're in the hut," said Nada doubtfully. "Surely I'd have seen them if they were?"

"Do not worry, Nada. I have put them in another place."

Nada looked puzzled. "But where could you?"

Angelique's smooth brow wrinkled in a frown, and she looked round at the circle of curious faces. "I wish that it would rain," she said.

Nada knew then that for some reason or other the subject of the jewels was taboo.

Basset jumped in quickly and changed the subject. "I'm going to see if I can get a turtle tonight. Who's coming?"

There were no offers.

Fifteen

It was the seventh day without rain but in spite of that spirits ran high as the catamaran was launched. Palm log rollers had been laid over a distance of fifty feet in the direction of the lagoon, and the survivors were pushing the catamaran forward and down onto the logs.

"Now!" ordered Jos, his shoulder taking the weight under the starboard bow while Ezekiel's took it on the port side. The others pushed from the stern.

Slowly the catamaran slid forward and down onto the logs. When they had trundled it over the first fifty feet towards the lagoon they stopped, picked up the logs and laid them ahead again.

This process was repeated many times until, exhausted and dripping with perspiration, they got the catamaran to the water. They anchored it fore and aft in the shallows with lumps of coral on the ends of fibre ropes. It listed over to port, but Jos explained that the outriggers would hold it on an even keel. These were carried down and laid athwartships after which the securing pegs were driven firmly home and lashed with fibre rope for good measure. As Jos predicted, the catamaran now floated on an even keel. It was mid-afternoon when the mast was stepped and the stays and shrouds brought up taut and secured. The lagoon was in the lee of the island and little wind reached the catamaran, so they hoisted the lugsail.

Then they stood back and watched with shining eyes. There it was at last! The catamaran on which they had laboured so hard and for so long, and on which they had for so many weeks placed all their hopes of rescue.

To each of them it was the symbol of deliverance. They were conscious of a tremendous sense of achievement. While it was building it had not seemed real, just a great palm log on which they worked endlessly. Now it was finished and it looked good and seaworthy, and though Jos and Ezekiel had done most of the work and planning, they all felt that the catamaran was the fruit of their own labour.

The sail was lowered and Ezekiel, Jos and Sebastian spent the rest of the afternoon paddling the dugout in the lagoon, hoisting and lowering the sail, and shipping and unshipping the steering oar. About fifty feet off-shore they felt the wind and found that with the halyard secured well forward on the gaff, the catamaran could just sail into wind though it made heavy leeway. They knew then that they would have to choose their weather carefully; preferably a day when the wind was more southerly than easterly, and even then beats to windward would have to be helped with vigorous paddling.

The steering oar kept jumping out of the thole pins. To stop this they rove a rope strop through a hole in the gunwale next to the pins.

Basset was a keen observer of these trials. Suddenly he remembered something he'd learned at boat drill in the *Bulolo*, and he shouted to them that the catamaran would sail closer to the wind with a man well forward in the bows. They found he was right.

*　　　　*

Inevitably the conversation that night was of the coming journey.

Canning was at his most amiable. "Well, Jos, what do you think? Is she ready?"

Jos looked into the fire. He didn't like Canning's face. "When we've made those adjustments she'll be okay."

"Is she up to expectations?"

"She's okay," he said guardedly. He knew that she far exceeded them. Somehow he'd never thought the catamaran would be so responsive, so easy to handle. When they were working her down to the water he'd been appalled at the deadweight, but once in the water she'd come alive. A creature of the sea, buoyant and stable.

Angelique sighed. "When will you be going?"

Jos looked at her thoughtfully. "We'll have to leave her in the water for a few days for the wood to take up. See whether any cracks show up. Then we'll have to provision her. Then," he shrugged his shoulders. "It's up to the weather. I'm not going unless it's dead right."

The African leant forward on his haunches and poked at the fire with a stick. Cascades of sparks climbed into the darkness.

"Jos is right. Weather's the vital factor. We'd be mad to try unless it's right. Another thing is water. The life-jackets are down to quarter-full now. We shouldn't go until it's rained and they're full again."

Jos nodded. "Must have three in the catamaran. We need plenty of water in case anything goes wrong."

They talked until late that night and when they got up to go to their huts the fire had burnt itself out. They had agreed eventually with Ezekiel's suggestion that the journey should not be undertaken until the rain had come.

        *   *

It was hot in the hut. Jos found sleep difficult because of that and because his mind was full of the coming journey. He knew it would be hazardous with that wind and those currents to contend with. Once or twice he dozed off, but then he'd find himself lying awake, his body wet with perspiration, plagued by prickly heat, his mind never still. There was an acrid smell of sweat in the hut, and the air was foetid with the odour of human bodies. He gave up the attempt to sleep, got up and pulled on his shorts. In a shaft of moonlight which lay across the floor he saw with surprise that Canning had gone.

Outside, he was about to cross over to the path to Bikini

Beach when he saw a dark shape at the gallows where the life-jackets hung.

The moonlight in the open clearing was laced with the shadows of many palms and in this patchwork he saw Canning's podgy figure. Jos moved quietly towards the gallows. Canning was filling a cup with water from one of the life-jackets. Jos stopped in his tracks and watched him raise the cup to his lips and drink.

Jos reached him in a few quick steps and knocked the cup out of his hand. "You bloody bastard!" he growled. "You're stealing water!"

Canning spun round, terrified. He saw it was Jos. "How dare you call me that!" His voice was querulous as if he'd been done the most heartless injustice.

"Stealing water, hey!" Dumbfounded, Jos repeated the charge. "You thieving bloody bastard!"

Canning's mind worked quickly in his terror. He shrieked, "Help! H-e-l-l-l-p!" and then with a frantic little run he was on the far side of the gallows.

Slowly the big man realised the significance of the cry for help and gave chase. Canning skipped round the gallows and made a headlong dash for Mecky and Basset's hut. Jos was too quick and a huge arm grabbed Canning round the neck as he reached the entrance. Then there was the sound of voices and out of the darkness came Ezekiel and Sebastian. Soon after Mecky and Basset appeared at the entrance with frightened, puzzled faces.

"Help!" cried Canning and there was no doubt about his fear. "Help me, for God's sake!"

Jos let go of Canning.

"What's the trouble?" It was the African's voice.

"Lombaard was st-stealing water," Canning's teeth chattered. "I caught him in the act. Then he attacked me."

With a roar of rage Jos shook him like a rat. "You lying bastard!" he growled. "It was you stealing the water and I caught you." He turned to the others. "He filled his cup and was drinking from it. There it is under the gallows!" The women came out of the darkness, their faces white in the moonlight.

"What's the trouble?" Nada's eyes were round with surprise.

Canning explained how he'd found Lombaard helping himself to water, but he'd not gone far when Jos laid a heavy hand on him. "Stop lying, you crooked bastard, or I'll kill you."

Canning yelled at Mecky and Basset. "Stop this maniac! Quickly! *Stop him*! Get the gun!" His voice rose to a scream.

Mecky turned away slowly. He noticed that Basset was no longer there. Must have slipped off in the darkness to fetch the gun, he thought. For some moments he stood undecided, then he moved towards the plantation with slow tentative steps as if he hoped they might not be noticed.

"If you're after the gun, save yourself the trouble," Ezekiel shouted. "You won't find it."

Mecky hesitated. Then he walked on and was lost in the shadows.

"Why don't you stop him, Zeke?" Jos's voice was urgent.

"No point. They can't find the gun."

"What d'you mean?"

"I'll tell you later. It's okay."

Jos looked down on Canning. He still held his arm in an iron grip. Shaking him once more, he flung him away violently so that the podgy man staggered.

Jos's eyes narrowed. "If you steal any more water or tell any more lies I'll beat you up. Even if you are fifty-five. D'you understand?"

Canning looked from one unsympathetic face to the other and then, hopefully, his eyes searched the darkness of the plantation for signs of Basset and the gun. But Basset didn't come. Acutely conscious of his humiliation, Canning walked back through the shadowed moonlight to the hut. Jos told them again what had happened and then in ones and twos they went back to their huts, until only Jos and Ezekiel were left. Jos looked at the African and frowned. "Sure it's okay about the gun?"

"Sure," said Ezekiel. "They'll never find it. I'll tell you to-morrow."

Jos laughed grimly. "So that's the end of Canning's leadership."

"Just about," the African drew a deep breath. "You know the fundamental law of politics. Nothing's immutable. Everything changes."

Jos gave him a hard look.

*   *

"Stumbled onto it a week ago," said Ezekiel. "Near the cairn. My toe struck something in the sand. It wasn't actually showing. Then I pushed the sand away and saw the bit of dinghy material. Pulled on it and out came Basset's automatic."

Jos eyed him curiously. "What d'you do with it?"

"Buried it again." The African looked round to make sure they were alone. "Not far from here."

"And now," said Jos slowly. "What?"

The African fumbled in the pocket of his shorts and brought out a cartridge-clip holding six rounds of ammunition. "Took this from it. If they find the gun it's no good to them now. Here . . ." he held it out to Jos. "You keep it."

Jos looked puzzled. "What's the idea?"

"The gun's dangerous. I know where it is. You don't. You've got the ammunition. I haven't. *With* the gun they can take charge. We can *without* it. If there's no ammunition the gun's nothing. It *could* be a bone of contention between you and me. It's better that neither of us has both."

Jos frowned, thinking deeply. "Okay. We'll leave it at that." After a pause he added. "So we're the bosses now."

"Yes," said Ezekiel. "*We* are. But you take charge, Jos."

The big man looked puzzled. "Me? Why not both of us?"

"No. You take charge. I'll support you." He paused. "It's better that way. They're your people."

"And when we go off to Smoke Island who'll take charge here?" Jos scratched at his black untidy hair.

"Canning, I suppose. He's a miserable bastard but he's shrewd. He's better than Basset and Mecky. Anyway we won't be away long . . . I hope." He added wryly.

"I hope," echoed Jos.

*   *

At the evening meal Jos told the others that he and Ezekiel had the automatic and while they had no intention of using it they'd made sure no one else could. There were not going to be any more elections or any nonsense of that sort.

"We tried democracy and it didn't work . . . because you people," . . . he shot fierce glances at Canning, Mecky, Basset and Sarah Tripp, "You people ganged up against the rest of us . . . on a race basis. And look what you chose as leader." He cocked a derisive thumb at Canning. "He couldn't lead a span of donkeys."

A bank of cloud obscured the moon and the wind blustered in the palm tops drowning Canning's indignation as he moved away from the fire.

"Come back!" roared Jos, "Or I'll skin the hide off you."

Slowly, awkwardly, Canning came back.

Mecky showed his disapproval by yawning loudly, but his eyes gave the lie to this gesture of boredom.

"Any orders that have to be given around here," went on Jos, "'ll be given by me. When I'm not about, Zeke'll give them."

He glowered at them. "Understand?"

A brilliant flash of lightning was followed by thunder which reverberated across the island. The rain started to fall. Large isolated drops at first and then, as the wind swept through the palms with the noise of an express train, it came down in sheets.

Next morning the catchment was full and the island sparkled like a jewel. Everywhere there was the fresh fragrance of sea and sand and trees washed by the rain.

*   *

227

Canning wiped the sweat from his forehead and fixed his watery eyes on Goldsworthy. "Why didn't you tell me what was going on?"

"I didn't know, sir."

"You *didn't know*! That's a fine thing to say! You're always hanging round Lombaard and Wanalu and now you expect me to believe that you *didn't know* they'd found the pistol."

"They never mentioned it to me, sir! *How* would I know?"

"You idiot. Don't you realise what this means? That brute Lombaard in charge! That nigger backing him up! Thanks to you, we're now at their mercy!"

His indignation rose. "You stand there like a mute, but you know damn' well you've failed. You're *useless*!"

Humiliated, Sebastian looked away. This was the cross he'd always had to bear. Ever since it had happened. In his misery he thought of Mary and little Timothy, and a picture of them— vivid and real as if they and not Canning were in front of him— was in his mind's eye. Then it faded and he saw only the puffy red face of the Chief, the sunburnt pate, blistered under the wisps of white hair, the flabby chest and protruding stomach and, starting somewhere below the navel, the ragged ridiculous shorts.

It occurred to Sebastian for the first time in his seventeen years with the Company that he hated Canning. A hate that was monstrous, indecent . . . something that had no place in a Christian. His humility returned.

"I'm sorry, sir," he said humbly.

*   *

Jos was sitting in the shade of a tree watching the sea-birds down at the southern end of the island. This was a peaceful place and almost always he had it to himself. But not this afternoon it seemed, for out of the corner of his eye he saw someone approaching. Those long swinging strides, the floppy sun hat and the flashes of sunlight on the glasses, were unmistakable. It was Sarah Tripp! He shrank back into the shade of the tree.

She was singing something from *Pinafore* high and toneless, but she was evidently happy and though he didn't like her Jos was glad. She was almost on him now and he could no longer ignore her. He said: "Hallo, Sarah."

Evidently she'd not expected anyone there. She shied like a horse. "Good heavens! *You!*" With a dramatic gesture she put her hand on her heart. But she soon recovered and didn't look at all pleased. "What are you doing here, may I ask?"

"My favourite spot." He indicated land, sea and sky with a flourish. "I come to watch the sea-birds."

She regarded him with suspicious eyes. "*You!* Interested in sea-birds! Well. Well."

"Sit down," he said gallantly. "If we're quiet for a few minutes you'll see what happens."

She sat down stiffly, keeping her distance. Around them the noise of the sea-birds rose above the thunder of the surf on the reef. A cacophony of shrill cries, of squawking, of chattering and grunting, as hundreds of them came and went. The musty smell of their droppings hung about the place.

A line of gannets swept across the sea. Jos touched her arm. "Watch!" he whispered. As he spoke the leader climbed, the line following. When they'd got height they made a steep turn to seaward, peeling off into plummeting dives. They came clear of the water with the silver gleam of fishes in their beaks and the frigate-birds dived down to snatch the prey.

Jos explained it all to her; she was interested in the terns. Finally he told her what went on in the colony in the trees.

"The wonderful thing," he said, "is how they all live together here, all mixed up. *Deurmekaar* as we say in Afrikaans. Yet you'll never see a gannet mating with anything but a gannet, and the same with the frigate-birds and the terns and the others. They keep to themselves."

"H'm." She was non-committal.

Jos's eyes narrowed and his bearded chin pointed skywards as he looked into the branches of the takamaka tree.

"*Apartheid*, you see. That's nature's way."

Sarah Tripp got to her feet.

"I've no desire to talk politics." She eyed him coldly, remembering how he'd rejected her advances. Now she could hurt him and she wouldn't let the opportunity pass. "Pity you don't practise a little *apartheid* yourself." She was supercilious.

He got up from the sand. "What d'you mean?"

"Making a fool of yourself with that *coloured* woman!" Sarah Tripp's lips curled.

Jos was livid. "You mean Angelique? *She's not coloured*! She told me herself she's half-French and half-Greek." He said it with passionate conviction.

"And you believed her?"

She turned on her heel and as she walked away she sneered at him over her shoulder. "You poor clot!"

*　　　　　*

Nada sighed. She was depressed. Perhaps it was the anti-climax. The knowledge that soon the catamaran would set off for Smoke Island and after that . . .? Well, what?

They might be rescued, or not make it and never be seen again. Who could say?

Whatever it was she felt miserable. Lately she'd thought a lot about Iles and Karin and Hughie and the others. It was terrible to think they were dead. She knew them so well. They'd been such gay and vital people and always full of fun. Even Hughie who was Captain of the aircraft and nearly forty. Forty seemed so old when you were twenty-three. That's the trouble on this island, she thought: Only I'm young. There's such a gap between me and the others. Who would that be anyway? Angelique, she supposed. But she must be about thirty and that seemed awfully old, too. She began thinking about their ages. Sarah Tripp! Thirty-six or seven. Jos? About forty. Ezekiel?

Thirty-something; terribly difficult to say with a black man. Basset . . . what? Forty or more? Mecky about the same or a little younger. And Canning? Well, one knew his age because he was always using it as an excuse to get off work. Fifty-five! Then there was Sebastian? Hard to say, but probably early forties. The beards made the men look much older.

She was lonely. She longed for other young people. For fun and high spirits and laughter. It would be wonderful to be with young people like Iles again. She thought of his face. For an agonising moment the picture wouldn't take shape and she felt disloyal to him. To think that she could forget so soon. It was only two months since she'd last seen him. She wondered what his face looked like now that he was dead? It was an awful thought; probably fish or some unspeakable creature which lived down in the bottom of the sea had eaten it away. She put her face in her hands and cried. She knew that she loved Iles: that she'd been in love with him all along. Why then had she been so beastly to him and why had she allowed herself to be infatuated with that dreadful Dieter creature? Was it because he had money and a good job with some standing? Because he represented *security*; whereas poor Iles didn't. It was a mystery to her. More than that. It was a nightmare!

*   *

The necessary adjustments were made to the catamaran and after further trials they were pleased with the results. The provisions and equipment she would carry had been thoroughly discussed, and in deciding quantities they had assumed the worst: failure to reach Smoke Island, or to get back to their own island. Water and provisions for two weeks would be taken and the better of the two fishing lines. The fish-traps were working well and would provide all the fish needed for those left behind.

Ezekiel and Jos were quietly confident that these precautions were unnecessary, and that if they chose their weather they could reach Smoke Island without undue difficulty. This confidence was based on a number of things: upon the catamaran which was stoutly built and, with its outriggers, thoroughly seaworthy; upon themselves, their strength, skill and endurance; and finally upon Providence. For Jos this meant belief in the Almighty, and for Ezekiel faith in the spirits of his ancestors.

The catamaran lay at anchor in the lagoon, but the mast, sail, paddles and steering oar were kept on the beach where the palms began.

When the weather was right they'd provision and equip the dugout. This would be done on the eve of departure, so that they might sail at first light the next day. The early start was vital because Smoke Island had to be reached in daylight.

There was a calao party that night to celebrate the final trials. Nobody quite knew who suggested it and, because there was no particular enthusiasm for it, it got off to a creaking start. But to those who really did want to celebrate—like Ezekiel, Angelique and Nada—and to those who wanted solace like Mecky, Sarah Tripp and Canning, the calao proved to be equally acceptable.

Jos and Canning sat apart from the others. Jos was in no mood for gaiety. For one thing he was in love with Angelique and what had so recently been an enthralling romance, had again become an intolerable burden on his conscience. Sarah Tripp had sown an ugly seed of doubt and he was consumed by it.

He looked at Angelique's lovely face, her red lips and flashing eyes as she talked to Ezekiel, and wondered if she were the sort of woman who would deliberately tell him an untruth? *Of course* she was dark. She'd been born and brought up in the tropics. He looked round in the firelight at the suntanned faces of the others. They were all dark. Of course it was the sun!

Angelique saw him watching her and frowned. What was wrong with Jos? Why'd he been so gloomy and uncommunicative recently? Kind and considerate still, but in some intangible way withdrawn and different. This made her sad. She was very fond of Jos. Because of her loyalty to Kwan she could not admit that she loved the Afrikaner, but she did. Despite his rough exterior and huge frame, Jos was to her a small boy, kind and gentle, and these qualities went to her heart. She knew he couldn't act a part; he was deeply sincere. Because he was unhappy she was too, although she laughed and chatted with the others.

Ezekiel had noticed Jos's moodiness, and he was worried because there was a bond now between him and the Afrikaner.

The calao flowed and tongues loosened. After two cups drunk in gloomy silence, Jos cheered up and threw himself into the spirit of the party.

After all, there *was* something to celebrate! At last the cata-maran was ready! Any day now the weather would be right, and they'd be off to Smoke Island. He was sure that would be the beginning of the end of their exile. But it would be the end of other things too. He looked at Angelique again and felt sad.

All good things had to end some time or other. Rescue meant getting back to Soetwaters and to the children, and picking up the threads of life on the farm. Anyway; Angelique was married and there was nothing he could do about that.

"Hey!" he shouted to Sebastian, flourishing his cup, "Hey, Sebastian! Give me another one, man!"

*   *

Canning began the party in a mood of deep depression. It was two days since he'd been so disgraced over the water supply business, and deposed from the leadership which meant so much to his self-esteem. And the manner of his fall had been so humiliating, especially the way in which Jos had ignored the majority decision of the election and simply taken charge.

For a moment Canning had thought of getting Mecky and Bas-set to attack Lombaard and Wanalu with the fire-axe one night while they slept, but he'd discarded the idea as absurd. In due course they'd all have to account for their actions, and in any case the Afrikaner and the African were so powerful physically that nothing but a gun could be counted on to be effective.

He had a premonition of approaching disaster. Somewhere along the line something would go badly wrong, he was certain. He couldn't believe that the catamaran would reach Smoke Island and bring them help. This thought persisted, and although Sebastian was going with them the apprehension remained. His thoughts turned inwards and he felt a wave of self-pity.

With bleak resignation he went across to Sebastian and had his cup filled. He joined Mecky and they stood in the shadows muttering, sharing their misery, their fears and their hates.

*   *

Sebastian was enjoying the party in his own quiet way, drinking coconut milk now that he knew calao was alcohol. His interest in his fellow beings carried him along happily, and tonight moreover he felt important in a humble self-effacing way, because he'd been chosen to make the catamaran journey. He'd often felt unwanted in the past but life was making up for that now. He had friends here and they'd shown they thought he was a useful member of their community. What was more the Chief had insisted on Sebastian going in the catamaran, which saved a lot of unpleasantness. Fortunately, Sebastian didn't know that Jos and Ezekiel were taking him because they needed his weight in the bow when the catamaran reached to windward. He had a vague feeling of apprehension about the coming journey—he was not a good sailor—but his confidence in Jos and Ezekiel made up for that.

At this moment, however, Sarah Tripp occupied Sebastian's attention to the exclusion of all else. She was on her third cup of calao and her speech was blurred.

"Thing is, Sebastian, it's a jolly good effort your going! I mean, you're not one of those muscle-bound hulks." She looked with disapproval at Jos and Ezekiel. "One of those fleshy morons! I mean you're a gentle person." She raised her cup. "Well done, Sebastian!" Her eyes were bleary.

He was embarrassed. "Really, Sarah! You do say the funniest

things! You know," he whispered into her ear. "You really *should* look after yourself. That calao's strong stuff. I'm *sure* too much of it's bad for you."

"Bad?" She was incredulous. "Did you say, bad?"

He nodded emphatically.

"Rubbish, my dear man. It's very good for me. Makes me forget I hate everybody an' that they hate me." She raised her cup. "Here's to calao!"

"Everybody doesn't hate you, Sarah," his voice was severe.

"*Who* doesn't?"

Sebastian gulped. "I don't for one." He looked round to see if the others were listening. "As a matter of fact, Sarah, I like you very much."

"My dear Sebastian. How kind you are!" She blinked at him happily through her glasses, nodding her head. "You know what, Sebastian, I like *you*! You're different!" She glared at the others. "Yes! different."

"Oh, not really, Sarah."

"Yes . . . you are . . . you know . . . like all those sweet little presents you've given me. The fan-shell necklace . . . an' that lovely big cowrie shell!"

Sebastian looked away. "They were nothing, really. But there's one thing I want you to take, Sarah. To keep for me. Until we get back from Smoke Island. It's this."

He pulled the signet ring from his finger.

"It belonged to my mother. Please take it."

Sarah Tripp gave him a strange look. "Have you no family . . . no relations at all, Sebastian?"

"Only my father. He's very old."

"But of course I'll keep it for you."

Sebastian fancied that in that moment Sarah Tripp's eyes changed. In place of the calculating, cynical look he thought he saw just the smallest trace of happiness.

Sixteen

A NUMBER of important and closely related things happened the next day. They started with the sighting, just before noon, of the smoke spiral from below the horizon. As always, this caused tremendous excitement in the camp.

Then, during the afternoon, the catamaran was provisioned and the compass, paddles, steering oar and sail were put on board. All was now ready for the journey.

Jos and Ezekiel spent some time at Casuarina Point testing the current and checking the direction of the wind, and the weather generally. Everything was right but the wind, which was too much in the east. But they knew that it was usually more southerly in the forenoons and more easterly in the afternoons. On many days it blew from the south until about two o'clock, when it veered to the south-east. It was these conditions they hoped for on the next day when the tide would be rising during the greater part of the forenoon. The sky was solidly overcast with the cloud ceiling lower than usual, but the strongish wind was steady. It was good sailing weather.

That evening Jos announced that they would make their final decision the next day at first light; if conditions were right they'd be away at sunrise.

Conversation round the fire that night was mostly of the coming journey but as always they speculated about the smoke. It was not an occasion for levity, and though they were excited a sober vein ran through their discussions. The others were heartened by the quiet confidence of Ezekiel and Jos.

Even Canning was infected by it; but Mecky, withdrawn,

236

morose, obsessed with his hatred for Jos, hoped only for disaster. The only pleasure he derived from the coming journey was the possibility that it might be the last he would ever see of them.

The night was muggy and after the evening meal they went to Bikini Beach to swim. They left Nada behind because she had a headache, and Basset who was to try for a turtle at The Strand.

Alone in the camp, Nada lay in the hut with her eyes closed, racked by the headache, and longing for the aspirins which she knew she couldn't touch. It had long ago been agreed that those in the first-aid kit were for serious illness only.

The stuffiness in the hut and the throbbing pain in her head became too much for her, so she went outside. For a time she stood uncertainly in the clearing. Should she go over to Bikini Beach to watch the others swim, or to Hook Point where she'd be alone? She was in no mood to talk, so she decided on Hook Point. In the darkness she felt her way through the palms, past the catamaran site until she was clear of the plantation. She walked along its edge skirting the beach.

The overcast sky darkened the night and she walked slowly, unable to see more than a few yards. She had not gone far when she heard something ahead: the sound of scraping in the sand. She wondered if it were a turtle burying its eggs, but then remembered that they never used this end of the beach. She listened, puzzled, before she moved forward. Suddenly, she was almost on top of a kneeling figure. For some reason she thought it was Mecky. She said: "Hallo, Chris, what are you up to?"

"Christ!" The dark shape sprang up and she saw that it was Basset in the same instant that she recognised his voice behind the frightened oath.

The Australian peered into her face in the darkness, breathing hard.

"How long've you been there?" He spoke slowly, menacingly. She experienced a sudden unreasoning fear.

"Not long, Art. Why?" She looked down at his feet and could

just see the hole he'd dug and the heap of sand next to it. Behind him, towards the plantation, there was nothing but the blackness of the night.

For a moment he watched her. Then he spoke again in that strange voice. "Look!" he pointed to the hole. "I'll show you." He knelt down. "Come and have a dekko! You'll be surprised!"

Uncertainly she knelt in the sand. She could see nothing in the hole. She reached out to feel the bottom. Instantly he snarled, "No, you don't, my gal!" In the darkness she felt the sudden, terrifying clutch of his hands at her throat, fingers tightening on her windpipe. Her last terror-stricken recollection was of his ferrety eyes blazing in the dark within a few inches of hers, his warm breath on her face. Then, with daggers of white-hot metal turning in her lungs and jagged lights flashing before her eyes and a bursting and unendurable pain in her chest, she passed out.

*   *

In no time, it seemed, she came to and the pain was with her again, agonising beyond description. She writhed and called out feebly but there was no reply. She felt her throat and retched and after that she lay there sobbing. She wondered for a frightening second if she'd been raped, but reassured herself that she hadn't. Disjointed thoughts came and went. A vision of Basset's eyes just before she lost consciousness; the hole in the sand; fingers at her throat. With new terror she wondered if he were still there. Desperately she sought for a reason why he should have attacked her with such sudden savagery. She gave up and lay still. Later she tried to get up but was still too weak to stand. After another rest she crawled slowly up the beach towards the camp. It was dark. She had no idea what the time was, only that she'd left the hut at about eight o'clock.

Often she stopped and rested, and twice again she retched— the second time all over her skirt. With handfuls of sand she tried to wipe the sickly mess away. She heard Ezekiel calling.

238

She tried to shout "Here!" but it wouldn't come, only a hoarse nothingness. He called again, much nearer this time. She saw a dark shape a few yards away, closer to the water than she was. With an effort she croaked "Zeke!" He stopped and looked about him, and she called again. Soon he was down on his knees beside her.

"My God, Nada, what's wrong! What's happened?"

When she found she couldn't answer she began to cry. Ezekiel picked her up and carried her as if her weight were nothing. She fainted again on the way. Then she was in the hut with Angelique next to her. Jos and Ezekiel were there, too, looking grim in the flickering light of the oil lamp.

They gave her water first and then some calao and it was that which seemed to help most. As the fiery liquid moved down inside her the warmth came back to her body. The agony in her throat and chest eased.

She asked the time, and when they said eleven o'clock she shook her head. It seemed like half an hour since she'd left the camp to go to Hook Point.

"Listen, Nada," Jos's face was grave. "I know it's a helluva'n effort. But tell us! Quickly! What happened?"

In short, wheezy sentences, with prompting when she stopped, she told her story. She'd scarcely got out the words: "And then . . . Art . . . suddenly," she sobbed, ". . . began to throttle me . . ." when Jos said: "Come on, Zeke! Quick man!" His voice was like a lash.

For hours, working separately, they searched the island—but in vain. There was a cold, frenzied anger in their hearts and had they found Basset they would have killed him with their bare hands. But it was impossible to make a thorough search in the dark. At one o'clock in the morning a violent storm broke over the island, the wind increasing to gale force, and they called off the search. They took turns as sentry in the rain-soaked shadows behind the women's hut, in case Basset returned.

The violence of the storm increased. At daybreak the sky was solidly overcast, angry black clouds racing past in close order, the rain coming in gusty squalls and the palm tops whipping and lashing to the scream of the wind. As far as the eye could see the dark water was streaked with spindrift, long foaming lines reaching down to leeward over the racing seas.

The first hours of daylight revealed this desolate storm-ravished scene, and the shattering fact that Basset, the catamaran and Angelique's jewels had disappeared during the night.

✷   ✷

Step by step they reconstructed what had happened. It required no great skill. Angelique identified the hole on the beach towards Hook Point as the spot where she'd buried her jewels. She explained how Basset had advised her to do this and given her the idea of a secret formula. Soon after that she'd gone out one dark night and buried them. No doubt he'd been a hidden observer.

Then Basset, caught in the act of lifting the jewels, had panicked and attacked Nada before wading out to the anchored catamaran. He'd cut the fibre anchor ropes in his haste to get away.

He must have paddled the catamaran out through the break in the reef opposite the anchorage, and then set sail. They remembered with what special interest he'd watched the catamaran trials, and the many questions he'd asked about wind and tides and currents.

"But what's his motive?" asked Sarah Tripp. "How on earth can he expect to get away with it?"

"He's a bloody crook!" Jos's face was grim. "He reckoned on making Smoke Island himself. He'd have said nothing about us once he got there."

"Yes," agreed Canning. "He'd have told some cock-and-bull story. That he was one of two survivors. How they'd built the catamaran and put to sea where his companion was lost overboard. Some such thing."

Jos looked at him under lowering brows and thought; You wouldn't have any difficulty in thinking up a story under any circumstances would you, my friend. But he said: "That's right. And when he got back to civilisation he'd have thousands of pounds of jewellery to start him off."

Ezekiel stroked his beard thoughtfully. "I suppose he reckoned that when we were rescued eventually, he'd have a good start on us."

"Bloody bastard! He half throttles Nada, then he steals the catamaran!" Jos's face was black with anger. "You realise what this means, Zeke?"

"Sure I do."

Mecky began to titter. "I think it's damn' funny! We work like beavers for weeks and weeks building the thing and . . . and then . . ." He was near to hysteria ". . . and then . . . of all people . . . our much despised Australian pinches it! And you two . . ." he pointed an accusing finger at Jos and Ezekiel. "You two muscle-bound morons are left . . ." His laughter got shriller, more uncontrolled; he shook like a leaf. "Are left sucking the hind tit!"

This was too much for Jos. A large bare foot landed a resounding kick on Mecky's backside. "*Voetsek, jou donner!*—Get out, you no good!" he bellowed. All the pent-up rage and frustration of the last twelve hours was in it.

Mecky disappeared at the double. Sarah Tripp beamed with pleasure. "Well done, Jos!" she said. "Couldn't have done it better myself."

Canning cleared his throat, rubbing his hands together. The loss of the catamaran affected him least of all. "Tell me," he asked blandly. "Will Basset—er—make Smoke Island?"

Jos watched him with withering contempt. He looked at the sky and the sea and then at Canning again. "Basset's had it. Might've been okay for the first few hours. When this gale hit him he couldn't've lasted an hour. He was a dirty rat and he got his deserts," he added dryly.

The dark eyes searched the storm-torn horizon. "The catamaran's somewhere down there. Broached to! Waterlogged! Maybe forty miles away now. Before half that distance the seas would've swept him overboard."

"Amen!" said Sebastian.

Jos gave him a hard look. Then he went to Nada.

Seventeen

IT WAS not until the next day that they experienced the full shock of Basset's disappearance. For nearly two months all their hopes had been centred on the catamaran. It had become the symbol of rescue, dominating each waking moment of their lives. Suddenly, on the eve of the vital journey, it had been snatched away and now the ugly implications of its loss were distressingly apparent. But not all of them were shocked: to both Canning and Mecky, although for different reasons, the loss of the catamaran was not serious. Canning, because he'd been dubious from the start about the venture, and Mecky because for him escape from the island would not really be escape at all, but a change from one uncongenial environment to another.

Jos had more or less disappeared since the theft of the catamaran. First, he'd fallen into a mood of black despair and refused to speak to anybody; then he'd gone to the southern end of the island where he spent the greater part of three days at the seabirds' roost. He would come back late in the evenings for a meal, morose and withdrawn. If he were spoken to his replies were monosyllabic. No one, not even Angelique, could break through the hard crust of this uncompromising mood. Then, on the afternoon of the third day he joined the rest of the party at Rescue Beach; he came up to them whistling and announced that the smoke was again showing and that they must start on another catamaran right away.

With shining eyes he stood looking at them, his hands on his hips, the strong face above the black beard burnt the same deep brown as the rest of his body. "Come on," he said in that basso profundo voice, the r's heavily rolled. "Let's get cracking."

"Jesus!" said Mecky, "Not *another* catamaran."

Jos glared at him. "Listen Mecky, cut out that blasphemy unless you want trouble! Who are you to take the Lord's name in vain?"

"That last catamaran took us six weeks." Canning looked at the callouses on his hands and shuddered. The thought of stripping more bark with a pocket knife was a grim one. "Think it's worth going through all that again, Jos? And with one man less?"

"What d'you want to do? Sit on your fat arse all day and do bugger all?"

Canning winced. "Nothing of the sort. But I'm convinced that it's only a matter of time before the island's visited by whoever's responsible for it. Then we'll be rescued without all this . . ." he flourished his hands, "all this back-breaking business . . . building a boat . . . hazards of the journey to an island we can't even see. You know what I mean."

"Who asked you to do any hazardous journey?" Jos's eyes burned into him. "Who told you this island'll be visited? There're no signs that anybody's been here for two or three years. How d'you know it won't be another two or three years?"

"Most unlikely. That's not the way business works, and you may be sure this plantation belongs to business men."

Canning always used the words "business" and "business men" with reverence, as if he were referring to a Higher Power.

"Business my foot!" Jos looked at Ezekiel. "What d'you think, Zeke?"

The black man contemplated the wide expanse of indigo sea reaching to the horizon. His eyes came back over the rows of charging white horses whipped along by the south-east trades, until he was watching the reef where the breakers curled in, wheeling undulations of blue-green water with foaming crests. He nodded. "Better build another catamaran. We can't just

244

sit around." But he thought, What I'm saying's true enough for them, but I could easily sit around and do no more than gather food and live for the day. My people have been doing this for thousands of years. But these whites aren't conditioned to doing nothing . . . it'll sap their morale. They don't understand leisure. It can destroy them.

Mecky interrupted his thoughts. "I'm blowed if I'm going to waste my time messing about with another catamaran." His long nose twitched.

"Listen Mecky," said Jos. "You'll do what you're damn' well told, whether you like it or not! That goes for you too, Canning. Understand?"

Once again the chores were allocated: the collection of food, the weaving of sails, the plaiting of fibre ropes, the stripping of bark from the takamaka branches: to be done by Canning and Mecky, while Jos and Zeke worked alternate shifts on the hull with the fire-axe. These matters having been settled, Jos said to Ezekiel: "Come on, man! Let's go and look for a palm trunk."

Ezekiel's smile emphasized the gap left by the missing tooth. "Okay, Jos!"

They walked off into the plantation.

*   *

Within the hour they were back, having found the palm they wanted. But grave news awaited them. The fire-axe had disappeared. Despite a thorough search there was no trace of it. Jos scoffed at the idea that it couldn't be found but hours later he was forced to accept that it had gone. The fact stunned him.

"Basset must have taken it," said Sarah Tripp.

Mecky was lugubrious. "Of course. It's obvious he took it."

Jos sat on his haunches, running his hands through his sweat-sodden hair. "Bloody bastard!" he growled. "Drowning's too good for him."

He got up and walked off into the plantation, fighting his despair, determined to pray as he'd never prayed before.

Sarah Tripp scratched her ear. "That's put paid to any more boats." She seemed curiously unperturbed.

Sebastian shook his head. "Poor Jos! He's worked so hard. He counted so much on getting to Smoke Island. It must be a terrible blow."

Sebastian wondered why he himself was so little upset. Was it because rescue meant a return to Fenchurch Street, to the dreary round of dealing with the Chief by day and coping with a lonely life in the room off the Finchley Road by night? Or was it because rescue meant he'd never see Sarah Tripp again? One way and another she was beginning to be rather important to him.

*   *

Jos sat under a takamaka tree brooding.

Without the axe they were helpless! They couldn't build a boat, or even a raft! They could do nothing! Even firewood had to be broken by hand. The Lord had enjoined him to build a boat and he'd obeyed. But the catamaran had gone and they had no axe.

He knew why this disaster had been visited upon them. He had departed from the ways of the Lord. He had sinned grievously. There had been no sincerity in his daily prayers. He fell upon his knees and prayed for forgiveness and deliverance. When he'd finished he sang the Thirty-Eighth Psalm: the one his father and grandfather and those before them had sung in times of distress, of drought and pestilence, or defeat by their enemies—particularly their political enemies. Jos knew it as well as he knew the Lord's prayer.

Later, with a sense of humility and the feeling that he'd shed a burden, he began the long walk back to camp. He'd made his peace with God and now he must wait for a sign. He had no doubt it would be given. They would be delivered from their distress.

*   *

From where he was sitting under a palm tree on the edge of the camp, Ezekiel could see the others; they too were sitting about listlessly. It was strange, he thought, how the loss of the fire-axe had affected their lives. A curious lethargy had settled upon them, for there was nothing to do. The food for the day had long since been gathered. It was not even necessary to catch fish because the traps did that now. They were all there except Jos. Ezekiel supposed he was down at the sea-birds' roost. It was unlike him to be idle, and yet what could he do without the axe.

It was comfortable under the palm tree. Ezekiel stretched his legs luxuriously and let his forearms rest at his sides in the cool sand. He had eaten well that forenoon and slept soundly the night before. Now there was nothing to do but wait for the late afternoon when the worst of the sun had gone. He'd go to Bikini Beach then and swim in the lagoon. After that would come the evening meal. Some calao perhaps, and a long talk round the fire; then they would go to their huts.

It was a good life, he reflected. Many people would give much for it.

He half closed his eyes. He was thinking about motivation. The African had slumbered through history . . . the advance of civilisation had passed him by . . . he'd not even thought of the wheel. Ezekiel knew these clichés by heart and he was sick of them. It hadn't been one long slumber. The women had always worked: tilled the fields, reaped and ground the corn, cut the thatching grass, carried the water, collected the firewood. The children had minded the cattle, and the men had built the huts and hunted and fought and got drunk and made love. They'd been an aristocracy. A leisured class. They'd understood leisure just as the European aristocracies had understood it when the serfs toiled in the fields and minded the cattle, and their masters hunted and fought and got drunk and made love.

The African still understood the leisured life and basically that had been his fight against the white man: the struggle to retain it.

Ezekiel conceded that the white man had some special motivation which the African lacked. What was it? Physiological? Environmental? From the beginning a difficult climate in which to subsist? The cheerless inhospitality of the high latitudes? Work or die! The machine age had come first to the white man in the cold regions of Europe.

Now the white man no longer understood leisure. He had a deep-rooted fear of it. Suspected it; equated it with the spectre of unemployment. Leisure was dangerous. *The dignity of labour*!

But in Africa it had been different. Africa with its vast spaces, its plentiful sunlight, its generous earth, its great rivers, its herds of game. Everything had conspired to provide an easy subsistence. Leisure had been possible and practised for thousands of years. The wheel hadn't been discovered because it wasn't necessary.

Ezekiel switched at the flies with the twig of leaves. Life on the island was easy. They subsisted with little effort. Leisure was possible. That was why he was so comfortable under the tree, and that was why he was not much worried about the loss of the fire-axe.

But the others seemed dominated by the desire to get away. Jos for example. He was the most energetic of them all. Yet he was a farmer, the son of generations of farmers. Just as I am the son of generations of farmers, thought Ezekiel.

What's he got that I haven't? Is it that he is white? What makes him the leader of this little community? Why is he always driven by something so that he must be up and doing?

Is it the desire to see his children? The smoke on the horizon?

Ezekiel moved on his buttocks to get more comfortable.

What is it that drives Nkrumah and Kaunda and Nyerere and Banda and me and all the others, he asked himself.

If the African lacks motivation, what motivates us?

Education? Knowledge of the processes of organised society? Communications? Awareness of the world outside and what it is thinking? Long ago thinking and saying that Africans should be fighting for their political rights when Africans . . . because they had no conception of rights outside a tribal society . . . had been doing no such thing, but since it was expected of them, coming at last to do it?

Or was the spur discrimination?

The day to day irritations, frustrations and humiliations of being told that you were inferior and of being treated as inferior?

The spur was a compound of all those things, he supposed, but in his heart he knew that discrimination was its most important element . . . it was more than a spur, it was a goad.

He wiped the pools of sweat from under his eyes and switched at the sand-flies again.

Rescue would come in due course, he had no doubt about that; he would be back among his people, caught up once more in the turbulence of African politics. But there was no worry or urgency about it.

He fell asleep.

*　　　　*

Down at the far end of The Strand, Sarah Tripp and Sebastian were searching in the white sand between the sea and the undergrowth lining the beach. It was here that the turtles buried their eggs.

They'd found some and though it was late afternoon it was still hot and they were perspiring and tired. Sebastian mopped his face with the back of his forearm.

"Phew! Sarah. Hot, isn't it?"

She straightened up, looked at him and nodded.

"Damned hot!" With the edge of her worn skirt she wiped her glasses. "Let's pack up."

He pointed to the eggs in the palm-leaf carrier. "I think so. We've got enough."

Picking up the carrier he offered her his free arm with a shy gesture and they set off along the beach. When they reached the water's edge they formed single file and splashed bare-footed through the shallows: Sebastian tall and gangling, no shirt, patched and tattered shorts, skin stained a deep brown by the sun, blue eyes twinkling behind steel-rimmed glasses, forward jutting beard heightening the effect of the domed head, bald pate shining in the sun.

Sarah, skipping along ahead of him in a shabby skirt and worn brassière, was just as brown. She had an orange tape from a life-jacket tied round her hair and she was whistling. Sebastian's eyes shone. How attractive she has become now that she's happy, he thought. She's quite a different person. And Sarah, who was a different person these days, was thinking how Sebastian had changed. From the pale self-effacing London clerk of the early days in the dinghy, he'd blossomed into a healthy, sunburnt man who was even gay at times. He's come out of himself, she thought. For the first time in his life he's living. If only he could get away from that wretch Canning who paralyses him with fright. She decided to tax Sebastian with this.

She waited for him to come up.

"Sebastian! There's something I must talk to you about."

"What is it, Sarah?"

"It's important." She pointed to the palm trees. "Let's go and sit in the shade."

"Now you mustn't be upset, Sebastian, but I'm coming straight to the point. Why are you so humble and servile with Canning?" She sat bolt upright, her chin in the air, eyes searching him.

He looked embarrassed. "It's . . . it's not servility. . . ."

"Oh, yes it is. You're *terrified* of him. Why? You're a much better man than he is."

"He's managing director of the Company, Sarah. I'm a very junior person. His personal assistant. I . . . I have to be . . . polite."

"Polite—fiddlesticks! You're *abject*! You *grovel*! Do you call doing his washing being polite? It's nauseating! Now come on

Sebastian, be honest. There's more to it . . . much more than you say." She looked at the signet ring she was wearing. "I'm *very* fond of you, Sebastian. You know that. Now tell me the truth."

The shock of learning that Sarah was fond of him was almost too much for Sebastian. It was so long since he'd heard anything like that, he felt a little dazed.

Swallowing, he said: "Sarah, *I* am deeply fond of *you*."

It did her good to hear that and her eyes shone, but she was determined not to be put off. Sebastian needed help and she would see he got it. "All the more reason why you should be truthful, Sebastian. Now come on! What's the trouble?"

There was a pause. He took a deep breath and looked away from her. "It does me no credit, Sarah. You'll be shocked."

"I'm sure I won't. Carry on!"

"It was many years ago. I was married to a fine woman. A wonderful wife. Her name was Mary." He hesitated. "We had a little boy, Timothy. Such a dear little chap." There was a catch in his voice and there were tears in his eyes. A wave of contrition swept her.

"Stop, Sebastian. I shouldn't have asked you. I'm . . . I'm *terribly* sorry."

"No!" He shook his head. "It's all right. I'll tell you. It was a long time ago." His shoulders went up in a despairing shrug. "It may help if I tell you.

"When Timothy was four we went for our first real holiday; to Brighton for two weeks. We had very little money. It was Whitsun. Timothy hadn't seen the sea before. How he loved it! He had a little bucket and spade and he was very proud of them. We were so happy! Then the Chief sent for me. There were some urgent matters to be attended to."

"What! On your holiday?" She was incredulous.

"Only for two days. He said I could extend my leave by two days afterwards "

"How nice of him," she said sarcastically.

"While I was away, on the first day, a terrible thing happened." His eyes were shocked. "Timothy . . . *poor* little Timothy . . .," he put his face in his hands and his voice broke. "They had come up from the beach . . . crossing the road . . . when he was run over by a car. Killed in front of Mary."

Sarah Tripp felt quite sick: all that she could say was, "Oh, how terrible!" but it sounded grotesquely inadequate.

He went on. "The shock did something to her. She was ill for a long time. We had doctors and specialists—psychiatrists, too. She spent nearly two months in a home. Most of the time she didn't recognise me." He sighed. "She was terribly ill. All my savings had gone. I'd used everything in the provident fund; borrowed from the pension fund. I wanted to give her everything of the best. She was in a good private home. Then they said I must take her to a warm place for a holiday. It was late in October, so we went to Cornwall. To a big hotel on the sea front. Mary loved the sound of the waves." Something occurred to him. "She'd have liked it here, you know." He went on. "I'd used up all my leave and had to ask for compassionate leave. The Company was very good. They gave me another week. That was thanks to Mr. Canning."

He looked at her and she saw that his face was taut. "At the end of the week I had to leave Mary in Falmouth and go back to the office. She seemed much better. Three days later she telephoned me and I knew that something was wrong. She was hysterical. Kept saying, 'I *need* you, Sebastian, I *need* you.'

"I told her it would be difficult to get leave again so soon, but that I'd see the Chief at once and phone back.

"The Chief was very busy and he couldn't see me until late in the afternoon. When I explained the position he said I couldn't go the next day because there was a board meeting, but I could the day after."

Sarah Tripp choked with indignation. "Inhuman monster!"

"No!" said Sebastian gently. "That's not fair, Sarah. He'd

been very good to me about leave. In a big organisation you can't always let people go just when they want to."

"Rubbish!" she said firmly. "It wasn't just that you *wanted* to. You *had* to."

"When I phoned Mary that evening she listened to me without saying anything, then . . ." His fingers were clenching and un-clenching and she saw that the flesh over the knuckles was white. "Then I heard her sobbing and after that . . . before I could say anything . . . well, the line went dead."

"Couldn't you get through again?"

"Yes. I did. But it was too late. She'd thrown herself into the street. From the fourth floor. When they picked her up she was . . . dead."

Sarah was appalled. "My poor Sebastian! How ghastly!"

He sighed. "It was a long time ago."

Sarah was silent. Then she said: "I still don't understand why these dreadful tragedies make you so terrified of Canning."

"That came later, Sarah. At the end of the year the auditors found that I'd taken more than £200 of the Company's money." The tone was so matter of fact that she felt sure he didn't appreciate the implications of what he was saying. "You see all my money'd gone. For all the things that were needed to make Mary better. I'd have taken twice that amount if it'd been necessary. I suppose . . . I was a little unbalanced. I intended paying it back."

"Of course," she said.

"When the Chief heard, he took the matter into his own hands. Told the auditors there'd been a mistake. That I'd taken the money with his authority. He wrote out his own cheque then and there for the missing money. Made it payable to me. Told me to bank it and pay it back to the Company the next day. He made me sign a paper in which I acknowledged that I'd misap-propriated the money, and he gave me two years in which to pay him back. He didn't charge me a penny of interest. He's kept me on as his personal assistant ever since."

There was a long silence broken only by the cries of the sea-birds.

"Did he give you back that paper when you'd repaid the money?"

Sebastian shook his head. "No. He still has it. When I asked for it he said he'd better keep it. In my own interests, he said. If there were no record of what had happened, he felt I might be tempted again."

Sarah Tripp shuddered. "My God! What a sadist!"

Sebastian seemed not to hear. "Let me see," he said dreamily. "It's all of eleven years. Yes! Eleven years. I was twenty-eight when Mary and Timothy went."

* *

"I tell you, Zeke. You can't beat Afrikaner cattle as beef producers." Jos sipped the calao.

The African shuffled on his haunches to get nearer the fire and away from the midges.

"Ever tried Aberdeen Angus?"

"*Ja!* Very fine beef producer, but not so resistant to disease."

"Of course my herd aren't any *particular* strain. What you'd call scrub cattle. But they're strong. There's fine grassveld at Gensa."

"Wouldn't it pay you people to improve your herds? Easy now with artificial insemination."

Ezekiel raised his cup with both hands and drank. Drops of calao clung to his beard, glistening in the firelight.

"We can't afford it, Jos. One of these days we'll be able to."

"Yes . . . of course. Not so long ago that my people couldn't afford it. Some still can't."

There was a silence. The others had gone off to their huts; all but Canning and Mecky who sat on the far side of the fire, muttering to each other. Jos was sure that he and Ezekiel were the subject of their conversation.

"How'd you like a nice piece of wildebees steak, Zeke? *Braaied* in a wood fire." Jos's eyes shone. "Hell, man! I can nearly smell it."

Ezekiel nodded. "With good stiff mealie meal . . . real *putu*."

"*Ja!* And meat gravy to dip it in. Plenty of salt."

Ezekiel grunted approval.

Jos went on. "Or a good mealie?"

Ezekiel sighed. "And the smell of African wood burning. The wood here's got a weak smell."

"*Ja*. Musty, hey?"

"Must be the sea or something."

A muscular arm, almost as brown as the coconut shell it was holding, thrust towards the African. "Hey, Zeke! The calao's next to you."

The African reached down for the calao and filled Jos's cup and his own. They looked at each other and raised their cups.

"*Gesondheid*! Zeke! Good health!"

"*Gesondheid, meneer*!"

They tasted the calao. Jos yawned. "Sometimes I get tired of nothing but the noise of the wind and sea. It's okay in the day, but at night . . . well . . . I get fed up with it."

"Me too." Ezekiel's eyes were drowsy. "You can't beat the night noises of the bush. The jackals calling to each other . . ."

"The howl of the hyenas . . ."

"Sometimes at Gensa you can hear the leopards cough."

The African imitated the sound.

Jos laughed, "Then the baboons start growling and screaming because they're frightened."

"The cry of the bush babies . . . d'you remember?"

"Their eyes in the dark . . . like little green lamps . . . so bright."

After a long pause, Ezekiel said: "The bird noises are good too." He wiped his mouth with the back of his hand. "The *kiewietjies* and the *dikkops* . . ."

"Bush partridges calling to each other," Jos half closed his eyes. "Like a squeaky pump."

"That's right."

Jos stretched his arms and yawned again. "You know, Zeke, you're the only man I can talk to around here. Sebastian's okay, but I can't talk to him about these things. He wouldn't understand. As for the others . . ." He looked across at Canning and Mecky, and spat into the fire.

Ezekiel pulled at his beard. "We can talk like this, Jos, because we're both of Africa. We understand her. *We* are Africa, Jos."

The Afrikaner sighed. "*Ja* . . . I suppose so." He seemed lost in thought; then he said: "Come on, man! *Huis toe*! Let's go."

As they moved away Mecky, made reckless by too much calao, said: "Thank God! The hairy ape's off to bed."

This remark, made in a low voice, was not meant to go farther than Canning, but Jos heard it. He turned round slowly and walked back until he stood over Mecky. "Say that again?" His voice was ominous.

Mecky looked at him with undisguised loathing. The calao worked on his hatred for the big man and he was rash: "Oh, for God's sake leave me alone!"

The blasphemy was too much for Jos. With his knee, quite gently, he pushed Mecky off his haunches and onto his back. "If you hadn't been drinking, Mecky, I'd have cracked you!" His dark eyes narrowed until they were slits. "You better look out, man! One of these days you'll get hurt!"

He went, leaving Mecky lying in the sand; a lean humiliated figure burning with an inward fire, the flames licking into his brain.

*   *

Earlier in the evening Angelique had gone to her hut to see Nada. She was worried about the Australian girl: apart from the bruises on her throat, she was still suffering from the shock of Basset's attack.

Before Angelique reached the hut she heard sobbing. Inside,

Nada was sprawled across the bed of coconut leaves, her head on her arms.

Angelique put an arm round her shoulders. "Nada, my little one. What is wrong?"

She repeated the question several times before Nada sat up. In the flickering light Angelique saw the tear-stained face. She took the girl in her arms, cushioning the tousled head on her breasts. "What is it, *ma chérie*?"

"Oh, it's so *hopeless*," sobbed Nada. "This terrible island! We'll never get off it! I know I'll *die* here! First it was Canning . . . then Basset. Something *terrible* will happen . . . I know! I'm being punished!"

In the next ten minutes she poured out her heart and spoke of her remorse because she had treated Iles so badly.

Angelique stroked her hair, holding her tight. "There, my little one. It's your nerves. Of course we'll be rescued. They will come and save us, just as you saved us in the dinghy."

She kissed Nada as if she were a child and let her down onto the palm leaves and lay close beside her. "Now we will sleep. Tomorrow the sun will shine again and you will feel better. Before long we shall have left this island."

Angelique would have been amazed had she known how accurate her prophecy was.

Eighteen

It was hot and sultry with no wind, and under the overcast the beach shimmered in the morning heat. Beyond it the sea reflected the intimidating colour of the sky and the swells were oily undulations of grey, low and uncrested. The shrill cries of the sea-birds were muted as they gathered on the beaches and reefs to watch the weather which held the island in its thrall.

Mecky sat on his haunches near the water's edge, arranging small shells in a pattern. There were four vertical rows in a rectangle and he was worried about their symmetry. So worried that his nerves jangled as he tried to get the lines parallel. He would move one shell to the left, only to find another was now too far to the right. The task was excruciating. At times he held his breath in an agony of indecision, his body trembling. Something in his mind would burst, if he couldn't get the lines straight.

Sometimes he would just sit and glare at the shells while he picked absent-mindedly at a spot on his forehead, or trimmed his short fingernails with his teeth. Then he would go back to his compulsive task.

While he was doing this he was thinking and what had been an untidy mental turmoil earlier in the day slowly resolved itself into a course of action until, as the morning wore on, he knew Jos must die.

Twice now this ape had attacked him, used violence, as if the moral assault of its being were not enough. First the kick on the rump the morning after Basset had disappeared and then, last night, the knee against his chest pushing him onto his back. These humiliations had driven him beyond breaking point.

Jos must die! That night! In the storm which was brewing. The Afrikaner's removal would create a new environment into which a refreshed and cleansed Mecky, his mind at peace, could properly fit. Everything would change. Not only for him but for the others. And since the act of killing Jos would destroy the African, they would be freed of a dual tyranny.

The decision made, his mind at last clear of non-essentials, he stood up and kicked at the pattern of shells, scattering them over the sand. The compelling need to arrange things into neat patterns . . . the other compulsions against which he had for so long and so hopelessly fought . . . would disappear after this thing had been done.

With the back of his hand he wiped the trickle of saliva from his chin, squared his slight shoulders and walked up the beach into the plantation.

* *

There was no moon outside the hut and he worked in darkness. The heat was stifling and there was no movement of air to relieve the heavy atmosphere. Occasionally a distant flash of lightning would momentarily scatter the darkness and thunder would follow, its reverberations amplified by the low clouds as it crossed the sea.

Mecky was on his knees in the far corner of the hut. First he pushed aside the palm leaves, then he scooped away the sand until he felt the hardness of the thing and pulled it out. Wiping it clean, he ran his finger along the blade. It was still razor sharp. Ezekiel and Jos had always insisted on this.

He stood in the hut in the darkness feeling the weight of the axe, wielding blows at imaginary targets. The luminous hands of his watch showed after two o'clock. Jos and the African had gone to their hut at half past ten: they should be sound asleep. He went outside and rehearsed his movements several times until he was satisfied with their speed and accuracy. He knew what to expect in the hut. Canning and Goldsworthy on the left; the

African and Lombaard on the right; the African nearest the entrance. Elation removed the last trace of fear. The excitement of danger! The moment had come! He felt remarkably clear-headed.

He was naked. It had been too hot to wear anything and there was no point in dressing now. The whole thing wouldn't take seventy-five seconds, including the walk to and from the hut. He would strike within fifteen seconds of entering their hut; thirty seconds later he would be back in his own feigning sleep. In the morning, or sooner if the alarm were raised, they'd find the axe next to the African. Wanalu wouldn't know it was there. Not until daylight came and they saw the handle sticking out from the palm leaves where he lay. There'd be blood on the blade.

Grasping the axe in his left hand he stole towards the hut, keeping to the centre of the clearing where there were no dried palm fronds to tread on. A flash of lightning threw the hut ahead into vivid relief and he saw that he was aiming too far to the left, so he altered direction. Near the entrance he heard snoring and stopped, waiting for the lightning. After the flash he moved forward slowly, scarcely daring to breathe. He trod on a twig and the crack, magnified many times by his nerves, made his heart jump. He groped cautiously for the entrance . . . another step forward and he felt the matting wall . . . to the right the opening. The odour of human bodies, of sour sweat, assailed his nostrils. The snoring was loud now . . . two snores . . . a deep extended grunt and a mixture of grunt and whistle. Mecky shivered.

Lightning flooded the scene in the hut, and it was engraved on his mind. There they were as he'd expected: Ezekiel on his side, back to the entrance; Jos beyond him, on his back.

Transferring the axe to his right hand, he took a long step forward, lowering his foot gently until it touched a palm leaf.

Carefully he shifted his weight, raising the axe. Then his left foot went forward, and down painstakingly, until he felt the palm leaves. Again he transferred the weight of his body. Now he was straddling the African. The next step would bring him within twelve inches of Jos's head.

His heart thumped as he tightened his grip on the axe and began the movement of the right foot. Gently, in slow motion, it went out—and down—and took his weight. Distant lightning reflected its thin effulgence in the hut. Jos's head was a little to the right, so Mecky turned slightly in that direction.

Now!

As he started the downward blow, bands of steel clamped around his left leg and he screamed—he felt himself jerked violently backwards. With mad energy he deflected the axe-head towards the hold on his leg. There was a shouted "Christ!" and his leg was released as he was thrown backwards out of the hut. He picked himself up and ran blindly through the clearing towards Second Beach, still holding the axe. Behind him he heard voices. Lightning turned night into day and he heard Ezekiel's shout: "I see him!"

* *

Ezekiel didn't know what woke him. He had felt that someone was standing above him. At first he'd thought it was one of his hut-mates.

Then the lightning came and he saw a man standing over Jos about to strike with an axe. Locking his hands round the nearest leg he pulled the man away. Instantly he felt a heavy blow on his wrists followed by burning pain. With a curse he let go and yelled: "Look out!" as the man fell out of the hut. The others woke and everybody began shouting at once. Ezekiel ran outside and stood there, trying to penetrate the blanket of darkness. But he could see nothing until a sheet of lightning revealed a lean naked figure, running down the path through the plantation to Second Beach. Ezekiel shouted, "I see him! It's Mecky!"

"Who . . . what's going on?" Jos was next to him.

"Mecky! He went for you with the axe! I pulled him away! He's making for Second Beach! I'm going after him!"

Ezekiel ran off into the darkness. Jos shouted. "Look out, Zeke! Don't take chances!" His voice was drowned in a rumble of thunder. The lightning came again. Then the roar of wind and rain as the storm broke.

Jos ran across the clearing to the heap of coconut husks beyond the water gallows. He dug frantically until he found the ammunition clip. Then he remembered he didn't know where the automatic was buried. The clip was useless! He took a heavy stick from the brushwood by the fire and ran into the plantation.

It was raining hard and there was more lightning so that he was never in darkness for long. High above, the palm tops rattled and screamed in the wind and the plantation vibrated with the storm. When he reached Second Beach he stopped and in the intermittent flashes he searched for Ezekiel and Mecky.

It was low water. In the lightning the reef stood out across the lagoon like a break-water; beyond it the sea was torn into a white scurry by the wind, long trailers of foam streaming inshore.

The light went again and there was nothing but the blackness of the night until in another flash, away to the left, he saw Mecky, still holding the axe, splashing through the shallows with Ezekiel following close. Jos hurried off in the darkness towards them. They'd reached the reef now and were moving across it towards the sea. Jos increased his pace. They were a hundred feet ahead and he wanted to get to them before the African closed in on Mecky and the axe.

As he started along the reef, the sharp edges of coral cut his feet, but he scarcely noticed this. The gale was mounting and he leant against the wind, rain streaming down his naked body, blinding his eyes.

A shout, eerie and sudden, came down in the wind. It sounded like Ezekiel's. Night became day again as a blinding flash of lightning flickered across the sky. Jos saw that Ezekiel had caught up with Mecky. They were facing each other, Mecky with his back to the sea, holding the axe with both hands while the African had one hand on it, the other held high, ready to strike. Their backs were arched as they strained. To Jos it looked strangely unreal—a ghostly tableau. But it ended as Ezekiel struck out suddenly with his foot, catching Mecky in the stomach. Mecky let go the axe, his arms went above his head, and his high scream rose above the noise of the storm as he reeled backwards into the sea.

Everything was lost in darkness. Jos hurried on. The sky lit up and he saw that he was near Ezekiel.

"Hey, Zeke!" he shouted. "You okay?"

The gale drowned Jos's voice and the African made no reply. Then they were together, looking out into the blackness over the sea.

"You okay, Zeke?"

"Sure. Mecky's in the sea!" The African had to shout above the wind. He was still holding the axe.

"I know. Saw him go!"

The sea and sky lit up and in that split second they saw Mecky swimming slowly through the wind-lashed water, away from the reef. Beyond him a big sea reared and broke in a frothing jumble. Then darkness swallowed the scene. In the next flash they saw that the wave had almost reached the reef, but there was no sign of Mecky.

They turned their backs to the wind.

"Come on!" shouted Jos. "Let's go!" He took the axe from the African.

Ezekiel began to feel the pain in his wrists, forgotten in the excitement of the chase. With his fingers he explored the deep cuts, felt the spurting blood before it was washed away by the rain. There was a weakness in his knees and he was sleepy. He fought against the drowsiness. He had to keep going.

The lamp was flickering in the hut when they got there. There was no sign of Canning or Sebastian.

Ezekiel held his hands out towards the light. His voice was hoarse. "Hell! Look at this!"

The Afrikaner turned and saw Ezekiel facing the lamp, his hands extended, drenched with blood which was pumping from the wrists. Jos looked at them like a man in a dream. As the African slumped down, the white man walked out into the storm.

*   *

Jos's blind instinct was to escape from the hut, but through the fog of horror in his mind something led him stumbling through the storm to the other hut. In the dim lamplight he saw the women with Canning and Sebastian. They were huddled together on the floor. At the sound of his voice they looked up with taut faces.

"What happened? Did you get him?" they cried.

Jos looked at them blankly. "In our hut! Zeke! Help him!" With the same dazed look on his face he disappeared into the darkness.

The rain beat down and the wind shrieked in the palm tops, tearing at the fronds as he staggered on into the plantation, aimlessly, without direction, trying only to get away, his mind numbed by the shock of what he had seen.

It was not the ghostly black shapes of palm trunks glistening wetly which he saw in the lightning, but the dingy charge-office in the police station at Eerstewaterfontein.

He had come in through the pouring rain, his eyes wild with fear, his old felt hat jammed on his head, water streaming from it, his sodden jacket and trousers clinging to him, boots squelching. He saw the impassive face of the sergeant, eyes mildly curious.

"*N'aand, meneer! Kan ek u hulp?* Evening, sir! May I help you?"

"*Ek is Joshua Lombaard. Waar's my vrou . . . wat't gebeur?* I am Joshua Lombaard. Where's my wife. . . . what's happened?" There was an urgent note of entreaty.

The sergeant's face softened. He came from behind the counter and stood next to the big man. "It's bad news, sir. Very bad," he said gently.

"She's dead, isn't she? Don't beat about the bush! I know she's dead! I knew as soon as they told me to come!"

The sergeant nodded. "Yes, sir."

"My God!" Jos slumped into a chair and buried his face in his hands. "My God!" he said brokenly and his body shook. He steadied himself. "How? Where? Where's she now?"

The sergeant laid his hand on Jos's shoulder. "She was staying with her sister at the small holdings . . ."

Jos interrupted. "I know! But what happened?"

"She went into Johannesburg to shop. She caught the 5.10 p.m. back. There was a power breakdown and it was forty minutes late. When she got here it was nearly dark. The station-master saw her. She must have taken the road through the blue-gum plantation. It's a short cut to her sister's place. Two natives attacked her . . . pulled her into the plantation . . ." The sergeant held out his hands in a hopeless gesture. "She put up a strong fight. We found the evidence."

Jos's eyes were imploring. "They didn't . . . I mean . . .?"

The sergeant looked away and nodded. "Yes . . . afterwards they strangled her with one of her stockings then . . ." he hesitated, looked at Jos and drew his finger slowly across his throat. "With a knife . . ." It was almost a whisper. He'd broken bad news before, but it had never been quite such a shocking tale. It was no use beating about the bush. Better with a man like this to administer the catharsis in one strong dose.

Jos shrunk down in the chair, crushed, defeated. He stared at the sergeant. It was a nightmare and he was confronted by a ghost. "How d'you know . . . that there were two?" It was more of a croak than a voice.

"The footprints . . . fingerprints . . . their hands were covered in . . ." he hesitated ". . . blood. They touched the bluegums.

Don't worry, we'll get them. It was this time yesterday we found her . . . long before the storm began." The sergeant looked out through the open door of the charge-office to the darkness beyond; the rain was pouring down, a shimmering curtain of smoke and silver in the lightning.

"Where . . . where's she now?"

The policeman looked at him with compassion. "Body's in the mortuary at Benoni." He added, "Any children?"

Jos stared at him with glazed eyes. "Two . . . two small ones." With his hands he indicated their size, as if they were fishes. His arms fell slackly against his sides.

The sergeant was right. On the third day the police arrested two young Africans and later the case was heard in the Supreme Court, Johannesburg.

Throughout the trial Jos was in Court. When the death sentence was passed he hurried out to where the Black Maria was waiting to take them back to the Fort. He stood a few feet from it and as they were hustled out from a side entrance to the back of the big van he was near them, an inconsolable grief in his heart, an unquenchable hatred in his eyes.

They held out their hands, wrists together, palms uppermost, for the police escort to examine the handcuffs.

Jos saw the black wrists, the pale skin of the palms, the truncated fingers, the projecting ends of the nails.

Black hands . . . covered with blood!

His mind reeling, he leant against a palm tree, the rain beating against his naked body while the wind clutched and tore at the island.

Nineteen

SOON AFTER daylight the storm had blown itself out. The clouds began to disperse and the sun shone fitfully. At first light Jos went back to the hut to get his shorts and sandals. Sebastian was asleep, but not Canning. He raised himself on one elbow and watched Jos with puzzled, bleary eyes.

"Where've you been?" he croaked.

Without turning his head, Jos said tersely. "Looking for something."

After a quick glance at Ezekiel who was sleeping heavily, bandaged wrists on his chest, Jos started off for Second Beach.

There he took off his shorts and swam over to the reef. He searched its seaward side for Mecky's body but found nothing. Not that he really expected to find anything. The sharks would long ago have dealt with that.

Back on the beach he put on his shorts and went down to the south, away from the camp. He walked slowly because he was tired, his nerves were exhausted. He would have to get this thing out of his system. It was three years now since Anna's death, but still the hatred was in him. He knew it was wrong. All races had their murderers. He couldn't go on holding his personal tragedy against the entire African race.

Black hands had killed Anna, but they'd also saved his life. Three times. They'd got him out of the well when he was a small boy. Ezekiel's hands had pulled him into the dinghy after the crash. Last night Ezekiel's hands had again saved him. As he walked, Jos brooded. It was Ezekiel's support which had helped him run things on the island on a more or less reasonable basis. The African was the only man among the survivors whom he really understood and with whom he could talk reasonably and, what was more, in his own tongue. He was the only man upon whom he could depend absolutely.

Sheepishly Jos had to admit that he liked Ezekiel. He was a man. He was resourceful. He had dignity and courage. Jos worked his hand over his jaw. Ezekiel could fight!

What should he do?

The answer came to him as he neared the sea-birds' roost. He must find Ezekiel and thank him. It was not easy, but it would have to be done.

First he would rest. He stretched himself out under a tree and fell into a deep sleep.

*   *

In the late afternoon he found Ezekiel sitting on the beach near Hook Point, his head on his arms.

From a short distance, Jos called. "Hallo, Zeke! How's it, man?"

Ezekiel looked up and saw a hollow-eyed Jos watching him, his black hair tousled, his beard unkempt.

Ezekiel smiled, holding up his bandaged wrists. "Better. Except for these."

"Anything bad?"

"Angelique thinks a tendon might be cut. In this one." He lifted up his right wrist. "But I'm not too bad. Lost a bit of blood. That's why I passed out." His tone was apologetic. "Where've you been all the time?"

Jos avoided the African's eyes. "Looking for Mecky's body."

"Find it?"

"No. Sharks must've taken him." Jos sat down. With a piece of driftwood he scratched in the sand.

"Zeke!" the gruff voice was hesitant. "Thanks a helluva lot for . . .," he stopped and looked at the African. "Well, you know,

268

man. I mean . . . pulling me out of the water that time after the crash, and . . . for stopping Mecky last night."

"That's nothing. You'd have done the same for me."

Jos nodded. "I would have. But it's not nothing." He patted Ezekiel on the shoulder. "Sorry you had to get hurt."

The African smiled shyly. Jos was not demonstrative. "I'll be okay. Can't help on another catamaran yet."

Jos scratched his hairy chest. "*Ag!* Don't worry. We'll make a start. When you're fit you can help."

For some time they sat in silence looking at the sea.

Jos threw the driftwood away.

"You know something, Zeke?"

"What's that?"

"Basset and Mecky used that deserted hut."

Ezekiel nodded. "I know."

"And they're both dead."

"It was stupid of them, Jos."

"*Ja!* Funny how ignorant these city people can be."

"It is," said Ezekiel with conviction.

*   *

A few days later a start was made on the second catamaran. Jos worked like a man possessed, with Sebastian and Canning helping him. The women collected food in the mornings and made fibre rope in the late afternoons. Ezekiel rested most of the time, Angelique seeing to the dressings on his wrists. The wounds were healing and there were, after all, no cut tendons.

At the end of the fourth day of work when they were sitting about dispiritedly wondering whether to go for a swim, Nada came running into the camp.

"Come quickly! There's a boat! There's a boat!" she screamed and ran back towards the beach.

Like a pack of hounds after a fox, they streamed in her wake . . . laughing and yelling: "Where? Where?"

When she reached the beach she pointed to the south. "There! Look!"

They saw a pirogue with a lateen sail, low in the water, about a mile off the beach. It was heading to the south-west, away from the island. In the sternsheets they saw people. There was a brisk breeze and the pirogue was moving quickly.

Despite the distance, and the wind which was carrying their voices away from the boat, the survivors waved and shouted. Nada raced back to the camp for the two-star-reds, and Jos yelled to the men: "Wood! Quick! Make a fire!"

The sun had almost set and the light was fading.

Nada was soon back. With despair she told them that the two-star-reds had gone. Taken by Basset.

"Forget them," said Jos. "Let's get the fire going."

Ezekiel arrived with embers from the camp and in no time the wood was well alight.

To seaward it was almost dark and they lost sight of the pirogue. But they were certain its occupants must have seen the fire. When the boat was last visible it was less than a mile and a half away.

While they stood round the fire talking excitedly, Jos thought of something. "We must pray," he said in that deep voice; firmly, in a way which they knew meant it was a command.

They knelt in the sand facing the sea and Jos led them in a prayer of passionate entreaty for deliverance.

As they echoed the "Amen," he jumped to his feet.

"Come on!" he said briskly. "More wood! Let's have a helluva big fire!"

They remained at the fire feeding it and keeping a watch to seaward. There was no moon, and over the water nothing but a wall of darkness.

Occasionally they shouted and coo-eed, listening in anxious silence for some answering sound. But none came.

As the night wore on their spirits sagged. In the early hours of morning the lack of sleep began to tell. They took it in turns to

lie down on the sand, close to the smoking fire where the midges
did not worry them.

*   *

Dawn came with tropical suddenness and there, less than a mile
away, their brown sails spread, two pirogues were heading in
towards the island.

Jos and Sebastian were on watch and they shouted excitedly.
At once the survivors were talking, pointing, laughing, dancing—
thumping each other in their wild excitement.

"*Never*," squeaked Sarah Tripp with tears in her eyes, "have I
seen grown-up people behave so idiotically!"

But Jos was taking no chances. "Come on!" he roared. "Green
leaves for the fire! We want smoke now, not flames!"

With wild energy they fed the fire, piling on leafy green branches
torn from the undergrowth. Billows of white smoke curled into the
morning air.

The pirogues drew closer. The survivors ran down The Strand,
waving and shouting as the boats made for the coral jetty.

The pirogues closed the beach and their sails were lowered.
There were three people in one and four in the other. With long
bamboos the crews poled the boats in through the shallows, too
busy to return the survivors' excited signals.

Just short of the jetty the pirogues anchored and the crews
came ashore, wading through the shallow water behind a gnarled
old man who seemed to be their leader. After him came a heavily
built man of middle age. The rest were young, and one was a boy.
Angelique saw that they were Creole islanders and her eyes were
moist with tears because it seemed to her, watching them, that
she was at last coming home.

The leader clambered onto the jetty and Jos shook him warmly
by the hand. The old man's mouth folded in a toothless grin and
he babbled away in a language Jos couldn't understand. None
of the rescuers could speak English, but Angelique understood

their Creole patois. Once they'd reached the beach she acted as interpreter.

Speaking the curious island French, her calmness and serenity deserted her. She became voluble, gesticulating with her hands, her eyes flashing. In this animated state she was to Jos more beautiful than ever. He sighed.

She explained to the old man, whose name was Emile, how three months ago they had crashed into the sea in an aircraft bound from Mauritius to Perth, and how after eleven days in the dinghy they'd drifted ashore on the island. She told him how they had collected food; of the catamaran they'd built; how Basset had stolen it; of Mecky's mad attack on Jos, and his disappearance afterwards during the storm. She told them, too, of the smoke they had sighted and of their plans to reach it.

Her story was often interrupted by Emile's questions, and by the islanders' exclamations of surprise.

Canning fidgeted impatiently, his jowls working. "What's all this talking about, Angelique? Haven't you arranged for them to get us help? Explain that we'll pay well."

Angelique frowned. "We have not discussed that yet. I have been telling him how we came here. They are very interested."

The old man explained that he and his men were from a neighbouring group of islands—Egmont Islands—about twenty-five miles away. The island the survivors were on was Eagle Island. It had been abandoned in 1935 and was on rare occasions inspected by employees of the company which held the island concessions. The old huts they'd found in the camp had been built three years before by islanders who'd been marooned there after a cyclone had destroyed their boats. The island below the horizon from which the smoke had come, was one of a small group called the Three Brothers. They were uninhabited, but islanders from adjoining atolls visited them occasionally to collect sea-birds' eggs. The smoke was from fires lit by these people.

The island they'd first sighted from the dinghy was one of the Egmont Islands, probably Ile Lubine, and the island between that and Eagle Island was Danger Island. It, too, was uninhabited.

All these islands, he explained, were on the great Chagos Bank, in the Chagos Archipelago.

When Nada heard this she cried: "*Of course!* How *stupid* of me to forget! I've seen that name on the charts."

The old man told them that the currents and tides between the islands were treacherous. Without local knowledge, journeys by small boats were dangerous.

Angelique translated for the survivors. When she'd finished Jos suggested that they should all return to camp for breakfast. The old man consulted his companions and eventually after they had agreed to leave one of the men with the pirogues, they made for the camp.

* *

The fire was lit and the women prepared a meal of fish and birds' eggs, while the men showed the islanders the huts, the water catchment, the gallows with its life-jackets and their few other possessions: notably the fire-axe, the trestles where the hull of the new catamaran was taking shape, and the remains of the emergency and first-aid kits. It occurred to Jos that there wasn't really very much to show, although their belongings had seemed adequate enough these last months.

This conducted tour was done by signs and gestures because Angelique was too busy cooking to act as interpreter. When the meal was ready they breakfasted together, Angelique and Emile keeping up a rapid conversation. At times she'd stop to translate.

She held up her hand. "Listen! Emile says they can take three of us in one pirogue and two in the other. They already have many birds' eggs and fish they must take back."

Canning was alarmed. "But there are *seven* of us! Tell them to throw away the eggs and fish. We'll pay for them."

"He says," explained Angelique, "that in a few days, if

the winds are still right, a pirogue can come back to take off the other two. But he cannot possibly take more than five when they leave. Also he will not throw away the eggs and the fish. He does not understand such a suggestion."

"That's okay," said Jos. "What say, Zeke?"

"Sure. Five on the first trip, two on the second."

Jos looked at Angelique. "Ask him why they came here."

She spoke to Emile.

"It seems," she said, "they came for fresh water. They saw our fire last night, but it was too late to land. They spent the night fishing farther out and came back at daylight."

Canning stood up, the horn-rimmed glasses low on his bulbous nose. He peered over the rims.

"Ask him," he said importantly, indicating the old man with a podgy thumb, "what communication his island has with the outside world?"

Angelique translated. The old man was voluble again, the information exploding out of him.

"He says that soon a schooner will sail from Egmont Islands to Diego Garcia. It is about sixty miles distant. We can go in the schooner to Diego Garcia. Some days later a steamer will leave there for Mauritius."

At this news the survivors could scarcely contain their delight.

"Tell him," said Canning blandly, "that *I* am very pleased with him, and that I *personally* shall see to it that he and his men are *handsomely* rewarded." After a short pause he added, "perhaps you'd better explain that I'm an important man in the City."

"What city?" asked Sarah Tripp icily.

Canning frowned. "London! London, of course!"

This was too much for Jos. "Forget it, Angelique," he said gruffly. "Ask what time we sail?"

The old man looked at the sea and sky before he spoke.

"He would like to go soon because the wind is more in the east than the south. That is good for the journey."

"Tell him we're ready any time he is." Jos looked round the camp. "There's nothing to take except water and a little food."

After further discussion with his men, Emile announced that they would leave in an hour's time.

*　　　*

It was while Emile and the islanders were filling their water bags from the well-stocked catchment that Angelique, prompted by the others, asked the old man where he would have got fresh water if the catchment had not been there.

He beckoned to them to follow, took the path through the plantation towards Rescue Beach and brought them at last to the coral cairn.

They gathered round and the old man talked away to Angelique, very emphatic about what he was saying.

She spoke to the others. "There is a well under this cairn which used to supply the small settlement here in the old days. The water is a little brackish, he says, but quite good enough."

They started back to the camp, Angelique and the old man talking incessantly. He was obviously delighted with the important role he was playing.

"He says," she flung back over her shoulder, "that when they saw our fire last night they thought we were islanders collecting eggs. They would not have come back this morning, but for the water.

"He says, also, that we must take water, coconuts and fishes with us in the pirogues. Enough for several days, because although he hopes to make the passage to Egmont Islands in under twenty-four hours, he cannot be sure. If the winds are wrong it may take several days."

"I'd like to get this quite straight," said Canning looking apprehensive. "Are we doing the right thing? Ask him if we're not taking unnecessary risks by making this journey in his boats?"

Angelique spoke to the old man. Then she translated.

"He says they have done these journeys many times and they

are still alive. Also, that you *are* taking risks because people who use small boats against the sea are *always* taking risks. He says, do you not know the fisherman's prayer? He told it to me. It is very beautiful:

> '*O God, be good to me,*
> *Thy sea is so wide and*
> *my ship is so small*'."

Canning was more interested in ensuring that undue risks were not taken now that rescue was at hand, than in the beauty of prayer. Fortunately, however, the weather was fine and he realised that the important thing was to get off the island: the sooner the better. But there was a nagging problem in the front of his mind and he realised he must deal with it soon. An opportunity came just before they reached the camp. Angelique and Emile were in the lead with Ezekiel, talking to Nada; then came Sebastian and Sarah Tripp with two islanders; Canning and Jos and the rest of the islanders brought up the rear.

Canning felt he could rely on Sarah because his plan would be in her interests. Sebastian, of course, would have to support him. He hurried and caught up with them.

"Sarah! Sebastian! Just a moment! There's an important matter we must settle." He spoke urgently. They stopped.

Canning looked back. "Let's wait for Jos. He must be in on this." He was a bit dubious about Jos because although the Afrikaner would benefit from the proposition he was quite unpredictable.

Jos came up and joined them. Canning spoke guardedly. "Jos! There's something we want to discuss with you."

"Yes. What's it?"

"Shouldn't we settle this question of who remains behind before we get back to the camp? I've given the problem quite a bit of thought. You see it may be some days . . . weather and that sort of thing . . . before a boat comes back."

"So . . .?"

"Well! The two left behind should be a resourceful couple with . . . er . . . shall we say . . . plenty in common. You know, congenial to each other."

"I thought we *all* had rather a lot in common after these last three months." Sarah Tripp's eyebrows were raised.

Jos was becoming impatient. "Come **on**, Canning! We haven't got all day."

"Well, the point is . . ." Canning's voice was at its blandest. "I thought that we . . . *white* survivors should go today, and that the two *non-whites*—Ezekiel and Angelique—should wait here for the second trip."

Jos was seized by a strong desire to wring Canning's neck, but the day was too important for that. They'd been found: they were at the beginning of their journey home. He wasn't going to spoil it all at this stage.

Instead he said in his deep guttural voice. "That'll be the day, *mister* bloody Canning. You're not fit to lick Ezekiel's . . ." he paused, discarding the word he'd all but used, ". . . . boots. And as for Angelique . . . mention her name again and I'll break your *bloody* neck."

If it were possible to go white under dark sunburn, Canning would have done so. He'd never dreamt of this angry reaction to what he considered a perfectly reasonable proposal.

As he moved off along the path Jos said with absolute finality: "The three women'll go off today with two men." Canning was hurrying along behind, arms flailing, desperately worried now that his plans looked like miscarrying. "But—Jos—*please*! How'll we decide *which* two men stay?"

"Wait and see!" Jos strode grimly ahead.

Canning's heart started to beat so fast and he felt such a surge of panic, that he slackened his pace. He knew from articles in *The Director* that he was very much in the coronary age zone. It was important to avoid over-strain, physical or emotional.

When they got back to the camp, Jos called them together. "You know that the pirogues can take off five of us today. This means two must wait until a pirogue comes back. That may be a few days. We'll decide which two men remain behind by drawing lots. Okay?"

There was no answer, but out of the corner of his eye he saw Canning wilt.

Jos picked up four twigs. With his back to the others he shortened two of them, and then held all four in his clenched fist with only their tops showing.

"There's four twigs here," he said. "Two short and two long. Those who draw the short ones stay behind. Okay?"

"Who has first turn?" Canning's voice trembled.

Jos gave him a steely stare. "You . . . if you like."

Canning concentrated on the twigs as if under a hypnotic spell. Several times he reached forward to take one, then withdrew, his hand fluttering indecisively towards another. At last he made up his mind and chose one. He looked at it fearfully. "Is it long or short?" It was a hoarse whisper.

Jos shook his head. "I don't know. Wait till we've all chosen. Then you'll see."

Sebastian drew next; then Ezekiel. Jos had to take the last twig.

They compared them and there was a low moan from Canning when it was found that he and Ezekiel had the short ones.

He looked at the African, frightened, appalled. He'd be left alone on the island for days . . . perhaps for years if a disaster overtook the pirogues . . . with this black man whom he loathed and feared. He couldn't, he wouldn't face it! Not at his age! It wasn't fair! It was un-British! His mind worked quickly, and soon he saw the solution. He'd wait until they got to the jetty. There wouldn't be time for argument there.

The camp became a scene of bustling activity as those who were to go set about collecting their few bits and pieces.

They each took a life-jacket from the water gallows. Two spare ones—Mecky's and the dead Italian's—were filled to provide extra drinking water in the pirogues. Coconuts were put in carriers, and fish from the traps were threaded onto the spikes of palm leaves. The fire-axe and the emergency and first-aid kits were left for those who were to remain.

They took a last look round the camp, perfunctory and unsentimental, for those who were going were too excited to feel any emotion or regret at leaving. When they reached the jetty they waded out to the pirogues and embarked with the help of the islanders. Angelique, Nada and Jos got into Emile's pirogue which had the smaller crew. Sebastian and Sarah Tripp went to the other one. Sarah had been helped on board by Sebastian when Canning, knee-deep in water next to the boat, touched Sebastian's shoulder. "Sebastian," he said in a you'll-do-as-I-say voice. "I want you to *volunteer* to take my place on the island so that I can go off today. I shall see that there's no delay in sending a boat back for you and Ezekiel." He looked over to Emile's pirogue where Ezekiel, up to the waist in water, was talking to Jos.

"It's important," said Canning, "that someone with my authority should get to Egmont Islands as soon as possible, to ensure that we are returned to Mauritius with the utmost despatch. I do it in the interests of all," he added with a sacrificial air.

"Very well, sir." Submissively Sebastian shrugged his thin shoulders and took off the life-jacket. "You'll need this. You've left yours in the camp."

Sarah Tripp's voice was cold and incisive. "Sebastian Goldsworthy! You'll do no such thing! I've never *heard* such a suggestion. You drew lots and you'll abide by them." She looked at Canning with such loathing and contempt that he blanched. "As for you . . . you *eel*—you vile creature—how can you *sink* to such foul depths—you—you . . ." she spluttered to a stop, lost for words.

Canning's hand went up in an imperious gesture. "Stop that,

woman!" He glared at Sebastian. "Now, come on! Don't let's waste time, Sebastian! Let me have that life-jacket." He lifted a foot over the gunwale and clambered in. Sebastian gave him the life-jacket.

Sarah Tripp stood up in the boat. "Sebastian!" she shrieked. "For heaven's sake show some guts! Don't grovel to this *worm*! Be a man!"

Sebastian looked at her with imploring eyes. "It's all right, Sarah! I'll be joining you in a day or so."

Canning beamed approval. "That's right, Sebastian. I knew you'd understand." His voice dropped to a whisper. "Wouldn't sound too good in the City if they heard you'd left your old boss on an island alone with a *nigger*, would it?"

Sarah was standing in the sternsheets. "Ezekiel!" she shrilled. "Come here!" She climbed out of the pirogue and stood in the shallow water next to Sebastian, untying the tapes on her life-jacket.

Ezekiel waded across. "What's the trouble." He saw with surprise that Canning was in the pirogue instead of Sarah Tripp and Sebastian.

"This creature!" she said pointing at Canning, "has *ordered* Sebastian to remain behind so that dear *Mister* Canning can go off now. Sebastian, of course," she looked at him with disapproval, "has meekly obeyed. So," she lugged the life-jacket over her head and passed it to Ezekiel, "*you* are to go in my place and *I* shall stay here with Sebastian and tell him what a spineless creature he is." She looked at Sebastian affectionately. Then she turned back to Ezekiel. "You, on the other hand, can keep a close eye on this nasty piece of work!" She jerked a contemptuous thumb in the direction of Canning, who blandly ignored her.

Ezekiel argued with Sarah but she would have none of it, so he went over to Jos and explained what had happened. Jos's first instinct was to throw Canning out of the boat, but then Sarah came across and hissed in his ear, "*You fools! I want* to stay with

Sebastian! It suits us both very well. We're . . ." She hesitated for a moment, looking at the signet ring she was wearing, "We're *actually* sort of engaged."

Jos's eyes twinkled. "Okay, Sarah. We'll send a boat for you soon." They shook hands, and she and Sebastian waded ashore.

In the pirogues the anchor stones were hauled aboard and the crews poled their craft out through the shallows.

Clear of the lee of the island the sails were hoisted and with main sheets hauled taut the pirogues came close to the wind, heading out on a long reach to windward.

Looking back at the shore the survivors saw Sarah Tripp and Sebastian on the end of the coral jetty, arms linked, waving.

The wind freshened and the pirogues slapped into the head sea, sluicing showers of spray over their crouching occupants.

Twenty

AFTER AN unpleasant journey, with much seasickness, they arrived at Egmont Islands late the next day. They found a small settlement with an overseer and his wife, and they were treated with every kindness. The women were put in the overseer's cottage and the men in a hut nearby. The language of the islanders was the patois which their rescuers had spoken.

There were only a few people in the settlement, but somehow they managed to find enough odds and ends of clothing for the rescued who shed most of their rags. Wearing old cotton print frocks and sandals or shoes the women, at least, began to look more civilised.

Jos's size was a problem: they found a shirt which, though skin-tight and too hard stretched for buttoning, at least covered his shoulders and most of his chest. But trousers were impossible, so he wore a piece of printed cloth folded round his body from the waist down, a sort of half toga, and an imposing figure he made. With scissors and a razor the men shaved their beards and looked strangely unfamiliar to their companions. Canning emerged with a new blandness; Ezekiel seemed to shed ten years of his age. Jos, too, looked younger; the firm mouth and chin under the small black moustache, and the thick dark hair still long and roughly trimmed, proclaimed a man of character. Angelique was secretly very proud of him, although still sad and puzzled by his behaviour. For the last ten days on the island he had been avoiding her.

The schooner in which they were to travel lay at anchor in the lagoon. It was due to leave in two days but the overseer decided that rather than send a pirogue back to Eagle Island for Sarah Tripp and Sebastian, the schooner should pick them up en route to Diego Garcia. This would add the best part of a day to the journey.

The overseer had a radio transmitter and was in touch with the company's office in Diego Garcia. He had reported the arrival of the survivors and his intention to transfer them there for onward passage to Mauritius.

The effect upon the survivors of their rescue was difficult to assess. The Egmont Islands were too like Eagle Island to make any great impact, and although they found it curious to be using familiar domestic objects again, like cutlery and crockery, and to see books and lamps and all the other ordinary things that they had not seen for so long, they were conscious only of general feelings of relief and expectancy. The great moment of excitement, of psychological shock, had been the first sighting of the pirogue. Everything that had happened since had had a curious inevitability about it. Indeed, they were already chafing at the delay in getting to Mauritius.

It was pleasant, of course, to see other people but as the islanders couldn't speak English, only Angelique talked to them. For the smokers, the supply of cigarettes and tobacco was a major event.

Perhaps the things they now enjoyed most were the feel and scent of real soap and the news broadcasts from Mauritius. On the second day they heard the first announcement that: "Seven survivors from the T.O.A.L. aircraft which came down in the sea between Mauritius and Cocos—Keeling in September have been found on an uninhabited island in the Chagos Archipelago. They have been taken to Egmont Islands en route to Diego Garcia and Mauritius. They are said to be in good physical condition, but two men who reached the island with them originally are reported missing, presumed dead."

"How can they know so soon?" Ezekiel frowned.

"Radio!" Angelique pointed at the overseer. "He told Diego Garcia and they passed the news to Mauritius. It will be all over the world now." Her eyes shone.

*   *

In due course they boarded the schooner and made a quick passage under sail to Eagle Island. There they anchored off The Strand and sent a small boat in to the jetty. Jos and his companions stood on deck and looked across the water to the low flat island, covered with palms and indigenous trees, which for three long months had been their home.

But there were few nostalgic thoughts. They might come later. Now that they'd been rescued they had an overwhelming desire to get home.

They watched the small boat make the journey inshore, its crew poling slowly across the blue water until it reached the shallows. Sarah Tripp and Sebastian were nowhere to be seen, so the captain of the schooner produced an old bellows fog-horn and honked it. A few moments later the missing couple appeared on the beach near Hook Point and, waving furiously, ran towards the boat. They were soon on board, a little coy and embarrassed, but delighted to be with their companions again and full of praise for their smart appearance.

Course was set for Diego Garcia, almost a hundred miles away, and a day later they reached the island having used the auxiliary engine most of the time. It was a vast horseshoe of land, with three islands at its open end, enclosing a superb lagoon about twelve miles long. It had, they were told, a population of some six hundred people. Once again they were treated with much kindness and were put up in the manager's house and adjoining cottages. There were stores where they were able to clothe themselves more effectively, the manager having generously given them credit. Slowly but surely they were acclimatising themselves to normal living. At first the change in diet, particularly the increased intake of fats, upset them but they soon became adjusted.

In Diego Garcia they found awaiting them a peremptory message from Mauritius, requesting full particulars of all survivors and of the two men reported missing. This information was sent, but it was their first reminder that they were again subject to the machinery of organised society.

The days were spent talking, exploring the island, sleeping and eating until at last, four days after their arrival, a small steamer anchored off East Point. The next day they went off to it in a launch and towards evening they sailed for Mauritius. For the first time they felt that they were really homeward bound.

*   *

Jos had had a frustrating time since their rescue. Neither on Egmont Islands nor on Diego Garcia, nor now on the steamer, had he been able to see Angelique alone for more than a few minutes. The need to do so had become pressing. He'd thought a lot about her lately and realised that he'd treated her very badly.

She'd explained to him who her parents were and then, just because of a cruel remark by Sarah Tripp—who couldn't possibly know—he'd disbelieved Angelique and avoided her. He'd seen that she was hurt. He was furious with himself! Kind gentle Angelique who'd done so much for him and for all of them. Angelique who'd never done or said anything which entitled him to think that she hadn't told the truth.

After much brooding it had dawned on him that Sarah Tripp was jealous. That was it! Jealous because Angelique was so beautiful. That explained why she'd tried to put him off by sneering at the Mauritian and saying she was coloured!

Consumed by the desire to get Angelique alone and to make amends for his inattention—though quite how, he didn't really know—Jos on this second night in the steamer was searching everywhere for her. She shared a cabin with Nada and Sarah, but his knock on the door produced only Nada who smiled kindly. "No. She's not here, Jos."

"Man, I wonder where she is?"

"Try the lounge," suggested Nada.

Running his hands through his hair in a gesture of desperation, he tightened the toga round his waist and continued the search.

It was nine o'clock and most of the passengers had gone to the lounge after dinner or were on deck enjoying the comparative cool of evening.

But Angelique was not in the lounge or on deck. It was maddening how she could disappear in such a small ship.

It was while he was standing on the boat deck near the bridge that he heard voices. They were speaking French. The man said something and then Jos heard the delicious tinkle of Angelique's laughter. It came from the bridge. He moved forward until he could see them in the moonlight. They were leaning over the bridge rail not twenty feet away, looking towards the stern. With a sudden flush of jealousy he saw that the man was the Captain. Jos had noticed that the Captain had paid much attention to Angelique from the moment they came on board. In the saloon, for example, he had insisted that she sit on his right. Jos was profoundly suspicious of all foreigners; especially Frenchmen, whom he regarded as having only one idea about women. He stood in the shadows glowering, listening to the conversation which was punctuated with laughter and many chuckles, and he cursed his inability to speak French.

"*Mais pourquoi, mon Capitaine?*"

"*Parce que vous êtes très belle, Madame.*"

"*Non, non!*" she protested, holding up her hands in mock disapproval, her eyes shining with pleasure at the compliment.

Jos decided that it was time to act. He cleared his throat and strode out of the shadows. But he tripped over a ringbolt and fell heavily against the bridge ladder below them. From above came a surprised, "*Mon Dieu! Q'est que c'est que ça?*" Struggling to retie the toga which had unfurled in the fall, he got to his feet. He cursed the toga. Neither on Diego Garcia nor in the steamer had he been able to find a pair of trousers large enough. A member of the crew who had a sewing machine was now making him a pair of outsize shorts, but these were not yet ready.

"Jos!" cried Angelique, "Are you hurt?"

"Yes," he growled, "Come and help me. You—not *him*," he added pointedly.

Angelique bade the astonished Captain good night and hurried down to Jos where he stood next to a life-boat, rubbing his thigh and looking angry.

"Now," she said. "What have you done to yourself?"

Without a word he took her arm and they walked aft along the boat-deck to the rail behind the wireless cabin.

It was the only secluded spot in the ship, and on an early reconnaissance he'd marked it down for an occasion such as this.

They leant on the rail and looked over the stern down the luminous path of the moon. From the engine-room skylights behind them came the mechanical clanking of the engine; that, and the swish of water down the side, were the only sounds to break the silence of the night.

The rail vibrated beneath them and wafts of funnel smoke, warm and acrid, drifted down. The ship rolled to a gentle swell, and the arch of the sky was bright with stars.

"You are hurt, Jos?" She looked at him anxiously.

"No," he said.

"And so why you disturb my very nice conversations with the *Capitaine*?"

"To hell with the Captain!"

"Why? What is wrong?"

"He's a Frenchman!" He said it with great authority as if it were an all-embracing explanation.

"Of course! But what difference does *this* make? The French are very nice people. I am half French."

He realised he'd said the wrong thing. Their shoulders touched. She turned to him. In the moonlight he could see her face. She was very beautiful and she smelt of jasmine. His blood raced.

"I'm fed up, Angelique."

"Why, Jos? What is wrong?"

"I haven't been able to see you alone for—for—well since they found us on Eagle Island."

"Why should you wish to see me alone? The last ten days on the island you did not wish to see me?"

This was too much for Jos. He took her in his arms and kissed her passionately. "Because," he said, still holding her tightly, "I love you! *And* you know it!"

She made no attempt to free herself. Instead she twined her arms round his neck and pressed her lips to his. He felt the warm round of her breasts through his thin shirt.

"And, I Jos—I love you. But we must forget this. I am nearly home and I have a good husband waiting for me."

Jos's arms tightened. "You've no children, Angelique. Leave him. Marry me."

She tried to push him away, but he wouldn't let her go.

"One cannot do such things, Jos. Douglas loves me—and I him." Her eyes were misty.

"How can you love him *and* me?"

"Don't ask me, Jos. This is very difficult to explain."

A shrill, familiar voice interrupted them. "*There* you are!" Sarah Tripp strode out of the darkness, Sebastian behind her. "We've been looking for you *everywhere*."

"Hell!" muttered Jos.

*   *

Nada had staggering news. There'd been other survivors from the crash. The Chief Officer remembered reading about it at the time. No! Unfortunately he could not recall the details. One dinghy had been found, of that he was certain. He thought it had been damaged. There had been only a few people in it, but they were picked up by a steamer a few days after the air-craft came down.

Nada's eyes were bright. "Were they passengers or crew? Men or women?"

He shrugged his shoulders, holding out his hands. "Both perhaps? It was three months ago. How can I remember?"

"Is there anybody else on board who would know?"

He smiled sympathetically. "You can try. Ask anyone you wish. I will ask also."

But no one could remember and Nada was left to wonder and to worry and to pray that by some miracle Iles was safe. Then she had another thought: three months was a long time and in the excitement of rescue and the return to Australia he might well have married. He'd always said that if he couldn't marry her he'd remain a bachelor, but she'd never given him any encourage-ment. Anyway, he didn't even know she was alive. She and the others must long ago have been presumed dead. She stifled the thought. Here she was sick with worry because Iles might have married. She should be hoping and praying that he was alive.

*　　　*

During the short voyage to Mauritius, Canning tried hard to be friendly and polite to his companions but he made little progress and, apart from Sebastian, none cared to be in his company a moment longer than necessary.

It was evident he'd impressed the Captain with his importance, for that good man treated him with much respect. Canning sent many wireless messages and these brought lengthy replies which he could be seen reading wherever there was an audience. Once or twice they were delivered to him in the saloon and then, smilingly apologetic, he would read them with profound pre-occupation.

Ezekiel had retired into his shell. He spent much time seated in a canvas chair on deck making notes. He'd cultivated the wireless operator who tuned into English language broadcasts, so that Ezekiel could listen to the world news. He did this avidly showing particular interest in what was going on at U.N.O., where the Afro-Asian bloc was in full cry after the remnants of colonialism, real and imaginary.

In the evenings Ezekiel would relax and talk and laugh with Jos or Nada. When she chided him for spending so much time listening to the news and writing, he smiled apologetically: "I'm trying to re-orientate myself. Rediscover my cause." He looked worried. "I've forgotten how to hate."

Nada frowned. "I don't know *what* you're talking about, Zeke."

"I suppose it'll come back," he said cheerfully.

*　　　　*

They arrived at Port Louis at nine in the morning. Long before that they had been up on deck watching the distant mountain peaks: Peter Both—its naked sides reaching up to a pinnacle surmounted by a ball of stone—and Le Pouce near it, looking like a grotesquely swollen thumb. There had been heavy rain and the tall flanks of basalt rock gleamed with reflected sunlight.

As they neared the shore they saw the clusters of buildings about Port Louis, the slopes of the mountains rising steep and green behind the town.

A pilot boat came out and the engines were stopped. The boat came alongside and the medical officer of health and the pilot boarded. Soon they felt the throb of the engines again and the ship started down past Fort George to the inner harbour. The ships alongside and in the roadstead sounded their sirens, and the survivors saw that many of them were flying gay streamers of bunting. With almost embarrassed surprise they realised that the sirens and flags were for their benefit.

As they approached the wharf they saw that it was crowded with people waving gaily. The strains of a brass band floated across the water. They were soon alongside and customs and immigration officials, port authorities and agents swarmed up the gangway. Among them was the T.O.A.L. representative who introduced himself as Jack Lund. Nada didn't know him. He'd only recently been transferred from Bombay.

The formalities seemed to take a long time, but at last they were completed and with Canning in the lead, followed by Jos wearing his new shorts, the survivors and other passengers started down the gangway.

The brass band broke into "See the conquering hero come." A ripple of cheering went up from the crowd and cut off suddenly as if they were not quite sure whether this was the right moment for it. Photographers darted about and TV and ciné cameras, flown across from South Africa for this morsel of world news, whirred busily.

At the foot of the gangway a master of ceremonies sorted out the survivors handing them over to a municipal official who presented them to the Mayor, a representative of the Governor, the Chief of Police and other dignitaries including an Anglican parson and a Roman Catholic priest.

The Mayor launched into a speech of welcome in which, inevitably, he referred to their experiences as: "An unparalleled feat of survival which will take its place among the great ocean epics, including that of Captain Foster and the crew of the *Trevessa* who, in 1923, reached this island after a voyage in open boats of more than 1,700 miles!"

When the cheering and clapping had subsided there was an awkward pause. Then Canning stepped forward and bowed graciously to the Mayor.

Wearing the white linen coat and trousers he'd acquired on Diego Garcia, freshly shaved, his white hair trimmed below the bald pate, he was a benevolent figure; considerably fitter, less podgy and more bronzed than when he'd stepped into the aircraft three months earlier.

As was his custom, he rubbed his hands together slowly. His

pale eyes swept over the little assembly. "Mr. Mayor, ladies and gentlemen, we are deeply touched by your welcome and by the wonderful tributes which you, Mr. Mayor, have just paid us. As our *elected* leader I am sure that I—er—speak for all of us when I say how glad we are to be here today. Little did we think three months ago when we left Mauritius bound for Australia that we should return to your lovely island by such a —er— devious route."

There was clapping and a chorus of "Hear! —Hear!"

Canning beamed. "We have had to battle with the elements! Fight to survive! But thanks to God's good grace . . ." he dropped his eyes reverently, "all but three of us have survived."

Who's the third, thought Ezekiel? Then he remembered the young Italian.

"I think, I may say, that it required—ah—courage and stead-fastness to come through." He turned and with a wave of his hand indicated his companions who were listening dumbfounded. "I want to take this opportunity to pay my—er—humble tribute to my colleagues without whose exertions we could not have survived. It would be invidious for me to single out any member of our team. Every one played his part . . ." he smiled at Nada and Angelique. ". . . or *her* part. It was *teamwork* that did it. Teamwork, ladies and gentlemen—and if I may say so—the British . . . ah—fighting spirit." Canning stopped, flummoxed by the audible "Drop dead!" from Sarah Tripp who was immediately behind him.

Then he bowed to the Mayor and there was a prolonged burst of clapping and cheering.

Sarah Tripp looked at Ezekiel. "My God!" she whispered. "Isn't he *dreadful*!"

Ezekiel smiled. "He'd make a good politician."

The official welcome over, the representatives of the Press, *Time* and *Life*, *Paris Match*, and the international news agencies, closed in on the survivors, notebooks at the ready. Ezekiel

Wanalu, M.P. and Herbert William Canning were their main targets.

* *

Much happened in the next few hours.

After a medical examination they were whisked off to police headquarters where affidavits were taken about the disappearance of Basset and Mecky. Each survivor was questioned separately and the police soon knew all they wanted to.

The survivors read the cables and letters awaiting them, including various offers for exclusive story rights; then they went off on a shopping spree with Jack Lund, who invited them to fit themselves out at the expense of T.O.A.L. and to draw such money as they needed.

They had to decide that day on their destinations. Sarah Tripp and Nada wished to continue to Australia, but the others wanted to return to Johannesburg. Ezekiel en route to Salisbury, and Canning and Sebastian to London.

Jos had sustained a severe shock soon after Canning finished speaking. Throughout the ceremony the Afrikaner stood next to Angelique, who smiled constantly at someone in the crowd. He could not see who it was but presumed it must be her husband and he became suddenly and unreasonably jealous. Then a small, middle-aged man, olive skinned and almond-eyed . . . unmistakably a Chinaman . . . came forward. Angelique ran to him and they ended in each others' arms, locked in a long embrace. Quietly, unostentatiously the Chinaman whisked her away before she could say good-bye to her companions.

Jos reeled! So that was it! The husband was a *Chink*! Sarah Tripp was right! Angelique *was* coloured. She'd deceived him. Filled with chagrin and mortification, his mind confused by the recollection of his love, angry and puzzled, he allowed himself to be pushed and jostled as the Press closed round the survivors.

* *

The time in Mauritius was to be short. It was Friday and Jack Lund told them that the aircraft for Johannesburg would leave on Sunday morning, and that for Australia on Monday night. This pleased them enormously because they were consumed by the desire to get home—all but Sebastian and Sarah Tripp who had other plans.

The shopping spree over, they were taken by car along roads hedged with clipped bamboos, through endless fields of sugar cane, to the Park Hotel in Curepipe. There they were shown to their rooms, and were soon enjoying the luxuries of civilisation from which they had for so long been separated.

* *

Among those who had met them on arrival at Port Louis was Gustave Maurice, the agent for Canning's company. Canning's importance was at once evident from the attention the Frenchman paid to him.

"Nothing ees too much trouble," he assured him. "You 'ave but to say, an' you shall 'ave."

Canning revelled in this return to an environment he understood, and his commands to the agent were many. Long cables for Winifred, for his chairman, for Porrit, for his married son and daughter; others to Johannesburg and Melbourne; details of various onward bookings and other matters he desired attended to.

But most important of all was his last request. They were sitting in Canning's suite in the hotel, a silver tray on the low table between them, on it a bottle of Martell Five-Star, soda-syphon and crystal glasses, and a plate of smoked salmon and caviar snacks.

Canning gulped his Martell and soda. "I want to put on a very special dinner party tomorrow night. For my companions. A farewell gathering, you understand. I would like you to make all the arrangements. A private room. *No expense to be spared.* French menu. French wines, French champagne . . . Flowers of course. Printed menus, printed cards for seat places. Try and arrange for a round table," he added. "One small point . . ." Canning exhaled the smoke from his cigar and closed his eyes. "All the accounts are to be made out to *me*. But you will pay them. Forward them on to me in London and I shall arrange with the Company for your reimbursement. But . . ." he smiled, "I shall want all the receipts . . . *made out to me* . . . before I leave. Got that?"

The Frenchman nodded understandingly. "Of course, *m'sieu*! Of course!"

Canning dismissed the agent and sighed with satisfaction. The dinner would be a great success. He'd already persuaded Sarah Tripp and Sebastian to come and when he had expressed to them his fears that the others might not, Sarah's eyes had glinted. "Leave it to me!" she said. "They'll come!"

Canning lifted his left foot from the floor and crossed it over his right foot, at the same time undoing the waistband and top fly-button of his new trousers so that his stomach might more comfortably distend. He belched gently. The dinner party was a brilliant idea! They would all part on the best of terms. By-gones would be by-gones, and they would remember only how they had suffered and survived together. He could hear them saying: "Good scout, old Canning! Remember that fabulous dinner he gave in Mauritius."

*   *

The taxi jolted along the narrow road which wound down from Curepipe through fields of sugar cane and maize, occasional clumps of banyan trees and scattered native villages. Along the road there was a never-ending stream of buses, bicycles, and humanity of varying shades and their children, dogs, and poultry. Fourteen miles of this brought the taxi to the outskirts of Port Louis where balconied houses, mellow and charming, rubbed shoulders with others squalid in wood and iron and brick. The place teemed with life which seemed predominantly Indian, and a pungent smell of the Orient, of spices and curries and oils, lay upon the town.

They turned into the Chinese quarter and after negotiating several side streets stopped before a pink house standing apart from its neighbours. The wooden shutters on the stucco walls were shut, and the absence of any sign of life gave the place an air of austere privacy.

"Mr. Lee's house," said the driver.

Jos got out, paid the fare and the taxi moved off.

He stood there uncertainly, wondering what to do next. Where he was the street was empty. He started up the hill. Outside a shop a knot of Chinese stood in the road chattering. Occasionally they stepped aside for a honking car, then joined ranks again behind it.

Jos looked inside the shop. There were several customers and behind the counters two Chinese assistants. Near him an elderly Chinaman was writing up an account book. Jos stopped before him. "Good afternoon!"

The Chinaman looked up, showing his teeth in a faintly interrogative grin. "Good afternoon!"

Jos shifted his weight from one foot to the other. "I'm from the South African Press. Over here to cover the return of these survivors that came in yesterday."

The Chinaman's face was expressionless. "Yes?"

"I'm looking for background material. About the lady from Mauritius. Mrs. Lee. She lives around here, I understand."

"Mrs. Kwan Lee?"

Jos shook his head. "Mrs. *Douglas* Lee."

"Same lady. Husband's Cantonese name Kwan. Business name for Europeans, 'Douglas'."

"What's his business?"

"Import export merchant."

Jos took a deep breath. "This lady . . . she's a fine-looking woman. Saw her at the docks when they landed. Not Chinese, is she?"

The Chinaman looked at him curiously, as if he were seeing him for the first time. "No. Live long time with Chinese family before she marry."

"I heard that." Jos looked round the shop as if the point didn't really interest him. "Who were her parents?"

"Mother, French lady. Work in Port Louis shop. Shop belong Chinaman."

"And her father?"

The old man shrugged his shoulders. "Mother very pretty. Many friends. Not marry."

Jos stood there awkwardly, tongue-tied, while the implications of what he'd heard sank in. He was dazed! Confused! What about the Greek? Had she lied to him?

"Sure she had no father?" He tried to sound casual.

"She *had* father," the Chinaman grinned. "But who?"

Jos stood there talking for a few minutes, but he wanted to escape now. He wanted to get out of the shop. Things had taken an unexpected turn. He wished now he'd not started on these inquiries. They hadn't helped.

The old Chinaman was saying something: ". . . look same like other one . . ."

"What's that?" . . . Jos tried to concentrate.

The old man's face puckered. "You look same like picture survivor man I see newspaper."

Jos started. "Yes," he said dreamily. "He was a big chap, too."

He walked out of the shop.

*   *

In another part of Port Louis, another survivor was busy making inquiries.

Nada had gone to the offices of *The Mauritas Times* where she introduced herself. "We heard on the steamer coming over from Diego Garcia that there were other survivors from our aircraft. Can I see copies of your paper which has news of them?"

The woman she spoke to nodded sympathetically. "Of course."

The copies were soon found and Nada read the first report, date-lined Perth, which announced that an R.A.F. Sunderland from Gan had reported picking up signals from a dinghy on the second day. By late evening the dinghy had been sighted.

The two nearest ships had been directed to the position but were not expected to reach it in less than forty-eight hours. During the night the Sunderland had to leave, but other search-aircraft had taken over.

The Mauritius Times was a weekly and the next report appeared seven days later. It was quite unsatisfactory because it did no more than record that the six survivors in the dinghy, including a baby, had been picked up by the steamer *Northern Star*, expected in Perth two days later. The survivors were, the report said, suffering from exposure and in some cases injuries. There were no names. Nada was desperately frustrated. Then she thought of Jack Lund, the T.O.A.L. man who had been so helpful during the morning. Why on *earth* hadn't she asked him when she had the opportunity? In the oppressive heat of the afternoon she hurried round to his office only to find that he was at the airport. She telephoned him there. An Indian clerk got the number, but the airport said Lund had already left. She asked to be put through to any T.O.A.L. staff on duty. A cheerful voice with a strong Australian accent came on the line. Nada told him who she was and what she wanted.

"I don't remember the details," he said. "Hold on a sec. I'll look it up."

In the long wait that followed her heart raced. The suspense was awful. Why did it have to be dragged out like this?

It was hot in the small office. With the back of her hand she wiped her forehead. She looked at the Indian clerk: at his dark spaniel's eyes and his delicate hands. She realised she was staring at him, so she looked at the tyre company calendar where a grinning red-head sat on a stool displaying lots of leg and bosom. Nada prayed silently, urgently, that Iles should be safe. He was in the tail unit. If others had got out they must have been in the tail unit. Iles *must* be one of them. He was so big and strong. Oh, God! *Please* let him be one of them!

The T.O.A.L. man's voice interrupted her thoughts. "Okay," he said cheerfully. "Here it is."

She heard the crackle of papers at the other end of the line.

"What's it say?" she tried to sound normal.

"There were six of them in the dinghy," said the distant voice. "Three men, two women and a baby."

"Any crew?" My voice'll pack up, she thought, and her heart pounded.

"Yes—the steward—Charles Iles."

She felt suddenly faint. The relief was too much. "Thank God! Oh, thank God!" she said.

There was no reply from the other end and she was about to put down the receiver when she heard his voice again. Not cheerful now but quiet, steady, measured: "He didn't make it, sister."

Didn't make what, she thought? *What* was this disembodied voice saying?

"What?" she said dully.

"He died of his injuries. Before the ship reached Perth."

She put down the receiver blankly, upsetting a filing basket. The Indian clerk was saying something, but she couldn't hear him.

She shook her head. She couldn't cry. Her heart was pounding and she felt she would choke. She must get away from this place. Somehow the news had made it obscene.

The Indian clerk spoke to her again. She turned away. "Oh, God!" she said brokenly. "Oh, God!"

He put his hand on her shoulder. She brushed it away and stumbled out of the office.

*   *

It was a busy afternoon for the survivors. Ezekiel Wanalu, M.P., was in his room at the Park Hotel preparing the speech he would deliver that night at a dinner to be given in his honour by the members of the Legislative Council. Its theme would be "The African Mind in a Changing World." It was a speech he had made before, but it was being modified. He'd learnt a lot in the last three months.

Canning had made calls at Government House and at the Mayor's Parlour. He was now busy in his agent's office, dictating instructions for a reward to be sent to Emile and the islanders. It was, Canning said, to be charged in the first instance to himself and he would thereafter arrange reimbursement through the Company, which in turn would claim on the airline.

"The receipts," Canning blew a cloud of cigar smoke at the ceiling and looked speculatively at the pretty French secretary who was taking notes, "are to be made out to 'H. W. Canning' and forwarded to me *personally* by airmail.

"That's all. Put my name at the bottom. Soon as it's typed I'll sign it." His eyes travelled over the French girl again. Pity they were leaving on Sunday morning. So little time. Dinner at Gustave Maurices' tonight. Farewell dinner at the hotel tomorrow night. Pity! She was a lovely girl!

*   *

Sarah Tripp and Sebastian, trim in their new clothes, deeply tanned by the sun, stood in front of the Park Hotel waiting for a taxi.

Sebastian looked at Sarah with adoring eyes. How attractive she was with her hair properly done and wearing those feminine clothes. She sparkled with a new kindliness, glowed with well-being. There was no doubt about it, Sarah was happy.

300

When the taxi arrived she looked at her watch. "We've got thirty-five minutes. I made the appointment for three-thirty."

"What a wonderful organiser you are, Sarah."

"Lucky one of us is."

She pinched him playfully.

Twenty-one

CANNING glanced at his watch. "I think, ladies and gentlemen, that we should go into dinner." He looked for Angelique who was to sit on his right, but she was in a corner talking to Jos and he couldn't catch her eye. Had it been anyone but the Afrikaner he would have interrupted them. Despite the heat and humidity, spirits were running high in the ante-room where the survivors were gathered. Gustave Maurice the agent and his wife, and Jack Lund the T.O.A.L. representative were there, too. Canning had invited them because he felt that the presence of these outsiders would be a steadying influence; a restraint, perhaps, on what might be said. But he had few fears now. His guests were in excellent form. An Indian wine-steward was serving drinks, and the noise and flushed cheerful faces showed he'd done his work well.

Angelique dominated the gathering. She was statuesque in white with a red carnation in her high-piled black hair. Her skin glowed with vigour, the dark eyes calm, the full mouth red and inviting. To Jos she had never been more beautiful.

Through the door in the private dining-room the round table sparkled with silver and glass. Silver candlesticks stood at the four corners of a magnificent centre-piece, a reproduction of Eagle Island in icing sugar, chocolate and other sweets. The palm trunks were marzipan, their fronds green angelica, and the reef awash at low water was nougat. The sapphire sea was icing sugar with wave crests of whipped cream. On either side frangipani and hibiscus blooms floated in silver bowls. In the corners alabaster vases on white *guéridons* held ferns and carnations. At the ends of the room oval mirrors in gilded stucco frames created the illusion of a gallery with endless round tables.

"Ladies and gentlemen!" Canning shouted to make himself heard. He masked his irritation with bonhomie. "The feast awaits us!"

In the dining-room he went to the far side of the table and stood behind a chair with his hands on its back. Everyone was talking at once. He held up his hands, clearing his throat. "You'll find place cards on the table. Please be seated." Beaming at Angelique he pointed to the chair on his right. "You're here, madame." His manner was ingratiating, but not the slightest attention was paid him or the place cards, and his guests sat where they pleased. Canning found Madame Maurice on his right and Sarah Tripp on his left.

Nada was the only absentee. No one had seen her since the day before. She had gone down to Port Louis that morning and not returned. A message had come to say how sorry she was not to be with them.

The dinner was superb. The wines, chosen by the manager with impeccable taste, were exquisite. Canning turned to Gustave. "I must say," he puffed his cheeks, "the dinner's been very well done. Really excellent!"

The Frenchman was delighted. "I am so 'appy. The wines? Do you approve?"

"I couldn't have chosen 'em better myself."

Gustave Maurice looked thoughtful.

Canning took another mouthful of the *bouche* of shell-fish. "You always get the best if you're prepared to pay for it," he said to the Frenchman.

Sarah Tripp could not restrain her curiosity. She pointed to a table against the wall. On it were six gaily-wrapped parcels. "What are those?"

Canning chuckled. "Ha, Ha! That's a secret, Sarah. All in good time."

The chatter never ceased and the wine-waiter was assiduous. As the dinner proceeded Canning's morale rose. It was proving even more of a success than he'd hoped. The *Beefsteak à Bigarade* came and went.

Canning tapped on a glass. The talking stopped. He stood, raising his glass. "Ladies and gentlemen, '*The Queen*'!"

The toast was drunk and cigars and cigarettes were lit. Arms were crossed and crackers were pulled. There were shrill cries and laughter as the spoils were examined.

Paper hats, bright and bizarre, adorned their heads: Canning's, a pirate's hat with skull and cross bones, was much admired. He sat under it smiling blandly, slightly befuddled by alcohol.

An Alaska Surprise, blue flames darting from it, was carried in and served as the Brut '59 was opened.

Jos stood up. "Hey! Where's the turtle meat and coconut?" His speech was thick. There was loud applause and he slumped back into his chair beaming.

Canning rapped on the table.

There were cries of "Shoosh! Silence!"

"The leader will speak," said Sarah Tripp reverently.

"*Sieg heil!*" cried Ezekiel. "Silence for the führer!"

Canning beamed. They were a good lot. No rancour here. The dinner'd done it, of course.

He rose, a glass of champagne in his hand. Behind the horn-rimmed spectacles his watery eyes gleamed.

"Ladies and gentlemen, it is my privilege as your host tonight—and, if I may add, as your *elected* leader—to propose the main toast at this, our last gathering together. Tomorrow most of us leave for Johannesburg. On Monday, Nada and Sarah fly off to Australia. I won't make a long speech but . . ."

There were shouts of "Hear! Hear!"

Canning gulped. A fair intake of drink had made him forgetful. "Ah, yes," he recollected. "I don't . . . I mean I do . . . *want* to say that we could not have survived our ordeal . . . had it not

304

been for teamwork. The pulling together. Our determination
never to give in. Each one of us played his part and—er—while
the future often looked black, we *never* gave in."

There was some table thumping.

Canning became more serious. "*We* survived. *We* are cele-
brating. Soon we shall be with our loved ones."

"Jolly good!" shouted someone.

"But *others* did not survive." He put his fingers together.
"Many perished in the sea. The Italian died in our dinghy."
He paused, eyes downcast. "Mecky and Basset died. We must
not be harsh in our judgment of them . . . nor of anyone for that
matter. We were under great stress . . ."

Jos started off lustily: "For we are jolly . . ."

"Shush, Jos!" Angelique put her hand on his arm. "Not yet."

Canning pressed on. "We must never forget . . . when we
get home and describe our hardships . . . our fight to survive . . .
to speak well of one another. Remember that we were a *team*,
pulling together, and that we came through!"

They banged the table. There were "Hear! Hear!'s", a
"Bravo!", an "*Olé!*" from Sarah, and a deep "*Hoor! Hoor!*"
from Jos.

Canning called them to order. "Now, ladies and gentlemen, I
give you a toast."

The guests shuffled to their feet. "I give you," he repeated,
"the toast of . . . '*The survivors*'. God bless us!"

"*The survivors*," they echoed.

When they sat down, the conversation and laughter was once
more general. Ezekiel and Jos were arguing good-naturedly
across Angelique, Jos illustrating his point with the nougat reef.
Sebastian and Sarah talked solemnly; her speech was slurred.

Canning looked across to Jos with a mild gesture of interrogation. Surely Jos would reply, if only to thank his host.

But Jos shook his head. Canning got the same gesture of refusal
from Ezekiel and then, when the delay was becoming embarrassing

and he was about to call on Sebastian, he heard the table being rapped. It was Sarah Tripp. In answer to Canning's whispered, "Will you?" she nodded.

Canning sprang up. "Pray silence!" He was perspiring. It was a hot night. "For Miss . . . Sarah Tripp."

Sarah Tripp got to her feet, swaying slightly, breathing heavily. Behind her thick spectacles she smiled at her companions. "*Mrs.* Sebastian Goldsworthy," she corrected. "As from three-thirty yesterday afternoon."

There was noisy applause, much banging on the table and stamping of feet.

"Nice work, Sebastian!" yelled Jos.

Sebastian blushed.

Canning looked anything but pleased. He glared at Sebastian. How dare he go and get married on the sly! And to that bitch of a woman!

"My speech," announced Sarah thickly, "is divided into two parts. First—I want to say how grateful *we all* are to Nada." (Cheers) "For the way she took charge in the dinghy. Especially that first night when she and Ezekiel pulled us out of the water. I only *wish* she were with us." (More cheers.)

"Good old Nada!" shouted Jos.

"Then I must . . . thank Jos and Ezekiel for all they did in the dinghy *and* on the island. We wouldn't have had a hope but for them."

There was applause, in which Canning rather reluctantly joined.

"Wait a minute," Sarah smiled. "Haven't nearly finished." She looked at Sebastian and her eyes softened. "Then I want to thank Providence . . . for giving me Sebastian." Sebastian blushed.

"Finally . . . I must say how grateful we are to those who rescued us an' looked after us, including Jack Lund and Gustave Maurice." Sarah raised the glass. "Thish then is to—*Our gratitude to all who helped us.*"

"*Our gratitude to all who helped us,*" everyone mumbled.

They sat down amid a lively buzz of conversation but Sarah remained standing. She held up her hand. "Shoosh! I told you my speech was in two parts. . . . Now I must deal with the second part.

"Once upon a time the sea washed up onto a desert island a medusa or sea-nettle . . . jelly fish to use its more common name. Well . . . thish was a rather special sort of medusa."

She spoke thickly, making airy gestures with her hands.

They were listening to her in silence, wondering what on earth she was talking about. Canning had pulled his chair well back. His cigar was glowing and he was smiling . . . not at what Sarah was saying, he wasn't really listening, but because of the rude shock his rescue must have been to Porrit, notwithstanding the fulsome cables of congratulation. He was thinking, too, what a splendid tale he had for Rotary.

Sarah went on. "The normal habitat of this invertebrate is not as you might think . . . the Chagos Archipelago. Indeed, no!" she swayed, grinning happily. "It is *normally* to be found in a plush board-room in the City. It is, however, the subject of my next toast."

She lifted her glass. "To you then . . . Herbert William Canning." She looked down on him. "Our gratitude for having so often . . . and so ably . . . reminded us, how very decent other men can be."

As the significance of what she was saying pierced the incipient inebriation and general euphoria which enveloped him, Canning's smile changed to frightened anger. He grasped the arms of the chair to get up.

But he was not quick enough. Out of Sarah's glass, well above him, came a golden stream of Brut '59. From his bald head, bubbling rivulets snaked down his forehead, were held for a moment by his bushy eyebrows, then overflowed and splashed onto his plate.

There was a shocked, "Sarah!" from Sebastian and a hoarse belly laugh from Jos.

White with anger, Canning hurried from the room followed by the Maurices, whose faces were blank, emotionless, but for the Frenchman's wink.

When Canning had gone they really let their hair down, and with Jack Lund acting as a sort of master of ceremonies the party reached great heights. Abdul Felipe, the wine-waiter, could not recall a busier or more enjoyable night.

Sarah's curiosity was satisfied when the parcels on the side table were opened and found to contain electric razors and vanity cases.

It was assumed by the survivors that these gifts were intended for them from Canning; but in spite of Sebastian's assurance that the dinner and everything connected with it would be charged to the Company—at least once and probably twice—they felt they could hardly accept the presents. Rather sadly, they left them on the table.

"You know, Sebastian," said Jos gravely. "Sarah's buggered your chances with the Company. Thought about that?"

Sebastian beamed through his steel-rimmed spectacles. "I'm resigning from the Company, Jos. Soon as we get to London. Drawing all my money from the pension and provident funds and," he smiled shyly, "I'm going out to Australia to join Sarah."

Jos patted him on the back. "Helluva good idea, Sebastian!"

In the early hours of the morning they decided to call it a day. Having agreed that Sarah should try to bring Nada to the airport next morning to see them off, they went through the ante-room and down the stairs.

The last to leave were Angelique and Jos. He took her arm and they went down the stairs. At the first landing they stopped. The light was dim and they stood facing each other.

His voice was husky. "Will I ever see you again, Angelique?"

She shook her head. "I don't think so, Jos."

"I wish," he said urgently, "that I had a ring or something to give you. Something to remember me by."

She put her hands on his shoulders and stood on her toes to kiss him. "*Mon Chéri!* That is not necessary. I shall never forget you. Always *something* will remind me."

They heard Jack Lund's voice calling from the foot of the stairs. "Hey! Come *on* you two!" He was to drive Angelique back to Port Louis.

Jos looked at Angelique, holding her away from him. He wanted to remember her beauty.

Angelique said: "Good-bye, my darling." She was crying.

Jack Lund shouted again. Jos took a deep breath. Then holding her arm, he led her down the stairs.

*   *

In the private dining-room the wine-waiter shut the door on the darkened room.

A few minutes later it opened again and someone tiptoed into the room. There was the flare of a match by the low table and a hand reached down and picked up one of the parcels.

The match spluttered and the room was in darkness.

The silence was broken by the closing of the door.

*   *

It was dark in the bedroom. She had been talking to Kwan in a low voice, answering and asking many questions. There was so much to say. They had single beds with a small table between them. She lay on her side facing him but she couldn't see him in the darkness.

She had just finished telling him about the loss of the jewels. It had not worried him; to have her back, he said, he would cheerfully have given all his fortune. That was not easy for a Cantonese, but she knew he meant it.

Now was the time to tell him the other—the most important thing. It would require courage but it had to be done. She was not really frightened but she didn't want to hurt him. He was so kind and unselfish.

She propped herself up on an elbow. "There is something else I must tell you, Kwan. It is *very* important."

"What is it?" He was indulgent, like a parent talking to a child who exaggerates.

"Do you remember once . . . when I was unhappy . . . you said that if I found a good man . . . he," she paused and drew a deep breath, "he could father my child?" The last sentence was almost a whisper.

"I remember." Kwan's voice was even.

"You said," she went on gravely, "that if I did this, you would not want to know who the man was."

There was silence. Outside in the street a car hooted and its lights lit up the room as it passed. When Angelique spoke there was a catch in her voice. "I am going to have a baby, Kwan."

"When?"

"In about seven and a half months, I think."

There was another silence. He was thinking of the survivors, the men, trying to remember their faces as they came down the gangway onto the wharf.

"Will you see him again?"

"Never, Kwan. Tonight at the dinner was the last time."

"Does he know about the child?"

"No. I did not wish to tell him. It is better so."

Kwan thought again of the faces of the men on the wharf. "What will the child be like?"

In the darkness under the sheet Angelique's hands were on her bare stomach feeling for signs of life, although she knew it was much too soon.

She felt happy and secure now in this room with Kwan. She knew from the way he had taken the news that he was not upset. Nor was he pleased. He had just accepted it. Later the child would mean much to him for it would transform their lives.

But she must answer his question.

"It will be a boy, Kwan." She spoke softly. "Of that I am *sure*. He will be big and strong, and his skin will be much fairer than mine." She paused. "He should be gentle and kind—and very brave," she added proudly.

Kwan sighed in the darkness.

So it *was* him.

Twenty-two

It was a clear day with occasional patches of fleecy cloud. They were flying at 14,000 feet. Below them the ragged line of the Madagascan coast, edged with the white of surf breaking on sunlit beaches, met the blue waters of the Mozambique Channel. They expected to sight the East African coast at three o'clock. Then they would strike inland somewhere between Vila de João Belo and Lourenço Marques. The estimated time of arrival at Jan Smuts was four-thirty.

The aircraft was a South African Airways DC7B. For Jos it had been like coming home when he embarked at La Plaisance and found himself among his countrymen again. After the take-off he went up front with the Captain, told him about their experiences and got from him news about the rescue of the other survivors.

Jos and Ezekiel were sitting together, silent now after much talking. The African stood up and lifted a blue flying-bag from the rack. From it he took a small black and white box. He opened it and there was a gleam of white and grey and silver. He grinned: "How d'you like my new razor?"

Jos looked at it, then at the African and his eyes narrowed. "You old bastard!"

Ezekiel stood up. "I'm going to shave. Don't tell Canning. Spoil his lunch."

Left alone, Jos tried to sort out the turmoil of his thoughts. He lived through it all again. The time in the dinghy. Landing on the island. Building the catamaran. The fight with Ezekiel. The fish-traps. The moonlight walks with Angelique. Basset's disappearance. Mecky's death. The rescue. Egmont Islands, Diego Garcia. The island steamer. Mauritius. The farewell dinner. Much had happened. They'd come a long way since the night of the crash!

Then he thought of getting home to his children and Soetwaters. He would be there the next day. He was tremendously excited. Nothing could be more wonderful than that! Nothing? He thought of Angelique, and became sad and melancholy. It would have been wonderful if he could have brought her back.

Would it? He heard again the voice of the old Chinaman in Port Louis. "She *had* a father, but who?"

Would she have fitted into his world at Soetwaters? Could he have broken up her marriage? He thought about those things, trying hard to be honest with himself.

He sighed. It all seemed a long time ago.

Something else started to worry and nag. It had happened just before lunch. He'd been sitting with Zeke and Sebastian, reminiscing about life on the island, about all that had happened in these last few months. They'd knocked back a good many beers and gins and tonics, and there'd been a bit of backslapping and plenty of laughter. Maybe they'd made more noise than they should. But hell! How would the other passengers have behaved if it had happened to them? It wasn't every day that you crashed into the sea, got stuck on a desert island, then rescued months later. It wasn't the sort of thing a man could be expected to be calm about; to be given a second chance of life; to be on your way home to your children, to your farm, to your people and your country.

Then this thing had happened that was worrying him. He'd been in one of the toilets in the after-end of the cabin when he heard a woman talking to a man in Afrikaans.

"That Lombaard's very friendly with the *kaffer*. Moving into the seat next to him. Laughing and joking and hitting each other on the back."

"Yes," agreed the man. "Some of the passengers have noticed it. He's a farmer. He ought to know better."

"Been away too long," said the woman. "You've got to be careful with these black politicians. They're the worst of the lot."

When he came out of the toilet, Jos saw the steward and air hostess and realised it was they who had been discussing him. He was shocked. The conversation had reminded him of things he'd forgotten. Perhaps he *had* been away too long. He supposed he *had* behaved rather indiscreetly.

But they didn't know Ezekiel. He wasn't like that. He was different, he was educated. He was more than that. He was a man . . . a fine man and a good friend. Not just because he'd twice saved Jos's life, but for many other reasons. Jos realised that there were things one could do on a desert island that one couldn't do at home.

After lunch he let the back of his chair down and made himself comfortable. To hell with it, anyway! He'd have a sleep and stop worrying. Soon he'd be standing on the stoep at Soetwaters, Marietjie and Dirkie in his arms, looking over the valley to where the escarpment dropped down into the Lowveld.

It was early December. The fruit would be setting on the trees in the orchard; beneath them the wild strawberries would be flowering; the raspberries would be putting out new canes and behind the house the cordoba vines would be burgeoning.

It was the season of thunderstorms in the valley. He wondered how the road was, and if they were putting back the gravel the rain washed away.

In the plantations the *Piet-my-vrous* would be laying their eggs in the thrushes' nests and calling to each other in high silvery cadences. Down by the river the grass and the willows would be green and the gurgle and splash of the water would be drowned every now and then by the screech of the guinea fowl and the cackle of the ibises.

Along the banks the warblers and wrens would be flitting in and out of the *graspols*, and the masked weavers would be building their nests in the willows, far out over the stream beyond the reach of snakes and other predators. Above the long grass the *sakabula* birds would be trailing their scythe-like tails in slow adumbrated flight, and the sheep would be grazing on the koppies.

The beer and gin began to take effect and Jos fell asleep. He slept fitfully, waking at times with a start and looking out of the window where there was nothing to be seen now but cloud, and then going off to sleep again.

The last time he woke was when the engines throttled back. He looked up and saw the notice "Make your seat belts fast," and then he heard the hostess announcing that they were about to land at Jan Smuts; eighteen minutes late because of head winds.

From then on things happened quickly.

An official boarded, checked the yellow fever and inoculation certificates and sprayed the aircraft. The passengers went down the gangway and walked across the tarmac towards the airport building. There was a fair crowd up on the main balcony and a lot of people waving. Jos hoped it was not going to be another official reception.

During the flight from Mauritius, Canning had avoided his companions, even Sebastian whom he had now presumably written off. But at this moment of arrival he was at pains to be friendly and to effect a certain bonhomie. "Wonderful moment this, isn't it," he observed as they got near the entrance to customs and immigration.

"*Ja!*" said Jos. "It certainly is."

"Very exciting indeed." Ezekiel's voice was school-masterly. With the arrival his manner had changed; he had become rather prim.

They were given priority in customs and immigration and quickly cleared. When they had finished an airport official came up and said: "Are you four gentlemen the survivors from Mauritius?"

While he was talking to them they were joined by a man in a dark suit who introduced himself as an official from the Department of External Affairs. His special assignment seemed to be Ezekiel, for after the introductions he said: "Mr. Wanalu, the Department has asked me to give you any assistance necessary. You're booked on the Salisbury flight. It leaves in about fifteen minutes, but there should just be time for the little ceremony outside. Your luggage is going on board now."

Jos groaned. "*Ag!* Man! Not another ceremony?"

The airport official smiled. "This'll be short and sweet. We heard you had a big show in Port Louis."

There was some delay while they looked for Canning who had melted away. Eventually he was found and they hurried through to the V.I.P. lounge where they were greeted by a score of people, among them reporters, photographers, ciné and sound men.

The man from External Affairs introduced them in turn to the Mayor of Kempton Park . . . in whose borough the airport lay . . . an official from the Department of Transport, the Consul for the Rhodesian Federation, the Airport Manager and other dignitaries.

The Mayor started speaking, the floodlights went on, the cameras whirred and clicked.

". . . we can imagine," the Mayor was saying, "the ordeal through which you have passed and I . . ."

At that moment Jos heard the External Affairs man's urgent whisper to Ezekiel who was next to him. "Afraid you'll have to come now, Mr. Wanalu! They've called the Salisbury flight for the last time."

Ezekiel whispered "Okay!" Out of the corner of his eye Jos saw the African move away.

". . . we have been filled with admiration for the courage and fortitude which you all displayed. It is with pride that I recall that two South Africans shared in this great epic."

The Mayor gave Jos a warm smile. "I'm sure that you, as a farmer, Mr. Lombaard . . ."

But Jos was not listening for a great fight was going on inside him. Was he going to stand there and let Zeke go out of his life like this without a word of good-bye, or was he going to say to hell with the consequences, to hell with what these people might think, and do what his heart told him?

He saw that Ezekiel, the Rhodesian Consul and the External Affairs man had almost reached the far door. With a muttered, "Just a moment, your Worship. I'll be back," he broke away from Canning and Sebastian and ran across the room, reaching the African and his escorts as they got to the door.

The Mayor stopped speaking and watched in astonishment as Jos placed a huge hand on Ezekiel's shoulder and swung him round.

"Hey, Zeke!" he cried. "You can't push off like that without saying good-bye, man!" He put out his hand and closed it on the African's. "Thanks a helluva lot, hey?"

The floodlights and cameras trained on Jos and Ezekiel, and the long arm of the mike reached over towards them.

Ezekiel said: "It was good to know you, Jos." His dark eyes shone.

The Afrikaner's voice rose as if in defiance of his listeners. "Any time you're down my way you'll be very welcome, Zeke." He boomed. "When you get to Dullstroom, just ask for Lombaard of Soetwaters. They'll direct you."

The External Affairs man was looking at his watch and politely tapping Ezekiel's shoulder. Jos still had the African's hand in an iron grip. They were facing the cameras and the knot of people round the Mayor.

"I won't forget you, Jos!"

"Good-bye, Zeke. *Alles van die beste, hoor!*"

317

"*Totsiens*, Jos! I'll miss you."

The Afrikaner looked into the African's eyes and pressed his hand for the last time. "Zeke," he said solemnly, "you're a white man."

The African frowned. Confused. Puzzled. Afraid that some oblique insult lay buried in the remark. But Jos's steadfast gaze reassured him. A chord of memory struck! Brownson at Jesus! Zeke's eyes wrinkled, the full lips curled back and his face creased into a huge grin, its centre marked with almost geometrical precision by the missing tooth.